MONDAY NIGHTS

stories from the creative writing workshop at the university of new orleans

edited by fredrick barton and joanna leake

UNO Press
Manufactured in the United States of America

ISBN: 978160801129
Cover photos: Corinne Green
Book and cover design: Alex Dimeff

UNIVERSITY OF NEW ORLEANS PRESS
unopress.org

MONDAY NIGHTS

stories from the creative writing workshop at the university of new orleans

Narratives by Graduates and Faculty
Of the Creative Writing Workshop
Celebrating Twenty-Five Years
Of the Master of Fine Arts Writing Program
At The University of New Orleans

For Joyce and David

The editors would like to thank our esteemed colleagues in the Creative Writing Workshop at the University of New Orleans for their tireless dedication to our students over the quarter century since we taught our first classes in the fall of 1991.

And we would like to thank our amazing students, all our students, those whose work is exhibited here and those whose work might have been, for spending three years of their lives with us. These students have come to us from almost every state in the Union and from countries all over the world. And while here they have built, sustained and strengthened a community that stands as the proudest development of our professional lives.

—Fredrick Barton and Joanna Leake

CONTENTS

faculty

Introduction

BY ABRAM SHALOM HIMELSTEIN

When I enrolled in the Creative Writing Workshop at the University of New Orleans in 1997, I took its existence for granted. Of course, there was a university in the biggest city in Louisiana. And of course, they taught creative writing there. The CWW felt like such a substantial institution; I was unaware that it was then only six years old.

And I had no idea, of course, that my professors, Rick Barton, James Knudsen, and Joanna Leake, along with poetry professor John Gery, had willed the Workshop into being, building the program over a painstaking decade, from a single sophomore-level course into a full graduate program offering an MFA in five genres. The establishment of this new degree program was accomplished despite the glacial movement of the university bureaucracy and the skepticism of many, some of whom later numbered among its biggest fans. Today, the CWW is among a handful of UNO's most distinguished programs.

In my years in the CWW, now two decades in the past, fiction workshops met on Monday night as they still do today. Like the other writers, when a story of mine was discussed around the conference table, I sat silently and took notes while my colleagues did their best to improve my stories and my writing. This is a bedrock pedagogical premise of the CWW: the purpose of each workshop for every story is not to judge but to assist. We all did heavy lifting for each other, and most felt lifted by the process. At the very least, we had sympathetic readers to give us the thoughts others had while reading our work; test markets were in short supply for many of us who were finding our voices as writers.

The after part for workshops was at Parkview Tavern on Carrollton Avenue, where the workshopped writers were allowed to break silence, and often did. After the stories of the day, we moved on to the other texts of our lives: new books we were reading, the search for affordable rent, job possibilities. For me, these Parkview sessions bore tremendous fruit. I shot pool with a neighbor who soon became my printer as I entered into the world of self-publishing. Two thousand dollars poorer, I had 500 books in my trunk, and the beginning of my adult career.

These were our Monday nights. For me, these were Monday nights for the five semesters I was a fiction student at the Workshop. But for the professors, and then for an ever-growing list of alumni, these were Monday nights into perpetuity. Parkview has become part of the CWW institution. Current students are still there on Monday nights, often joined by alumni, like the graduates included in this book, who still reside in New Orleans.

As the CWW observes its 25th anniversary, it is hard to imagine modern-day, literary New Orleans without the UNO's Creative Writing Workshop. A key measure of what this program has produced is a burgeoning library of its graduates' books, now numbering more than one hundred, and many other writers plying their trade in journals and magazines.

Many alumni are working all across America. But many others have decided to remain in New Orleans where we are legion, earning our livings, as our fellows elsewhere, as college professors, high school teachers, journalists (in print and online), singer/songwriters, filmmakers, playwrights, technical writers, copy writers, and others, like me, who have become publishers, applying our way with words in any and every way we can imagine. And noticeably, the Creative Writing Workshop begat leaders and founders for other influential institutions. To name a few: *Bayou Magazine*, The Greater New Orleans Writing Project, NOLA Fugees, *Quaint Magazine*, the Neighborhood Story Project and the University of New Orleans Press. To speak the language of university administrators, business leaders, and politicians nationwide, the Creative Writing Workshop at the University of New Orleans has produced for its city an enormous economic impact.

I graduated in May of 2005, the end of an eight-year process, seen through by Joanna and Rick. In August of that year, the levees failed, and the CWW, like every institution in New Orleans, had to slog through the flood waters of Hurricane Katrina. The campus was flooded; the staff and students found shelter and footing where they could. After the initial shock, the professors and students regathered themselves, willing the program back into being, defying first the flood and then the thousand cuts of budget decreases from Baton Rouge as the state of Louisiana turned a cold shoulder to higher education.

Today, a second and third generation of fiction professors has arrived to staff the CWW as its enrollments have grown. Barb Johnson and M.O. Walsh lead workshops once headed by James Knudsen, and later by Joseph Boyden and Amanda Boyden. Meanwhile, our book's editors, Rick Barton and Joanna Leake, retired as full-time faculty, but immediately returned to the CWW front lines, still professors of fiction writing, still coming out on Monday nights to sit around the conference table and join their students at Parkview to talk writing.

Monday Nights, with its display of imaginative and inspiring fictional prose, stands as a wonderful portrait of the Creative Writing Workshop in this particular moment in history. Thanks to the astonishing and talented writers in these pages, the Workshop moves forward with a proud tradition behind it and a bright future ahead.

GRADUATES

The Ending of the Duck Joke

LINDSAY ALLEN

Colette sprinted up the stairs and crammed into the hallway outside Mae's kindergarten classroom along with all the other nannies and mothers who were already waiting to gather up lunch boxes and wrap kids in hats and scarves. She was right on time, but some of them gave her the "you're late" look. East Village parents could be so liberal when it came to recreational drug use and politics, but parenting made puritans of them all. Even Colette seemed to have lost something she once had, and when the noisy, reckless wave of arms and legs and moving mouths poured into the hallway, Colette almost toppled over from its force.

"Mom, we made puppets," Mae said.

"That's great," Colette answered, struggling to gather up her purse and Mae's lunch box, jacket, backpack, and scooter.

"Mine's a shark." She attacked Colette with cardboard fangs.

"Mine too," Mae's friend Sasha said. Polly and David were out of town, and Colette had agreed to watch Sasha for the night.

"Ooooh, so scary."

"No. Mom. Not scary. He's hungry, and you are the food. It's not scary. You get eaten—that's all that happens."

Colette felt the implied, you stupid idiot.

"Yeah. That's all," Sasha chimed in.

Colette sensed the beginning of her slow, painful death as Sasha and Mae grew into malevolent teenagers, hands on hips, scowling at her. Normally Andrew picked Mae up from school and took her to the park on Houston for a few hours; then Colette met them after work, dragged Mae home for dinner and put her to bed. "You can't count on that," her mother said when Colette told her about Andrew's duties as an afternoon dad. Ever since 911 she begged Colette to get out of the city. "Mae needs to be able to bike up and down the driveway." A perfect example of why Colette would never leave the East Village.

"Look, Mom," Mae said, thrusting her pointer finger in Colette's face. "It hurts."

Colette squatted down. A slice of nail crowned the top Mae's tiny finger. Raw, pink skin peaked out. "It's a hangnail. Let me cut off this ragged part."

"Cut it off?" Mae snatched her hand back, knocking Colette to the floor and skipped away down the hall singing.

Colette dug through her purse, searching for her keys with the little pink pocketknife key chain. She dumped the contents of her handbag on the floor. Where were they? Had she left them somewhere? The orange elementary school walls seemed to close in on her. Probably at the dry cleaners. She stared at the shark puppet's oily, white, pastel-crayon, cardboard fangs and exceptionally small, glued-on, bouncy, plastic eyeballs. Had she forgotten them at the cafe? She'd had a meeting with a possible patron for her dance company. To keep her NYU teaching gig, she had to continue producing avant-garde, Off-off-Broadway, experimental performance pieces. Her last reviews in *The Times* had been so disappointing that she now needed to prove that she was as brilliant as the critics had once thought she was, not a weird, stroke-of-luck-amateur, artistic fluke.

But she didn't feel brilliant. She felt broke and tired. She needed to raise money and soon before Amex cut her off. If she didn't get this project going, she would never be able to raise more money for other experimental and possibly more lucrative projects. She'd get fired and have to move to a subdivision in Jersey and teach ballet to spoiled, pigeon-toed nose-pickers. She could ask Andrew for help, but the agreement was always that he would cover college and she would take care of everything else.

Mae and Sasha skipped back and circled her. "Ashes to ashes, we all fall down," they sang and joined her on the floor. In the next breath, they were on their feet again.

* * *

Waiting in line at the dry cleaners, the kids made faces and stuck out their tongues then touched tongues. That was a new one. She couldn't really imagine her daughter turning into a woman who kissed women, but if that were the case Colette would be an open-minded, supportive parent. "Well, you like women. That's okay," she imagined herself saying. "I've done it. We've all done it. It's a common thing in college to go around kissing girls. Sure, I'd like to meet your girlfriend." She pictured shaking hands with a butch lesbian, whom she would treat like a man. She would let this lesbian open doors for her and fix broken things. That's probably how it would be. If, that is, Mae turned out that way. Or Mae would be the butch one! More likely Mae would turn out like Colette, a desperate, hopeless romantic, who could not stay focused on one man at a time or keep the ones she wanted. Fortunately Colette had her books, wine, friends, television, art openings, and her work. She wasn't in need, not in that way, except when she craved the physical part. Hence Trip.

Except now Trip was to blame for this mess. He occupied far too much space in her brain, so much space that there wasn't room left for remembering her keys and balancing her checkbook. She thought of his smooth back and the way he had stood on the bed, turning for her, doing that impersonation. He was unusual and witty and far too young. Colette was pretty sure Trip woke up each morning looking energetic and handsome. She was pretty sure he wouldn't want to wake up next to a five-year-old, snarled and tangled in a nest of stuffed animals and baby blankets.

As if he could feel her thinking about him, her phone vibrated. *I want to open u up and eat u.* Clearly not a poet, but he was direct. *Right now.*

"No keys. Not here," the man behind the counter said. "Sorry."

"Okay, thanks," she said, ushering the children out.

Are u ignoring me? Only makes me want u more. Come over later. Colette had to stop acting like a teenager, propping up pillows in her bed, leaving the TV on, locking, double locking the doors, and sneaking down to his apartment. It had to stop. Leaving Mae to creep off for a quickie made her a terrible mother.

Mae grabbed at her crotch. "I have to go," she whined.

They could go to the Tompkins Street Library around the corner, but the homeless people showered in the sink. She once saw a man emerge from the ladies' room, completely drenched, without his shirt. Starbucks was always filthy. Perhaps, they could pee at Life Café. She peeked through the window, hoping Clarissa—or was is Larissa?—was working. She was not. Well, Colette would have to walk them to the back, with purpose, as if she was looking for someone, and then scoot them out quickly when they were done. Colette kneeled so she was eye level with the girls. She wiped a booger off Mae's nose, and Mae squirmed away.

"Okay, when we go in there, follow directly behind me."

"Can we have milkshakes?" Mae asked. "Daddy lets me have a milkshake."

"Yeah, well, then let Daddy be responsible for your sugar addiction."

"I want one now. Pleeeeeeeese."

"Darling, listen," she said, exasperated. "Here's why you can't have a milkshake. Number one, you just had a sucker and a bagel. Number two, they're expensive. Number three, too much milk gives you a monstrous stomach ache. Number four, they have no nutritional value, and so you'll be eating loads of empty calories and though you're young and will burn them off, someday you won't and you'll get fat." Now she sounded just like Polly. She was losing their attention, but she held on as they squirmed. "I'm not done. Number five, we're going to have a race as soon as we go in there and go to the bathroom, and you'll lose, if you're filled up from a fattening milkshake."

"But you're fat, and you don't eat milkshakes."

"Mommy is fat because she doesn't exercise enough because she's taking care of you." She shouldn't have said that last part. She shouldn't blame her child. She shouldn't have brought up fatness in the first place. She wasn't actually fat. She complained about getting fat in order to prevent it from happening, as a reminder that at any moment she could become that way if she wasn't careful. Or could Mae see something she could not?

"That lady is fat," Sasha said, pointing at a woman in a big overcoat, waddling past them. Colette slapped her hand down, but it was too late.

"She's not," Colette said. The overweight woman glared at her. "I'm sorry."

"Yes she is," Mae whispered. At least she whispered it.

"Don't be rude. Apologize right now."

"Sorry," Sasha said. She fondled the zipper of her jacket.

"Girls," she began, "you never, ever, under any circumstances tell a woman she's fat. It's not nice. It's like saying ugly. Women are sensitive. There could be a thousand reasons a woman is fat. She might be pregnant. Or have diabetes or bad genes. Or be in an unhappy relationship. Or have a tragic eating disorder. You just don't know. So, do you get it? Women are not fat."

They nodded in unison.

"Now, when we go inside please follow directly behind me. Do not speak to anyone. Do not pass go. Do not stop to collect two hundred dollars."

"What? Two hundred dollars?" Sasha said, the little capitalist.

"It's a joke. From Monopoly. Seriously, though, please not a word to anyone. We're going in, and we're going to use the bathroom. No talking to anyone, understood?"

The girls nodded. Perhaps they could feel the exhaustion in her voice. As she pushed the door, it jingled, and then she heard her name.

"Colette, is that you?" a man asked, rising to hold the door open for her. "Henry."

"Oh, hi. Yes."

"How are you? It's been … you look great."

She didn't look great. He looked great, exactly the same as when they'd met a decade ago.

"Your twins?" he asked. The girls held hands and covered their mouths.

"Oh, yes. No, not twins. This is Mae, my daughter, and her very best friend, Sasha. Say hello, girls," she instructed, remembering that she'd just ordered them into silence. They shrugged, helplessly, giggling through their fingers.

"Say hi. Stop that no-talking rule for a minute. Please."

"Hello, Mae. Hello, Sasha," Henry said.

His dark hair and glasses made him look just as intelligent and mysterious as he had appeared to her the first time, many years ago, when they'd met at some recital on the Bowery. He was an aspiring musician, and she, well, an aspiring dancer, a bartender really. Or was she working in that health food store back then? She gave up on getting the girls to say hello.

"So what are you doing here?" she said, hoping that he was, perhaps, still a bachelor. "You live in the neighborhood?" She briefly entertained the thought of a reunion.

"No. Actually, we're out in LA. I got married two years ago. Crazy, huh? We just bought a little place in the Hollywood Hills. Nothing extravagant, but the price was right. So many deals when the market fell out. I actually have a mortgage. Can you believe it?"

She said she couldn't, and he went on about the good old days. Romanticizing their youth in that way was dangerous. Those nights were far more sinister than he made them sound; they drank, exchanged partners. Some exchanged needles. A whole group of them, all lost, trying to be something they'd never become, but it was fun, sure, if you distracted yourself from being poor and confused. They had all hated the establishment, and now they worked in it, for it, were consumed by it. They'd grown up. Now, at least, her life had purpose. She had Mae to look after, and when everything else seemed chaotic, that responsibility grounded her.

As he spoke, she watched the girls play a silly game of zipping their mouths shut, then opening them for a split second to produce unintelligible sounds, before zipping them up again. They pretended to toss imaginary keys behind them, scamper around on the floor looking for them only to discover another set of invisible keys in each other's pockets.

"Better for musicians out there, right?" Colette said.

"Well, I'm producing now."

"Good for you … Mae, stay near me, please. And your wife, what does she do?"

"Well, she's pregnant. Actually."

Being pregnant. What a great occupation.

"Congratulations."

"We love it out there. So much space and it's sunny. I mean New York is great, but winter and subways and walk-ups . . . " He sounded like her parents. He must have realized mid-sentence that he was backing himself into a corner and changed directions, quickly. "But you found a way to make it work. Tell me. What are you up to these days?"

"Doing choreography now. I have a company actually. And I teach. NYU."

"Your husband must be a saint."

She didn't quite understand his meaning. Why would her husband be a saint? For marrying her? For taking Mae when she was at rehearsal? If he was her husband, wouldn't that be his job?

"Oh, right," Colette said. "Yes. Mae's father is an angel." She didn't feel like getting into the whole story with Henry. Andrew wasn't her husband, had never been her husband, and would never be her husband. Colette and Andrew were friends. They were purposely *not* together from the start. Eventually she would have to tell Mae that her existence had been carefully considered. Andrew had wanted a child. So had Colette. They'd decided they'd better hurry up and do it before she stopped producing eggs.

"Well," she said. "These girls have to go." Let Henry wonder why she didn't wear a ring. Let him find out through the grapevine sooner or later. Made no difference. Mae grabbed her crotch again. The Michael Jackson move. This conversation could only be torture for a five-year-old. "So good to see you again."

"You too." Henry leaned in to give her a peck on the cheek and then another like the French, but she wasn't prepared for the second kiss and turned her head the wrong way. His lips grazed hers and landed close to her mouth. She could smell his aftershave. He lingered for a moment too long. "I'm staying at the Soho Grand," he whispered before he pulled away. He said it so quietly and looked so at ease, she thought she had imagined it. Both Mae and Sasha were uncharacteristically quiet, watching the awkward goodbye. Colette smiled. She felt her cheeks flush as Henry, calm as ever, sank into his seat to enjoy his newspaper and a cup of coffee. What a luxury.

In the bathroom, Mae wrapped her arms around Colette's neck, and Colette squatted down, holding Mae's little, pink thighs, so that Mae was suspended over the toilet seat. They waited for the tinkle.

"Mom, who was that?" Mae asked.

"An old friend from a long time ago."

"Was he your boyfriend?"

Children could be so intelligent and intuitive when they felt like it.

"Yes. No. Not exactly. I don't know. It was a long time ago."

"So, why don't you have him anymore?"

Colette wondered about this question. Mae was good like that. She got straight to the point. No easy questions. Oh, no. Why don't the subways follow a schedule? Why are mean people mean? What color is vitamin C?

"Because your daddy's my best friend."

Mae's question tugged at her. She never fully understood the real reason she and Henry had fallen apart. Maybe Henry, when he was dating Colette, had sought a diversion from the path his life should take just so that he could some day look back and reminisce, as he just had, about the days when they lived amongst drug addicts and punk rockers. They'd gotten along well and spent endless hours walking through Chinatown, Little Italy, the West Village, the East Village, with their arms linked, planning their impossible futures. His had turned out well. Although not as he had hoped. He'd wanted to be a rock star, but probably, underneath it all, he always wanted to be the one behind the scenes. And hers had turned out well also. Though not as she'd planned. Or exactly as planned? Better than planned? She'd always wanted to be a dancer. But that was the thing about it—she'd never made a plan. Things came at her, and she avoided them or confronted them. She'd been fun, but apparently not the kind you marry.

"Mom. Mom. I'm done."

Colette realized that Mae had been pinching her neck.

"I think Daddy is my best friend," Mae said.

"What about Sasha and me? That doesn't make us feel very loved."

"Well, you can be seconds. Daddy buys me milkshakes."

She let it go. She let Sasha and Mae hash it out about best friends, the requirements, the privileges and duties of such a title. She was happy that they had each other, and she wasn't going to worry about buying milkshakes. When she pulled down Sasha's tights to hold her over the toilet seat, she realized that she was too late.

"Whoops. You had an accident."

Sasha burst into tears. Colette kissed her forehead.

"It happens to all of us. Accidents happen. Even I had an accident today."

"You did?" Sasha said.

"Well, I only went a wee bit in my panties, but I had to go sooooooo bad and someone made me so excited, and it just came out."

Sasha felt better now. Colette could tell.

"But the really big accident I had today," she said, as she tried her best to wrap wads of toilet paper around Sasha's undies so she wouldn't feel quite so uncomfortable, "was that I forgot the keys at home."

"You did what?" Sasha said, as if trying to understand how someone could make such a mistake. She really was just like Polly. "I know," she said, always a serious thinker, "let's go to my house, and then we can check the message machine and see if my mom and dad called."

"Only thing is. I forgot those keys too!" Colette smacked her own forehead like a clown and said, "Silly me!" This didn't seem to make Sasha feel better.

"What are we going to do?"

"Don't worry. I have a plan. In fact, I have a surprise," she said. She had to say something. Sasha's bottom lip quivered. "You must behave like little angels if you want to find out what it is."

Why had she brought up any of this in the first place? The children didn't need to know that she was worried about the keys. What had she done all day? Maybe she could make a few phone calls. She'd taken Mae to school, picked up her dress at the dry cleaner's, grabbed a coffee, changed in the bathroom of the Starbucks, taken the subway from St. Marks up to 23rd, been fifteen minutes late to her meeting, lamented the lack of funding for the arts and the precarious position of modern dance, headed downtown to critique a student's final project, eaten a late lunch at that falafel place in Soho, stopped by the studio, picked up tampons at the bodega, and walked over to Mae's school. It was possible, she thought, that her keys could be home, inside the apartment. They had one of those doors now that locked automatically, and this morning had been hectic. She had her hands full. Yes. Most likely they were sitting on the kitchen counter.

* * *

While the girls climbed up and down the steps of someone's brownstone, Colette sat on the stoop and made a few calls to confirm that she'd not left her keys at any one of those places that she'd been to earlier. She'd have to call a locksmith or the building manager. She'd scribbled down the new super's name and stuck it on the fridge.

Lately, it seemed that every day was like this, containing some sort of dramatic event: losing, finding, forgetting, bumping into or discovering something. There was none of the gentle lull that the summer had brought, where all the days were essentially the same, lazy and long, easy to understand. The world seemed to conspire against her, and she wished, briefly, that she had a little bungalow in West Hollywood, where she could put a key under a rock and know that she was always free to go home.

She really didn't want to deal with her landlord, but she had no choice. She called him. No answer. He screened his calls. She was sure of it. Who else did she know in the building? Trip. Her salvation. She texted him before she could stop herself. She needed help. This would be the end of things for sure. *In a bind! Do you have the number for the super?*

He was always home at this time. Half of his apartment was devoted to his work. He photographed food. He spent all day adjusting lighting for a glass of milk or a chocolate chip cookie. Ridiculous! He was an artist, but this was how he made money, and now the money-making part had taken over—it always did.

Trip knew that she had a child, but he didn't really get it. She never talked about Mae. He never saw them together. As far as he was concerned, her daughter was a magnificent excuse for anything she did or didn't want to do. This daughter made it impossible for them to have dinner dates. This daughter made her seem wise. This daughter ensured that nothing would ever become too serious. He liked this invisible daughter, but meeting her would change everything. Seeing her in person would make Colette a real mother with a real daughter. Colette would cease to be the mysterious dancer down the hall and become instead maternal, old, boring. Not to mention, how it might confuse Mae if Colette had Daddy as her best friend and this other man as her second best friend.

But Mae was only a child. She would get over that. Colette hardly remembered anything from age five. Trip wrote back: *anything for you. Come and get it.*

He was persistent. She liked that. And he had the number for the super.

Mae balanced on the third stair. Colette wanted to stop her but let her jump. When Mae scrambled back up to jump from the fourth one, Colette watched Mae swing her arms and rock onto her toes, drawing up courage and momentum. She flew, landed on her feet, and pitched forward onto the concrete, scraping her hands. When she stood, the knees of her tights were dirty. Colette pretended she hadn't seen the fall. Sometimes if she didn't react, Mae brushed herself off and continued playing. Not this time; she wailed and held out her hands. Colette held her until she calmed down.

"Come, girls, let's walk home," she said, thinking about surprises.

* * *

Colette heard the sound of running water, the shower, coming from the other room, but Trip had told her to walk right in, and so they did. Despite a little voice that told her not to, she entered, only to find Trip naked in the kitchen, talking on his cell phone, looking at a tiny magnet calendar on the fridge. His exposed, firm buttocks stared back at her. She quickly turned to cover Mae and Sasha's eyes, but they'd already seen his nakedness.

As he swiveled around, holding up a finger over his lips to tease Colette and put her off for one more minute, they saw the rest of him, including his erect, now half-erect, penis.

"What the?" Trip said. He reached for a dishtowel to cover up.

"Oh no!" Colette said. "Girls, come." She led them into the hallway. He disappeared into the bedroom.

"I think his thinger is bigger than my dad's," Mae said to Sasha.

"Why was he naked?" Sasha asked.

"What I want to know is why dads all have hairs on their butts."

This should make her laugh. Later, she might laugh, but instead she felt a sickening tightening in her stomach: guilt about exposing her daughter and her friend's daughter to Trip's nudity. But why should she feel that way? Was nudity such a bad thing? Europe is full of nude beaches. She wished they lived in France where naked people could run free amongst children. She'd spent a year in Paris in her twenties. Perhaps Europe held the answers to all her problems: health care, education, sexual liberation. She and Mae should move to a villa in France.

What would she tell Polly? Nothing. Everything.

"Trip was about to take his shower," she said. He probably thought that she was coming over to romp around before she ran off to pick up the children. It wasn't such an insane gesture. She might have done the same. In fact, she was almost certain that, before Mae, she had done the same thing. She should have told him that she was with the kids. "And then he got an important phone call, and his phone was in the kitchen, so he didn't have time to put on some clothes before he ran out to answer it."

The simple explanation seemed reasonable enough.

"Then why did he buzz us in?" Sasha asked. Sometimes she was too smart for her own good. Colette didn't have an answer. For some reason an image of Lana Turner in *The Postman Always Rings Twice* came to mind, and she wanted nothing more than to be back in her old apartment with a big bowl of buttered popcorn watching the movie channel while Mae slept next to her.

"He must have thought it was the mailman dropping off a package downstairs."

"But who is he?" Mae said. "Where's his kids?"

"Where *are* his kids? He doesn't have any."

"Why not?" Sasha asked. This seemed to disturb her even more than his nudity.

"I don't know. You'll have to ask him. He's just a neighbor, and he's going to help us get into our apartment."

Trip returned, wearing jeans. He seemed agitated but invited them into the living room, which looked very different than she remembered it. His bookshelves didn't hold books but rather expensive camera equipment and a strange collection of super hero toys, while all of his large coffee table photography books lined up in a neat vertical stack against the exposed brick of the non-working fireplace between the windows. They were too neat to have been read.

"Don't touch anything," Colette said. The girls sat in the high stools at the breakfast bar, spinning left and right.

"Sorry. I've had a horrendous day," she said. "Really. I ran into an old friend and I had this thing, this meeting. And the keys on top of all that."

He nodded as he searched through his phone for the number of the superintendent of the building.

"I thought that, you know," he said, raising an eyebrow in the direction of the girls, and continued, "that you were coming alone."

He was not apologetic. He seemed irritated.

"I'm sorry," Colette said.

Finally, he found the number and dialed for her. He handed her his phone and when the man answered she explained her situation, pacing around the room near the stack of books. She noticed that they were arranged alphabetically.

In the kitchen, Trip tried to make conversation, asking names, ages, basic information, and Mae answered quietly, while Sasha drew pictures with her finger on the counter top. Then she heard Mae ask, "You don't have any girls like us?"

"I only want boys," he said, laughing at his own joke. "Just kidding."

But he didn't answer the question, or if he did, Colette didn't hear his response. She made plans to meet the super in an hour and prepared to take the girls elsewhere to wait, but Trip offered to make them a frozen pizza.

"If you don't mind," Colette said. Polly would kill her. Bagels for a snack. Pizza for dinner. At least she said no to the milkshake. He turned on the oven and opened a bottle of wine, poured a glass for himself and one for Colette. He fiddled around with his music and stepped into the other room to answer a call. A stale, burnt curry odor seeped from the oven.

There were only two stools so the girls sat while Colette leaned. Trip glided into the room and popped the pizza into the oven before it reached the preheated temperature. Colette restrained herself from commenting, and while they waited for the pizza to cook, Mae told the only joke she could tell.

"A duck walks into the store and says, 'Got any gwapes?'" Mae began.

"And the owner says, nope," Colette said, who loved the duck joke and had taught it to Mae. Watching Mae tell a joke was painful because Mae had to get every word right. She was reminded of that first time Mae had glided away on her scooter in the church parking lot. If Mae missed a beat, the punch line was ruined, and there was nothing Colette could do about it.

"I'm telling it," Mae said, kicking her feet against the stool under the counter. "Then the duck goes back the next day, and he says, 'Got any gwapes?' and the owner is getting mad, and he says, 'I told you yesterday, I ain't got no grapes, and if you ask me again, I'll nail your beak to the wall. So what do you think happens?" Mae said.

Trip shrugged.

"Take a guess."

Andrew always wanted Mae to postulate on how things might turn out.

"I don't know. Maybe the duck asks for apples," Trip said.

"Nope, you're wrong. The duck goes back and says, 'Got any nails?' and the owner says, 'nope,' and so the duck says, 'Got any gwapes?'"

They laughed. Colette sighed in relief.

"Get it?" Mae said. "If he doesn't have any nails he can't hammer his beak."

The super was late, and they watched TV, sitting around like a family. Trip choked on his wine while doing Donald Duck impersonations, and it squirted through his nose, which the girls found hilarious. Colette hoped it would help them forget everything else from earlier. This, she thought, was how something sexual turned into something more. The roadrunner zoomed through the desert. She wanted to reach over and take Trip's hand but didn't. As they were leaving, Trip leaned over and whispered that he already knew the ending of the duck joke. "Thanks for pretending," Colette said, squeezing his bicep as she stepped out into the hall.

The keys were on the counter, just as she'd suspected. They were all exhausted, but she stripped the kids down and forced herself to give them a bath, which took up a good part of the evening. They fell asleep after some whining and stories, and she was at last alone with her nightcap and her book. She wondered if Trip would text. He didn't. Before she went to sleep, she sent him a message: *You were gweat.*

But he didn't write back.

* * *

That Sunday when Polly and David returned and took Sasha home, Colette and Mae sprawled out in their urban emptiness. They devoted the afternoon to nothing. Mae had been wearing her pink tutu since Saturday morning and was still prancing about casting magic, happy-princess spells with her wand. Stretched out across the hardwood floor underneath a "castle" of pillows and bed sheets, Colette dozed off with an unread newspaper. The afternoon light blazed through the open window.

Mae slid under the sheets and into the fort next to Colette. She put her face so close that Colette could feel her hot, deep breaths. Colette opened her eyes, and Mae stared back.

"My stomach hurts," Mae said, with great sincerity, and Colette opened her eyes wider, yawning, roused with concern.

"Like how? Where?"

"Here," Mae said, pointing to her bellybutton and circling it. "I need a milkshake."

"You do, do you? Would that make your stomach better?" Colette reached for Mae, wrecking the fort. "You're full of it." She blew a raspberry on Mae's belly.

"Full of what?" Mae asked.

For dinner, they walked over to Avenue A, sat down in a booth at Odessa, and ordered a large chocolate milkshake with two straws.

Spit

JAMIE AMOS

John shouldn't have brought the girl here. They stand facing each other in his tiny kitchen, Billie watches him, and John's eyes flit from her bright red hair to her chin to his cabinets and back. He can't tell if she's pretty or just very young, but there's a difference, and he can't figure it out until they get older and their faces sag. All women are young once, but only a few are truly pretty.

He hands her a glass of tequila which she sets on the counter so she can twist her hair into a ponytail, revealing a substrata of roots disguised by that clownish red dye. He wonders what she looks like beneath all her paint and color, a visual barrier between Billie and the world. He cocks his head, concentrating.

"What?"

"Tell me what you'll do next semester."

She talks and talks but has no plans. At least that John can tell. Her dreams are like half-deflated balloons, the colors leached from them by the sun. She'll quit the copy center at the university where John has taught for the past ten years. She'll find a job, she tells John, maybe bill coding, probably across the river where her father lives, maybe not. Just a job. And then. She hasn't thought much about then.

"You should talk to the career counselors."

Billie blinks. "Hmm," she says.

"No, you should. I mean—" He studies her, the hard way she stands, arms crossed, one hip cocked, a playfully defiant smirk masking her inability to hold his eyes. It seems like all the girls in his classes stand like this now: both insecure and confrontational, daring old men like John to want them. They linger near his office, perch at his desk with accusatory eyes. They're so angry, and he can't understand why—they have this whole big world, all for them.

He grabs more limes from the fridge and slices them. Billie lifts a wedge to her mouth and licks, and the delight in her expression conjures his daughters before he can stop himself, Ashley, cross-legged in her room, building kingdoms out of construction paper, Brianna, probably on the couch, reading, her bangs touching the bridge of her nose. Somewhere Linda moves through the house, like an apparition, the miracle of laundered, folded clothes and dusted shelves unnoticed by the girls. Place him there just a couple months ago, and he is sequestered in the home office, on his fourth beer, embarrassed every time the naked woman on screen looks directly into her web cam.

Billie wanders his apartment living room, pausing to consider a stack of books by the couch. If she finds this place shabby, she doesn't say so. His first week here he considered it a sanctuary. The bare walls, the secondhand couch, all of this the Spartan neatness of someone who lives alone and on very little. But now, in the glaring light of a bare bulb, this place looks desperate, sad in a way he denied each time he returned here in the evenings.

She stops at his CD case and thumbs through the few CDs he brought with him. "What's your favorite?"

This is a test. A measure of his age, his ability to navigate current culture. If he answers with a band she's never heard of—the Pixies? Yo La Tengo?—he has the advantage of sounding knowledgeable about obscure music. But it could also date him, sending them both careening back to the late eighties of his college days when Billie was probably still in grade school. "You're my guest," he says, "You pick," and she turns her back to him, a faint sigh registering her disappointment as she plucks Nirvana from its case.

When the music starts, they both sit on the couch, Billie with her feet tucked beneath her, the glass still in her hands, John at the opposite end. This is what you don't expect: the awkward silences, a stinging self-consciousness. You forget, being married so long, the aching quiet of two people unfamiliar with each other.

John coughs. "Do you like the copy center?"

She reaches into her purse, a small clam-shaped one with sequins, like one of his daughters might play with. “I can smoke?”

His place will smell for days, maybe even his clothes when he drives to the house tomorrow to see his kids. Brianna will smell the collar of his sports coat when he hugs her, and she will stiffen. She will say, when she is older, that this is the moment she knew.

“Sure,” he says.

Billie blows a long stream of smoke to the right of her face, and it clouds the air between them. “It’s better than waiting tables. And my boss is okay.” She grins and considers him for a moment. “You should hear his ‘Dr. Professor’ voice. He does it for all of you.”

“What do you mean?”

“The professors. He does this impression of all of you.”

“What does he say?”

“About you?”

“Yes, about me.”

“We mostly talk about the other ones. They all want their copies that day or they have all these stupid orders for things we don’t do. I think about you we just said your sweaters look like Muppets would wear them.”

“Muppets.”

“Yeah, like Sesame Street. But it works on you.” She grabs a ceramic coaster—a paw print Brianna made him for Father’s Day—and wipes her ash on the lip before setting it back down. She scoots closer to him. “I wasn’t trying to hurt your feelings.”

He thought they’d been flirting. Both of them. He walked into the copy center one day, inhaled the powdery chemical smell of paper reams, and handed her his slip to pick up his copies. He could feel her watching him from behind the cabinet as she thumbed through the orders. She smiled the way women do in movies—all teeth and flesh, nothing hidden—and he wanted to make her laugh every time he saw her. He started drawing smiley faces on his copy orders, then dinosaurs flying airplanes, then robots holding flowers. She drew notes back. He brought her books. A dog-eared copy of *We Don’t Live Here Anymore*, ink marks in the margins, his thoughts almost twenty years old. When she gave it back to him, she looked him right in the eye and said, “That man doesn’t seem sorry for sleeping with his best friend’s wife.”

"He's not," John said, voice steady.

Billie stands. "Tell me about teaching. Do you hate your students?"

"I like teaching."

She heads toward his bedroom before he can stop her. She emerges from the hallway, drops her cigarette in her glass, and leans against the wall. He doesn't feel drunk, just warm. She smiles, but she doesn't look happy.

"The kids on your dresser," she says. "How old are they?"

"I'm sorry?"

"The picture. Like they're skiing."

Colorado, last year. Linda packed hot chocolate in thermoses for them, and Ashley tripped, spilling hers on the snow. Brianna picked up Ashley's thermos and poured half of her own hot chocolate inside. A small moment, but in it he and Linda felt that they had done everything right. "They're twelve and eight."

Billie grimaces.

"What?"

"Nothing. I'm just—" She leans back and looks up. "I thought they were much younger."

This surprises him. They *are* young, practically still babies, nowhere near the age of this girl. But he knows better. Earlier this spring, Linda was folding laundry on the couch while he graded papers. Out of the corner of his eye he saw her pick up a flimsy bra, just two white cotton triangles and elastic straps.

"What is that?" he asked.

Linda rolled her eyes. "John, she's almost thirteen."

He tries to look at Billie again, to return to this limbo space that is his home and not his home. But he thinks of Linda leaving the room with the laundry basket, that bra folded neatly inside. He left his papers in the chair to find Ashley and take her to his favorite used bookshop. Up and down the aisles she smeared snake trails in the dust, searching for books about adventurous girls doing improbable things like flying or going on safaris.

"Your wife looks nice," Billie says, "in the picture." He'd snapped the photograph right when Linda had called his name, and it looked like he'd captured her laugh. He loved her laugh, always, the way she swallowed each one halfway through. But that inward and shy quality had changed over the years, intensified, so that John felt as if his wife presented a fortress and pretended it was her face.

"My wife is a really good person," he says for no reason, "but we're more like roommates now."

"I'm sure." Billie nods. "Most wives are."

Billie reaches down and draws her short skirt up her thigh. There, puckered like raised rivers on a map, are the tender pink scars of trauma and then the delicate black lace of her panties. "You're old enough to be my father," she says and laughs, a lone blue fingernail disappearing beneath the scalloped edge.

He wants to ask her what happened to her, her whole life, but he doesn't think he'll understand any of it. He senses a menace in her, acute and pointed where it was unfocused before. Linda said to him once when Brianna painted her fingernails black and uglied her face with her mother's makeup that there are two impulses warring inside every young girl: one who wants to spit and one who wants to be spit on. What do women see that he can't? What is waiting for his daughters?

Billie unbuttons her blouse and tosses it to the ground. Her skirt and underwear next. She straddles him, her small breasts guarded by the lace of her bra. He closes his eyes and waits for that moment of entering this girl when she will gasp as if wounded.

Names on My Tongue

REBECA ANTOINE

The last time I saw my mother, she had Aunt Vivian on the brain. My mother and I were sitting side by side at the slot machines at the Indian casino when she turned and looked at me.

"Last night I dreamt of Vivian again." She turned away from me then and slipped another quarter into the machine. That's the way she likes to do it. One quarter at a time.

"What was she doing?" I asked. My mother often offered dreams for interpretation.

"We were just girls. Sitting behind the old oak tree, looking out at the cotton field, smoking one of Poppa's pipes." She pulled down the slot machine's arm.

"They have buttons for that now," I said. I always reminded her of the button.

"I like the arm," she said. "Feels like I have more control."

"There's no difference." I put a bunch of quarters in and pushed the button. Five quarters gathered in the machine's gullet. I smiled, winked at her, then asked, "But in your dream, you were young and blissful?"

She nodded. "You look so much like her." She ran her finger down my cheek. "Especially when you were younger. So much like her." My mother got a wistful, faraway look in her eye, and I hoped she would not tell it again. "We had such good times together."

I know the story. My aunt Vivian moved up North years before my mother did. Vivian was fifteen and came up to New Haven with my aunt Ginny, who was twenty at the time. Ginny had a particular affection for alcohol and men with conked hair and shiny cars. The two of them worked in white people's houses. Vivian was a nanny to a doctor's children and went to school, while Ginny was the maid for a bachelor lawyer and got to sleep in her own home at night. The doctor Vivian worked for used to come to her room at night and mess with her. I've always admired Southerners' uses of euphemisms. "Messed with" sounds so much easier to take than "raped." After a while, Vivian got used to the doctor; she figured that white men liked to mess with black girls. That was the way her own grandmother was conceived. Vivian stayed one whole weekend with the children because the Missus was out of town visiting her people. The doctor let his friends have at Vivian as well, and one night six men raped her. This she thought was too much, and she told Ginny, who in turn told their mother. Vivian never went back to the doctor's house, just left all her things, nice dresses and all. Grandma Penny came up and got her, but Vivian was never the same. She had trouble sleeping after that. My mother used to say that Vivian had bad dreams and always thought someone was after her. Turned out that she was pregnant, and when she found out, Vivian couldn't sleep at all and was always trying to hurt herself. Grandma Penny knew a woman in the next county who could get rid of the baby, and so they drove three hours to the woman's house. Aunt Vivian was just starting to eat normally again when my mother found her face down in the creek behind their house. My mother always ended that story saying, "Vivi never did learn how to swim."

But my mother did not tell me that day. Now I wish she had, so I could have heard it just once more from her. She tells it better than I do; she has a certain flair with her words, a cadence that camouflages the tragedy of it. Instead, she just turned back to her slot machine, fed it another quarter, and pulled down the arm. She came out ten dollars ahead that day. That was three weeks ago, and I didn't know my mother was dying. Not in the way that we're all dying, life seeping out of us day by day, but dying in the way that something faulty inside consumes you.

I never met my aunt Vivian. She died a lifetime before I was born. To me, she is forever a girl smiling up from a grainy black and white picture. The girl in my mother's dreams. And she is my namesake.

"Repeat after me, Vivian," the doctor says. "My name is Vivian Rogers."

The doctor seems not to understand that if I could do such a thing, I would not be sitting before him dressed in paper.

I open my mouth, but only a low, guttural sound comes out. I pick up my notebook and write, *I can't.*

Jean, my husband, is in the room as well. It seems lately that he has seen me more inside of hospitals than out. At least this time I don't need a D&C. In the two years we've been married, I have had four miscarriages. I just kept trying again, hoping something would happen. Like suddenly I would no longer have an inhospitable uterus. Despite these recent misfortunes, Jean still manages a soft, empathetic look when he sees me this way. His head is slightly tilted as he shakes it, always maintaining eye contact with me. I offer him a smile, and he mirrors my weak gesture.

"Look," he says. "Vivian says she can't talk. Aren't you supposed to figure out why?"

The doctor turns around and begins speaking to Jean. Now it is the two of them, talking about me as if I am not here, as if I do not exist. I have faded noiselessly into the background. I close my eyes and listen to them. Jean is French, and despite his years in America, he holds onto a thick accent. Words sound so much better coming from him. My name sounds like music, broken, staccatoed, with a flourish at the end.

"I told you last time," the doctor is saying, "I didn't find anything *physically* wrong with her." He is trying to whisper, but I think my hearing is better since my speech is gone.

"You said some time," Jean says, "but it's been weeks now, and I'm worried."

I open my eyes and tap my pen loudly on my notebook, and the men look at me again, both with soft, empathetic looks, and I wonder if they've practiced those looks over time, that these are the looks found to bring the most comfort to damaged women.

The doctor sits in front of me again. He is convinced that my muteness is psychosomatic.

* * *

I found my mother's body lying on her living room floor, just a few feet from her phone. I imagined that she had fallen there on her way to answer my weekly call to confirm our slots date. That was our mother-daughter time. Sitting at slot machines. When I didn't hear from her that night, I worried, drove over to her house and there she was. I took care of the arrangements, we buried her next to my father, and when the first handful of dirt landed on the coffin, I opened my mouth to ask my husband for his handkerchief, and I couldn't say a word.

When I am at work, people pretend nothing is wrong. I realize that talking is overrated. I do everything by e-mail; at staff meetings I go unnoticed. My assistant takes messages. Most things work themselves out without my interference. It is when I get home that the trouble begins. Jean constantly tries to prompt me to speak, as if he can just wear down my will and fully formed words will magically appear in my mouth.

* * *

"So there's nothing wrong with you, Vivian," Jean says over dinner one evening. He has taken me out to a nice restaurant where they place several types of wineglasses on the table, then remove the ones that are inappropriate for the wine you order. I have brought my notebook and pen so that we might not spend the entire evening in silence, so to speak.

It's something, though.

"So, what shall we do?" he says, and punctuates his question with a sigh. He has been sighing more often lately. I believe my silence frustrates him because it makes me no longer a willing partner in his games. With Jean, it's always talking. Talking about things we'll do, things we'll be. Jean has the habit of asking me questions that he knows I cannot really answer. He'll look up from the Travel section of the Sunday *Times* and say, "Why haven't we been to Cairo?" as if we'd ever actually spoken about going to Cairo and perhaps decided against it. Then we go back and forth, intermittently, all day on the pros and cons of going to Cairo.

"Is it just me you don't want to talk to or is it everyone?" he asks, sipping from his ballooned wineglass.

It's not my choice.

Nevertheless, we spend most of the evening gazing over each other's shoulders at other couples who are laughing, smiling, and playfully touching each other's noses. Jean seems to find comfort in his sighing. I find it strange, the stagnation our relationship suffers when we cannot play these games, when I have nothing to offer my husband but my mere presence. When he looks at me, it's as if I'm far away, just a blurry image.

* * *

My mother left me her photographs. There are a number of pictures of my parents and my brothers and me. But there are also photographs from my mother's childhood, the photographs Grandma Penny left when she died. I am sitting on the bed, pictures spread before me, trying to choose which ones will be framed, which ones will be digitally reborn, and which ones will simply return to the velvet-lined box my mother used to keep on the top shelf of her closet. Jean lies down next to me and runs his fingers along the scars on my thigh. He kisses a spot of reformed skin and pulls me into a firm hug.

"I think I fell in love with your scars," he says.

I reach for my pen and paper and scribble, *???*

"When I first saw these scars, I thought that you must be a risk taker." He gives me a little squeeze, and I pull away from him.

Clumsy. That's all.

"I don't believe you've ever been just clumsy." He fingers a dark spot above my knee, about three inches long. "Tell me, how did this happen? Every scar has a story."

He's right, maybe. Up and down each of my legs is a multitude of scars, and every one just might have a story. Not all of them good ones, I know. Jean rests his fingers on the spot again; his eyes plead with me to tell him something.

I remember the pain I felt before the skin grew back. I remember the blood.

The last week of every June, my brothers and I stayed at Aunt Trudy's up in Windham. She had two girls around my age and a boy the same age as my oldest brother. On that day, I'd been upstairs with the girls, and they had been trying on clothes. They wouldn't let me try on any of their dresses because they said that maybe some of my black would rub off on them. They were all light-skinned beauties, and their mother wouldn't let them out in the sun. The girls called me Hershey's Kiss because I was dark like chocolate, and they called my oldest brother Hershey's Special Dark because he was even darker than the rest of us. That day I sat on the bed, watching them preen in the mirror until they pushed me out of the room. I ran out into the yard and followed the boys up the tree. But I lost my footing and fell right onto the boulder that sat at the tree's root; a sharp, jagged piece of rock scraped deep into my thigh. I probably should have gone to the emergency room, gotten stitches or something, but Aunt Trudy sprayed it with antiseptic and told me to keep it covered with Band-Aids. I never spent time at Aunt Trudy's after that.

Jean is still looking at me, waiting. "I can tell you're remembering. Aren't you going to tell me?"

I kiss his forehead and quickly scrawl, *I fell*. There is only so much that I can write, and I find myself forced to issue terse replies.

"But how?" he asks. "How did you fall?"

Doesn't matter.

Jean sits up, kisses my cheek. "Maybe some other time, then."

He leaves the room, and I am alone, faded photographs in my palms. The pictures remind me of the stories my mother used to tell, and the stories keep going around and around in my mind. They are a history of my mother's family, my family, our lives. Jean doesn't know these stories; I haven't had occasion to tell them. He knows that I love red wine, and I am not such a good listener most of the time. He knows my family as the working-class New Englanders we remade ourselves to be, people whose prized possession is a Weber grill that we pulled out systematically on Memorial Day, the Fourth of July, and Labor Day, as people who vacation on the Cape in the off-season. This is who we became, and it all seemed so easy.

* * *

We were sitting at the slot machines when I first told my mother that Jean and I were engaged. She told me the story about her cousin Mansy, who thought she would marry up by not marrying black and spent years living with a man from Ireland who ended up killing her when she was pregnant with their second child.

"He killed her but good," she said.

"I don't think I'm too good for anybody," I said.

"I wasn't talking about you."

"And Jean's not Irish."

"Didn't say he was," my mother said, pulling down her machine's arm.

My mother had a sad story for every occasion. I guess that's what happens when you live long enough, or your family's large enough.

* * *

My great aunt Tookie smiles up at me from a faded photograph now limp with age. She stands beside a man who holds a saxophone, and I wonder how they met, what they were doing that day, whether they were lovers. On the back of Aunt Tookie's picture, someone has written "Tookie with Arthur Ruddy."

I pick up my pad and write, *Tookie*. I compare the handwriting on the back with my own, noting where the gentle slopes of my cursive match that on the photograph. The handwriting is decidedly feminine, and I wonder whom it belongs to. My writing is identical to my mother's. I write the name again, *Tookie*.

Tookie was a spinster. She was always the pretty one, high yellow and good hair. She probably could have passed like some of her sisters did, but Tookie was too proud for all that. Too proud to always worry about being found out, to worry about what color her children might turn up. But white men sometimes don't care about having children; they're happy with pretty wives and money and vacations in Paris. Tookie could have been a doctor's wife. In 1921, Tookie packed up her hats and moved to New York. She was nineteen, should have been married and pregnant by then. Should have been married to Rue Kingsly, who lived about five miles down the road. He was a nice boy with golden skin and a few acres his family owned outright. Tookie took a shine to Rue, but two weeks before she got on that train to New York City, Rue's daddy found him hung from a tree on their property. Sheriff said it must have been suicide, that Rue must have been upset over a lady friend or whatnot. Tookie cried a little and packed up her hats saying that she wasn't going to have any children just so the white men could kill them with nothing she could do about it. Tookie danced in clubs in Harlem, drank whiskey like a man, smoked cigarettes, and never went to church. She said it wasn't worth her Sundays for a God that did nothing for her. Tookie didn't say, but she never did get over Rue, and she never married or had children. One man whose name escapes me courted Tookie for a while and wanted to take her away from that life, but she never could settle. Tookie always used to say "Love well, or not at all."

Jean reaches over me and pulls the picture from my hand. "Earth to Vivi," he says. He reminds me that since my voice left me, I have the tendency to let my jaw go slack, and I stare off into the distance with my mouth hanging open.

He holds the photograph up to his face, then flips it over to read the back. "What kind of name is Tookie?" he asks, inspecting the faded writing.

I flip to the next page in my notebook. *Her name was Anna Beth*, I write.

"They just called her Tookie?"

I nod my head.

"Why?"

Why not?

Jean concedes this and leaves me once again in silence with my mother's photographs. I watch him as he leaves the room. He walks slowly, stopping to pick up a pen from the dresser as though that is what he came to the room for in the first place. He stops again at the door, takes a lingering look back and smiles. He reminds me of the last episode of a sitcom, where the characters always seem to be moving from where they live. This always signals the end; we apparently cannot follow them outside of the world of that single space. They stop, turn, and look back on what was before they embrace what will be. This thought amuses me slightly, and I smile. Jean thinks I'm smiling back at him, and his smile grows wider before he saunters down the hallway.

I don't know the answer to Jean's question, why they called Aunt Tookie by that name. But it seems that everyone had another name back then. There was the name they were given at birth and the other that they earned. Grandma Penny's real name was Lacy, but when she was three years old, she almost choked to death on a penny. They used to call my mother Funny because she never liked to be near boys; they thought she'd grow up to be a lesbian. I used to be called Bunny because I liked to jump up and down. Nobody calls me Bunny anymore.

* * *

I have an appointment with a new doctor to discuss my options. Much to Jean's dismay, I have been putting this off. I wonder maybe if this is the source of his sighing, not my lack of vocal communication. My new doctor is a woman. She is five feet tall at the most, and the chair in her office has clearly been made for a much larger person. It is brown and leather and sturdy. She sinks into it, and she looks to me like a child playing dress-up. Jean sits beside me holding my hand, patient and assiduous; he wrinkles his forehead pensively as the doctor speaks.

"The HSG your previous doctor did came up normal, but when we performed the hysteroscopy it showed that you have some scar tissue on your uterus."

My stomach sinks even though the doctor's voice is quick and light. She gives me the empathetic look, though I believe she is smiling too much. She is staring at me as I nod my head. I gather that she expects me to say something, but I have left my notebook in the car.

"My wife has laryngitis," Jean offers.

"Oh. For how long?" the doctor asks.

"A month now," Jean says.

"Have you seen a doctor?" she asks.

I nod.

"Well." She flips through my file and explains that the scar tissue is what makes my uterus a bad place for a baby to grow. She tells me how I would have been able to tell there was scarring and how cases as minor as mine can be easily missed but can cause horrible damage to a pregnancy as we well know. Jean wants to know what we can do about it, how we can make my body safe again. "This could have happened after your first miscarriage," the doctor adds. "Possibly why they did the HSG in the first place."

Jean appears satisfied by this answer. That everything has been explained away. We have a new lease on life. He turns to me, smiling, his brow still furrowed. I nod thoughtfully, though I fear my smile to be as inappropriate as the doctor's. I immediately know where this scarring came from. I remember the pain instantaneously.

Jean tightens his grip on my hand as the doctor explains the surgery. She uses the words doctors usually use, like "simple procedure" and "routine." She spouts off risks and percentages and chances of conception post-surgery.

"This can be extraordinarily successful for you," she adds. "We can go in with a scope and repair the tissue."

"That simple?" Jean asks.

"Pretty much. Of course I can't promise everything will be perfect." The doctor smiles at me.

Jean holds my hand tighter and looks at me, smiling. "You see, Vivi. Simple."

I motion to the doctor for a paper and pencil. She looks befuddled for a moment, then hands me a pad of Post-it notes.

I will have to think about it.

Jean's face falls farther than I have ever seen it fall before. He seems as confused as I am. I begin to ask myself if this is my penance for past deeds done. Perhaps I do not deserve to heal. I wonder if maybe I've liked the slow torture of it all. Perhaps everything has worked itself out for the best.

* * *

Late at night, Jean and I are lying in bed in the dark, turned away from each other, pretending to sleep.

"I think Barbara is a good name," he says.

I grunt my acknowledgment. The name is barely recognizable in his accent. He says it Bub-a-rah, with the emphasis on the final syllable, and I imagine that we'd call her Bubby.

Jean rolls onto his back and sighs loudly.

"When my father died," he says, "I was devastated."

I turn toward him and see the silhouette of his hands reaching for his face, and then I can hear his heavy breaths collecting in his palms.

"I was twelve years old," he says, "and I didn't know how to be a man yet. I had to learn. But you're a grown woman now, Vivi. You can't just retreat."

I flip on the light on the nightstand and grab my notebook, knowing that he expects an answer. I write slowly, rip out the page, and hand it to him. I watch him as he reads.

I have written, *It's the weight of it all.*

Jean crumples the piece of paper, sighs again, then tosses it towards the wastebasket, but the ball of paper lands to the left. I turn off the light, lie back down, and close my eyes. I feel Jean's arms wrap around me.

"What do you think about Barbara for a girl, huh?" he says and gives me a quick hug.

I grunt again. I wonder why Jean insists on keeping up this charade. He doesn't seem to understand that this is a game that I no longer want to play, that I do not want to talk about our children and the names we'll give them or the instruments they'll play. Everywhere I look, there are women, swollen, mocking me. I have failed to do the one thing my body is built for, and I feel as though I am a husk, as if I am closed up, cut off, as if something has crawled up inside me and grown over all that was there.

Jean rolls over again. "I love you no matter what," he says. When I don't offer him anything in return, he sighs.

I hear his breaths slow as he drifts off to sleep.

I know that I am not blameless as the doctor implied; it is my fault, this scar.

* * *

My mother didn't tell me that she was sick. She told my oldest brother and his wife, but not me. Apparently she found out about the cancer while Jean and I were visiting his family in Paris. It was just after my first miscarriage, and my brother said that my mother didn't want to upset me in my own time of need. She opted not to get treatment. She spoke quite often about the natural course of things, that we should not mess with our lives, that God would take care of things in his own way. My mother died of a massive coronary; the cancer didn't have enough time to eat her whole.

* * *

I am sitting cross-legged on the bed surrounded by photographs. I feel as if I can hear them calling to me. To my left is Aunt Gracie, who died in childbirth after being beaten by her husband. To my right is Grandma Penny, who had fifteen children, twelve who lived past their first birthday. Before me is my mother, a woman who allowed her body to be eaten by cancer without a fight, only to be killed by something else. In the picture, she is pregnant with me; my brothers stand at her side. My father's finger is to the right of the frame. She's not smiling; instead, she looks as if she's saying something. Most likely she's yelling to my father to get his finger off the lens just like she always did. I am still making piles. The largest is of the pictures to be fixed. They are cracked, some of them a little torn. Fragile. I want them to be new again so that others can see them after I take my own inevitable plunge into death. On the top of this pile sits Aunt Vivian, still smiling, her body not violated, her lungs not filled with water.

Jean enters the room and stops at the edge of the bed. He holds a bouquet of flowers in his hands, my favorites, Gerber daisies. Jean surveys the bed and hands me the flowers. I mouth a thank you, and he kisses my cheek.

"So when will this end?" he asks. "When will this little project of yours be done?"

I shrug, although I know that I am almost finished. I have surveyed the bits and pieces of my relatives' lives. As far removed as I am from them, I realize that my life is not much different. We all swim in a river of loss. And now, every time I open my mouth, I am inexplicably tripping over these names on my tongue, the stories that I am obligated to share. I want to give them air and life so they do not fade away into some uninhabited void. There are lessons to be learned; I am sure of it.

"Damn it, Vivi," Jean begins. "Just talk to me." He pushes aside some pictures, and they float onto the floor beside the bed. He sits, quiet for a moment, then strokes my hair in the way he always does when I'm sick. "The doctor said we could get pregnant, that you could have this procedure and everything could be okay. Don't you want that? Don't you want to try?"

No matter what happens, everything will not be okay. The doctors can remove the evidence, but the memory will still be there.

"I don't care if you never say another word to me." He kisses me lightly on the lips. "But I need to know if you want to try to have a child or not. Just a yes. Or a no."

Yes or no. These seem like terms I no longer understand, that whatever answer I could give would be more than that. The answer would have to be more than that.

"Yes or no. Either way, I will still wake up beside you tomorrow."

I look in his eyes, and I know that he loves me, that he wants us to be a family, that he is simply trying to traverse this silent chasm between us. It is time for me to open; the memories are there forever whether I speak them or not. I look down at the piles of photos that surround me; these are the remnants of lives already lived and deeds already done. I still have the chance to unmake one of the tragedies of my life.

"Okay," I whisper. "Let me tell you a story."

Addressing You

TAD BARTLETT

1.

Amy, I'm addressing you. It's me, Joe Alsobrook.

I want to reach out to you, write you, call you, google you, friend you, email you, text you, see you, talk to you, touch you, tell you that I love you. Tell you I love you in a simple sentence, no modifiers or qualifiers. No silliness, no triviality, just real, transcending, complicated, miserable, hand-holding, fall day, summer sweat, knees weak, relating, elating, love.

We let them get to us.

Not that "us" was more than two months of teen-aged soap drama, high school seniors, twenty years ago. What the hell am I doing even looking you up online? Your family pictures, your smile, your children, while my children call up to me from downstairs. Fuck all.

It's been so long, I'm mostly convinced I dreamed you, dreamed us, dreamed them. Probably dreamed me, too—probably still am. Fuck all.

2.

Old hate-filled hometown, I'm addressing you now, your heart and history heavy with strange fruit. I deny you now, you know. Deny that I have anything to do with you, or you with me.

Do you remember the start of it? Band practice, the week before the first game of the season, on the practice fields across the back street from the high school, hot, August 29, 1988.

It's sweat I remember first. Sweat because it was hot and we had been out there marching and playing for two hours. But mainly sweat because I was a nervous teenaged boy about to play a song for a girl I had worshipped for almost three years, since we were freshmen, wandering the halls, lost, each from our junior highs on our own sides of town, now in the same high school, the one public high school sitting on Broad Street, the road separating the east and west sides of town, what was black from what was white.

Not that Amy would know I was playing for her. She likely didn't know I existed, or so I figured. I raised my trumpet to my lips, pressed the cold, hard metal of the mouthpiece against my tightened muscles, felt the blood feel good as it flowed fast into that damned vein that popped out on my forehead whenever I blew real hard, hard like I had to blow to play a crazy love song for a girl who'd never said a word directly to me, whose body moved in ways that made me feel God, to play it loud enough to rise over the band departing from the practice field, to reach the ears of the lithe majorette practicing her baton throws on the sidelines, Amy Jones.

And then she said it, and I know you heard it just as clearly as I did. "Joe's just about the goofiest-ass white boy I ever saw," she said over her shoulder to one of the other majorettes. That could have meant anything for my chances. It could have meant that I'd touched her heart, that she would be mine forever until the end of time. It could have meant that she thought I was goofy and an ass, and white, and not in a good way. It could have meant she thought I was funny. Or that I was a pervert or a bug. Anything. But the one thing I knew it meant for sure was that she knew who I was, that she knew I existed, that she heard my song.

3.

Google search entry: "Joseph Alsobrook." 6,690 results.

Google search entry: "Amy Jones." 763,000 results.

We could be anyone.

Google search entry: "Amy Jones Alsobrook." No results found.

4.

I think I found you, Amy.

Saw you have a video-chat account. I could totally just click a link and see you, talk to you. But what would we do then? It could only be one of two things: Awkward small talk that ruins everything I hold in this memory of you. Or you see in me what I see in you, we realize the same things about time and history and mistakes, and we smile knowingly, feel a rush of physical pleasure and danger. But then what are we? What am I? Just another clown pulling his pants down for a webcam. I'm not that guy. I'm not him. Forget I even thought it.

5.

And so it was always you, my hometown. You were always looking, watching, waiting for your moment to pounce.

After the first game of the season, you were there. We were all mixed in together, the band members, the majorettes, the cheerleaders, the football players. Combined, we were you, our town. We were at the municipal stadium, headed for the buses for the ride back to the parking lot behind the school.

My uniform tunic was unbuttoned, my black concert T-shirt underneath drenched in sweat, my trumpet gripped in my right hand. I was walking next to Shaun. He was draped in his sousaphone. I had talked to Shaun at least a thousand times about Amy. But now we weren't talking at all. I was watching Amy as she walked in her majorette uniform just ahead of us. Shaun was looking at me and shaking his head. He knew what was going on.

In my head, Amy turned around and caught my gaze, but she liked it, liked me. She was all smiles between lips like soft berries. In my head, she said, "Stop staring, goofy-ass Joe, and kiss me already," and her arms were around me, pulled me against her body, and then here's the unbelievable part, I knew what to do, I kissed her, just like in the movies, with assurance and manliness, and I wasn't just one big quivering erection and anxiety, but I was suave. I knew things. And she knew I knew things. In my head.

"Dude," Shaun said, "take a picture, bruh, right?"

I dropped my eyes. I was not suave. Amy kept walking on in front of us, elbowing her friends, talking about things I would never know about.

"Damn, Shaun, what do I do?"

"Don't do anything. Don't be a freak. That song the other day was one thing, but man, don't make her feel stalked, or like you're some kind of weirdo."

"I've been invisible for two years."

"Relax," Shaun said as we got up to the band bus. Then he looked over his shoulder at me. "Come to Johnny's tonight. She'll probably be there."

You know about Johnny's house. After every home game, it's where half the seniors and juniors went to hang out and party, the black half mainly, except for the occasional white football players thinking they could score some weed there easier than on their side of town. They always left empty handed but feeling cooler, somehow in on something. They never stayed.

"You think it's cool?" I asked Shaun.

He looked back at me in the aisle of the school bus, crinkled his brow, exhaled sharply. "Man, please."

6.

You have lost it.

I am addressing you, Joe Alsobrook, aging face in the mirror, googler of old girlfriends and wives never married, ignorer of family, betrayer of customers, progenitor of fatherless children.

I saw you the other day, shuddering in fear as you drove through the wrong part of town. I saw you lock your doors at the downtown intersection. You can't escape me.

7.

Amy, I love you.

You know I'm not the clumsy jerk I make myself out to sound like, right? That's just some personal myth, the myth of the regular white kid. It goes like this: I was a slob at Johnny's. I was clueless, dressed only in the clean T-shirt and jeans that I had stashed in my car, while everyone else was dressed sharp. Tailored, low-cut, high-cut, unbuttoned, relaxed; skinny neckties, just enough cleavage, shiny shoes and heeled sandals; hints of cologne and perfume; hair in perfect fades or elaborately sculpted curls. And me, the goofy white boy.

But you knew that was just myth, that there was a man inside of this boy waiting to be looked at, talked to. I saw you sitting on a sofa on the other side of the room, squeezed in between friends, surrounded by noise and pressing bodies, and you were looking at me, only at me. Shaun said something to me, and I smirked something in response, but I don't remember now, and I doubt I knew then, what we were talking about.

And then he pushed me across the room, a hand in my back, me his puppet, across the carpet and through the crowd. Nobody cared I was there, except, it turns out, you. And then Shaun grabbed the hand of the girl next to you, a piccolo player, and pulled her up, said something about the ragged formation of the woodwinds on the field, and you were left looking up at me, waiting for me to say something, and then I did it, I spoke.

"Hey, Amy," tasting your name as if I hadn't said it countless times to Shaun, to myself in the mirror, to you in dreams, because I had never actually said it to you. I tripped over my big sneakers into a sitting position next to you.

"Joe. What was that song you were playing the other day?"

"I don't know," I lied, "just something that had been stuck in my head. Best way to get it unstuck, you know."

And you laughed, and then you nailed me. "Sounded like 'Just the Two of Us.'"

And then I laughed, too. "Huh, maybe it was. Must have been on the radio or something. I was probably hitting the notes all wrong."

"No, I thought it was cool." And then you looked around the room, like you were as nervous as I felt, though I couldn't take my eyes off you.

"Well, my embouchure was shot," I said. "I don't know. It was nothing."

Then you looked back at me, steadily. You put your hand on mine. "You want to go outside?" you asked. "It's not so crowded out there. It's stifling in here."

Even me, oblivious, goofy Joe Alsobrook, even I knew this was a time to move.

8.

Old hometown, can you believe that Amy was the first girl I ever kissed? A senior in high school, that's right, and never laid lips on a girl before that night out behind Johnny's house, Shaun honking his horn out by the street because his curfew was coming up. If you had known, maybe you would have tried to stop us sooner.

For a good while after I left Amy behind, and Shaun behind, and you behind, a voice in my head opined how strange a white girl tasted. But then it struck me one night a couple years later, kissing a white girl in the old cemetery behind my white college, that that whole business about the taste of Amy's kisses was just you talking, not me, that skin tastes like skin, lips like lips. Like my son tells me now, "Underwear is underwear."

9.

You, Shaun. You stuck by me through a lot. Or maybe I stuck by you. Or maybe we were kids, and we were in the same place at the same time, and it was just easier not to be repelled by each other. But you were there that night when Amy and I kissed for the first time.

I thought you'd be steamed at me when I made my way around the side of the house and out to the street where your heap sat idling. You had a midnight curfew, something we had pushed many times before, but never shattered in the way we did that night. But you weren't mad. You were grinning, actually, looking at me sideways as I slipped through the passenger door.

"Whoa, cuz', what's that all on your cheek?" You grabbed me by the jaw and swiped a rough thumb over Amy's lipstick marks.

"Just a little something. It's nothing," I said low and into the floorboards, before I cracked a grin myself, "Wow."

"Damn, Joe."

We drove through darkened streets, going slow over potholes and one unpaved block on our way back to where my car was parked at the high school. As I climbed out of your car, I could tell you wanted to say something, the way you didn't smile. "What?"

"Joe, not to discourage you or nothing, but you know what this town is. You know how people are, right?"

"Yeah, I know."

"Well, just be sure you know what you're doing."

"I am."

"Then, good luck."

Of course, I didn't know what I was doing. I was seventeen and had just been kissed for the first time. You knew I was off the rails.

"Joe, really," you said. "I know you think some folks are down with you. I know you think it doesn't matter what anyone else thinks."

"I could give two shits about what the other people think. This fucking town."

"Well, I'm just saying that you got to have your own back sometimes." And then you smiled again. "Just be careful what you do, Joe."

10.

Amy, do you remember the first week? It dreams in my memory like a year of sunlight. On that Monday, I jumped from my chest waiting to catch sight of you in the morning parking lot, to see if you would smile, or if you would glare, or if you would just walk on by. It almost didn't matter which, because it would all be happening in a different world than any smile or glare or snub before.

Twenty minutes later, your dad's minivan stopped next to the chain-link fence separating the lot from the street behind, and you stepped out, looked around, and spotted me. Then you headed straight for me. Do you remember what you said to me?

"You didn't call me," both anger and hurt on your face at the same time.

I stood there smiling, an asshole. "I didn't have your number. I looked, really. I even thought about going through and calling all the Joneses in the book asking to speak to you, but have you looked you up in the phone book? There's like a half a page of Jones."

"You could have asked somebody."

I could feel a thaw, maybe. I kept smiling, not meaning to, not planning to, but just smiling anyway.

And then that was it. The last ice floe sloughed into the warming sea. You slid your hand into mine as the bell rang, and we walked, holding hands, backpacks slung over our shoulders, into the bandroom, jostled on either side as we went through the door, our arms touching.

11.

Old hometown, you couldn't let that first week end like that, five days of warm breezes and cool nights, holding hands and late-night telephone calls when our fathers were sleeping. No, you couldn't just let kids grow, learn from each other.

"Nigger lover," remember? Scrawled on scraps of notebook paper slid under my books on my desk in American History class, or balled into a crumple and stuffed in my backpack, or muttered under your breath in the cafeteria. Remember? Sometimes I don't. Sometimes I'm not sure I even caught it those times to begin with, nonchalant and oblivious, just trying to *be cool man*, as Shaun never forgot to remind me.

That first Friday, lunchtime, Amy grabbed me by the arm as our lunch/study class walked down the hall toward the cafeteria, and pulled me down a set of stairs, laughter silent on her face.

"What are we doing?" I asked.

"Let's have a picnic, Joe, out on the side steps where nobody goes. I packed some sandwiches. We can get away from everyone."

I looked back up the stairs at the last of our class going down the hall. I didn't want trouble. I looked back at Amy.

"Come on," she said. "We never get to be away from everyone looking all the time. Let's go."

Out on the side steps, away from you, we laughed and talked easily about people we had known and things we had done over the past three years, realizing we both knew all the same people, and both went to a lot of the same places, and both listened to the same music, and read the same books, and felt the same way about things, and both were too shy to ever talk to each other, and found out that we both had a thing for each other all that time, and we tried to trace it back to the particular point in time and event that made us realize we had that thing.

For Amy, it was something I said in ninth grade biology class, or the way I slouched in my chair, all cool without knowing I was cool, something vague, really, that I didn't quite get. But I laughed and felt good about it anyway when she recounted it for me there on the steps. For me, it was easier, no vague sense of anything. More like thunder following lightning right on top of you on a summer night. It was the moment I saw her for the first time, walking through the hall with her first-semester schedule gripped in her hand, the way her hair swayed down her back, the way her large, almond-shaped eyes took in everything before them, heavy-lidded and confident, the shape of her body, the stride of her walk. She was freaking Venus; it didn't get much simpler than that.

So there we were, talking like that, knowing each other, inching closer to each other each chance we could until the full length of my leg was pressed against the full length of her leg, and our hands touched each other's hands as we talked, and our breath mixed as we laughed, and we didn't have the awkwardness of the lunch table around us, and we were happy.

And then you were there, and you saw us. You were in a late-60s Mustang speeding noisily up the side-street beside the school, and you yelled out the open window, "Kiss her, nigger lover!"

I dropped Amy's hand, spilled my sandwich remains from my lap, and was on my feet before I knew what I was doing, what I was saying. "Fuck you, asshole!" I yelled at you.

"Cool down, Joe," I heard Amy tell me. Then we stuffed things into the backpack, and we tried to get back inside to the cafeteria before somebody came to see what all the yelling was about, but we were too late. We both got a day of detention for skipping lunch. I got two more days for cussing.

12.

Your arms were strong, Amy, when you held me in the front seat of my car, on that dirt road north of town, as I shook and you told me, softly, to calm down, that we didn't need to worry about anyone else.

"Fucking McDonald's," I spat, "fucking assholes."

"Baby, it wasn't the Big Mac, and it wasn't no McDonald's. Those people are jerks no matter where we might have run into them."

"I don't care. I don't care." The stars were layered like rime across the black sky outside my car windows.

You kept holding me. I don't know why you held me so long or held onto me so long. It was two months before the end, but if you had any sense maybe it should have been two days. I couldn't help it. Those people, that town—I had never experienced fury like that before. I was used to being the oddity, the one who was picked on, excluded, whatever. I had developed a tough skin. But this was different. This was me in love with someone who loved me, or at least who kissed me and held my hand, and now they were aiming their arrows at you.

You remember the McDonald's that time. Another couple of Friday nights into our dating, after another football game, everyone headed to get burgers and Cokes before whatever parties started. We were there when the football team from the seg academy came and saw us together and made comments about how they could pay you better than what I was but only if you would do better things for them. I swear, if I knew how, I would have killed someone. But then our football players were there, too, white ones and black ones together, and you pulled me, yelling, out the side door as the punches, and the blood, and the ketchup started flying.

13.

You poor soul, Joe Alsobrook, you poor scared kid.

Homecoming night. You danced with Amy held close in the darkened gymnasium, hoping it would never end, the darkness of the dance, the rotating sparkles of lights from the disco ball hung from the rafters by the decorations committee, the smell of Amy's hair as she nestled her head against your chest. You didn't want it to end, but you knew it would, knew this was the night that she would lead you out of there early, right after you had your pictures taken to prove to her parents that you were there like you said you would be, that soon you would be in your car on that dirt road again, that she would have your pants all the way off this time, not just pushed down where she could touch you, that her dress would end up folded neatly on the back seat to avoid getting wrinkled or worse, that she would be naked in front of you, that you would be afraid to really look at her, all of her, that you would kiss the skin of her throat, and her chest, and her neck, and her ears ,and her cheeks over and over, not quite sure what to do or where to go, how far down, what to touch, what was OK, what was forbidden, what was both.

And then it was too much, and there it was, the desperation, the clumsiness, the expectation, and she pulled you toward her, on top of her, the car seat reclined back as far as you could make it go, and you tried to go places you had never even properly seen, had no idea how it all worked, how it all fit together, and she coaxed you, shifted you, trying to make it right, and then you both forgot who you were doing it for, and then, just as you were trying to figure out how to laugh it off, find a way not to do it but not to hurt her or hurt you or, God forbid, never get the chance to do it again, and when she sounded like she was ready to give up, too, you were in.

It must have been half an hour of complete foolishness to get there, but then it was better than any hand, hers or yours, had ever been, so different, so clearly like what the pursuit of life for the rest of your life would be about. But you didn't think about that then, because once you were in you wanted nothing more than to stay in and nothing more than to be out, and you were filled with the fear of every sex ed class you had ever taken, sperm and eggs, and money, and desperate afternoon phone calls, and beige clinics, and babies or not babies, and parents' disappointment and furor, and your own shame, and forget about college, and grad school, and a decent job, and cocktail parties where you would be the hit of the evening, and forget about art movies in a big city with sophisticated friends, and forget about concerts with your lover by your side, her hand in yours, and forget about leaving this place or the places like it.

And then Amy was catching her breath short and you were back there with her on that homecoming night, senior year, your blue 1978 Japanese hatchback creaking on its springs, the windows fogged up, Amy sweating underneath you even though the night was cold, and you opened your eyes, which you just then realized had been squeezed shut tight, and her face was loose and her eyelids open, but her eyes rolled back in her head, and you felt her hands on your naked butt, and felt her legs moving under yours, and you realized that your whole life was about to end, and you said, quietly, "Amy, no, I can't," and then you backed down off of Amy to the floor at her feet.

And then she laughed and twined her fingers in your hair, and you realized you had no idea what a woman is or what a woman wants, but you knew that this was enough, whatever it meant, whatever it was.

14.

Of course, hometown, you couldn't have that. Maybe you saw us slip out of the dance. Maybe you figured out why. I think at that point you were already counting the days until the end, knew it would come soon enough.

I think you must have got to Shaun. Maybe you threatened to beat the crap out of him, or offered him a job, or maybe a twenty. Maybe you told him he had a shot with Amy if I was out of the way, that she belonged more with him than with me. Or maybe Shaun was just with you the whole time. Whatever it was, you sent Shaun to do your dirty work.

It was the Monday after homecoming. Amy and Tonya had gone over to their desks to look up something in the textbook, and Shaun and I were alone at our lab table.

"What the hell are you doing?" Shaun whispered.

"About what?"

"You and Amy. Y'all kissing, and holding hands, and being all nice on each other, that's one thing. But are you fucking her now?"

I felt cold sickness drop into my stomach. "Maybe that's none of your damned business," I said. "I love her, Shaun. Shit, you shouldn't be surprised."

Shaun looked down at his hands, turning his next words over in his head before he said them. Then he looked back at me, right in my eyes. "You a nigger lover?" His whisper broke a little too loud.

And then there was Amy, standing behind him, the textbook in her hands, her mouth dropped open. I couldn't say anything back to Shaun's question. It didn't feel like him anymore, but like you.

But then I was on one side of the lab table looking at Shaun on the other side of it, and Amy was on that side, too, and I couldn't say anything. Amy herself had told me repeatedly the word was nothing. But maybe coming from Shaun, it was all upside-down and inside-out.

You got what you wanted. It's a blur, the time between that chemistry lab and the official end of Amy-and-me. A blur of flat-voiced conversations, avoided eye contact, lifeless hand-holding. But there it was one day, after lunch. In the time it took to get from the cafeteria to the lockers in the bandroom, Amy laid it out.

"Look, Joe. We need to be friends."

"But we are friends. Are you dumping me?"

"I just don't think it's working out."

"Is this because of homecoming night?"

"It's got nothing to do with that."

"Is it because of Shaun?"

"You don't get it, Joe. It's not working out." And she turned and walked in another direction through the halls. That was it.

15.

You. I don't know what to do with you.

I don't know what to do with you, Amy, though I suppose even now I have to let you go, again.

I don't know what to do with you, Shaun. When I remember you, I really only remember you as a friend, and I don't remember that one day in chemistry except when it's dark out and I've been awake too long or I've had too much to drink. Maybe it wasn't you who fucked it all up. Maybe I screwed myself up, with how bad a lover I was, or how I couldn't stand up to people for Amy, or how I was just a dork, or maybe we were just seventeen, and this is how things start and end for seventeen-year-olds everywhere, no matter what it is that makes them different from each other.

And you, hometown, what do I do with you? Mainly I hate you, and I don't feel bad about it. But maybe you deserve better? That's a question, not a statement, and I don't know the answer.

But the biggest question mark is for you, Joe. I don't know where you are sometimes or who you are. Are you still that kid?

Or are you someone, something else? Look at you. You are these things you hate and love. Maybe you feel good to sit back after twenty years and assess it all, like you're removed from it all, above it all, beyond it all. Or maybe you're down in it.

Myrmecology

ROBIN BAUDIER

"Becca, get out while you still can." June's voice crackled through the phone. "Why are you doing this?"

It was the afternoon before Hurricane Isaac made landfall, but the sun was shining, and my pre-storm data looked great. Clad in hip waders, Danny valiantly climbed overboard into the marshy shallows and dragged our boat the last couple of feet to solid ground.

I shouldn't have answered the phone. June and I had already hashed out all of her arguments for why I should have evacuated the evening before: my niece would love to get a visit from me at June's mother-in-law's in Meridian; I was living in a death trap over a river that was definitely going to flood; it was the seven-year anniversary of Hurricane Katrina, and how could I put her through this; I was going to die.

I had laid out for her all the reasons why I didn't think I needed to evacuate: Hurricane Isaac was just a Category One, and it would likely be downgraded to a tropical storm as soon as it hit land; the raised fishing camp I was renting would be higher and drier than most of the state; I had evacuated for Hurricane Gustav four years before and got stuck in traffic for eight hours; the only thing that sounded worse than that to me was her mother-in-law's in Meridian; I was not going to die.

"Just tell me," June snapped, "what it is that you are doing that is so important it can't wait a couple of days until after this hurricane has passed."

"Danny and I hit all of the other areas we monitor in the past couple of weeks," I explained. "Once we finish checking on our ant populations here in the Manchac Wilderness Area, I'll have a beautifully complete and up-to-date data set for before the storm."

Danny's narrow shoulders bowed with the effort of hauling the boat onto shore. He had started out as my means of transportation, a neighbor with a boat and a willingness to drive me around in it all day for gas money and minimum wage. I had hired him as my field assistant after only a week of tedious coordinating with undergraduate assistants commuting from Baton Rouge. It was the best decision of the whole field season.

"If I stay here, we can get right back out as soon as the flooding goes down." I heard her inhale and cut her off. "I have to go, June. The ants have seized our technology and are rising up in violent revolt." I hung up.

Danny and I pulled on our gloves and got to work. We used the handheld radio scanner to track down the ant populations we'd already tagged with radio receivers, logging their GPS location before combing the fields to find more. By the end of the day, we'd found all of the colonies in the reserve we'd previously tagged and tagged two additional colonies of fire ants and acrobat ants. Tagging consisted of getting the ants to bite onto your gloved finger, dabbing their backs with glue using a matchstick, and using tweezers to attach the tiny, lightweight radio receiver. It really wasn't hard, but we had to isolate the freshly glued ants for an hour afterwards to make sure their receivers weren't dislodged before the glue was finished drying.

We were sitting next to a decaying tree stump, watching some freshly glued acrobat ants dry. Danny doffed his baseball cap and wiped the sweat off his forehead with the back of a hand. He refused to wear sunscreen, claiming he tanned easily. He did, but whenever we were out for more than four hours, his skin got the pinkish undertone of a pig on a spit.

"Do you think these little guys are going to be here after the storm?" he asked.

"Some of the colonies will be." I tapped my gloved fingers lightly against the plastic enclosure. The ants arched abdomens over thoraxes at unnatural-looking angles. "Most won't. These acrobat ants are awfully close to the water. I'll be very surprised if they're here when we come back."

"Doesn't it bother you?" He squinted even though the sun was setting behind him. "Your work is basically studying animals and then watching them get washed away."

It did bother me. That was the point.

"It'll make for more dramatic findings if most of them don't survive." I turned on the receiver to see the signals of the ants in the enclosure on the display. When I came back to check on them, these blips of light and their movements would signify the colony had survived. Now they were so close together, they registered as one large, shifting blob. "If populations are more decimated than in other post-disaster studies, it could support a correlation between shrinking wetland buffers caused by global warming and increased ecological disruption."

"You know, you could come to my mom's with me." Danny's voice was casual, calloused fingers folding and refolding a blade of cordgrass. "She's baking a turkey tonight, so if the power goes out, there'll be plenty of food for sandwiches."

"Thanks," I said. Part of me meant it even though his mom's house in Ponchatoula was way more likely to flood than my raised fishing camp. The rest of me panicked. Danny was ninety percent of my human contact in the long months I spent in rural Louisiana. We tagged and tracked ants, played cards, drank beer. But outside of the time and space we shared, we really didn't know much about each other's lives. Meeting his mom would end that. It felt like too much to risk.

"I'm actually looking forward to watching the weather from my place over the river though. Then in a day or two, we can get right back out here and check on these little guys." I laughed to hear myself parrot his words; calling ants little guys made it sound like they might get together a game of T-ball.

"You're looking forward to a hurricane?" Danny shook his head. "I'd just as soon pass."

I did some math and guessed that he must have been about fourteen when Katrina hit. Too young to remember the big ones before that. He wouldn't understand.

The way the entire city stopped. Huge waves splashing over the seawall, over benches, over bridges. Water spouts moving up and down Lake Pontchartrain, so far out they looked like giant creatures running up and down the Causeway bridge. Wind so strong that if you were small enough and you jumped high enough, you could sail backward a yard or so before floating down to the ground. How it felt like flying.

We sat in silence for a bit. Danny tore the cordgrass and folded it into the shape of a football. “Why ants?” Danny flicked the football at me, but it unwrapped midair.

“Because I’m a nihilist.” I picked up the unwound blade and started tearing it into pieces.

“Seriously though. Why ants?”

I shrugged and scattered the pieces of my shredded blade of grass. “Funding, mostly. A lot of entomological funding. The grant paying for this study is from the pesticide industry. There’s a lot of interest in killing ants.” I lifted the lid off the ant enclosure and tipped them back out onto the ground. “It’s not *not* a nihilistic area of study.”

“So inside every myrmecologist, there’s a frustrated E.O. Wilson?” Danny asked. I raised my eyebrows, and he leaned back on his elbows, clearly enjoying himself. “Google tells me he’s the father of what we’re doing out here. Myrmecology. Did you know that he was into eugenics? Because that’s pretty fucked up.”

“Early Social Darwinists were into eugenics. Wilson wasn’t.” I pulled off my gloves and wiped my sweaty palms on my pants. “He just saw ants sacrifice self-interest for the good of the colony. So he said that human morality might have evolved because altruism and self-sacrifice can help a human colony’s DNA get passed on, even if it is detrimental to passing on an individual’s DNA. Looking at human beings as DNA’s way to make more DNA disturbs people.”

“What about everything people do that doesn’t help society pass on DNA?” Danny got up and starting packing away our gear. “What would E.O. Wilson say is the evolutionary purpose of tagging ants?”

“I don’t know. That it’s a manifestation of my biophilia?” My sweeping gesture took in the sun-scorched cordgrass, the rotting stump, and the August sun beating down on us. Danny laughed even though it seemed unlikely he was familiar with the term. Maybe a word ending in “philia” was enough to guess, if you knew words like pedophilia and necrophilia. That put a whole new color on 'the urge to affiliate with other forms of life.' I laughed and Danny, as dehydrated and more sunburnt than I was, continued to laugh, harder than merited. When we got back to the boat, I turned on the tracker, but the blip of the acrobat ants was almost out of range. By the time we were far out enough that Danny could turn on the motor, the blip was gone.

* * *

That night, I went to sleep with a soft patter on my roof. The following morning, I woke to sheets of rain thrumming against the walls. I was nursing my second cup of coffee, standing just inside the door to my porch, when June called again. From where I stood, I could watch the fast coursing of the Tangipahoa River without getting more than a stray raindrop or two in my mug. The river looked alive, splashing up on the other few camps I could see downstream and kicking off the river bend. It was as if the water knew it didn't belong onshore and was racing to get back out to the gulf. I didn't want to move from where I stood, but until the storm passed, not answering the phone was not an option. I retrieved my cell but carried it back out to the open doorway before answering.

"Good news, I'm not dead yet." I took another sip of coffee and waited for June to explode.

Her quiet took me off guard. "That's not funny, Becca. Seven years ago today, you were stuck in your attic, hoping someone would come by in a boat and pull you out of there."

"Yes, I was."

I could still see the wall of water rushing down my street from the 17th Street Canal breach. As if Moses had decided to stop parting the Red Sea. I was lucky that I heard a rumble and looked out the window or my first warning would have been my door blowing off of its hinges. I watched from the hatch of my attic door as all of my furniture was pushed by the tide of water to the back of my apartment. I lost everything except for the phone I was holding. A stranger in a boat pulled me out of a hole I kicked through an exterior wall with my bare feet.

"They're saying on the news that the Percy Quinn Dam might break. Tell me again. How many miles north is that of where you are?"

"This thing's just a tropical storm by now." I looked across and down the river to see the water had almost risen to the bottom of Danny's one-room shack. I was a good four feet above him, so I was still safe, but I hoped he'd had the good sense to get anything he wanted to keep off the floor before heading over to his mother's. "Besides, it's too late. It wouldn't be safe for me to be on the road now. I'll be fine. I promise. How about I call you later and tell you again that I'm still alive?"

"You can't do this to me again." June was angry now. "I still have your voicemails. The ones you left from your attic. What kind of person almost drowns in her own living room and then decides to wait out a hurricane on a river with a leaky dam?"

"People deal with things differently." I heard the edge in my voice but couldn't seem to smooth it out. We'd both lost everything. First with the storm, then Dad dying of a heart attack less than three months later. June had been married and pregnant with her first child within a year. I'd left New Orleans and, other than a shared office for post-docs at LSU, had never really settled anywhere since. The beauty of field science was that it didn't really matter where you paid rent if you spent most of your time on government reserves.

Below, I saw movement in one of Danny's windows. The oval of a face flashed in the glass. "I have to go. I'll call you later." I hung up without waiting to hear June's response and called Danny's cell.

"Hey, Rebecca."

"Hey, Danny, is someone in your place? I thought I just saw something in your window."

"Yeah, I am, actually." The face returned to the window. "My mom's boyfriend and I got into a fight last night, and I just couldn't stay there. So I came back here."

The river had risen flush with the bottom of Danny's shack. "You're going to be standing in water soon."

"Yeah." Danny gave a tight laugh. "If you take the word 'soon' out of that sentence and replace it with 'now,' I'd say that's one hundred percent accurate."

"Do you think you can make it over here? Safely?"

"The road's flooded. I tried to go back to my mom's about half an hour ago, but I couldn't get through."

I leaned out over my railing and could see that his boat was still tethered to the common pier downstream. My hair was plastered to my face by the time I leaned back in. "What about by boat?"

Danny's window opened, and his curly head craned out and got similarly plastered by the rain. He leaned back in and answered, "I could probably do it."

I didn't realize my boat launch was a few inches underwater until I started down the stairs under my house. I thought about going back up for my shrimp boots, but then Danny came into sight, his little motor struggling to make it upstream. I wanted to be there to help guide the boat in, so I stepped out onto the launch and heard an awful creaking. I slithered along the slick wood boards under my feet, holding onto the support piers as I waded out to him. He was still a few yards out.

A moan, muffled by the water, reverberated up through my feet. Then a sharp, loud crack. The river must have undermined the supports, or dry rot could have finally given away. All I really know is that when the wood broke underneath my feet, my hand slipped from the post, and my world went sideways. Water slapped against the length of my body, and then I was under, and the current was pulling me down and towards the pier wreckage. I tried to push off against the boards, but my foot pushed through a layer of mud into a pocket of ragged wood that cut through my jeans. I didn't realize I was trapped until I tried to pull free.

A band tightened around my chest. I wanted so badly to let out the scream I had swallowed before I hit the water. But I couldn't let the air out. If I did, I wouldn't be able to resist sucking water back in. I embraced the burn in my lungs and clawed at what was left of the boat launch, but my left leg was caught like a fish on a hook. I kicked my shoes off and ripped open the button and fly of my jeans. With every hard-won inch of leg I got free, I wished that it weren't a universal truth that jeans are the worst thing to get in or out of when wet. Still, I hadn't breathed.

The jeans were trapped behind me in the murk, and I was swimming upwards towards the shadow of the boat when I couldn't hold the air in any longer. Bubbles burst out of me, racing ahead to the surface. There wasn't far to go. I was less than a second behind them. But when Danny stuck his head into the disgusting water and reached for me, when his wiry arms dragged me up the last inch through the surface, I felt saved.

Danny's shirt and one shoe were off. He'd been halfway through stripping to jump in after me when he'd seen the bubbles rising and me not far behind them. I couldn't have been down there as long as it felt like. Just long enough to think I was going to die.

Seven years before in my attic, looking down on the parade of all of my earthly belongings, my bed, my bookcase, my television, floating past before slamming against the back wall of my shotgun house, I remember thinking my home looked strangely empty, even as it became more and more full.

Seven years later, looking up at Danny, I realized what I must have always known: *I* had been what was missing from my house. I knew my home as the space around me, defined by my peripheries. There was a terrible wholeness to the experience of being submerged, water filling that space, trying to fill the spaces inside of me. A negative void made positive. I recognized this completion with a horrible: *of course*. Of course, this is how it will end.

But then it didn't. I kicked and swam. And I didn't end.

Danny maneuvered us in under my house until he could grab my stairs and tether his boat to them. We climbed directly from the boat to the stairs, not trusting the little bit of launch that was still attached to their base. Then we were back inside my house, dripping onto my kitchen floor. I didn't have any pants on, but how bare and raw I felt had nothing to do with clothing.

When he wrapped his arms around me, we were in shock. He was warm, and I was cold, and it felt good. But when his thumb found the side of my face, brushing a wet clump of hair away from my eyes, shock started to feel like an excuse for not thinking things through. I let myself hold him for half a breath longer, then left Danny standing there. I didn't even offer him a towel or anything, just grabbed my phone and called June.

I carried the phone outside onto my porch and sat with my back pressed up against the rough, varnished siding. There was an overhang, but the rain angled in to mist me with its impact against the porch. For my own sake, I wanted to tell June what had just happened. But I knew that would be cruel, that she would be a wreck until I made it out of the area. So instead, when she answered, I apologized for what I thought she was really upset about.

"I promise I will never say goodbye by voicemail again." I pulled my wet legs against my chest, trying to hug some warmth back into them. Pain shot down my left calf, and I realized there was a bloody gash down the length of it. "I promise to do my best to live forever."

"Christ, Becca," June said, her exasperation clear. "It's not that you tried to say goodbye to me. I mean, yes it was horrible, but I would have treasured that. It's that you laughed. You told me you loved me, and then you said, 'I guess this is goodbye' and you laughed! How could you laugh at the worst thing that had ever happened to me?"

I laughed again, knowing it was the worst response to what she was saying. My brain was too frazzled, too fuzzy to put into words that my laughter seven years before and my laughter right then were the sounds of my letting go. You get hurt when you brace yourself in a car crash; that's why drunk drivers don't get whiplash. Letting go, accepting death, was how I had gotten through the worst day of my life. Studying hurricanes and the complex communities of insects they destroy, that was how I got through every day since. I made a study of death, and I accepted it. That it would happen, and I would be powerless against it. And I hoped that if I could just find a way to completely let go, maybe I could stop being afraid.

I couldn't tell her that today I hadn't accepted it. I had fought for air, and I lived. So instead I said, "I promise not to laugh next time."

Becca sighed. I knew her sighs well enough to recognize it as forgiveness. "Do you remember Hurricane Andrew?"

"I was just thinking about it earlier today." I was calmed by the memory. Andrew had started as a Category Five, but tearing across Florida had knocked it down to a Three before it got to us. "I was scared, so you built that hurricane shelter in your closet for us. We crammed it full of your books and my stuffed animals."

"But you were still afraid. So I went and told Dad, and he pulled us out of there, bundled us up in ponchos and took us out to the lakefront. So illegal."

I laughed. "That was the part I was thinking about. Remember flying?"

"I remember. You were so small and the wind was so strong, you couldn't make it over the top of the levee without holding my hand. And when we jumped holding hands, it felt like we were flying backwards. You were lighter and were getting more airtime, so I let you go to see how far you could fly. Then you landed so far away from me, and the wind kept pushing you. It looked like you were running backwards."

I remembered this. Feeling like my feet couldn't quite get hold of the ground. June running after me hands extended, my arms wheeling to stay upright.

"I ran after you as fast as I could, trying to get to you before you went down the other side of the levee and out into the street. It was terrifying. Not because you were actually going to get hit by a car—no one was out on the roads—but because it made me realize Dad wasn't really watching us. I was the only one there to protect you, and that scared the crap out of me."

I thought about this. I couldn't remember how hard I'd really been trying to stop. "You're not responsible for me, June. I am."

"Fine. Let me be selfish then. If you died, I would survive. But I'd lose all the things I forget about myself until you're around. Please help me keep you alive. For me."

It sounded dysfunctional, but I understood. How someone could become a weight-bearing wall in your life without your even noticing you'd built them into it. "I promise. I'll help."

* * *

Back inside, Danny was still standing where I'd left him, his expression guarded. I felt like a royal asshole, so I insisted he take a shower to get warm. By the time he came out with two inches of leg showing at the bottom of a borrowed pair of my sweats, I was bandaged and dry. I gestured to a second mug of coffee on the kitchen table and hunched farther over the tracking receiver.

"What are you looking at?" He crossed to the table but ignored the mug. I could tell he was feeling uncomfortable in my house, in my clothes. Around me.

I turned the display towards him. He leaned in, squinting. I wondered if he needed glasses or if that was just his thinking face.

"I thought that receiver had a pretty limited range."

"It does," I said. "I turned it on because it occurred to me that we might see some of our ants floating by if their colonies got washed out upstream. It was pretty unlikely, but—"

"How can they still all be together like that?"

I grinned. "Want me to show you?"

We were careful going back down the stairs, and we didn't go very far. Just low enough to see the fire-ant raft clinging to a post next to the bottom step.

"It looks like a ball made only of ants." Danny sounded mystified. "How is that floating?"

"Only fire ants can do this." I braced my hand on his shoulder as I leaned past for a better look. He reached up and covered it. "They use their mandibles, claws and the adhesive pads on the ends of their legs to cling to each other. A fire ant's outer layer is water-repellant and rough, so when they're immersed, tiny pockets called plastrons get trapped. When they grip onto each other, it works like weaving waterproof fabric. They can trap enough air between them to stay buoyant for months. You're just seeing the top layer. The ones on the bottom will be able to breathe from their plastrons for a while, but even as they die, they'll hold on so that the others can live." I rubbed my fingers against his shirt and could feel the texture of his skin through it. It felt outrageous and good. "Evolutionary altruism."

"You'd never see that with people." Danny looked back over his shoulder. "If we evolved good impulses, we sure as hell evolved even stronger selfish ones. Which is fine with me. Sure, going down the river in a death ball looks badass, but if it comes naturally, it's not really a noble sacrifice, you know? It's not choosing to live or die for someone else. It's just dying."

"Yeah." I paused. "Death ball?"

"I expect credit for coining the term." Danny crept down to the second to bottom step, the one we had clambered onto together from the boat less than an hour before. "Would it screw up your experiment if we pulled them out?" The rain and water splashed onto Danny's pale, vulnerable feet, up past the tan lines on his ankles to make his sweats cling to his bird legs.

Shaking my head at myself, I went down the steps until I was even with him. I pulled a shard of broken wood out of the debris around the stairs and tossed it slightly upriver of the ball of ants. It floated past them without catching on their post and continued downriver. I reached for another one.

"What happened to your 'more dramatic findings'?" Danny teased but joined me. The river current fought us, but a flung plank finally drifted towards their pier at just the right angle. It caught between the ant raft's post and another post closer to shore.

After that, we went back upstairs and turned off the receiver. The ants might crawl down the length of the board and reshape themselves into a new formation that could reach the shore. Or they might miss their chance and float down the river, buoyed by the last breaths of their dead. For one day, I didn't want to know. Too soon, we'd be back out in Danny's boat, searching for too few blips. But for the rest of the storm, we could sit side by side and listen to the wind rattle the glass, and the rain hammer the roof, and pretend we could all survive.

When the Crazy People Get Their Checks

ANDREA BOLL

It's four o'clock, and Joe's Cozy Corner is bursting with lunatics. Lots of them are outside. People barbecuing pork chops and sausages. Turkey necks boiling. Already too many people lost in their past and future lives. The drinks are that strong. I know because I've died in this bar a thousand times, slipping off my stool into hell and waking to Persephone spitting pomegranate seeds at my face, only to be born again in its bathroom that never has any toilet paper. And usually, the Crazy People make it all the more tragic with their shiny, crazy eyes, their desperation and sharp claws. But not today. Today the Crazy People have received their money. Today they are Presidents, High Rollers, Recently Crowned Miss Americas.

Inside, it's a narrow bar with four walls. Bigger than a breadbox. Big enough for dreams to be created and destroyed. Sitting at the bar is Olga. We have the same name. Until I moved to New Orleans, I never met anyone with that name. This Olga is the third Olga I know here. There have been days when we are all at Joe's being Drunk Olgas. I don't like being one of three Olgas. It makes me feel like I have personalities I don't know about, that I do things I only remember in dreams. I also don't like one of the other Olgas because she's always getting too drunk and saying stupid things. I like this Olga though. I find her at the bars where the lights are dim and the drinks are cheap. This Olga has a shaved head and a thin goatee she ties with a blue bow. I also have hairs on my chinny chin chin, but I pluck them because they don't grow long enough for a goatee.

She buys me a gin and tonic. It's exactly what I want. Olga the Mind Reader. She's already drunk with her right eye squinting at me as if she's looking through a telescope, as if I'm a faraway planet or the man on the moon hiding in craters.

It's crowded in here, she says.

Because the Crazy People got their checks today, I tell her.

Really? It's already the fifteenth? She looks around for confirmation. A calendar would be nice, but there are no calendars here. Only a clock without any hands.

Yep, I say. Olga is crazy but not because the government gives her checks. She's crazy because she has 353 hearts and each one has been broken twice. That's what she told me the night we got so drunk we ended up in bed together, and I lost my underwear. They were nice too, black satin with lace. She might have them on right now. I was drunk, but she was the sort of drunk when you can see all the Fallen Angels mangled in gutters. But mostly what I remember from that night was what breasts felt like: Soft Solid Happiness.

You alone? she asks.

I don't know, I tell her.

I mostly came here because the Crazy People like to buy drinks for the other people who aren't crazy enough to receive crazy money from the government, but I mostly come here because I'm hoping to see my boyfriend, Atlas. I haven't seen him for over a month, since the day he shaved off all his hair, even his eyebrows. Without them, he looked disturbing, a ghoul possibly or a troll under the bridge waiting to gobble up silly little children.

When I first met Atlas, he was only a little crazy, and that was okay because a little crazy only makes life more interesting. We met by the river. I'd fallen asleep, and when I woke up, he was waiting for me. He offered me a beer and asked if my mother had breast-fed me. I told him no because she hadn't. He wasn't breastfed either and had a theory that babies who were raised on formula grew up to be crazy. But he wasn't sure if it was because a formula baby never sucked from its mother's breasts (Soft Solid Happiness) or because the first taste of this world is artificial.

Sometimes I would call his house, and he wouldn't know who I was. That's when I first realized he was a little crazy. I'd say, Atlas baby, it's me. And he'd say, Who? Who?, his voice slightly hysterical and slightly angry. Made my teeth hurt, that voice. And then in a couple of days, he'd call me and say, Olga, pussy cat, where you been at? You find yourself a new man? And I'd I have to tell him he had forgotten me again.

The worst part about it was that I could never help him figure out why it happened because he could never remember forgetting me. But this drama of ours was okay because afterwards, we'd go to his apartment and have sex that would split me wide open. All my guts would just spill out onto his floor with all the dirt, and hair, and germs of shoes. He would gently clean off my insides and place them back inside of me. But always all wrong. The last time this happened, my heart came stumbling out, and he deliberately put it above my pussy. He thought that was funny. But now I'm all fucked up. My brain barely gets blood at all.

I turn to Olga. I'm hoping Atlas will be here with new eyebrows and a new mind, I say.

She nods. Olga the Mind Reader.

We both smoke a cigarette and watch the bar in the mirror. Really, you can't tell who's crazy and who's not. Everyone is drinking, and laughing, and spitting, and forgetting.

You want to know what my dad said before he abandoned me? Olga asks.

What's that?

You'll see.

What do you mean, I'll see?

That's what he said. He got down on his knees, gave me a hug, and then he said, You'll see, Olga. I was nine.

That's fucked up.

She nods. Yep. She finishes her drink and then puts her hand on my shoulder. I ain't seen Atlas around, she says with sorrys in her eyes. Not here. Not anywhere. She leaves.

I would have still loved Atlas with his hairless head insanity, but he didn't want it. He said he was too far in the hole and wouldn't take me down there with him. This was hard for me because I wanted to believe I somehow made him less crazy, but I think it was the opposite. The men I love always seem to slip into insanity after being with me for a while. They start off as sweet angel boys and end up as angry, drooling monsters. I don't even notice it's happening until they're all the way gone, until we wake up one day and they speak in tongues, or can't speak at all, or only speak in curse words. The first man I ever loved told me that I was the worst thing that ever happened to him. He said I was the bubonic plague and he was a peasant in Europe. He said I was a herd of angry bulls and he was a china shop full of brides trying to register. He said I was salt in the hand of a cruel child and he was a snail. He had a list of one hundred analogies, but I'll stop at three because that's how many it took for me to get the point. After he listed the one hundred analogies, he took a wire hanger, untwisted it, and tried to pluck his heart out. When he couldn't (it was too big), he shaved his head and walked to Mexico. A year later, I got a postcard from him that said:

Dear Olga, I have died a horrible death. Finally. Hell is closer than you think. Please do not try to contact me in this life or the afterlife. Marco.

And that was that. I raise my glass and yell, CHEERS! to all the crazy people. They yell it back, and we drink.

Girl, what the fuck is you doing here acting all crazy? It's Penelope, my good friend.

Waiting for you to buy me a drink, I tell her. I know you got your crazy check.

Yep, and now I'm rolling, girl. Rolling.

Penelope receives a check in the mail because she drinks bleach. She drinks bleach so she can receive a crazy check. She orders me a beer and sits down. She has very white teeth.

He ain't gonna be here, she says. I been looking for you. Motherfucker just disappeared.

That's not even why I'm here, I say.

Shhiiiiiiiittttt. If you gonna lie like that, you might as well take your ass back to bed.

As we sit there, men start coming closer. Penelope has that effect on men. She says she's got a magnet in her pussy.

I got me a nickel bag, she says. You wanna smoke?

So we go outside to the now crazy block party, and she rolls us up a cigar. Girl, she says. I'm telling you. You lucky you found out now he fucked up in the head. Fuck. I married my old man, and within a month, he tells me he gotta go take care of business in Atlanta or some shit and then poof! He gone. Now look at me. A goddamn newlywed who need a vibrator. That what you want?

I already got a vibrator, I say.

She lights up the blunt. Atlas done you a favor, she says. Now all you need is some new dick and you forget all about him. She laughs, and it turns into a cough that turns into a sort of cry.

Some guy walks by. Hey cousin, he says. You looking good.

You ain't think I know? she says and then turns to me. Stupid motherfuckers. All of them.

I take a hit off the blunt and start choking.

I understand though, she says. Good sex make you feel like you belong somewhere. She takes the blunt and hits it again. Fuck it. I need to find some valiums. She passes it back to me. You can smoke the rest of that. Weed just make me horny for my old man.

She leaves, and I go back inside to order another drink. A man in sunglasses and a red baseball hat sits next to me.

Hello, he says. I'm running for mayor.

I'm trying to tell if he's crazy, but the sunglasses make it difficult. Eyes are one of the only ways I can tell if someone is truly crazy. I learned this from my mother's eyes because she is all the way crazy. Demons in her head who cackle and whisper in her ear of the sweetness of death crazy. And when they come, she gets this look in her eyes like she can see all the way into my head and see all my terrible thoughts. But she can't see me. Having seen this for my whole life, I can recognize it in others. Gradations of it. My father makes enough money so that she's only privately crazy. If not, she'd definitely receive checks in the mail. Then she'd be publicly crazy, spending all her money on drinks instead of electroshock therapy. She'd be right next to me, buying me beers instead of being tied down in the loony bin. Alcohol is cheaper than shock therapy, especially in New Orleans.

How would you like to go to the symphony with me tonight? he asks. I have to go because I'm going to be mayor. You could do worse for yourself than date the future mayor.

I look at his arms where possibly a child has scribbled green ink all over them.

I don't know, I say. I might be waiting for someone. I'll know in a little while.

My name's Minos Lee Wintercoat, by the way, he says and puts out his hand for a shake. Can I get you a beer? We shake.

Sure I say, and he pulls one out of his backpack. Minos the Magic Mayor. I could do worse.

What's your name? he asks, passing me the beer.

Olga.

No it's not, he says. You have a new name.

Really? I was just thinking I needed a new name.

Yes. He stares at me with a titled head. Your new name is Hecate. I know this because I'm Sioux Indian. I am the great, great, great, great grandson of Sitting Bull.

I don't think Sitting Bull was Sioux, I say.

He slams his beer on the bar. You're stupid. Stupid stupid stupid. I can't take a stupid girl to the symphony. Symphonies are for smart people. I'm going to be mayor of this town and then you're going to be sorry you're so stupid. Olga Olga Olga Olga. You aren't ready for Hecate yet. I'm taking it back. He grabs the air in front of him and puts it in his pocket. He jumps off the stool. And by the way, he says, he's not coming because you're so stupid. Then he leaves.

Who was that weirdo?

It's Venus, my best friend. She's just as beautiful as she's supposed to be: born from blond sunlight and blue-eyed waves. But today, she has on a pink veil covering her mouth. I can only see her eyes. They have traces of demons but only in the corners. They sparkle like stars. Venus with the demon stars in her eyes.

That was the mayor, I say.

When did he turn white?

I mean that's the future mayor. He asked me to the symphony, but I'm not going.

Why? That might be fun.

Because I'm waiting for Atlas.

He might show up, she offers, even though she knows it's not true.

What's with the veil? I ask. New boyfriend?

Venus has this problem. When she sleeps with a man, she has physical reactions to him. Not romance novel reactions of tingles and hard nipples but a different variety. Once she slept with a man who made her skin have a blue tint. Another man made her hiccup. And the last one made the theme song to Sesame Street play in her head for a week. We both agree she could probably get crazy checks for this, but we think the doctors might lock her up and run tests on her. Make her sleep with thousands of men. And maybe that wouldn't be so bad except for the locked-up part.

She lifts up her veil and around her mouth is a rash of what appears to be tiny pink daisies.

Whoa, I say and look closer. They're kinda cool, I say.

I don't know how I feel about them, she says. She lowers her voice. They also bloomed around my crotch. And I have to tell you. I've never been a big fan of daisies. Tulips maybe. Or Jasmine. Jasmine would be nice. I wouldn't mind smelling like jasmine all the time.

I turn to the guy next to me. My girl has daisies growing on her face. If you buy us a drink, she'll let you see.

He buys us shots of tequila. Venus pulls down the veil, but all he sees is her beauty. He buys us another round because she is so beautiful. And for the next thirteen minutes, everything is lovely. Life is good when you can get drinks with daisies.

At minute fourteen, everything changes. The police arrive with their angry, rational faces. They bring mayhem. People start crying, and screaming, and laughing. Someone yells, I'm dying. I'm a fish out of water, and I'm dying. He flops to the ground. Another man with long, thick locks climbs on top of the jukebox and says, Rapunzel, Rapunzel. I've got you hair sister! He bends over and picks out the next song with his nose. A good party trick. The chaos is put to music: *One sad morning when this life is over, I'll fly away. When I die, halleluia by and by. I'll fly away.* The fish out of water gets up and starts dancing with the soon-to-be mayor who has reappeared. They're both good dancers, spinning and kicking their legs like cheerleaders. I suddenly remember that Sitting Bull *was* a Sioux Indian. I see the Olga I don't like come out of the bathroom. I didn't even know she was here.

I'M WASTED, she screams. Y'ALL HEAR ME? DOUBLEYOU-AYE-ESS-TEE-EEE-DEE. WASTED. She returns to the bathroom.

Venus puts her veil back in place. I'm outta here, she says and leaves. Penelope comes back in. Fuck you motherfuckers, she screams at the police. One cop grabs her and shoves her against the wall. I like it when you use the handcuffs, she tells him. Shut up, he yells. ShutupShutupShutup. He is staring at her ass. *I'll fly away.*

This is all part of the game that is played every check day. The police wait until the Crazy People have spent all their money, and then they come. They scream, and slobber, and arrest the Crazy People. This is a good thing because if they weren't arrested, then the government wouldn't give them any money, and the Crazy People would still be crazy, but it would be much, much worse. With no check to buy drugs, and drinks, and cigarettes, the Crazy People would be angry and slip into the world of the faceless and soulless. They would run around squashing the normal people, thinking they were cockroaches.

One cop comes up to me. His whole face is red as a tomato. He might blow up into ketchup. You better watch yourself, he says to me. He has rotten egg breath. I've been watching you. You come here too much. I know your boyfriend too. He's no good.

Have you seen him? I ask. Is he in jail?

Maybe, he says and laughs. It's a black laughter with sharp teeth. The cop leaves, but his laughter stays.

And just like that, the song is over, and the bar is empty except for me, the echoing laughter, and the lingering souls of the Crazy People. The souls aren't ready for jail yet. Maybe they'll catch up later. Maybe not. They seem a little lost right now. Trying to pick up their drinks without hands. Trying to smoke burning cigarettes with no lungs.

I sit back at the bar and begin to drink one of the beers left behind. When I finish it, I let myself fall off the stool. I lie on the ground for what feels like a very long time. And then the door opens. And it's Atlas. My prince. My messiah. My armageddon. The heart above my pussy begins to pound, and I sigh.

Except it's not Atlas at all.

It's Persephone with her heavy black boots and frowning face of porcelain. She looks down at me and shakes her head. Frowns deeper. She reaches into her black bag and pulls out a half of a pomegranate. Then she smiles, but just barely.

Stuck Between Middle Management and Oblivion

CARIN CHAPMAN

After the plane takes off, the guy sitting in the middle of my row turns to me, in my window seat, and says, "So what's your name, and what do you do for work?"

Hot-damn-dog, I think. Airplane small talk is easily one of my all-time, top-five favorite things. If Jules hadn't left me, she'd be in that seat. Or, actually, I wouldn't even be on this plane. But I'm doing something, going somewhere, like she wants, so she'll come back.

I try to smile. "Daniel," I say. "And I'm an artist." Why doesn't he move into the empty aisle seat?

He grins. His wide nose is covered in red, broken blood vessels, and the line of hair he missed while he was shaving this morning borders the acne scars on his cheek. He forms his hands into a megaphone shape around his thin lips and says, "Painter on board! Danny the painter on board!"

I knew he'd assume I'm a painter. Everybody thinks that when you say you're an 'artist.' Still, he seems really excited about it. Nice enough guy. I almost hate to correct him.

"Actually, I do caricatures," I say. "In an amusement park."

"Like exaggerated pictures?" he says. He outlines the shape of a Coke-bottle, female form.

Uh-huh, I think. Objectifying women. That's my job. You nailed it.

He keeps talking. "That's one way to make money. Me?" he says, even though I didn't ask what he does. "Living the dream.

Got promoted to middle management." He spreads his hands out as he says 'middle management,' like he's reading his title off an office door. I can't tell if he's serious or so deadpan he might be a comedic genius. "But," he goes on, "the wife thinks I need to work on managing my own middle." He laughs at his joke and pats his butter-tub belly. It balloons out of his short-sleeved, white, button-up shirt like a cascading wave. I do a polite snort-laugh thing. Flip up the window shade. How long is this flight again?

As soon as the flight attendant announces, "Use of personal electronic devices is now permitted," Middle Management snaps open the computer in his lap. Excel spreadsheets and Word documents with long chains of numbers flash across his screen.

He pushes his laptop to the edge of his knees and angles it toward me, then elbows me. "All this?" he says and scrolls down a number chain. "The boss says it's got to be moved over here." He clicks open a spreadsheet. "By tonight." He elbows me again. "All this! By tonight!"

"Bosses," I say, thinking about the last two kids I had in my "Caricature Cabana" at work yesterday, one week exactly since Jules left. The little girl I sketched dripped her orange sherbet push-pop all over my pencils, and the boy hurled in my trash can, so I was enveloped by the familiar smell of a plastic garbage bag, warmed with hot-dog vomit, up until Rosco, the big mama elephant in the "Elephant Elysium" enclosure next door, once again projectiled her shit onto the roof of my Cabana, where it sat baking in the heat.

I couldn't do it anymore, so I marched to my manager's office and delivered her a chain of chicken-shit lies about how I needed to go home for my fifteen-year high-school reunion. I'm not even sure that's a thing, but I did the math, and I'm thirty-three, so it would make sense. Plus, I told her no one was going to come get a sketch because of Mama Rosco's shit-storm stench.

"They're caricatures. Not sketches," she reminded me again.

"I need a few days off," I said.

On the plane, the world's largest flight attendant shovels a drink cart down the aisle. He yells, "Elbows. Watch your elbows," not because of the drink cart but because he's about five feet wide, or would be if I sketched him. He rocks a high-and-tight, a slick moustache that stops in a straight line right before it touches his lip, and a furrow dug so deep between his black eyes you could rest a pencil in there. Something about his sharp, super-pro uniform reminds me of Mr. Baumgartner, my fourth grade teacher, who wore pleated khaki pants with matching khaki buttonups. Also pleated. For a second, I trust the flight attendant entirely, want him to read me *The Wind in the Willows* and tell me what to do with my life, how to get Jules back, and how fractions work. But then he's looming over me.

"Drink," he says.

It takes me a second to realize he's offering me a drink, not giving a command. "Coffee and orange juice," I say, then add, "and water." Can't forget the water. Jules always says, "Hydration is key." Key to what? I'm not sure. But if it's a key to her, then I need that key.

"Three drinks?" the flight attendant says. He pauses with the coffee carafe in mid-air and holds up three fingers, spread wide.

"I mean," I say, "if it's a problem—"

"No, no problem," he says. "Three drinks for everybody." He spreads his arms wide to highlight that he is, indeed, talking about every person on the plane. "That way, the last person will probably finally get their *three* drinks by the time we've landed and de-boarded."

I want to tell him how much time he's eating up by describing the situation. But First Sergeant Flight Attendant here has the coffee. I want the coffee. And then there's the fact we're trapped in a metal tube, hurling itself against oblivion, wherein he is the authority.

After we get our drinks, Middle Management leans over and whispers, "Hard ass, huh?" and points over his shoulder with his thumb, toward the retreating Flight Attendant.

"Probably just having a bad day," I say.

Middle Management thumbs his chest and says, "I know a thing or three about bad days. All this computer work makes me miss back when I made the product. And the hell I got from my wife today. Never had to travel before the promotion. She's got new curtains coming for the living room. Pink and brown stripes, she says, and nobody to put them up."

I try to nod, hope it looks enthusiastic. Middle Management thinks his day is bad? Try having my day. Try working coated in elephant crap. After Mama Rosco doused me, all I thought was: I've got to get home and tell Jules about this. I can endure my shit days solely because I turn them into stories that'll make her laugh. But then I remembered Jules wasn't home. She's somewhere in Alaska. She left me, so I can "blossom on my own," as she put it, followed by some lofty metaphor about her being the bigger tree blocking the sunlight I need. She is, in fact, a painter. With a reputation et cetera, et cetera.

Why did Jules leave? My real best guess? She's pissed I blew my try-out session at court. She knows my dream is to be a courtroom sketch artist. They're in there sketching history, man. Watergate? O.J. Simpson? Lindsay Lohan? All sketched by courtroom artists. At arraignments, you only get six minutes to see, decide on, and sketch the whole scene before the accused gets hauled out. You have to be a pit-bull. You can't back down. Or hesitate. It's a roller-coaster in there, and you're the train conductor, hopped up on blow, calling the shots. I could do it. I can make decisions. Pretty quick. I can certainly be hopped up on blow. But the night my buddy called and offered me a try-out for the NBC affiliate, I was getting shit-faced at Jules's latest gallery opening and woke up the next day so hung-over I forgot my pastels and had to sketch the arraignment using charcoals which, for me, is like swinging a three wood when I need a putter.

Middle Management tippity, tappity types on his laptop. The noise infuriates me. I don't know why. I stare out the window to get my mind off it, watch the shaking flaps on the wing. Which are totally sturdy, I'm sure. Though, I could convince myself easier if Jules were here. For her, I can be brave about stuff like the soundness of airplanes. I'm not afraid of anything when I have to take care of both of us. But really she's the brave one. Like this Alaska thing. She's never been there, doesn't know anybody there. But she hopped on a plane, like she'd planned this trip her whole life. I never get how she makes decisions so easy like that.

Beside me, Middle Management lets a snore rip. I glance over at him sleeping, his jaw gaping open and his hand still on the track pad of his open laptop. If it wouldn't be weird, I'd close the laptop for him. But then he'd think I was trying to steal it. Or think my hands were in his lap for some other reason. Best to leave things alone.

That's my M.O. Leave it alone. Let it work itself out. And Jules seemed to love that about me. Right up until she decided she didn't love it anymore and said I never accomplish anything. She packed her owl-shaped suitcase with her yellow scarf and her fur-lined Soviet hat, then held my scruff-covered cheeks between her hands and stared me down with those green eyes. "When's the last time you did something?" she said. I almost told her how I had done something that morning when I scrubbed out her leftover pasta pot. "You need to keep alive, move around," she said. So I'm moving around, going to the desert, a place where you have to *try* to keep alive.

The First Sergeant Flight Attendant stomps back up the plane so loud I'm sure he'll sink us out of the sky. When he gets near my row, I shoot a look over to make sure he isn't coming at me with a cat-of-nine-tails or anything, and that's when I see it.

I bolt up in my seat, my stomach sinks in on itself, and a dry spot scratches up in the back of my throat: Middle Management is watching porn. Right here, on his laptop.

What do I do? I fucking panic, that's what. I want to slam his computer shut, but he's still asleep, with his fingers grazing the track pad. He must've accidentally clicked on a Recently Opened QuickTime file or something. What the fuck do I do? The poor old turd. He probably needs regular doses of porn. If I had his stagnant life, I'd have porn loaded up, ready to go on my work laptop, too. If I had a work laptop. Which I don't. So I just have easily accessible porn on my personal laptop.

I don't want to embarrass him. Or cause a scene, which would get the Flight Attendant's attention. I'll just nudge his fingers off and close the laptop. I reach over, but as I do, Middle Management shifts in his sleep, and the computer starts to fall off his knees. I end up with a corner of it in my hands, which, all-fuckery-be, with the whole thing turned slightly toward me, it looks like I'm the one watching porn. Splendid. Absolutely splendid. Last thing I need is First Sergeant Flight Attendant catching me with porn. So I shove the machine back on Middle Management's lap. Am I sweating? Is that really sweat? I open the air vent above me. The Flight Attendant is one row away and then walks by without looking over. Take it easy, Daniel. Everything is cool. Nothing is fucked here.

I glance back over at the porn. Jesus, Middle Management. It isn't even good porn. And the guy left his socks on, which drives me insane in porn. I don't notice for long, but right at the beginning, before the sex starts, I'm thinking, take the socks off with the pants, man. It's probably because Jules makes me take off my socks, and I would do anything she wanted except she can never figure out exactly what it is she needs me to do. That or she can't tell me. I don't know which. Should I ask her? Should I maybe have asked her long before she left for the Arctic? Should I have done a billion things I didn't do? What good does it do to think about that?

The point is, I'm not proud of the fact I'm now half-chubbed on an airplane over some lame-ass, sock-wearing porn.

What do I do with this stiffy? I'll look away. Think about how Jules is probably riding a sperm whale in Alaska by now. A *sperm* whale? Really? That's a fantastic way to get my mind off the porno-box beside me. But probably she is riding a polar bear, or a helicopter, or a fishing boat. She loves to ride things. Ferris wheels, horses, dirt bikes. It's her long legs. They make her feel like she can control anything, ride it wherever she wants.

She's the kind of girl who wears the same earrings day in, day out and never does anything with her waist-length black hair except wash and brush it, and occasionally, when it annoys her, pile it on top of her head in a messy bun. I know a jazillion tiny things like that about her. She's easy to know because she's all definites and extremes, never uncertain. She can't understand me, why I do stuff like blow my one shot at being a courtroom artist. Which, yes, I did wake up hung-over and forgot my charcoals, but really, I blew it because I couldn't pick my moment. I deliberated, started five different sketches in a row. I choked. Because I can't make decisions, can't take action. I just let life happen to me. While I watch Jules make a way for herself, and I sit—

The growl of the Flight Attendant's approach stops me mid-thought. I peer around people's heads and spot him tromping up the aisle. This is not perfect news. Not, say, the best thing that could possibly happen right now. I'm still sporting this unfortunate chub. I need cover. A blanket would work. Remember how they used to give out blankets on airplanes in the eighties? What happened to the eighties? Could I cover my lap with Middle Management's computer? But what if he wakes up and sees what appears to be me watching his porn? Yeah. That's a great plan, Daniel, you fuck-scoot.

The Flight Attendant is coming. He already hates me. I'll probably go to jail for watching lewd content in a public space.

All right. Calm down. What are my options here? I could wake Middle Management up. I could squeeze by to use the bathroom. Close the laptop?

Damnit. The Flight Attendant's stomps get closer. I swear to god he's walking in slow-mo just so I have to panic longer. He's going to see the porn. He's going to see my chub. He's going to arrest me, mock me, tell the whole plane I'm a disgusting shit-stain on the proverbial panties of an otherwise ethical and moral world. Then he's staring down at me, and I know he's glaring at my crotch, and the laptop, and I'm going to airplane jail for indecency.

I snatch the in-flight magazine out of my seat back and spread it across my lap.

"Where is your trash?" he says. "You had three beverages." He holds up three fingers spread wide. How the hell is this not waking up Middle Management? There is a dragon screaming over him. There is a woman (and a dildo now) and a dude with socks still on, going at it on his lap. There is me, hyperventilating.

"I...," I say, and fumble around in front of me, grab the in-flight magazine off my lap. Promptly put it back over my lap. First Sergeant Flight Attendant leans farther into our row. Oh dear god. He's going to see the porn. But it's still slightly turned, so maybe his angle is bad. Meanwhile, trash? Trash! Where did I put the fucking trash?

He's so close now I can smell him. Like coffee and baby lotion. "On the floor," the Flight Attendant snaps. I start to get on the floor, thinking that's the position you assume when being arrested on an airplane, but then he says, "You threw it on the floor," and points at my feet, where my empty cups fell without my noticing. I grab them, hand them to him.

He snatches them away and says, "Put up your seatback for landing," while he tosses the cups into the transparent garbage bag he carries with him. I sink deep into my seat. Is there a vomit-bag in the pouch in front of me? I might need it. I try to open the air vent more. My wood has died down, at least.

The Flight Attendant's trash bag reminds me of my own work. I bet he has to deal with vomit-filled trash bags too. Poor guy. I bet he's got a Jules, too (or maybe a Mike or something), who leaves him feeling desperate to be a better guy. Or maybe he's got a wife like poor Middle Management here, who goes home to pink and brown living room curtains which might be the worst version of hell imaginable. I should have just shut his laptop a long time ago. I should've woken him up. I should've done something intentional. Long before Jules left. The seatbelt light blinks on, and the Flight Attendant gives the pre-landing speech.

Middle Management's going to wake up. I seriously should close his laptop now. He stirs, with his eyes still closed, and rubs at the drool pooled on the sides of his mouth. He's going to pop those eyeballs open any second. He's going to—

I throw my head against the window and close my eyes, pretend I'm asleep. I hear Middle Management sit up then close his laptop with the most "I'm-so-embarrassed-I-sure-as-hell-hope-nobody-saw-that" laptop closing sound ever. I wait until enough time passes that I'm positive he has completely put away the computer. Then I stretch awake. Yawn wide. Look over at Middle Management and say, "Whew, howdy. I must have been out like totally that whole entire time."

"Me too, partner," he says. "Good thing. The old laptop here decided to open up a little gentleman's video, if you're picking up what I'm laying down." He elbows me.

Does he know? Did he see me? Was this all on purpose? Holy shit. What do I say? I can't pretend like I didn't know. I mean, I can. Maybe I should? Damnit, if Jules were here we'd just laugh.

"Good thing nobody saw it," he says. "Would've been embarrassing for a second."

For a second? Really? This guy would...what? Blow it off and shut the computer like nothing happened? Which is, I guess, exactly what he is doing.

The plane lands. We stare out the window together. Light rain splatters the long strips of browning grass we taxi by.

Then he says, “Real pleasure, Artist Danny. Here’s my card. Sometimes we need graphic designers. You ever looking for work, we like spry kids like you.”

I mumble thanks, grab my carry-on from the overhead, and look at the card after he walks down the aisle. It has his name then says, “Management Team. Wood and Fur, International Distributors of Adult Entertainment.”

He’s a porno dude? I stare up the aisle even though he’s already gone. That was a work video? It dawns on me that maybe that guy’s actually got it together, way more than I gave him credit for. He’s got his wife. And his promotion. His confidence. He must’ve known I saw that video, and he wasn’t even embarrassed about it. I’m not saying I want his life, but maybe I want his life. He had to have seen how useless I am. Why would he offer me a gig? Well, sort of offer. I didn’t even give him my full name. Chances are, if I email him, he won’t remember me.

Still, I could email him. I could at least try at this and prove that I’ll fail. Or, maybe, sliver-of-a-possibility, not fail. I should do it. I could get my shit together, like Middle Management. I will do it. I’ll email him. Jules would want me to. That’s doing something. That’s staying alive.

I move up the aisle feeling a little lighter. First Sergeant Flight Attendant stands at the plane’s exit door, stiff, like he’s prepared to salute. As I walk by, he holds up three fingers.

“You’re one tough cookie,” I say to him. But not in a mean way. More like a this-is-just-how-the-world-is way. “But I still hope you don’t have to haul any vomit today.”

I head down the jetway. I’ll get to the desert. I’ll email Middle Management. Then I can tell Jules, and she’ll come home and help me get the gig. It’ll all work itself out.

excerpt from
Reap and Sow

HANNAH CHOI

Secretly in the darkness of a freight car to Manchuria, we speak our language and make a pact never to forget. We are three sisters, not by blood but country. It is 1941, and Japan is several years in a war against what seems to us like the rest of the world. Our only light during the long journey is bullet holes in the rusted metal walls. We count five different men guarding us, but there may be more. We hear their voices call to each other outside. I worked in the Magistrate's house of my village, where there were many Japanese guests, so I know our captors are Japanese. Occasionally, we see an eye, sometimes a finger, and even a tongue worms through the hole and swirls around. I resist the urge to crush the tongue like an insect. The last thing I want is to be thrown out in the middle of nowhere.

We think we are on our way to a factory in Harbin in northeast China where we will make uniforms for Japanese soldiers, but we are not sure. I am the oldest, and I am not used to having sisters. Il-rye is the bold one. She says she is glad to leave Korea and plans to marry a rich foreigner. She remains the cool alley cat, trying to catch the eye of the men whenever they look in. Sun-hee is only thirteen. She has never been on her own before and clings to my arm.

The train pushes northward, and we keep warm under thick layers of blankets, which are not an act of kindness on the part of the men but thrift. We'd bring no profit to them if we died of frostbite during the journey. I remember it is my birthday, and when I sleep, I dream of Mother. It rains where she is, and she worries about a mudslide pushing the graves of my siblings into the river. She clutches me to her side. I know it is a dream because Mother died when I was eight, and her long hair, which she tied in a bun at her neck, drapes across her shoulders and down her gray tunic. Her hair smells of mulberry and grass. Her grip tightens around me, and she tells me the same fairytale she told me when I was a child. You know the one. It lives in her, breathing beneath her skin, under her eyes, inside her mouth. She indulges in the details. The woodcutter's tobacco-stained fingernails. The black bristles on his chin. The blood soaked through his straw sandals from the climb.

Once, there was a poor woodcutter, Mother begins, who climbed to the highest peak of the Baek-du Mountains through a path in the forest, farther than he had ever gone before. He was from a small village in the Kang-won Province and traveled so deep into the forest that he did not realize how high up he was. He was almost at the mountain pass, which usually was a sliver in the clouds from his view below in the shack he shared with his aged mother. A smooth teal lake had formed in a valley dipping between the white peaks, and ancient pine trees surrounded the water. The sap was sticky gold, and green needles tapped in the breeze. The woodcutter picked a pinecone and found a single glowing nut encased in one of its shells. He slipped it in his mouth and let the buttery taste linger as he looked up to the sunlight filtering through the treetops. He took axe to trunk, and the forest shuddered. No human hands had touched those sacred trees. But how could he know? And why would he care? The woodcutter worked with pleasure, singing with the music of the blade as it sliced through the air and into the bark.

Mother paces from one sibling grave to another, her arm holding me close. She times her words with her steps, smiling because the slower she tells it the better it will be stomped into the soil, one day to grow from her feet. She can walk like that all day in my head, forgetting the weather. But I am restless, and she never stays for long.

Awake, I see my sisters' eyes glimmer in the darkness of the train car. I push my hands down on the metal floor. With every rattle and thrust, the sickening feeling grows. You must be dead if I am in Manchuria. You said this place was hell on earth.

At the Tumen River, more girls are boarded: four Chinese and two Filipina. Altogether, we are nine, but we stay in separate corners, our disparate languages soft in the stifled air.

Sun-hee murmurs to herself.

"What do you think she's saying?" I ask Il-rye, who braids and re-braids her long hair.

"She's praying in a funny language."

Il-rye nudges Sun-hee's shoulder, but she does not open her eyes or respond. She pulls the blankets from the young girl, and a small glass ball rolls toward me. I hold it to a bullet hole where it fills with light. Three women in white and gold huddle inside, heads bowed and wings perched up like petals. The world inside snows.

Il-rye looks over my shoulder. "What is it?"

"Heaven," Sun-hee replies and reaches up. "Big Sisters, please give it back. It's the only thing I have from home."

"Where did you get it?" Il-rye asks.

"The Catholic priest in my village gave it to me. Prayers fill it up with manna from heaven, and the angels eat it like bread."

"You sound like the mudang in my village," Il-rye mocks. "But she was possessed by her dead father, not by some foreign priest."

"I've seen a real possessed woman, and she had to be tied down," Sun-hee replies. "Her mouth foamed, and her eyes burned red. The priest saved her by ordering the demon out."

"How did he do it?" I ask.

"With holy water and holy book. I was there. Such peace filled her face, and she fell asleep for two days."

I peer through the dome's glass to see the women's faces. I shake the globe again.

The night of Mother's death, umbilical cord knotted around the neck of my brother, the shaman woman was there. Widow Moon walked across the paddies, holding a bundle over her head. She terrified me. Her lips were painted red. Her hair was white, but she looked very young, younger even than Mother. Her eyes were murky blue. Her presence was electric. She walked into the room where Mother lay dead with my brother. She told me to get rags and water, and I hurried to my feet, afraid to disobey her. We soaked up the blood with the rags. Then we cleaned their bodies and dressed them in white linen. It took hours, and by the time we finished, it was nighttime. The dogs and chickens cried outside, and the villagers who had gathered outside were gone. The shaman woman spread white rice over where Mother and baby brother lay, and I set Mother's favorite foods on a small table in the courtyard.

The shaman woman made a fire and prayed. From her bundle she pulled out a hollowed gourd and walked to the river to fill it. She returned and mixed ashes with the water inside. She took a paper branch of many strips and hung it on a mulberry tree, and the strips danced in the wind. Then she gave me a sip of the ashy water and told me to dig. The shovel was too big for me, so I used Mother's sickle. The shaman woman drank from the gourd and dug with the shovel. When she was done, she rested and sat under the tree and drank. She closed her eyes. I thought she had fallen asleep, but soon she opened her eyes and stood to dance, waving a small knife above her. Her hips pivoted like a broken clock. Silk slippers scraped the ground. White skirt billowed in the wind. I wanted to run into her blade so I could follow Mother to the afterlife, but I stayed where I was.

Afterward, seeing that I was alone, my father absent as usual, the Widow took me to her seacoast cottage and cared for me like I was her own. We spent several weeks as substitute mother and daughter, and she weaved stories for me in the sand and water. She spoke of love and her fisherman husband who had drowned many years ago. She told me that the greatest lesson in her life came when he died because that was the moment that she never stopped reliving. "He is the secret to my power," she said with a strange smile.

I imagined a happy kind of life as the Widow's adopted daughter, but my father showed up and reclaimed me. His wife and three children buried, I was the only family left, and he would have me. Someone needed to prepare his meals and look after his home.

"You can marry again," the Widow said, unwilling to let me go.

"Who will marry me?" He bowed before her, his knees pushing in the sand. He, like everyone else in the village, was afraid of her. "I am ill. That is why I cannot work. That is why I drink. I have hoped for a cure and paid the apothecary, but nothing works. Please. My daughter is the comfort in my life now, and you have no right to keep her from me."

Her grip tightened around me, but I felt her change. She turned my face toward her pale eyes.

"Heaven," she whispered, "has a mysterious way of rewarding obedience."

I did not know what she meant, but there was no time to ask her. Father took me away.

I remember she smelled like lavender, her white hair, her ivory neck and hands and even her clothes, which she washed in the ocean. Lavender protected her from the disease of dead bodies; it kept nightmares away and helped her sleep.

Widow Moon stood on the beach, facing the water, and I looked back as my father pulled me away, hoping she would change her mind. I wonder why she let me go so easily. What did she see in the ocean that day? She never turned around, not even when I cried for her on the wooded path. She was a small, white glimmer standing above the waves, and I was alone with my father.

The forest darkened around us. "My ancestors must pity me," he said. "Left with such a selfish girl." He had a way of bruising my shoulders with each embrace, of too much punishing tenderness. His hot breath close to my neck, he spoke his secret thoughts aloud to the forest, about the curses of his life, not even a son to carry on the family name. He used me like a pushpin doll for his emotions, and when I felt pain, he felt better. When I cried, he spoke kindly.

"At least I still have you," he said, as if I were his mirror. But inside, I resisted him, and in my struggle, I felt closer to Mother than before. I could name her as the sorrow rising within me. I lit the terrible darkness with her story, and the memories of her voice filled the forest. In this way, I quieted even the laments of my poor, luckless father.

* * *

When the woodcutter had chopped more pine than he could carry back to his village, he rested by the lakeside and imagined the house he would build with the prized timber. It would be more majestic than his greedy landlord's. Grander even than the Blooming Lotus temple where eleven monks lived at the foot of the mountains.

As he traced a calloused finger in the air, along the tall beams of his perfect house, he noticed shadows in the sky. He sat up, confused. It was an impossible sight. Three heavenly maidens descended from the mountain pass in translucent dresses with red and blue wings. Singing, they glided to the lakeside. They disrobed and hung their silks on the pine branches. The woodcutter crawled and hid in the grass. He sucked in his breath. He could taste the pine nut and bit down on his bottom lip.

The maidens dove underwater, and the lake's surface became a cool, still mirror. Laughter rippled and vibrated in the grass. A hand surfaced from the lake and was clasped by another then another pair of hands then another, and the three maidens, arms intertwined, swam in a large, slow circle.

* * *

The train stops near the Amur River. The freight car opens, and daylight burns our eyes. There is no factory. Soldiers line up in straight rows under a cold, sunlit sky. They wear heavy, green coats over their uniforms and white, fur-brimmed hats. A young man sits on horseback with the white and red Shinto flag waving above him, while an older man, with a graying moustache, rides back and forth. He turns to the young man.

"Why are they standing on the edge like a row of chickens?" he shouts in Japanese and points his gun at us. "Lieutenant Hata, get those girls off the freight car."

"Yes, Commander Akifusa," the young man replies. He dismounts his horse and looks up, spreading his arms as if to catch all of us. His fur hat hangs crooked, and he adjusts it. Then he turns back and orders a few of the soldiers to pull us down.

On the ground, we are tied to one another with the same rope used to wrangle horses. I still have Sun-hee's globe, hidden underneath my tunic. I don't think of you. I don't think of you at all. What can be changed now? I let you fade back with the infantry. I curse myself for not finding a way to jump off the train before the last white ridge of our Baek-du Mountains disappeared from view. The sky darkens, and a half-moon follows but offers little light or warmth.

*   *   *

The maidens dove underwater again, and the woodcutter took his chance. He ran to their dresses and grabbed the smallest one. The silken fabric felt alive and slipped out of his hands. He picked it up and rubbed it between his fingers. The blue and red wings were finely woven, gold-embroidered ribbons, and the dress itself, soft like the skin of butterflies. But it was durable; he tested it with rough, taut tugs, stretching his arms out wide. He hid the dress and crouched in the grass. The maidens emerged from the lake, and their supple skin glistened under the setting sun. Pearls of water slid down the curves of their hips and legs, and they retrieved their dresses. But the youngest maiden stood back, pointing a finger to an empty branch, with a question furrowing her eyebrows.

*   *   *

We reach a clearing where the rest of the infantry waits at an encampment. A fire glows in the parade grounds, and Akifusa orders us to kneel. Those meager embers already die under the winds that push through the trees. The scent of sorghum and barley mixes with rain and pine, while the men surrounding us smell of blood, sweat and gunpowder. Unlike the soldiers who met us at the train, these men are intoxicated and unruly. About seventy in number, they crowd us like jackals. Akifusa takes a long swig from a jug and, wiping his mouth, passes the drink to his lieutenant, who gives it to another soldier without taking a sip of his own. The commander stands on a makeshift platform and recounts Japan's latest conquests: a destroyed American fleet at Pearl Harbor, two sunken British battleships in Singapore, and the Philippines, Guam, Wake Island and Hong Kong have all been claimed for Japan. The soldiers yawp at every name. Their sacrifice is not in vain. Their country is winning. They deserve to celebrate.

Akifusa steps down and smiles at us. "Even young girls must prove themselves during war," he says and stops at the youngest of us. He unties Sun-hee, and she stands in front of him.

"What are you saying?" he barks. "Your babble is not allowed here."

Sun-hee's black tunic is ripped around the collar, and her white skirt is stained with dirt. She shivers and leans closer to the fire. She is in shock, as if only now seeing the surrounding barracks in the northern countryside. She blinks without recognition at the soldiers. Akifusa takes off his leather gloves and cups her heart-shaped face. I should protect the little one, but my knees stay frozen on the ground. Her small glass globe feels cold and heavy against my skin, and I remember what my father said about me. I am a selfish girl. I put myself first.

"I will call her Bara because she embodies innocence and naiveté," he proclaims. His soldiers laugh. He gathers her hair and pulls tightly, cutting it with a knife. "Everyone joins the infantry with a clean head. It shows purity and conformity." His men agree in unison.

Sun-hee reaches behind her shoulders and opens her mouth to protest, but he throws her dark strands into the fire. The flames jump and die back down. She looks like a white poppy after its petals have dropped, a cropped head dangling on a small body. Her large eyes search the crowd, but they express nothing. She touches her head and neck and feels for the locks no longer there.

Akifusa makes the rest of us stand and unties us. With cold hands, he sizes our bodies, one after the other, our breasts, thighs and calves, and he proceeds to cut our hair. He gives us Japanese names. The Filipina girls become Chuurippu and Ayame, and the Chinese girls are Yuri, Sakura and Hasu. Il-rye, who is the tallest of us and stands poised in front of him, becomes Beni. She surprises me by weeping when he cuts her hair. She hides her face and falls to the ground like an opened shell, her pride evaporated.

I am last. At eighteen I am determined to be strong, so strong that my father would not be able to recognize me. I return the small globe to Sun-hee, hiding it underneath her long skirt, and step forward to the commander. I clench my hands into stones, sharpen my eyes into daggers, and turn my mouth into an icy blade. Akifusa grabs my head, and I spit in his face. The soldiers' laughter stops. Guns cock. But the commander remains unfazed. He wipes his nose and moustache. "What do you call a poisonous flower?" he asks his lieutenant.

"The oleander is poisonous, sir," Hata replies. "It's red like a rose but potent enough to kill a man."

The commander sets his blade against my throat. "This girl cannot kill anyone." He pushes his blade down the front of my tunic. "Her heart beats like a trapped doe."

"You can call her Sumire," the lieutenant suggests. "Its fruits and seeds can be poisonous, but the blue flowers are safe to eat."

"Sumire," Akifusa repeats, and the soldiers whoop their approval.

The Commander moves his knife over the fire and sets the reddened blade on the back of my neck. I scream, and he holds me down and throws my hair into the fire pit. A shadow rises with the smoke, and I swear it is Mother's love rising to protect me. I hold my tongue and let my arms go slack.

"We will remember each other," Akifusa whispers and lets me go.

The lieutenant writes down our Japanese names in the inventory log and closes it with a leather string. The soldiers continue their celebration with song and wine. They parade us to a canvas tent, surrounded by a barbed wire fence. Two young guards stand at the entrance, and the infantry lines up outside. The officers come in first. It does not take us long to realize why we are there.

*   *   *

The naked, marooned maiden stood alone before the woodcutter.

"Where are your clothes?" he asked, pretending to look concerned.

His gruff voice made her run back into the water, neck-deep. He waded in and held out a blanket. "Since you can't go with your sisters," he said, "why not come with me?" His eyes flashed under the moonlight.

What could she do? The water turned cold. Arms around her chest, she shivered and looked up at the sky.

The woodcutter led the maiden out of the lake and covered her with his blanket. Under a waning moon, she stood in the darkness, her lips trembling. The man lit a lantern, and she focused on that light. She followed it through the forest, down the mountain and across the rice fields to the woodcutter's shack, where his old mother sat waiting for him on the porch, grinding red peppers in a mortar. The woodcutter had the maiden's dress hidden in his stacks, but she did not know. She kept looking at the sky for her sisters, but those were just stars burning through the night.

Over time, the woodcutter added two more rooms onto his shack. It was not the glorious house he imagined, but the sons he had with the maiden were enough to make his chin push up whenever his landlord came by.

One night, when he was drunk, he let it slip that he had stolen the maiden's dress while she had bathed in the lake with her sisters. She did not believe him until he lifted a plank from the bedroom floor and took out a small pine chest. He held up her winged dress, still slippery like oil and fragrant.

"Can I try on the dress, just once?" she asked.

He hesitated, but she kept asking. "Fine," he grunted.

Carefully, her hands shaking and closing her eyes because she did not need to see the dress to know it was hers, she exchanged her farming clothes for heavenly silk. At this point in the story, Mother always stops to laugh, a clean, pure sound that peals in the wind of the maiden's flight. The woodcutter did not even have the chance to blink before he saw the maiden and his three small children, gathered in her arms, flying away toward the mountain pass. He ran after them, but his legs never outraced her wings.

* * *

It starts to snow again. The guards give us old uniforms, underwear, socks and boots. I stare at the other girls weeping in their soldier hand-me-downs and do not know whether to love or hate them. Sun-hee kneels in her tunic, and her pale legs rub against the black dirt. She has not eaten at all from the large bowl of rice the guards left us.

"Sun-hee," I say in the best big-sister voice I can manage. "What the soldiers did, you can't let it weaken you. Virginity is something to lose. I lost mine when I was fifteen, to my father's gambling buddy. What could I have done when my father did nothing?"

Sun-hee bites her dirty fingernails. "He really did nothing?" she asks.

"He made me marry him," I reply. Steam hisses from the ondol heater as water boils through the pipes buried beneath us.

That boar-faced Constable Ahn, my father's devil. His cheeks turned red, rough skin as hot from the acidic soju distilled in large clay pots in his courtyard. One morning, I found him sleeping on the steps of our porch, his thick, stubby hands clutching my straw sandals. I pushed him over, and he fell to the ground. He rubbed his eyes and looked up. "I've been waiting for you," he slurred, his eyes heavy. "Your father couldn't pay, so now you pay."

I remember how he laughed as he pushed me into my room and the surprising grip of his hands pinning down my shoulders. Conquest sobered him quickly. He was a spineless, stupid man, a drunkard hiding behind a title and baton. And what did that make me, to be overpowered by him? He took from me what I had been saving for you.

When my father found me with the constable, he beat me until he was exhausted. Not one word of outrage against the constable. My father refused to look at me and stepped outside to the porch, where the constable waited and drank sullenly.

"I'll take her home with me," the constable said.

"You know you can't disgrace me like this," my father implored. "There must be a proper wedding, in front of all the village people. So everyone will think that I have done my duty as a good father. You must give me at least this."

The constable snorted but agreed, and the wedding date was chosen for the following week. I begged my father and confessed that I was waiting for your return from Manchuria. Surely, heaven would reward my patience and faith.

I told him all about you, the kitchen boy from the magistrate's house who grew up to become a noble soldier. I told him that I loved you, ever since we were children. He looked at me, bewildered.

"And you don't love me?" he demanded. "Am I doing such a terrible thing? Marrying my daughter to a respected man in the village, a man with land and money. Am I to be cursed for saving you from a shameful fate? How many unwed girls are taken for the Japanese? This way the constable can protect you."

What could I have said to persuade him? I search for the words in Manchuria against an army of fathers. What could I have said or done to make him see me?

* * *

Does my father mourn me now? Disobedient girl, fell right into the hands of the Japanese.

I ask Sun-hee about the small globe in her hand. "Why do you always make it snow inside?"

Her voice shakes. "Jesus, Jesus, Jesus, I pray. Feed me for one more day."

"Feed you what?"

"The Lord gives food that the world knows nothing about." Her voice grows louder as she tells me the story of her God, who came down from heaven as a man with blue eyes and golden hair. He wore simple, straw sandals and a linen robe. "He's scarred all over his body," she explains. She points to her wrists, palms, legs and feet and places a hand over her side.

"Why worship a wounded God?" I ask. "We have enough trouble."

"He pays for our sins. If the three of us believe, then I know he will hear us. Three is better than one."

Il-rye frowns. "I am not praying."

I do not pray either, but I am caught on her words. *He pays for our sins. He pays?* Sun-hee refuses to eat and fills her mouth with God, speeding through a torrent of her holy words. I lift the globe, and the maidens of Mother's story whisper, with frosted eyelashes and lips. Silvery white caps hide their hair, and wings flutter with a metallic sheen. Nothing can hurt them inside their pristine dome of glass. Jesus, Jesus, Jesus, I wonder if those are their names.

Sun-hee's small fingers dig in the ground. I have seen her do this before, but I do not realize until now that she is writing.

"What does it say?" I ask.

"The only certain thing is resurrection," she reads and wipes tears from her eyes.

"The dead deserve rest," I say, remembering what Widow Moon told me after Mother died. "We must learn to let go."

"Christ can awaken the dead," Sun-hee whispers.

She takes the glass ball from me like a small child who believes she holds the ocean in a seashell. But she holds echoes. Widow Moon taught me that. This world is mere shadows of unknowable mystery. The shaman woman had cataract eyes that gave her an appearance of blindness, but she saw very clearly. Nothing escaped her sight, not even the quiet rabbit hiding in the grass or a mosquito plotting for my neck.

But is she as powerful as Sun-hee's God? The Widow drew shapes in the sand and mimicked the rhythm of the ocean, but she did not write — that art protected by men so proudly. I remember how precious and divine the Magistrate's library seemed to me when I first entered his home as a child. His cedar cabinets were filled with aged rice paper scrolls. Rice paper prayers, I called them. I thought if I pulled a single sheet open, I would hear heaven's thunderous peal.

"Who taught you how to write?" I ask the young girl.

"The priest was from far away, but he knew our language. He taught me."

I wanted to go to school, but my father forbade it, saying that school made disobedient whores out of daughters. He dragged me from the schoolhouse one day, which was on the magistrate's property, and humiliated me in front of the villagers.

"So, you think you deserve better than your father!" he shouted. "That you should have an education while I slaved in the rice paddies since I could walk on my own!"

I remember the stones on the path as my knees dragged, my scraped skin and blood, his words, his hands. I watch Sun-hee unearth the powers of life with each stroke in the dirt, and I say nothing. But Sun-hee takes my finger and has me copy her strokes, and like that, without even knowing what I write, I feel wings flutter in my stomach.

That night, I turn away from an officer after he rapes me and push my face against the canvas wall. I open my mouth to scream, and I hear the northern winds hammer snow into the ground. I fall asleep to the sound and dream of Mother, who paces from grave to grave. Her arm holds me close. We finish burying another one of my sisters when it starts to rain.

"When I was young," she says, "there were two sisters who drowned and showed up floating side by side like bloomed lotuses. A mist covered the river where the girls were found, and every night the wind carried it to the village. Everyone was scared of the girls returning. But I knew the sisters wouldn't be back because I saw when they left. For months it'd been raining, and I was so restless being inside that I ran to the river to watch the current. I didn't care about getting sick or falling in or anything. And that's when I saw them flying up the mountain and disappearing through a narrow slit I never noticed before." Mother's grip is tight around me; then she lets go. I wake with the memory of white, jagged mountains through a bullet hole of light.

* * *

But we lose time in Manchuria. We lose the feeling of our bodies. We even lose our language, what we swore never to forget.

You are dead, I repeat. You are dead. I remember your cold hand in mine. Now that I have nothing, I do not care what happens to me. The soldiers use us as the mat to beat against. They care nothing about us, and we care nothing about them.

And this must be my lot of love. My punishment to endure. This cold emptying out every time another soldier is done with me. I lie back and stare at the canvas tears in the tent. This must be my portion of love. The constant absence of you and the longing. The hungry sorrow and the endless regret.

I imagine the Emperor's face, and I see my father, and his father, and his father, and his father. If he had let me go to school, if he had let me wait for you, if he had let me choose my own life, I would have never run away. But that's a child's way to think, *if*.

"You are a broken seed," my father said.

If I were born his son, could we have loved each other? But I am his underworld maiden. I am his buried girl, cast under his darkness.

No one is going to save me, not Mother or you. My father would be too ashamed to look at me, a daughter reduced to a slave. He is like a wolf that sniffs at a corpse then walks away.

You are dead, I repeat. You are dead. I remember your cold hand in mine. Now that I have nothing, I do not care what happens to me.

My fingers bleed from digging in the dirt. The blood tastes fresh and salty, and the taste of it reminds me of you.

The Distance

CHRYS DARKWATER

I am light, fire, burning, not only taking up the space inside my body but all the area around me, a symphony in my blood, woodwinds and brass and percussion pressed between muscle and bone, trying to escape, aching for crescendo, pushing out through the short hairs that rise out of my skin, tiny fingers of flame.

I throw slow punches in the air. Muscle-memory guides them, past thought, past memories, leads me to where I have to go.

Scheduled for twelve rounds, the Book lays odds the fight will be over in under six. Of course, I'm not expected to win, not expected to go the distance.

My girlfriend used to laugh whenever I talked about going the distance. She'd laugh, saying that she should be so lucky, and I'd throw her over my shoulder while she squealed, kicking her legs weakly, the silky burn of her hair against my back electric. I can still feel her smile against my skin, her words warm on my cheek. Back then, me and my baby, we could always go the distance.

Anything not right in front of me goes blurry, reduced to shapes, outlines. Sound becomes muffled like I'm underwater, voices like whale songs, undulating and distant.

He's knocked out everyone who's stepped in the ring with him, twenty-six straight, most in the first round. Good pop in both fists. Dynamite they call him.

I think of fighters who died in the ring. I never heard of anyone ever actually dying in the ring itself; they died from what happened in the ring. They died, later, hooked up to tubes and machines, with nurses and doctors and well wishers, in rooms full of prayers and flowers, so many eyes squeezed shut against the inevitable. Semantics never changed the ending.

I think about Beethaeven Scottland, Jimmy Garcia, Johnny Owen. Each of them twenty-four when their luck ran out. My blood thickens as the twisted strings of my DNA tangle and knot, snaking through me. My skin is too tight, hot, burning, and my vision blurs, and I have to close my eyes, tell myself to breathe, to force air into my lungs and to hold it tight before letting it out slowly, rising from the soles of my feet. I think about Cleveland Denny, Robert Wanglia, Willie Classen.

When I close my eyes, I can still feel my daughter's kisses on my skin, can still smell the sweet sticky candy lip gloss on my lips, on both cheeks, on my forehead as she wished me luck, her eyes bright as new quarters, shiny like that. She always told me to be careful, her voice slow and deliberate, sounding the way I sounded when I told her to look both ways before crossing the street. Her kisses echo through me, through the miles and years apart, bouncing between skin and bone. Closing my eyes erases all the years.

I think of the distance.

Twelve rounds.

My fists paw the air.

My bones remember fights where I had to go past the point where there was nothing left, where thoughts and memories blurred together, indistinguishable, like a fracture that healed wrong, a faultline of fused bone. What happened, or what I thought happened, or what I wished happened, all smashed together to where I'm not sure of anything. But the bones remember every punch, what was given and what was taken away.

My little girl told me to stop fighting. Her mother, a woman I was smart enough to ask to marry me, a woman smart enough to say no, never asked me directly. She'd slip it in, clean, like throwing a punch coming out of a weave, telling me to think of her, our little girl, our future.

I wonder what will happen the day when I dig down deep and find nothing. I tell myself that today isn't that day, but I don't know if that's a lie.

My cut-man slips his hands into the mitts and holds them up in front of him. His lips move around words that I don't hear, but I understand what he is asking.

My fists pop into the mitts, punches cracking like handfuls of thunder.

The familiar tension that runs between muscle and bone slowly melts until I am glowing, light. I'm lightning, crackling around the edges, filling the space around me.

My trainer stands behind me and to the side, watching. His eyes on me, heavy, I feel when he nods approvingly, a small dip of the head that matches the timing of my punches.

The sweat is coming good and thick now, the way it's supposed to. Warm and thick as blood.

My cut-man claps the mitts together, nods, a whisper of a smile on his face, as he slips his hands free and turns towards the door.

I follow him out, down the hall, down through the dark tunnel that opens up to a sea of dark faces. Below them, in front of me, the ring glows. The blue of the canvas is the blue promise of Caribbean seas and cloudless skies, the blue the color of dreams. The rest of the world disappears.

A spotlight brushes over us as we make our way toward the ring. Music plays, but I can't make out what song it is. Bass and drum push against my skin. I feel the music more than I hear it.

People lean over the railings, yelling, faces reduced to shadows. Compliments or insults, I can't tell. Maybe they yell just to yell, to hear their own voices, to feel the words swell up from inside them like a wave threatening to swallow the shore.

From behind, my trainer keeps his hands on me, whispers words of magic warm against my skin.

I walk, floating, my feet touching the ground solidly and yet not at all. I am hollowed out and yet full of the world. Empty and full, heavy and weightless, I am a contradiction on fire as I float above the ground even as I sink down deep, deeper, deepest, roots tangling all the way to the center of the world.

Mariposas

LEA L. DOWNING

Jake shivered as he fished out his uniform polo from a laundry basket heaped with dirty clothes and pulled it over his head. His water heater had been broken for almost two weeks. As fall came into full effect, the cold showers he'd been enduring grew more and more trying. He'd call someone to get it fixed that afternoon, while he was on his lunch break. The shirt was wrinkled, and he tried to smooth it out, his hand passing over the left side of his chest where his name was embroidered.

Jake's official title at Quicko's Truck Plaza was "Customer Sales Specialist," but all he did was run the cash register in the convenience store section of the sprawling building. Quicko's was much more than a gas station: it also had a barbecue restaurant, an ice cream parlor, an automotive shop, full-service showers, and a twenty-four-hour gym. Beyond that, however, it was the only service station adjacent to the interstate for more than fifty miles in either direction. Billboards along I-40 counted down to its arrival: "30 miles from Quicko's!" then "23 miles from your last chance for gas!" and finally, in giant neon text, "Wait's over! Exit now for Quicko's!"

State Road 15 crossed the interstate at the Quicko's exit and continued on to Marshall's small town center. Jake had grown up in Marshall. He'd only left the area a handful of times, mainly to visit his grandmother in Cranston. Marshall wasn't a place that people moved to; it was a place that people were born into.

Jake took the job at Quicko's earlier that year after his scholarship wasn't renewed at the community college. He had been studying a smattering of subjects, hadn't yet nailed down one to concentrate on. But Jake was hoping the little he was able to save working at Quicko's would make it possible for him to return to school the following year. College had made it clear to Jake that there was a great big world outside of Marshall, and he wanted to know more.

Jake pulled into the Quicko's parking lot and drove to the rear of the building, where employees were expected to park. He entered through the delivery bay, stopping briefly to clock in and collect his cash tray before he continued on to the front. Jake smiled at Kimmy, one of the graveyard shift, who stood behind the cash register.

"What're you smiling at?" she snapped. "You're late."

Jake looked at the clock on the wall behind the counter. "Only two minutes."

"Two minutes I could be asleep, asshole," she mumbled as she took her cash tray out of the register and pushed past him.

Usually Jake would not be so disturbed by Kimmy's poor mood, but in that moment he found himself oddly affected by it.

He didn't know anything about Kimmy. They had worked at the same place for several months, and he knew absolutely nothing about her. For all he was aware, she also could be dealing with a broken water heater and trying to save up for school. Instead of that thought making him feel comforted, less alone, it made him feel isolated. He couldn't even maintain friendly relations with a long-time coworker.

A young woman wanting ten dollars on number four shook him from his daze. Jake took her money and turned on the pump.

A few moments later, a pair of tour buses arrived and unloaded next to the front doors. Quicko's signs proudly announced it to "Welcome All Buses," but Jake didn't share their enthusiasm. Tours, especially ones made up of teenagers, came like tornadoes through the truck plaza. Lines in the convenience store would be ten-deep, and the barbecue restaurant would be full, with only one waitress to tend to patrons. Shelves would be left in disarray, and inevitably someone would become impatient and angry at Jake's inability to check people out faster.

These tour buses were filled with a high school marching band, which, according to the matching T-shirts that most of them wore, had just won a state championship of some sort. They congregated just inside the doors to the convenience store, where one of their chaperones announced that they had one hour to spend at the plaza, then it was "wheels up" again.

Many of the kids went into the barbecue restaurant, some headed back toward the bathrooms, and the rest swarmed through the convenience store, pawing at souvenirs and grabbing sodas and bags of chips. Soon there was a line in front of Jake that stretched all the way to the back of the store.

He worked as quickly as he could to check out the line, but after a student found she had misplaced her wallet and the line got stalled, some of the kids began to grow restless.

"*Cough* loser *cough*," came from the rear of the line. Jake looked up to where it had come from. Some kids snickered and playfully shoved the one who had spoken. The girl with the misplaced wallet stepped out of line to search through her backpack and Jake continued checking people out.

The line diminished, and the kids who had called out "loser" were at the register.

"*Cough* loser *cough*," came again. The group of kids tried to stifle their laughter.

Jake had assumed they had been calling out to the girl who'd lost her wallet, but apparently he'd been wrong.

"*Cough* jerkoff *cough*," a different one said.

Jake stopped checking the kids out and eyed the one who had just spoken. Without responding, he began checking them out again, this time as slowly as he could manage.

"Aw, come on, man!" one of them said. "We were just kidding."

"Oh, I'm sorry," Jake said, "it appears that we have a technical problem here with the cash register. Looks like you can't get your Funyons." He looked over the heads of the kids to where an older woman was standing holding a candy bar and a Gatorade. "Next."

The kids moved out of the way and jostled over to the front doors. "You *are* a fucking loser," one of them called. They broke into laughter and left the building.

Jake scanned the woman's purchases and said, "Five eighteen."

She handed him six dollars and leaned forward over the counter. In a soft voice she said, "You seem like a nice young man." She patted his hand, took her change, and left the store.

There was a possibility that Jake might be reprimanded for his treatment of the kids, but a certain boldness had come over him, and he found that he really didn't care if he got in trouble.

At lunchtime, Jake left his post and headed to the Bottomless Pit, the truck plaza's twenty-four-hour barbecue restaurant. He ate there every day, and Marlene always had his plate ready when he took his lunch break.

"Afternoon, Marlene," Jake said, sitting down at the Formica counter.

"Jake," she said, smiling. She set his food down in front of him.

He was taking a bite of baked beans when a man sat down next to him.

"Could I see a menu?" he asked Marlene.

The young man was no more than twenty, wearing a crisp, white tank top and black jeans that looked spray painted on. His auburn hair was combed meticulously, parted on the side. He wore grubby, once-white jogging shoes. He wasn't a trucker; that was clear. He also didn't fit the look of a young road tripper. He wasn't with anybody else, so likely not traveling with family.

Marlene pitched a menu on the counter in front of the man, giving him a sidelong look as she walked away. She returned with silverware and a glass of water, which she smacked down, sloshing water over the side of the glass and onto the counter. The man looked toward the glass, then at Marlene, then back to the menu.

"So?" she asked, leaning onto the counter, palms pressed flat.

"Lemon meringue pie," the man replied. "Please and thank you."

Marlene snatched up the menu and walked down to the pie case.

Jake eyed the man. His jaw was strong and his skin porcelain. His chestnut eyes held a relaxed gaze across the counter to where the chrome soda machine sat.

"I can see you looking at me," the man said, pointing to the broad, mirror-like side of the machine. "Anything you like?"

Jake's cheeks flushed, and he turned away.

"It's OK," the man said, "I know I'm pretty. You can look if you want to."

Jake realized what the man was. The truck plaza, being a locus for semi drivers and other road-dwellers, had a robust and revolving population of prostitutes: lot lizards, sleeper leapers, pavement princesses, asphalt cowboys. And while Jake could usually pick them out with ease, this man was different. He looked fresh, glowing even, not as worn out as the others.

Marlene returned with the man's pie and set it on the counter. She then turned away and walked to the kitchen, where she stayed.

"You can call me Ro," the man said, with a mouthful of pie.

"I don't know that I'm going to call you anything," Jake said.

Ro shrugged, Jake bit the inside of his lip, and the two men ate in silence.

Once Ro finished his pie, he took a crumpled five-dollar bill from his pocket, flattened it, and tucked it under the edge of his plate. "Tell her 'thank you' for me." He nodded in the direction of the kitchen.

"Sure."

Jake watched Ro stride across the restaurant toward the front doors. Before he walked out, he stopped at the jukebox, dropped in two coins, and, after a brief flip through the possible selections, punched a combination of buttons.

"Sam Cooke makes everything better," he called, winking at Jake as he turned and walked out the glass doors. Sam Cooke's "Bring it on Home to Me" filled the near empty restaurant.

"Sorry he was bothering you," Marlene said. She had returned from the kitchen and was collecting the used dishes. "Want me to turn his music off?"

Though Jake wanted to turn back to the counter, he watched Ro, the fabric of his shirt caught rippling in the breeze as he crossed the parking lot toward the diesel bays. Sam Cooke's imploring tenor called out to a wayward lover, begging her to return.

"No," Jake said. "Leave it on."

* * *

The afternoon passed slowly for Jake. As the end of his shift neared, he saw Ro get out of the cab of a semi parked at the back of the lot. The semi shook itself to life and rumbled out onto the road, leaving Ro standing in its exhaust. He brushed himself off, tied one of his shoes, and walked toward the convenience store. Jake's arms clenched. Something scurried in the bottom of his abdomen.

Ro entered without looking up at Jake and proceeded to walk to the back of the store, where the refrigerated cases were. He took a bottle of water out of a case and brought it back to where Jake stood behind the register passing time with his coworker Mike.

"You know," Mike said, "my uncle can take care of that water heater problem for you. He works down at Harry's Fix 'Em. I can call him right now if you want."

"Yeah, maybe," Jake replied. He turned toward the counter, where Ro stood.

"We meet again," Ro said, leaning across the counter with a kind of comical menace.

"Looks like it," Jake said, pushing his shoulders back. He took the bottle from Ro's hand and scanned it. "Two-oh-nine."

Ro held out three dollars, and as their fingers met, he bent forward and touched Jake's hand. "You got problems with your water heater?"

Jake pulled his hand back, flexing his fingers. He made change for Ro and placed it on the counter.

"Look," Jake said, glancing about to make sure no other customers or employees were watching their exchange. Mike was occupied with a young, blond girl at the opposite end of the counter. "No offense or anything, but I don't want—I'm not in need of your services, you know?"

Ro laughed. "You should be so lucky. I know a bit about fixing appliances." He waved a hand back over his shoulder. "Did it for work back in another life. I could do it for you cheap. Cheaper than his uncle." He gestured toward Mike.

Jake didn't know what to say. He wasn't sure that he wanted Ro in his house, but he also needed his water heater fixed, cheaply at that.

Ro pointed to where Jake's name was embroidered on his shirt. "Jake, right? Listen, when do you get off, Jake?"

Jake answered instinctively. "Half hour."

"OK. Meet me out back when you're done with work. We'll get you fixed up." Without waiting for a response from Jake, Ro took his water and strolled out of the store.

What had Jake been thinking? If he was lucky, maybe Ro would be late, and he could slip off before Ro even saw him. But then again, maybe Ro would be waiting for him outside the delivery bay, wearing those perfect clothes and disgusting shoes. And maybe that's what Jake wanted.

* * *

Ro was standing behind the building, wearing a backpack, when Jake came out. A few of Jake's coworkers sat on the ledge of the loading dock, smoking cigarettes and watching them. Jake hadn't planned on having an audience.

"What's in the backpack?" Jake asked. It was a forest green, standard school backpack, threadbare in many places. Jake figured it was probably full of condoms and lube. He hoped he wouldn't have to touch it.

"My life," Ro responded, hitching up the straps.

As they walked away from the delivery bay, Hermán, one of the older men who worked in the automotive shop, called out, "*Mariposa*." He then flicked his still-lit cigarette in their direction, hitting Ro on the back of his left calf. Ro didn't show any sign of having felt the impact of the cigarette, though Jake knew he must have. He looked back at the group of his coworkers, who stood laughing.

"And proud of it," Ro called over his shoulder.

Jake led Ro to the back of the parking lot where his car was parked. After they both had gotten in, Ro put his hand out to stop Jake as he reached to shift the car into drive. Ro's hand was warmer than Jake expected, rougher, too.

"I have an idea," Ro said, reaching into his backpack. He took out a tiny bag of white powder, holding it in one hand while he flicked at its bottom with the other. "What do you think?"

"Don't know," Jake said. He pulled away from Ro a few inches. "Haven't touched it since I was a teenager."

Ro reached into his shirt and pulled out a key that hung around his neck on a thin, blue ribbon. He opened the bag, scooped a bit onto the end of the key, and brought it to his left nostril. Jake watched as Ro inhaled forcefully, then leaned back and shook his head, eyes closed. With little more than a few seconds' respite, Ro took the key and scooped another small mound of powder from the bag, holding it out to Jake.

"Here you go," he said.

Jake snorted the coke, felt a burning sensation and the bitter drip coating the back of his mouth. He stared at the speedometer before him, wondering how exactly he arrived where he was. Doing cocaine in his car with a male prostitute, no horizon beyond the moment he was in.

"Fuck," Ro said. "Guy I got this from said it was good, but they all say that. He seemed like the kind of guy who would sell you stuff cut with shit. But this is good."

Jake was struck with the need to drive, to move. "Where do you want to go?" he asked. "I want to be going somewhere."

Ro looked at Jake. "Take me to the most beautiful place you can think of. The best place. I want to see the best place you know."

"The best place…" Jake considered their options. There were the bars down 15, but he didn't want to go there. He was feeling too good to put himself in a situation where some jackass could dim his high.

"Someplace where we can be outside," Ro said.

There was only one place Jake could think of that would allow them to be outside and not potentially cross paths with someone who would bother them.

"Well, there's a state park just up the road, Coyote Trace. People camp there sometimes, and the gates are always open, but for the most part it's pretty empty. There are some hills and a lookout where you can see all the way to Millsburg."

"Let's go."

Jake pulled out onto State Road 15 and picked up speed. It felt like going to Coyote Trace was going to be the best experience he ever had in his life.

Jake guided them to the park effortlessly, if a little quickly, and he parked near the campground pavilion, a dark mass in front of them.

"Let's go to that lookout," Ro said, zipping up his backpack.

Jake took a flashlight from the trunk of his car, and they set off toward the trailhead.

"It's going to be so nice," Jake gushed as they walked. "It's one of those places where you can see really far, and it kind of forces you to feel small. You know? Like you see Millsburg, and it looks small, but you know there are a few thousand people there, inside that small space. Which makes you feel small too."

"Yeah, I think I know what you mean. My favorite places are all out in the desert, with mountains and clear air where you can see really far. It gives you perspective. Makes you feel small, like you said."

Jake felt a sudden rush of affection for Ro. He knew it was the drugs that made him feel that way, but that didn't lessen the feelings.

The walk to the lookout took about fifteen minutes. As far as Jake could perceive, it could have been as much as an hour. It felt so full.

A steep incline dotted with loose rocks brought them to the top. Ro reached the clearing first, entering an outcropping of boulders. A dark valley spread out below. Small, bright grids of towns dotted the foreground. I-40 cut across the darkness beyond. Cars moved along their predetermined paths; the tiny dots of light came together as veins of red and white on the indigo landscape.

"That's Marshall," Jake said, pointing to a closer grid of lights. "That, over there, that's Millsburg."

"What's in Millsburg?" Ro asked, tugging his baggie from his back pocket.

"Not much. It's kind of like Marshall. Some of my family lives there."

"Do you have a girlfriend?" Ro asked, serving himself.

Jake shook his head. Ro extended the key to Jake, who gladly accepted it.

"Boyfriend?" Ro asked.

"Does that key actually go to anything?" Jake asked.

"To my home," Ro answered.

"Where's home?"

"Far away from here."

Both men sat facing the valley. Jake worked the edge of his Quicko's polo with his thumb. Ro fingered the key that hung around his neck.

Every time his high reached a lull, and before Ro offered him more, Jake fell into a brief realization of where he was, whom he was with, and what he was doing. He expected that it would shock him, but it didn't.

Their conversation felt effortless. It floated back and forth between them like a baseball in a casual game of catch.

"There was this one man," Jake said, smiling, "that hung around the plaza for a while. He was a traveler, you know, but also a little loose in the head."

"Familiar."

Jake nodded. "Yeah. Anyway, he would panhandle every day outside the convenience store, and once he'd gotten enough cash, he'd go into the barbecue restaurant. He always had this brown paper sack, and he'd sit down at a four-top and unload it. It was filled with troll dolls. You know, those raggedy naked dolls with the big hair?"

"Yeah. My sister had a bunch of those."

"Well, he always ordered the same thing, ribs, and he would share it with his dolls. His 'family' he called them. He'd take little bits of meat and smash it against their mouths. Then at the end of the meal, he would wipe their faces off, put them back into the sack, and leave."

Ro looked at Jake with gloom in his eyes.

"Now that I think about it," Jake said, his smile fading, "it's actually pretty sad."

Ro told Jake stories from the road: how he'd been working it for almost two years, that he was tired of it but not sure what to do to break out.

"I've almost died a bunch of times," Ro confessed. "I mean, I've almost been killed a bunch of times."

Jake nodded.

"When I get into a cab, I never know what the guy is going to be like. He could end up being friendly, or he could be violent. Lots of them just want to be held. Lots of them cry."

Jake didn't know what to say, so he stayed silent. He imagined Ro naked, tangled in a lustful frenzy inside the cab of a semi. The image was shocking to Jake. Somehow he had a hard time placing Ro in such a scene.

"One time there was this woman."

"A woman?" Jake asked, clearly betraying his surprise.

Ro chuckled. "Don't look so shocked," he said. "I'm equal opportunity. Anyway, she picked me up on her way out of Albuquerque. She had lung cancer and wheezed when she talked. Said that years of smoking while driving her rig had finally done her in. Didn't have but a few months left."

"Huh."

"Yeah. She told me a lot about herself, her family, and where she'd come from. Eventually she said to me, 'I just want to be fucked one last time.'"

Jake choked a little. "Did you do it?"

"Yeah. We stopped outside of Tucumcari. It was actually kind of nice. She seemed so happy to be touched." Ro flicked at the key and looked toward Jake.

"Sure."

Jake wanted the nighttime to expand, to stop, and open up, and allow them to keep doing what they were doing, feeling what they were feeling. The coming day felt ominous and lingering, ready to attack from just beyond the eastern threshold of the horizon.

Jake turned to Ro, who was already looking at him, his face closer than anticipated. Ro reached forward, put a hand on the side of Jake's face, and stroked Jake's cheek with his thumb.

Jake didn't push it away. Ro leaned closer and kissed Jake, who parted his lips to speak, and Ro slid his tongue into Jake's mouth, where it moved slowly against Jake's tongue. Jake felt as though they had closed a circuit, made something whole. He welled with desire.

Jake drew back, his body pulling away before his face did. His lips lingered.

"No," Jake said, looking at Ro. Jake gestured in front of himself as if looking for the right thing to say. When nothing came, he repeated, "No."

Ro nodded and turned away.

Jake's face burned with embarrassment. He wanted to say something to Ro, something that would make the previous moment funny or lighthearted in some other way.

"Why not?" Ro asked.

"I'm not like that," Jake said, knowing as the words came that he was unsure as to their truthfulness. "I just can't."

"You can't or you won't," Ro said under his breath.

Jake didn't respond.

Both men turned back to the valley. Its edges grew light. The stars flicked off, one by one. They were quiet. Ro didn't offer Jake the key again.

They left the lookout just before sunrise. The walk back was easier as the ambient brightness from the early sky made it possible to see the path without the use of the flashlight. The drive back to Quicko's passed with little conversation.

"Thanks, Ro," Jake said as Ro climbed out of the car. He leaned on the doorframe, looking out across the parking lot.

"Sure," Ro answered.

"How much longer do you think you'll be around?"

"Not long."

"Well," Jake said, "we should have lunch or something before you leave."

"Yeah, maybe."

At the other end of the parking lot, a semi flashed its lights three times.

"I should probably go," Ro said, turning to walk away.

"OK," Jake called after Ro, who gave a quick wave without looking back at Jake. Ro crossed the parking lot and climbed into the cab of the semi.

As Jake watched Ro disappear into the vehicle, he became aware of the fact that he was coming down hard, and his surroundings appeared to take on a pallid hue. Jake wanted more than anything to return to the belly of the night before, when he and Ro were swaddled in the security of their seclusion. He stared at the cab that Ro had climbed into and tried to rein in the bottomless, despairing sensation he had welling in his gut. Was it simple regret? Loss?

At the lookout, some part of Jake had cracked open, allowing just a sliver of light to escape. It was enough to show him that there were caverns of unexplored territory there, in him. Jake searched himself for any trace of the glow he'd sensed before but found none. He strained to see some flash of Ro and hoped with all of himself that Ro would emerge from the cab and come back. Across the parking lot, the cab sat still and concealed the happenings within, showing only a quiet darkness through its front windows.

What Cats Do

ZACHARY GEORGE

"How somebody gonna waste this?" Lionel says, reaching into the weeds of the cracked sidewalk and picking up a nail file.

Each step he takes causes pain, and bending his knees about kills him, but Lionel loves to find things. The best things are free things.

He keeps walking, passes the Charbonnet Funeral Home, and remembers his mama running a file across her nails. Lionel would paint, and she would blow the polish dry. He smells the remover she used to clean her cuticles and feels her dry nails on his bare back. Lionel sucks on the back of his teeth. His saliva tastes like her fresh-squeezed lemonade.

A car horn startles him. They can't even let an old man cross the street. Lionel coughs and gasps in front of the stoop of his old house. He hangs his cane on the railing. It's not his anymore, not since Allstate told him they didn't cover flood damage. Lionel sits and tries to catch his breath. Stray cats peek out from behind trashcans, looking up at him with needy eyes. His new landlord won't let him keep Mingus there, and his old cat looks skinnier each day.

"Hold on, Mingus," Lionel says, taking napkin-wrapped chicken bones out of his pants pocket. "Rest of y'all too."

Miss Katie opens her door and pulls closed her robe. "Who you talking to?" She shields her eyes from the sun. "You gone crazy?"

Lionel sneaks the bones back into his pocket. Miss Katie's staring, so he pulls out his rosary and rubs the red thread his mama tied extra wide for each Hail Mary. Lionel don't think he's gone crazy yet. Miss Katie's the one gone crazy.

"I'm about to string them damn cats up," Miss Katie says, slapping a wet towel against her door. "They don't quit playing in my garbage."

"They ain't trying to bother nobody."

"I'm a bring you out some breakfast."

Lionel taps his feet on the step below him and tries not to think about the pain in his knees. Mingus sits in his lap, purring, his tongue like sandpaper. "Ol Pops get you some better food," Lionel says, rubbing his old cat's clipped ear.

The Social Security check he receives each month barely covers the bills, and, now, three other kittens run around with the same spots of brown. They have friends too, friends that Lionel can't deny when they sit and beg like stray dogs trapped inside cat bodies.

Lionel's palms look different where the skin bends. There are white lines, deeper than those he used to get after sitting in the bathtub for too long. The darker flakes around the lines remind him of the paint that chips from his mailbox when he reaches in to check for a letter from Dontrell.

Lionel takes the file from his pocket. As he scrapes dead skin, he can hear Seraphin yelling in Spanish, waking his workers. He knows Seraphin only means to help. It's a good yell, a yelling makes Lionel think of his preacher and how he gets worked up at the people and sweats on his robe. Lionel remembers what the preacher says about how everything happens for a reason, and God never puts two people together and only helps one. Seraphin brought a world Lionel never known. Seraphin fed him *mixiotos* with lamb and told him stories about trying to survive all through America. He stood up for Lionel when the other Mexicans told him he couldn't sit on his old stoop anymore.

If he stares hard enough across the street, the paint job fades, the Mexicans leave, and the roof loses a few shingles. In this space of old, he sees the love that was the Jones family. Joe Jones yelling at his five kids, "Get your asses ready for school. Now!"

Lionel digs at the skin on his hands, wishing that this past, where everybody talked and drank and ate together, still existed.

Two teenagers, dreadlocks swinging like worms, walk down the sidewalk with a bicycle. The one pushing speaks gibberish Lionel can't understand.

"How you kids doing this fine morning?" Lionel asks, leaning down from the stoop.

The shorter one glares at him and says, "Mind your own business, old man."

His partner scowls at Lionel while gripping his belt buckle, holding up his pants like he's got something under there. If Lionel's mama ever heard him talking to an elderly like that, she'd have whooped his ass, but maybe that bike tire flattening put the frowns on their faces.

The Mexicans come out of the house. Lionel moves aside and lets them pass. Must be about fifteen of them, and there seem to be more and more coming each day.

Lionel tells them, "*Hola*."

They say, "What's up, Mr. Lionel?"

Some of them look real tired and red-eyed. The ones in their early twenties run through the streets, chasing each other and hiding, like America is just a game they're playing. Lionel wants to get up and run. He wants to play soccer. What he needs is a little job. When he turns his head, his vision seems wrong: he sees hundreds of cats struggling along the sidewalk.

Lionel smiles at two teenage girls carrying backpacks. "How you beautiful babies doing?"

They look down at the sidewalk like they're deaf. He knows they're not deaf. That's just their path in this life.

Seraphin walks out to the porch. "What you doing, my friend?"

"Got to clean off the dead," Lionel says.

"How your hands dead? You no working."

"I do whatever somebody give me."

"You go with my wife, *amigo*. She taking you the Wal-Mart. She speaking with them."

If he had a job, maybe he could buy some gifts for his grandbabies and get some of that cat food with the tops that pull off like the old beer cans.

Miss Katie brings toast and eggs on a paper plate. Lionel makes the sign of the cross. He sits in silence for a minute. Then he gums the eggs slowly and watches the Mexicans ride away.

* * *

Lionel wants to get up out of bed and go to church, but his head hurts. One of these days he's supposed to go and start that new job at the Wal-Mart. Nights keep killing his morning spirit. He feels so much better in the evenings when he drinks his beer, like all his cares and worries are taken away. He don't think about Dontrell in Colorado. He don't worry about Mingus. He knows that if he gets up and goes, he'll feel a lot better. There's something about preacher's words do the same thing the beer does. His words make Lionel believe everything going to be all right.

A black and white photo next to his bed shows him and his twin brothers Bony and Fat Tony when they was kids. Lionel stands in the middle, his older brothers looking proud of him as he holds the turtle he caught at City Park. They always found animals. When Lionel was nine, doves came and made a nest on an oak branch right outside the window. Waking on those days used to excite him. Bony always pulled the sheets off the king-size bed, and once Tony and Lionel stopped yelling, they always thanked him. Sure was something watching the Mama and Papa take turns sitting on those eggs. Lionel tried to scare them a couple times, pounding on the glass of the window, but them birds had no fear.

Lionel picks up another framed photo—Dontrell standing in front of a mountain in Colorado with his mother— and he remembers the night the two of them left. Over seventy years later the image still haunts him. Every time Lionel sees a blinking street light, he's reminded of Dontrell's squinty eyes and that last night when they kept flicking open and closed.

If Lionel gets up and goes to church, he'll light a candle for Dontrell. He'll light a candle for Mama, and Papa, and Bony, and Tony, and everybody who's gone already, but he don't want to move. His bed feels so cozy.

His knees crack on his walk to the window. Lionel tries to look past the vines and yellow flowers destroying the tree. Seraphin's wife, Damaris, on the sidewalk yelling up.

Lionel forgot. He yells down, "*Uno minuto.*" It takes longer to find the right hole on his belt because his waist keeps getting smaller.

Lionel has to stop a couple times to catch his breath on his way down the steps.

"*Hola*," he tells Damaris, putting his cane in the backseat. He gets in. "The door no closing."

"You must holding," she says.

Lionel grips the handle as the car bounces down Claiborne.

"I am very sad baby cat die," she says. "He looking like a baby Mingus."

"Thought you don't like cats."

"You feeding him. I no like him, but then the car, it come, and I am very sad for baby cat."

The silence makes Lionel feel uncomfortable. He's relieved when they pull into the parking lot.

Inside Wal-Mart, his boss walks toward him with his toes pointed in. Mr. David sounds like one of them sissy boys Lionel sees around the neighborhood sometimes. He says Lionel's name wrong, like it's three words: Li-o-nel.

"It's all yours, Lionel," Mr. David says. "You know where the bathrooms are if you need to go."

Lionel hopes he don't need to go. He came to Wal-Mart one time and saw an old man leaning against a walker in the pharmacy. The man was crying. His seersucker pants had a wet spot running down his leg to a yellow puddle on the floor at his feet. Lionel should have hugged him, but he didn't. He stood there, staring; he couldn't help himself.

Two women walk through the automatic doors pushing a basket.

"Welcome to Wal-Mart," Lionel says. "How you beautiful babies doing?"

"Good, you?" They smile.

"I'm pretty good," Lionel says.

They pass. A warm vibration rushes through Lionel's chest. Maybe that's why old folks like this job so much.

Mr. David puts his arm around Lionel's shoulder. He says, "Lionel, I know you're trying to be friendly, but instead of beautiful babies, how about you try this, 'Welcome. How are you ladies doing today? May I help you with anything?'"

A group of teenagers wearing Katrina Relief T-shirts walks past the potted plants. Lionel smiles and nods. "How you doing, children of God?"

The kids say hello. Mr. David comes up, and Lionel thinks he's going to congratulate him. "Lionel, I know you mean well."

"I made those children smile."

"And that's good." Mr. David fools around with a price tag gun. "We have some rules here. In the handbook. Me, personally, I got no problem with God, but Wal-Mart has a strict policy. It's under the section about separation between church and corporation."

"But....Them street cars a corporation. I seen advertising just the other day. Be a Christian."

Mr. David talks slowly. "Please, just say, 'Ladies, welcome to Wal-Mart.'"

Lionel thinks about telling Mr. David to take the walnuts out of his ass and live a little. Instead, he says, "Yes, sir." He rolls the words through his head like balls in a bingo blower. Lionel's focusing on the two bikers walking through the door. He's thinking gentlemen. He can see they're gentlemen, but he's got Mr. David's voice trapped in his head. "Hi, how are you ladies doing today? Damn....I'm sorry. I...."

"Don't worry about it," one of the bikers says with a big smile beneath his moustache.

* * *

Today's the Fourth of July. The cashiers hand out free flags at the Wal-Mart. Lionel sticks two in the back of his Saints cap before he goes home.

Damaris turns to him on the way out. "I no seeing Mingus yesterday," she says.

"I snuck him in," Lionel says. "Keep an eye out for the landlord."

"Maybe you find different *casa*."

Lionel laughs. The Mexicans have taught him things he never even thought about knowing, like *fuerte* and *amor* and *viva* New Orleans.

Lionel don't mind silence anymore when he's riding with Damaris.

He thinks of the homeless under the overpass. Not everybody gets to go to the Wal-Mart and talk to nice people. When he comes home these days, his pillow feels a little bit softer than it did the night before. Lionel feeds Mingus fancy can food, and the two of them curl up in his bed and watch black and white movies on cable TV.

Damaris pulls in front of his house. Lionel gets out and ties the passenger door to a hook in the glove box.

Finches fly around the tree in his front yard. Mr. David told him that as soon as one comes, the rest will follow. Lionel told Mr. David he didn't want any of them damn pigeons to take birdseed from his finches, so Mr. David recommended this special bird feeder with little posts sticking out on the side.

Lionel walks from his house toward his old stoop. The sun shines so strong that he tries to stare at the ground. Under the I-10 overpass, he feels dizzy and needs to sit. He's thinking that he's hearing sirens in the distance and voices of people he hasn't seen in years.

* * *

A crowd gathers in front of the Charbonnet Funeral Home. Lionel can't see just who the people are. He walks easier now; the sun don't bother him. Lionel looks for his reflection in a gold sousaphone, but all he sees are people swaying to the somber music. The Treme Brass Band plays "Just A Closer Walk with Thee" while two pale gray horses stand at attention. Six men lower a casket from the carriage, and a woman in a red dress climbs onto the long box. She cries and screams. Then she looks out to the crowd, raises her arms to the sky, and dances like her body needs to move, like the music bypasses her mind and controls her bones. Her face takes shape in Lionel's brain, and he seems to be the only one noticing her.

Once he realizes he's watching Mama, he reaches up to the hem of her dress. The cotton feels soft on his calloused hands. The sun seems so bright, so bright that maybe his eyes are failing him, but he don't feel hot. He can see his Pops standing next to a picnic table in Tuba Fats Square, swaying with his Gilbey's gin, tapping a drum stick against an almost empty bottle. Bony splashes Fat Tony in a puddle, and all of them are young again. They pull Lionel into the water. He squeezes between their bodies, and they hold him tight.

Lionel jumps onto Fat Tony's shoulders and claps as they pass abandoned houses. He bats at oak branches and reaches down to people drowned in the flood.

Seraphin leading all the Mexicans around, handing out plates of fish tacos he grilled on a barbecue out front. Dontrell's kids sweating like they never seen a New Orleans summer. Everybody stops and circles around Lionel's old stoop. Miss Katie looks beautiful in her black dress, bouncing the way only babies and old ladies can dance. Seraphin hands her a taco. Miss Katie kisses his cheek and drops a chunk of fish down to Mingus.

A little girl shakes the cowrie shells tied at the ends of her hair. She licks a red sno-ball and dances just like Miss Katie. "Whose cat that is?" the girl asks.

"Old Mr. Lionel," Miss Katie says. "Used to sit right there."

The girl says, "Old Mr. Lionel give me a praline once."

A little boy pulls on Miss Katie's dress. "I know Mr. Lionel. He a funny old man, Mr. Lionel."

Lionel don't know everybody, don't even know who knew him. Sometimes people just come for the music, and some of them don't even know who the jazz funeral for. Don't matter. Those horns blow because it's time to go. It's time for the horns to blow. It's time for *I'll Fly Away*.

The Cryptozoologist

SKIP HORACK

Hoop Snakes

Grandpa is easing along with a cane pole on his shoulder when up ahead a long, thin snake goes zipping through the short grass. Boys being boys, he gives chase. He dogs after it for a good fifty yards before the land starts to slope, and that snake latches onto the end of its own tail, comes popping up like a wagon wheel. Grandpa stops running, just stands there and watches as the snake rolls across the pasture, bouncing itself clear over a barb-wire fence before disappearing into some pine woods where a driving range now sits. My grandfather didn't tell tall tales—he wasn't that species of old man—and so I'd give anything to have been there with him in that pasture. If there was any magic at all in his own sad life, it happened on that day.

What magic I could find growing up came on a page. There was an old set of encyclopedias in the house, and I read through them like some boys read comics, finding more and more ways to humiliate myself at the science fair each year. My teachers would try to explain that what I was calling science was more like history, but I could never really see the big difference myself. Only the librarians in town would encourage me, happy to see any farm kid with his nose in a book.

The Mushussu

The Ishtar Gate was the eighth gate to the ancient city of Babylon. Constructed by order of King Nebuchadnezzar II in the sixth century BCE, the gate honored Ishtar, goddess of fertility, love, war, and sex. Her cult involved sacred prostitution, and Ishtar herself was known to be the courtesan of the gods.

The gate stood on the north side of the city. A massive stone arch decorated with glazed blue tile, bas-relief depictions of cattle and dragons. And it was those long-tailed, snake-tongued dragons, mushussu, that seduced Robert Koldewey. In 1902 Koldewey discovered the Ishtar Gate while excavating in Ottoman Iraq. The dragons—scaly, high-necked creatures with hind legs that ended in talons and the forelegs of a lion—were unlike any known beast. And yet for some reason Koldewey couldn't dismiss them as legend. Risking ridicule, he argued that mushussu might very well have been known to the ancients, that mushussu might even have walked among them.

Jenny Hanivers

Antwerp. All along the docks, bored and landlocked sailors pass the Renaissance centuries dangling shrimp-tipped hand lines, pulling man-faced rays and skates from the muddy bottom of the River Scheldt. At midday the stunned catch is laid out to dry on wooden planks, and here they bake and then harden in the sun.

Days later the dried dead are collected, and the sailors begin to carve. They work their rusty ship knives through stiff wings, transforming the river fish into whiptailed demons and devils. Satisfied, the sailors paint their creations with varnish and then stack them like shingles.

Finally the merchant comes for these jeunes d'Anvers, these young of Antwerp, and men haggle over the corpses until a deal is struck. The curiosities are sold in the markets of the city, then sold and resold as they move farther and farther from their place of genesis. They are ageless now, everlasting. London Cockneys take to calling them Jenny Hanivers, and as time passes so does the truth.

The Wolf of Ansbach

In the seventeenth century Ansbach was the main city of a principality of the Holy Roman Empire, a realm that existed for nearly a millennium in central Europe, stretching across and beyond most of the lands in which German is spoken today. The First Reich.

For many years Ansbach is governed by a very cruel man, a Bürgermeister despised by all. In 1685 the tyrant finally dies, and soon thereafter a wolf begins to prey on the sheep and the cattle of the peasantry. The livestock predations then give way to attacks on women and children. Rumors circulate. It's believed that this evil wolf is the reincarnation of the hated Bürgermeister, that the man has somehow become a Werwolf.

Hunts are organized, and at last the beast is driven from the forest by hounds. The exhausted creature leaps into a well, and when the hunters arrive, the Bürgermeister's second reign of terror comes to an end. The man-eater is paraded through the streets of Ansbach, but the carcass looks too much like a wolf for the satisfaction of the peasants. And so the muzzle is sawed off and the body dressed in the clothes of a man. A human mask and wig are affixed, a beard made of horsetail. The Bürgermeister is hanged by his neck from a gibbet, and thus placated, the crowd disperses.

The Batutut

War ended up being my college. I'm dying now, but I was healthy then. Choice pickings for the draft board. I was forced to lay down my books and leave Carolina behind.

May 2, 1974. We were at least fifty klicks across the border into Laos, in a place we shouldn't have been, doing things we shouldn't have been doing. I knew that even then. It was just me and Toomer and Leon up in the high jungle, checking in with some of the hill tribes, making the rounds. We were humping across this valley one morning when we got caught in a storm. We watched a creek turn into a stream and then a big muddy river. Finally we quit betting on things calming, and we made for higher ground, scrambling our way along a narrow ridge that ran like a spine up out of thc valley. We had our heads down, pushing, pushing, pushing, when this honest-to-God monkey man came screaming up behind us like he's got the same bug-out plan and we're blocking his escape. He was almost as tall as little Toomer. Five feet, maybe. Thick brown fur, a leather face. We were looking down at him, and he was looking up at us. We stayed frozen like that until the thing started uprooting plants and tossing them, flashing teeth. Toomer and Leon were in front of me, right in my line of fire, and I was yelling, shoot, boys, shoot, when Leon let fly with a double tap and sent that beast tumbling all the way down the wet ridge.

When I think about him now, what I remember most are his hands. How they were slapping at that water as the current pulled him away. A week later I tripped the grenade that killed Toomer and Leon both, and for over thirty years now I've had a scar on my chest to remind me I should've checked out with them. Before they died, we all agreed that Laos morning wasn't something we should ever talk about, but it's the best way I know of explaining why I fell back into my boyhood obsession. Why I went from soldier to searcher. Call that new life my penance.

The Altamaha-Ha

Southeastern Georgia. The Altamaha empties into the Atlantic, carving its way through a bright-green prairie of saltwater marsh. From time to time over the centuries a serpent has surfaced in the waters of the river and its many tributaries. Timucua and Tamathli and Yamasee. Spanish friars and riverboat captains. Plantation men and slaves and Georgia Crackers. Boy Scouts, sailors, fishermen, farmers. Two Reidsville state prison officials. They've all kept the legend alive.

1770. In a poem about a beautiful English village deserted and then destroyed, Oliver Goldsmith finds a moment to mention this river. Some of his homeless villagers have found themselves exiled to a distant colony:

Through torrid tracts with fainting steps they go,
Where wild Altama murmurs to their woe.
Far different there from all that charm'd before,
The various terrors of that horrid shore.

Goldsmith never saw the Altamaha or the Altamaha-Ha. He never saw America. At some point in the eighteenth century he booked passage—even planned to emigrate, some claim—but owing either to the poet's fear or confusion, in the end his ship left without him.

Giglioli's Whale

September 4, 1867. The Italian Royal Navy warship Magenta is sailing the Pacific Ocean, approximately twelve hundred miles off the coast of Chile. The ship is engaged in a government-sponsored voyage to circumnavigate the globe, and passengers include the zoologist Enrico Hillyer Giglioli, a man who would one day become the director of the Royal Zoological Museum in Florence, a man not given to exaggeration or delusion.

On this particular day Giglioli is making observations from the deck of the Magenta when a large whale is sighted. The whale is similar to a common baleen whale except for the presence of twin dorsal fins, a feature no known species of whale has ever been documented to possess. The cannons are manned, but this strange whale is positioned too close to the Magenta for the crew to risk a shot. For some fifteen minutes of detailed observation the whale swims alongside the Magenta, and though Giglioli later assigns the creature a scientific name, its existence has never been confirmed.

The Mongolian Death Worm

I was laid up at Walter Reed with the other Purple Hearts when Grandpa wrote me for the last time. It was just before he passed. He knew his days were numbered but promised to leave me enough that I could do anything with my life, though not so much that I could do nothing. I'm not sure whether he failed in that or not. On the one hand, I never married or had kids or held a real job, but on the other no one can say I didn't keep myself busy. Eventually I became the type of crackpot self-taught scientist other scientists laughed at. Indiana Jones in a Panel Van, that was the name I heard one of them call me. Still, those early years were good years, cruising this country in that Chevy, flying to far-off places, pissing Grandpa's money away. Things got darker in time, but the curtains fell so gradually that it took a long while for me to notice.

Olgoi-khorkhoi had been on my radar since I was a boy. Bloodred worms as long as a man's arm, as thick as a glistening stretch of cow intestine. They lived under the sands but sometimes emerged in summer rainstorms, ready to spew poison. Even I was dubious. The Gobi Desert is a moonscape where almost nothing can live.

But then one day, for reasons I can't even remember now—chupacabras, maybe —I found myself broken down on the shoulder of an interstate that cut across some American desert, watching black clouds gather on the eastern horizon. Suddenly I could hear the muffled screaming of Toomer and Leon, and in that moment I knew those worms to be real. A toxic species living just beneath the surface of things. Stirring now. Rising.

The Madagascar Tree

To believe in the killing tree you must first believe in Carl Liche. In 1878 the German explorer and his companion, Hendrick, hacked their way through a green jungle hell, guided by a party of Mkodo tribespeople. At the hottest part of the day they arrived at the bank of a stagnant stream, and the Mkodo began to chant. A giant plant or tree was growing there. Think of an enormous pineapple that stands taller than a man; believe in that too. Long, hairy tendrils and tentacles sprout from the tree's thorned surface. They dart and they slither.

The Mkodo selected a young woman from their band, and the two Germans looked on as they forced her at spear point to approach the strange tree. Three years later the South Australian Register published Liche's account of what he witnessed before fleeing with Hendrick:

The slender, delicate palpi, with the fury of starved serpents, quivered a moment over her head, then as if instinct with demoniac intelligence, they fastened upon her in sudden coils round and round her neck and arms; then while her awful screams and yet more awful laughter rose wildly to be instantly strangled down again into a gurgling moan, the tendrils one after another, like great green serpents, with brutal energy and infernal rapidity, rose, retracted themselves, and wrapped her about in fold after fold, ever tightening with cruel swiftness and savage tenacity of anacondas fastening upon their prey.

Some seventy years passed before another German determined through research that neither Liche nor Hendrick, nor the Mkodo tribe, ever existed. They were fabrications, all of them.

The Yeti

1959. The Irishman asks if he can borrow the skeletal hand, if the monks will let him keep it for a little while so that some tests might be performed. The monks refuse. The hand must never leave the monastery of Pangboche.

But the Irishman works for a Texas oilman named Slick. He has his orders. The monks make the mistake of leaving him alone with the hand, and he replaces a few of the bones with human ones. Nothing that the monks would ever notice. Soon the bones have been smuggled from Nepal into India, and they arrive in America hidden in the luggage of Jimmy Stewart. The oilman Slick is the kind of man for whom even the Hollywood famous do such favors.

Three decades later *Unsolved Mysteries* has the bones examined in a lab, but the scientists can only report that they are "near human." And then shortly after the broadcast the entire hand, the original hand, is stolen from the Pangboche monastery, another casualty of the illegal underground trade in antiquities.

The Loch Ness Monster

This fairy tale destroyed Marmaduke Wetherell's life. Ruined his reputation, turned him into a liar and a fraud. The *Daily Mail* was the newspaper that hired him. They needed a famous big-game hunter, and Wetherell was their man. He hadn't been but a few days at Loch Ness when he came across some tracks along the shore. Or at least so he claimed.

Later, the Natural History Museum in London concluded that the tracks Wetherell preserved in plaster were hippopotamus footprints, that most likely Wetherell or some other prankster had been messing around with a novelty umbrella stand. After that the *Daily Mail* showed its teeth. Wetherell was publicly ridiculed, and a man who had spent his whole life seeking fame turned into something of a hermit. If he did make those tracks, it was wrong what he did, but I can also sympathize. To want something so badly, I mean.

The Zanzibar Leopard

Unguja in the Zanzibar archipelago was cut off from present-day Tanzania by rising sea levels at the end of the last ice age, and the leopards living on this new island began to evolve separately from their mainland counterparts. The leopards of Unguja were smaller and more heavily spotted than those on the continent, an adaptation to their environment but also a consequence of the loss of genetic variation, which occurs whenever a new population is established by an inadequate number of individuals, isolated from the larger population.

And then agriculture came to Unguja. As the territory of these leopards was encroached on, the belief spread among villagers that many of these animals were in fact controlled by witches. In 1964 a leopard-killing campaign was initiated by a famous witch-finder, and though islanders continued to report sightings and the loss of livestock, most experts believe the last Zanzibar leopard died before the dawn of this century.

The Loveland Frog

May, 1955. Southwestern Ohio. The city of Loveland. A businessman is driving along the Little Miami River when he glimpses movement beneath a bridge. Three small frogmen, widemouthed and wrinkled, are squatting on the bank. One of them holds a sort of staff in its webbed hand. There comes a shower of sparks, and the businessman flees. For a long time afterward the area smells of alfalfa and almonds, but then seventeen years pass without further incident.

March 3, 1972. A bridge over the Little Miami again. Maybe the same bridge, maybe some new one. A policeman sees a thing he cannot put a name to leap into the river, but an official report is never filed.

Two weeks later the critter is encountered by officer Mark Mathews. Mathews fires his revolver but misses. Again no report is filed, but then someone circulates a false police description to the media:

The creature was three to four feet tall, fifty to seventy-five pounds, leathery skin, possibly wet-matted hair on its body that made it look textured, possible tail, a head and face like a frog or lizard, and could leap over the road's guardrail.

In 2001 Officer Mathews, interviewed via email, states:

It was and is no "monster." It was not leathery or [have] wet matted fur. It was not three to five feet tall. It did not stand erect. The animal I saw was obviously some type of lizard that someone had as a pet that either got too large for its aquarium, escaped by accident, or they simply got tired of it. It was less than three feet in length, ran across the road and was probably blinded by my headlights. It presented no aggressive action.

Officer Mathews went on to explain that he only fired his weapon for the sake of the policeman who'd spotted the lizard two weeks earlier. No one had believed his friend, and hell, a man's good name was at stake.

The Ropen

Not so long ago the remote jungles of Papua New Guinea captured the interest of certain outsiders: Christians seeking dinosaurs. They were searching for the ropen, a nocturnal, pterodactyl-like animal in which many of the natives believed. At night the ropens were said to leave those volcanic islands for the seas, feeding like gigantic pelicans on schools of ocean fish.

During World War II an American soldier claimed to have seen a ropen. The young man walked into a jungle clearing, and the ropen took flight. "It was a big one!" said the man from his home in Montana, some sixty years later. "I have a Piper Tri-Pacer airplane...and it appeared to be about that size."

And so in time these creationists arrived on the scene, eager to disprove mainstream scientific views on the age of our Earth.

The Lizard Man of Scape Ore Swamp

If you listen to enough locals, it seems like every thick swamp and dark forest has a Bigfoot-like ape-man—just like every deep lake has a Nessie of some sort—and chasing all those lies all those years had made me more than a little cynical. In my career I'd learned as much about people and their dishonest and greedy natures as I had about cryptids.

And perhaps that was why that supposed lizard man in South Carolina caught my attention, had me hoping that maybe, just maybe, there was something to this one. I mean, if a teenager was going to conjure up a story to explain how his daddy's car got all scratched up, I had a hard time buying that this was the fib he would go with.

Over the next month there were follow-up sightings, but no doubt that was just country people letting their imaginations get the best of them, plus a few frauds trying to con their names into the paper. I saw that all the time. No, it was the kid I was interested in. I truly believed that he believed, and so it was him I was thinking of when I put my hip boots on every morning and went off searching that swamp.

But driving home from South Carolina empty-handed yet again, I was forced to accept the facts. The big scary beasts on this crowded and shrinking planet have all been discovered. It brought me no joy to admit that. I was an alien hunter now. That was all I had left to look for.

The Monkey Man of New Delhi

In the spring of 2001, hysteria gripped the citizens of New Delhi. Police drawings depicted shiny red eyes. Metal claws. Sometimes a helmet even. The furry creature attacked late at night, when residents had gone to the cool of their rooftops to sleep. More than a hundred people reported being scratched, bruised, bitten.

Bands of vigilantes roamed the streets. It was a thing to see. They carried knives and sticks. Cricket mallets. Pikes fashioned from butchers' cleavers. A number of innocents were badly beaten, and screams from neighbors led to three deaths: a pregnant woman who fell down the stairs of her terrace, two terrified men who leaped from the top of a building. Scheduled power outages were halted. No neighborhood remained dark after sunset anymore.

Sanal Edamaruku, of the India Rationalist Association, said: "People in India often find it difficult to distinguish between fantasy and reality." There are approximately 330 million gods in his country.

The Barmanou

In 1990 the Spanish cryptozoologist Jordi Magraner moved to Pakistan to begin searching for the wild men long claimed to be living in the remote mountains to the north. With the encouragement of Bernard Heuvelmans, "the father of cryptozoology," for the next eleven years Magraner conducted his field research. He was fluent in the languages of the Kalashi, Chitrali, and Pashtun, and he used strict scientific methods in his witness interviews. Footprints were documented, and on two occasions Magraner heard strange, guttural sounds he believed could have been made by the voice box of a primitive primate. Traveling on horseback, he frequently slipped across the border into Afghanistan.

Enter the war. In August 2002 Magraner and his twelve-year-old servant were found with their throats slashed in the house Magraner had been renting. The Pakistani media reported that Magraner had "dubious links," while a police source noted that his home was furnished with sophisticated communications equipment. Another employee, an Afghan refugee, was said to be missing.

The Killer Badgers of Basra

In the aftermath of the Gulf War and with the encouragement of coalition forces, the Shia majority in southern Iraq took up arms against Saddam Hussein's regime. The Voice of Free Iraq radio station, funded and operated by the CIA, broadcast a message to the Iraqi people:

Rise to save the homeland from the clutches of dictatorship so that you can devote yourself to avoid the dangers of the continuation of the war and destruction. Honorable sons of the Tigris and Euphrates, at these decisive moments of your life, and while facing the danger of death at the hands of foreign forces, you have no option in order to survive and defend the homeland but to put an end to the dictator and his criminal gang.

Several weeks of unrest followed, but no military support came from the coalition. Tens of thousands of Shia were killed by loyalist and Republican Guard forces before the revolution was crushed. In southeastern Iraq the Marsh Arabs living in the Tigris-Euphrates wetlands were singled out for persecution. The twin rivers were diverted, the marshlands drained.

Another war. Following the fall of Saddam, dikes were breached and the rivers rerouted. Strange animals began to appear in the province of Basra. The local population accused the British occupiers of releasing these man-eaters, but it seems the fierce beasts were merely common honey badgers. The reflooding of the marshes had forced them there, into that atmosphere of distrust.

The Pope Lick Monster

Twenty years without so much as a checkup was a few years too many, and I went to Pope Lick Creek not so long after the doctors told me I was going to die. They say the monster lives alone in a dense thicket of woods, under the Norfolk Southern Railway trestle. Half human, half goat. A Kentucky satyr.

A certain type of tourist is drawn to that place. Legend-trippers, they're called. These pilgrims come at night to the trestle as if on a dare, scaling the high hurricane fence meant to frustrate them. Their empty bottles shatter against steel and timber, interrupting the electric chirpings of the cicadas below, the trillings of the toads. Spent cigarettes go spinning out into the darkness to then explode onto branches. The air smells of honeysuckle and kudzu, smoke and creosote.

One belief is that the monster uses hypnosis or maybe mimicry to lure people to their deaths. Some are smashed by trains; others leap without ever knowing why. But of course trespassing on a railroad trestle is a fool's game at best, and what some call murder others might call negligence or even suicide.

The Orang Minyak

The name means "oily man" in Malay. According to legend, the devil offered to help him win back a lost love if he raped forty virgins within a week. Naturally. The orang minyak was described as human, nude, and slathered with dark oil, and in the sixties he was said to be living in the vicinity of several small Malaysian villages. A mass panic ensued then, something like the one I'd witness myself years later in New Delhi. Unmarried women borrowed the sweaty clothes of their brothers to sleep in, hoping to trick the thing into moving along.

I guess it's not technically proper to call the orang minyak a cryptid, an animal, but in the first year of my death sentence I was still chasing down every lead that I could. No stone left unturned, as they say. I'd been told that if I saw another two birthdays I'd be lucky, and so I was like some aging criminal, desperate finally to pull off one big score. Reports of the orang minyak had continued off and on through the years, steadily declining until 2005, when a resurgence in sightings brought me over there. I was laid up in my hotel room feeling the cancer, when I learned that several men had been arrested. Rapists who were as of this world as the terrified women they preyed on.

I should be in the graveyard by now, but so far I've managed to cheat that fourth horseman. I made it home from Malaysia somehow, and I haven't left Carolina since. From the window of my office, I can see my grandfather's pasture, and then beyond it the rows of men practicing with their golf clubs. Of course my thoughts often return to his hoop snake. The idea of a creature swallowing itself to survive, bouncing on and on and on until it disappears into memory.

Mosaic

JENNIFER ANN KUCHTA

In Bellagio, Gustavo stands beside the Mercedes, my bags in his hands, alert and ready to take them into the hotel, but above and behind him I can see her. Seimone stands on a second-floor balcony looking across Lake Como towards the villas on the opposite shore. She is surrounded by red geraniums, and her white linen dress glows against the sky. The porter is directing us inside to the front desk, and Gustavo waits patiently for me to follow.

Gustavo—a man collected somehow in Rome when I was a child and re-collected every time my family sets down once again in Italy. As we grew, my sister Lauren and I joked that someday we'd have "Gustavos" of our own. We determined we'd ultimately have to "flip" for him when we left home, but who knew I'd win by default, a phone call and a life cut short.

My mother didn't think we should return this summer. She thought it was still too soon, and except for last year, we've spent at least a week in Italy every summer since I can remember. I may not recall exactly what we did or where we went, but we have always, *always* gone to Italy. It is July again, and I am back in Italy and, as always, accompanied by Gustavo as per my parents' request. We have ashes to scatter, lives to put back together.

"If you please, Melanie. The reception is this way."

Over the years Gustavo has nearly perfected his English, but I have never bothered to learn Italian. It could be laziness or lack of desire. Why learn it when Gustavo is there to speak for me? My father speaks it—mostly dictionary phrases about the cost of wine and authentic fakes.

At the front desk, Gustavo greets the woman behind it, telling her that *Signorina* Mueller has arrived and gesturing to me with his right hand. She smiles and asks for my passport. When she's done making sure all is in order, she smiles again.

"*Signorina* Francis has already arrived," she says, handing back my passport along with a room key. There is something else in her smile now, and I am not sure that it's not just me, always the paranoid American, fearing that my mere presence in her country somehow offends her. She tilts her head towards the bellhop, who has taken possession of my two bags, and tells me, in my language, that he will show me to my room.

I thank her, a single word in shaky Italian: "*Grazie*."

Gustavo puts his hand on my arm. "I will see you in the morning, yes?"

It's always a question with Gustavo. As if he must always check in to be assured that he will still be allowed to do his job. I know full well that in the morning he will magically appear in this very foyer or next to the Mercedes, which is always at the ready as if he knows exactly when I will want to go somewhere. Where he goes in the meantime, I have no idea. Lauren and I used to joke that he simply ceased to exist when we weren't around. We couldn't imagine him having a life without us or touring another family around Italy. Sometime between now and when I see him again, my parents will have arrived. And my sister, too, in a sense.

Nodding, I bid him goodbye and turn to follow the bellhop. I feel Gustavo's eyes watching me until I disappear out of his sight around the corner.

* * *

The last time I was in Italy, in 2001, Lauren and I stood in the piazza in front of the Milan Cathedral, staring awe-struck at each of its hundreds of turrets and spires and sculptures that reach Godward, extending endlessly toward the heavens. Scurrying masses filled the square pushing in on us as we waited for our parents to finish their tour of the cathedral. By that time I had sworn off entering cathedrals and temples of all types, fearing that I could only tempt God so many times before he dropped an ancient church on me, leaving my toes to curl up mercilessly under its tons of granite and marble. Each person in the square seemed to be trying to outshine the cathedral's beauty, each thinking himself a model or movie star. Boys in tight pants and tighter shirts swaggered around, talking on tiny cell phones, their eyes shielded by Gucci, their bodies sheathed in Versace.

I was wondering which was the greater sin, which the greater abuse of pride and vanity, the cathedral or the crowd, when Gustavo came rushing towards us just as my mother and father came out of the cathedral. He cut through the crowd of pretty young people, his dark suit and sunglasses making him look like Secret Service, and I played at being a Kennedy, if only for a moment.

He took my mother's elbow and hurried us through the pulsing crowd back towards the waiting car. The big Mercedes van always found a place to park among the ruins and a way through the sea of scooters that moved through the ancient, narrow streets like funneled schools of fish.

"We must hurry," he said as he slid open the side door of the van and helped my mother in. "The parade is coming this way; we must get out before it is impossible."

And as my father looked on, puzzled, it was then that I understood what the banners hanging all around the square had said. My sister looked at me knowingly and laughed as she climbed into the back of the van. I wanted to stand there and let us be trapped; I wanted to be accidentally part of something. It was something to tell Seimone later on a postcard of *The Last Supper*: Gay Pride in Milan. I glanced back at that cathedral. Perhaps God was sending me a sign.

Gustavo put his hand gently on my back, not understanding my hesitation. Why would he? My own parents didn't know then, didn't know about Seimone tucked away back home in New Orleans. Only Lauren knew.

He shrugged as he spoke, seeming to have trouble finding his words. "It is no big deal, yes?" He smiled and scratched his cheek. "It's just that they love differently than we do."

And as that silver door slid shut and Gustavo hurried around to the driver's side to whisk us away to safety, I could just hear the chants of the crowd and the drums beating as the parade neared the square. I imagined the banners coming down the street between the buildings. I pressed my forehead to the tinted glass, forcing myself to see a rainbow of colors, and when I was convinced I could, my throat broke, and I sobbed silently in the back of the van. But as we twisted and turned our way out of Milan, out of the concrete and billboards, Lauren's hand crept across the back seat and squeezed mine tight.

* * *

Seimone is still out on the balcony when the bellhop lets me into the room and follows me in with my bags. The room is crazy ornate, all gilded frames and antiques, something you'd expect to find in Versailles or Windsor Castle. My family has stayed at this hotel before, but I don't remember its being so luxurious. I guess we come to see things in a different light as we grow older. What has it been? Ten years? Have I changed so much since I was twenty-three?

I tip the bellhop and then slip through the open floor-to-ceiling doors, which are swung open wide, allowing the late afternoon breeze to blow in off of the lake. Seimone has her hand over her eyes, shielding them from the sun, but even without her fully turning towards me, I know she knows I'm here. A smile turns up the corner of her mouth as I come up behind her and put my arms around her, pressing my face into her bare shoulder and inhaling.

"When did you arrive?" I ask as she squeezes my arms to her chest.

It is chance that she should be here. She taught literature in Prague for the last month, so it made perfect sense for her to come here instead of heading straight back home. Our paths would have crossed somewhere high over the cold Atlantic.

"About an hour ago. The train was late."

"And how were the expatriates?"

She laughs and kisses my hands. "The same as they are at home. Bored."

Down below, beyond the fence, there is something of a beach, and people are swimming in the lake. A few women are sunbathing on a floating platform, but most are stretched out on chaise lounges, making the most of the dropping sun.

"It's so beautiful here," Seimone says, putting her elbows on the railing and leaning forward. "I can see why you wanted your family to come back here. Have you swum in the lake?"

I nod.

"It makes me think about *Frankenstein.* In which of those villas do you suppose Elizabeth was strangled?" She shivers with pleasure, looking me directly in the eyes at last.

Even though she is smiling, her gray eyes are not. Maybe it is too much too soon, or maybe it is nervousness or exhaustion. My parents are spending their retirement traveling. With so much of their time abroad and with Seimone's and my work schedules, there hasn't been much time for meetings among the three of them on any grand scale. Sure, there have been an awkward Christmas and a weekend or so here and there, but most of those meetings have been shadowed by Lauren's death.

"It is inappropriate," my mother said when I told her over the phone that Seimone would be in Bellagio. "This isn't the right time."

"Mother, I want her to be part of this. I need her to be. It's just the one weekend, and then we're going to Venice. She's never been to Italy."

As I waited for my mother's response, I imagined her shaking her head on the other end of the line, endlessly spinning her wedding ring.

"Besides, Melanie, we're going to Rome, not Bellagio. That's where we're taking Lauren."

"No," I said. "We've already discussed this. It must be Bellagio. You *promised* it would be Bellagio."

And at some point she and my father gave in, agreeing to meet me here after Wimbledon, before going on to Rome.

"It's going to be fine," I tell Seimone, taking her hands. "Just a few days here, and then we're off to Venice. You're going to love the Doge's Palace. I promise."

Her eyes cut away from me as she looks out at the lake again, and I feel a sinking in my chest.

* * *

In Pompeii, eight years ago, our tour guide was a fretful Italian man. His name might have been Bennie or Benito; I don't recall. Gustavo set him up for us; the man was his friend, and I wondered how many hundred thousand lire his knowledge would cost my father. Lauren and I had been there before as children, fifteen years before, perhaps, but all I remembered was the volcano and being afraid that it would suddenly spring back to life and envelop us in red lava. The guide looked us over, and I wondered what he thought of us. Did we represent nothing but another band of dirty, raucous Americans who would spit out our gum and scratch our initials into ancient walls?

The man wiped his brow with a thick blue handkerchief and prattled on at my mother's side as we headed into the ruins. Lauren marveled at the wagon ruts in the stone road, and she fawned over the black and white mosaic of a dog that remained in place forever, calmly panting his warning up from the ground.

"How could I have forgotten about him?" she whispered, squatting down to run her fingers over his stone coat when no one was looking. "He's so beautiful."

The dog was a stark contrast to the sick strays that wandered, as we did, among the ruins. They were thin and listless, probably struck with parvo and distemper. It killed Lauren to see them. She wanted to pick them up, to hug each of them to her chest and pick the fleas and ticks from their ears, to take each home with her and offer it a soft place on her bed.

She couldn't stop looking, her green eyes tearing up, but I looked away, sickened. Strays come in all forms on the tourist circuit of Italy. Over the years, we'd been warned about the pick-pocketing gypsy children outside of the Coliseum, but who would have expected stray dogs in Pompeii? Perhaps the ghosts of an entire city silenced at once keep them there, loyal.

Mount Vesuvius loomed over the city, its sides strangely flat, its caldera crooked against the sky. We ducked into another house, and then a bath, and then the remnants of what was once a shop. We looked dutifully into the holes and at the remaining bits of paint and tile. I wanted to see the underside of Pompeii, not the mummies forever frozen in time or the burned out jars or statues. I wanted to see the house painted with scenes of a Bacchanalian ritual, the fresco of a satyr weighing his manhood, not another villa or temple destroyed by time.

* * *

All of our summers have been Milan and Rome and Florence and Venice. It has been preordained that I should love Venice, being a moonchild born under a water sign. And there is *prosciutto e melone* and *caprese*. There are fortresses on the tops of every hillside and anxious priests and nuns checking the length of our skirts and shorts before we enter any cathedral, or church, or tiny chapel.

And between all of our destinations Gustavo has driven us across Italy faster than anybody I've ever ridden with. Over eighty miles an hour up and down and across the Italian plains and over and through the Italian Alps. Zooming through Tuscany and Campania. Careening around the curves of the Amalfi Coast on a road barely wider than the van. Sometimes he drove so fast I was sure I would die, and I closed my eyes and braced myself for the impact, prepared myself for the loss of life and limb, wondering who would identify us on the outskirts of Positano. But Lauren loved it, was thrilled by riding with her eyes wide open and seeing more of Italy than the rest of us ever did.

Then Gustavo would smile as he parked the car wherever he wished, always smiling in his suit as he let us out, calm and cool as if we'd just been cruising the Vegas Strip. Always smiling when he found something new for us to do. A private gallery in the basements of Vatican City. A private tour of a Murano glass factory. A stay at the Castello di Spaltenna. Always wanting us to see everything. To experience everything.

Those summers were always Lauren and I. Lauren and I buying tiny pink and blue glass poodles in Venice. Lauren flirting with the gondolier. Lauren on the lookout as I made out with a sweaty Venetian waitress, my parents sipping Chianti just yards away. Me convincing my parents that a month-long snowboarding trip to the Dolomites *was* in Lauren's best interest. That there was nothing wrong with my sister wanting to build a career out of rescuing strays and snowboarding.

The day after that last trip to Pompeii, Lauren swore that when she went pro and got famous that her first snowboard design would have *cave canem* written across the base: Beware of Dog. And there'd be a mosaic on the deck, a mosaic of a black and white dog, a faithful companion to guide her safely down the slopes.

"Or," she said to Gustavo, pulling his arm as we strolled around the Forum, "I'll put a picture of you on it." She paused near a broken column and pretended to take his picture.

He had scrunched up his face, looking confused at first but then saying, when he saw us laughing, heads together, "Oh, it is a joke, yes?"

And us falling all over ourselves. Lauren and I laughing and laughing and laughing.

* * *

Here I am, two years since my last summer in Italy. Two years since Gustavo opened my doors and looked through mirrored sunglasses at me. It's 2003. Almost a year and a half since Lauren was found cold and huddled under six feet of Rocky Mountain avalanche, her snowboard still strapped to her feet as if she would simply jump up and glide off again. But she had been there for hours, and she was so frozen, so cold.

She had called me, as she always did, at some point just before she took to the slopes, her hollerings full of static as she raved about fresh powder and no tracks. Nearly every weekend, she and her friends drove to the top of the pass and then took turns boarding down again and again and again, until it was too dark, too dangerous. But it was always too dangerous snowboarding out of bounds and away from the resorts.

"It's great, Melanie, no tracks as far as I can see. Just powder, powder—"

"Lauren?" I was sorting laundry, while Seimone sorted through the mail.

Her voice scratched in again, cutting in and out, and then I lost her, figuring she was out of range, too many mountains and miles between Loveland Pass and New Orleans.

Last summer was my family's first summer with no Italy. I sweated it away in New Orleans, feeling lost when I wandered beneath French Quarter balconies. No Romeo and Juliet there. No Trevi Fountain. No Spanish Steps. Just heat, heat, and more heat.

I spent a lot of time safely hidden behind drawn blinds, cooled by blasting central air, trying to recall our summers abroad. Searching for traces of Lauren's face in Seimone's for some reason but finding it impossible, finding it unfair to all involved. Gray eyes instead of green. Tangles of long dark curls instead of dirty blond wisps.

I would flip through album after album of photos. All of them taken on the various cameras I've had over the years. Some twenty years of photos, the earliest mere squares, barely in focus. Lauren a tiny figure in the center, pointing at something not in the picture, my parents two ants arm in arm near a brightly painted boat, the ocean in the background.

In one batch there were pictures of Lauren and me, I maybe twenty, she sixteen. Photos obviously taken by my father, the blur of his thumb in the corner as his signature. Pictures of Lauren and me wrist-deep in the gaping mouth of a large, round stone visage: the *Bocca Della Verita*. The Mouth of Truth. Legend says the mouth will close around the hand of the person who doesn't speak the truth while her hand is in it. Lauren's face glows with a toothy smile, but I look nervous, as if I know that mouth will suddenly clamp down and never let me go, leaving me exposed for all to see.

* * *

That evening Seimone and I dine in the hotel restaurant where we gaze out at the lake, watching its dark waters lap the shore. Then we walk around town, peering into shops and picking out treasures to take home, but strangely quiet in each other's presence. I chalk it up to our fatigue, her flight and train ride from Prague and my long flight from the States. Still, one would think that, not having seen each other in a month, we'd be filled with some sort of energy, sexual or otherwise. But there is only this polite quietness, this sense of impending doom. Maybe I am imagining it. We go to bed early, and I am grateful for the weight of Seimone's arm across my back.

During the night I dream of Pompeii and Herculaneum. Of Lauren and me running and running as Vesuvius erupts, Lauren desperately trying to collect the strays as the ash comes down, covering us like snow.

In the morning, Gustavo is in the foyer waiting for me, and he informs me that my parents have delayed their arrival in Bellagio until this evening. He tells me that he must go to Milan to pick them up, that they want to do some shopping there, and that they will meet me for dinner at seven here in the hotel dining room. He rattles all of this off so quickly and matter-of-factly that I hardly understand.

"I am sorry," he says, looking truly remorseful as he takes his car keys from his pocket. "Is there anything I can do for you before I go?"

And at that moment, while I am still sorting through his message, wondering why my parents didn't just call me, Seimone comes down the stairway, pulling her sweater around her bare shoulders and then lifting her hair out from under it. She catches both of us staring at her and winks, and Gustavo and I look at each other awkwardly.

"Gustavo," I say, touching Seimone lightly on the back when she stops beside me. "This is Seimone." Her gray eyes search Gustavo's face above her smile. "Seimone, this is Gustavo."

He smiles and takes her hand, clasping it tightly in his. For a moment, I am afraid that he will kiss her on the cheek or hand and she will swoon under his touch, but he doesn't, and she doesn't, and I feel the wave of insane jealousy subside as quickly as it came.

"I am very happy to meet you," he says.

She laughs lightly and puts her other hand on top of his. "Likewise. Melanie has told me so much about you. When she talks about Italy, it's always 'Gustavo this' or 'Gustavo that.'"

A touch of color rises in his cheeks, and he drops her hand and quickly pulls his sunglasses out of his breast pocket. "I am sure we will have time to talk later, but for now, I must go." He looks at me. "You will have a good day."

It sounds like more of a question, and I nod in agreement.

"Good," he says, excusing himself and heading out of the hotel as he thrusts his sunglasses onto his face.

We watch him drive away, the van glinting in the sun.

"Where is he going?" Seimone asks, pulling her sweater in tighter around her.

"To Milan," I say, still watching the space where the van had just been parked.

"Milan?"

I turn to her now, feeling something ugly starting to brew inside of me. "To pick up my parents."

She looks confused, looks around the foyer as if they are standing somewhere nearby or might suddenly appear from behind a counter or down a hallway. "What are they doing in Milan?"

"Shopping."

"But I thought they were spending the whole weekend with us."

"So did I."

She starts to say something, but she catches that something stirring up between us and thinks better of it. "Well," she says, trying to quell the beast. "Shall we get something to eat?"

I could have said yes, or I could have said I wasn't really hungry, but because I say no and because it comes out the way it does, the day goes from bad to worse very quickly.

We go our separate ways. Seimone chooses a boat tour of the lake while I wander aimlessly through the town and hillside, half expecting Lauren to pop out from behind a bush or building.

When I come out of the shower later that evening, Seimone is stretched out on the bed.

"You're watching television?" I ask, surprised.

She nods and fiddles with the remote. "There's nothing on but soccer and Italian music videos."

I sit down on the edge of the bed, wanting to make things right between us but not understanding why they went wrong. "How was your tour?"

"It was nice. Peaceful even. I didn't know the lake was so big."

"No Frankenstein sightings?"

She smiles and shakes her head.

"Well," I say, standing up to finish drying my hair. "I'm done in the bathroom if you want to shower before dinner."

Sitting up, she pulls her knees to her chest and straightens her skirt over them. "I think it would be best if I passed."

I stop toweling. "What? Why?"

She traces the pattern on the bedspread. "I'll just grab something in town. It's no big deal."

My heart starts knocking around in my chest. "It is to me."

"You haven't seen your parents in months. You should go by yourself." She flips one of her hands out at me. "Spend some quality time together."

"Seimone—"

She cuts me off, getting up suddenly. "I am not going to spend time playing nice with people who want nothing to do with me. I know why you think they didn't come earlier, like they were supposed to."

But before I can answer, before I can tell her that I was probably wrong and that they probably did just want to shop, she has grabbed her purse and rushed out the door. I look at myself in the mirror, wet brown hair sticking out in every direction. Even I don't believe me.

* * *

My parents are standing just outside of the dining room when I come down to dinner. They have their backs to me and are looking at a portrait of a buxom Italian woman with an array of lap-dogs at her feet. My father turns first, looking young and tan in his linen suit. He sees me and smiles, squeezing my mother's upper arm. She spins around, holding something shiny in her hands, something that looks like a golden ostrich egg.

"Melanie," she says, handing the object to my father as she comes towards me and then wraps her arms around me. "I've missed you so much."

I hug back. "I've missed you, too. What is that thing?" I ask over her shoulder.

My father looks down at it and then holds it up like he's testing its weight. "It's your sister," he says and jerks a thumb toward the dining room. "Let's eat."

And if my mother hadn't still had me in her clutches, I would have fainted dead away.

I spend the entire meal staring at Lauren's urn, half listening to my father's analysis of the state of American tennis. The urn *is* some sort of egg-shaped something I'm sure Lauren would be appalled by. A big brass egg. Brass. In between bites of prosciutto and cantaloupe, I can't help but wonder how my parents brought her on the plane, and, more importantly, what happened to the porcelain urn they had her in at home.

"We're going to tour all of the fountains," my mother says as she finishes her chicken. "They were Lauren's favorite."

Instantly, I remember Lauren laughing at the Trevi Fountain, flirting with one of the many policemen who had shown up to protect the fountain in the aftermath of the Rome team winning some big soccer game. Apparently the police didn't want revelers taking a victory lap with the river gods in Salvi's masterpiece, not even under Neptune's watchful eye. The streets were filled with billowing orange, red and black striped banners. Romulus and Remus suckled their she-wolf mother in triumph on flags hanging all over the place.

But then what my mother is really saying settles over me, and I stare at them. "You're going to put her in the fountains? Just like that?"

They nod, looking particularly pleased with themselves, as if this is some plan they had long devised. My mother puts her hands around the urn and closes her eyes.

"I was so happy when we found this this afternoon. It was in a beautiful antique store not far from that glass-roofed shopping mall. Oh, what is it again...the Galleria something or other."

"The Galleria Vittorio Emanuele, the *second*," my father says, holding his wine glass up to the light before taking a sip.

The urn is resting on the table near my mother's half-eaten salad. "You can't just put her in the fountains," I say.

My father wipes his mouth with his napkin. "Why not? Lauren loved those fountains when she was little. Both of you girls did. We could barely keep you out of them."

"But what if they clean them or refurbish them or something? What if she gets drained into some Italian sewer?"

"Melanie, lower your voice," my mother says, her eyes darting around the dining room. "We've made our decision. On Sunday, Gustavo is taking us to Rome and that is that."

I sit back in my chair feeling swimmy in my head. "But *this* is the last place we ever were with Lauren in Italy. Well, before we raced off to Venice and got on that goddamned train to Paris."

"It's the best thing for her," my father says, patting my arm. "For all of us."

My mother smiles at him, tears glistening in the corners of her eyes. "Yes."

He hands her his handkerchief, and she dabs her eyes with it, sniffling. She's trying not to cry, but all I can think about is Lauren being trapped in all of that snow and ice only to wind up being trapped in some fountain.

I take a long drink of wine, wanting not to be having this conversation and glad that Seimone isn't here to witness this. I can feel every drop of the wine as it glides down my throat. I close my eyes, take some deep breaths, and try to let the conversation cease, but I just can't.

"But, Mom, Dad, don't you remember Lauren *here*?" I tap my finger on the table. "At that villa we stayed at last time after driving up from Milan? Don't you remember? Lauren swore Bellagio was the most beautiful place she'd ever been. Better than Aspen or Paris, or *Rome*, for that matter."

They stare at me incredulously. How can they not remember? Even in this red dining room, I can still see Lauren standing out on the balcony of that huge estate, her blond hair dancing in the breeze. She was holding somebody's tiny mutt and whispering into its neck as they looked out at the lake. She'd been snowboarding in Australia. Had just lined up her first serious sponsor. Was one step closer to that mosaic.

"I can't believe you've forgotten," I say, quietly. "I just can't believe it."

We sit in silence until my father lets out a low cough and takes my mother's hand. "Why don't we let Melanie take care of Lauren for now, until we leave for Rome?"

My mother nods, a tight smile on her lips, and gently pushes the urn across the table to me. "She would have wanted it that way," she says, touching my cheek.

I take the urn in my hands, surprised by how warm it is, and with the blood pounding in my veins, I thank them for dinner, rushing away from the dining room before I can say something I will regret. It is only when I'm halfway up the stairs that I realize they haven't even asked about Seimone.

Upstairs, Seimone is sitting in bed reading *Jane Eyre* in the light of a single lamp. Her gray eyes go immediately to my hands.

"It's exactly what you think it is," I say, crossing the room in three or four huge steps and gently setting the urn on the mantle. "It's Lauren." I point at it. "Right here. In our room. My sister." The blood is pumping so loudly through my head I feel like I'm going to erupt, to stroke out.

Seimone closes her book and looks at me across the dark room, her hair tangled around her face.

"You know what they want to do with her?" I half yell as I start to unbutton my shirt, wanting to rid myself of any reminder of dinner.

She shrugs.

My fingers struggle to work the buttons out of their holes. "They want to dump her in the fountains. Just walk around Rome scattering her here and there like they're feeding pigeons."

She looks at her hands and then crosses her arms across herself. "And what's wrong with that? I thought you all wanted to scatter her ashes. Isn't that why you came here?"

"Yes, but not like that. Not in Rome. Oh, I don't know." I stop with the buttons, throwing my hands down in defeat. "I guess I don't know what I really expected. I just know I wanted it to be *here*. Something just told me. I thought it was right. *This* is the last place we were all together."

Suddenly it's all too much, and I cross the room and go out on the balcony. I sense Seimone behind me, but she doesn't touch me. Doesn't come close.

"What did Lauren want?"

I can't answer through the tears. I just shrug and shake my head. No one thinks about those things when they're twenty-eight.

Maybe she would have wanted to have been left in her snowy grave or dropped into some crevasse. Or maybe she would be happy in the fountains, which is surely illegal, but that's just not enough.

"She should be in Pompeii protecting the strays," I say finally, swiping at my eyes. "And in Sienna watching the horses race around and around the square. She should be getting big air in the Dolomites and drifting across Tuscany. To Lauren, Italy was about way more than those goddamned fountains."

Seimone touches me on the shoulder. "She's already doing all of those things. Those are just ashes, Melanie. Lauren's already gone."

"Don't say that," I say, pointing a finger at her. "Don't ever say that."

"Melanie?"

I stalk back into the room and pick up the urn as she calls me again.

"Mel?"

* * *

Outside of the hotel in the small courtyard where I arrived only yesterday, Gustavo is leaning against the van, smoking. He jumps when he sees me and immediately puts out his cigarette. It's the first time I've ever caught him off guard.

"Melanie," he says, brushing at his coat. "Your parents, they are inside having a drink in the bar. Shall I take you to them?"

I shake my head. "No."

He spots the urn, looks at me, and then drops his gaze to his feet before looking out at the lake. "Your sister and you...your whole family...you have always been my favorite." He reaches out slowly and just barely touches the urn with his fingertips. "Like my own," he says.

I smile at him because I cannot possibly speak. Suddenly I understand. There was safety in those painted landscapes Gustavo allowed us to see in Pompeii, in all of those flowers and cherubs and trees, and even in all of those goddamned cathedrals and churches. But Gustavo couldn't protect us from the worst of things.

I start toward the beach. In an instant Gustavo is there, opening the gate for me and following me to the water's edge. I pause for a moment, gazing out, before putting one foot, shoe and all, into the water and then the other. I look back, and Gustavo is standing on the beach, his dress shoes in the sand, his hands on his hips. He nods, and I turn and wade slowly into the water, knowing that he, at least, remembers.

And I swim out, some sort of bastardized doggy-paddle, Lauren held just above my head, the brass urn clasped tightly in one hand. There is no noise, just the lapping of the water around my chest. When I have swum out far enough, far past the floating platform, I stop and struggle to tread water. Never before have I felt such darkness, even with the moon bobbing alongside of me.

The urn is made of two pieces that screw together near the top. Shivering, I try to unscrew them, but my wet hands slip, and I nearly drop the urn. I clutch it to my chest, inhale water into my mouth and nose. Choking, I bob up and down in the waves until the top finally comes off. I hold the bottom half up above my head like a chalice. I toast my sister with a silent prayer and then gently tilt the urn.

Lauren catches on the slight breeze, the lightest ashes drifting into my nose and eyes and sticking to my skin, the heavier ones slipping into the lake. As she sinks, the gray ash spiraling downward in the moonlight, I breathe the last airborne bits of her in, imagining her flowing forever out of this northern lake, carried southward by the rivers, down throughout all that is Italy.

Ich

A.C. LAMBETH

It takes a drop of water ninety days to flow from the headwaters of this river to the delta. Glacier touches sea with a long, fish-muscled arm. We live on its shoulder, where the drop falls from whitewater into man-made lakes, where it mills about, waiting finless for that miracle to send it over our dams, along the wide dry valleys and past the moonscape of the Dakotas, through the heartland and the southland to reach and spread into bayous and swamps and find the sea. One season, and ice becomes ocean.

In our town, we make these distinctions, our lives marked by snow and fire, drought and flashflood, little ripples in population. The brief pauses in between are our still, safe places, like the calm when the college kids empty us before the tourists stream in, a peace that every new car disturbs coming off the interstate.

It was during such an interim one spring that we noticed the brown paper tacked up on the inside of the windows at the old hardware store. The place had sat dusty and abandoned for two years between Carlos' Tatoos 'n Piercing and the Christian Scientist Reading Room. Then suddenly, this brown paper. We weren't expecting Starbucks—no possibility for a drive-through, plus there were already three coffee shops in the three-block radius—or another Made in Montana store—no town wants to be West Yellowstone. Another bar was out of the question; in our town there are only a handful of liquor licenses, and those are passed down, like inheritance, father to son, native to native. The best we could hope for was some kind of boutique that might draw people away from the department stores, wives of senators who were used to shopping in Bozeman and Missoula and would grow giddy at our small-town prices. Once we knew who'd rented the space, however, knew the owners of that sleek green Tacoma with Louisiana plates and a rainbow decal above the sticker that read "I Brake for Salmon," we began to worry.

Becky Delong was the first to meet the women. When they first walked into the kitchen of the No Sweat Café to introduce themselves, she said she thought they were mother-daughter. Then the younger one, a tall, boyish girl with some kind of new-agey name like Shakira or Zena and a disarming tattoo of a dragon curling down the back of her neck, gave the other a definitely undaughterly squeeze of the hand before she headed to the bathroom. Maxine (Becky remembered the older, petite woman's name) hadn't seemed to notice the stares of the customers at the counter. Maybe she attributed it to her Southern accent. Maybe she was used to such attention, being a dead ringer for a brunette Jodie Foster with glasses. She'd shaken Becky's hand with a frank friendliness and said she looked forward to being neighbors. Left a big tip under a hunk of rose quartz. But she would not say what kind of store they were opening. It was a surprise, Maxine said. Something our town needed. Probably some kind of import shop where they sold incense and little Buddha figurines and books on natural healing, Becky figured. We weren't so sure. Becky always gave everyone the benefit of the doubt. She'd been a hippie herself when she moved here from the East Coast twenty years ago.

But it wasn't their outright homosexuality that bothered us. We're not that kind of place. There were people in our town everyone knew were gay, even if they did keep quiet about it: Donnie White, for instance, who ran the second-hand store at the end of the block (although he went to confession every week, it was rumored, and left the church in tears), or those women who taught Gender Studies at the college with their cropped hair and humorless faces. Nor was it their artistic bent that concerned us. There were enough young artists in residency at the Ceramics Center who worked in our restaurants with their green hair and facial piercings, not to mention the draft dodgers who settled here in the seventies on their way back from Canada, to keep us from being some kind of White-bread outpost like Great Falls or Miles City.

What disconcerted us was their secrecy. The women's mysterious perseverance. What were they building behind those papered windows? Why all that noise? The sawing and welding? The hammering, the drilling, the shudder of glass and metal? And the trucks that double parked on Main, delivering generators and other electrical equipment—what was it all for? Our whispers buzzed in line at the Ace Hardware, we bent over our fences to each other with conjecture, but no one guessed right. And when the purple glow lit the spaces above the paper and stayed on day and night, spilling out onto the dusty sidewalk like some kind of scented moonlight, and still the women wouldn't talk, our curiosity reached obsessive proportions.

Lindsay Hammond's mother wasn't the only one of us who hissed the phrase *adult entertainment*. That was more than water-cooler rumor, though she probably heard it at McIntyre and Finch where she had worked as a legal secretary since her husband ran off with that EPA lawyer from Denver. The sex shop idea was common gossip, giggled about in school yards, tossed around in the Downtown Fitness Center's locker room, considered under hair-dryers. And just as he had preached about forgiveness, letting his eye fall with stern compassion on the abandoned Mrs. Hammond and her teenage daughter doodling in the second pew, Father Stewart spoke the Sunday after the light's appearance of generosity. Generosity without judgment. Our faces burned, but when we gathered for the annual spring potluck at the rectory, even the good Father was heard to lament the inevitable stream of perverts from Deer Lodge and Jefferson City such a place would bring.

So we were vigilant. We kept a constant eye on that sliver of light and pricked up our ears whenever the women were around. But they let nothing slip. Would not be begged, threatened, or tricked into telling. Of course we didn't follow them, but we knew where they went; we noticed their habits and added them up, comparing notes. How they shopped every other day at the health food store, filling their baskets with tofu and brown rice and soy-milk (vegetarians, we nodded). We noted that they had not set foot in a bar except to use the payphone to connect their home service (a fact suspicious to some but promising to others). At breakfast every Sunday at the café they shared the paper:

Maxine always read the front section first, while Shatara (we finally deciphered her name) started off with the comics, whiffling through her nose, then read aloud from the horoscopes as Maxine *um-hmm'd*, engrossed in the business page (Shatara was a Taurus, Maxine, a Pisces, though none of us, not even Bonnie who ran the bookstore, could conclude much from that). Otherwise, the two drove straight into town from their cabin in Rimini every day and stayed behind those papered windows well into the evening. They left us to shuttle uninformed and restless outside, only barely distracted by the arrival of the first tourists or the brief blush of green upon our hills as summer set in.

Still, for all our watchfulness, no one knows how or when they met Guppy Sullivan, although the reasons for his hiring seem obvious, even laughable, now.

And no one would have known then about his job had he not told Lindsay Hammond, his best friend, who was also freshly graduated from high school and, as he was, half-heartedly looking for a job. Who else would have hired her, what with her attitude (though no one could really blame her for that)? She burned bridges before she even crossed them, her mother sighed at social functions. The only employer in town who hadn't fired Lindsay was Becky Delong, though it was at the café that she'd caused the biggest scandal. That time, at least, our town was saved from embarrassment, as Becky not only paid for Senator Lehman's suit, but also managed to persuade the sixteen-year-old not to go to the papers with her allegations. Senator Lehman was a family man, his grandfather settled this county, and although Lindsay was a precocious girl, and, it's true, she looked mature for her age, no one believed the stories she told. Now, after the tangle she got into with the new women, people aren't so sure. Not that she didn't lie, but that it wasn't as black and white as we thought. Maybe truth is found not on one side or the other, but in between. Maybe it is like a fish in a current, a flash of silver you only catch in the corner of your eye.

It's tempting to wonder what would have happened had Lindsay not entered the shop that day, but each of us has probably thought back to the first time we set foot inside the place and asked ourselves, *What if it had never happened? What if it were all a dream that we will finally, someday, wake from?* But even if it were just a dream, we'd still have the taste of it in our mouths. We would remember. How could we not?

And Lindsay did step inside the shop; Guppy did bring her there, unable to keep his secret, *Guess where I got a job?* And inside an hour she had forgotten the fight she'd had with her mother that morning, what had prompted her to discard her usual ripped jeans and skin-tight tank top for dress slacks and a real blouse and what had sent her on her way to interview with Frank McIntyre who'd promised to help the girl out. She must have forgotten all that, so swept away that she accepted a job for which she had no experience and that couldn't last more than a week or two. We tell ourselves, well, that's Lindsay, always diving in without a thought—*that artistic inclination of hers*—but any of us might have done the same, seeing the place the first time; any of us could have accepted the painting job just as easily, and found ourselves, not unwillingly, transforming that putty-brown store-front into a doorway to the tropics.

But at that point we hadn't been inside yet. We were subjected first to an explosion of turquoise and bright yellow trim. The blue of the Caribbean, a yellow that stunned the eyes. Creole colors, Maxine called them. Enough to cause two wrecks at the corner of Holter and Main alone. Enough to induce Fannie Pearson, when she came out of the Hallmark store across the street, into labor two months early. Enough that the Winterburn's herd scattered back into higher meadows, not ready for such heat. Lilacs burst into bloom before their leaves. Whole flocks of geese passed us up, keeping north.

Understand we are not a summer people. We do not amble down the street, sit on porches, or talk with a lilt. This color scheme was outrageous. Dangerous, we knew, even then. These were colors meant for a place where people slept afternoons, danced on sangria into the night, and celebrated Shrove Tuesday with much more than a pancake dinner at the church community center. These colors were not for people for whom summer began as a lukewarm thaw and ended in blazes and smoke.

And yet, despite our decent upbringing, regardless of our misgivings, the gaucheness of that store-front drew us to it. We found ourselves making unnecessary detours through town, taking after-dinner strolls to watch the colors spread, marking how the blue stretched like a canvas of sea, the yellow, bright strips of dawn sand. And even though we knew it was the unforgiving Montana light that beat the ruddy brown into her shoulders, that streaked her hair gold and freckled her face, Lindsay Hammond, standing on her ladder, brush in hand, herself grew tropical before our eyes. A girl of islands. Coconuts could have fallen at her feet or hula girls swished by, and none of us, Lindsay included, would have blinked. When we spoke to her, she turned her bronzed face at us and smiled a secret smile, as if we spoke a language she no longer knew.

Perhaps if it had been anyone but Lindsay, we would have been more worried. With another daughter of the town, we might have sensed the pull of loss. We might have tried to grasp at her, keep her from descending the bank towards those waters.

And maybe we expected too much from Guppy. He was, after all, not only her best friend; he was in love with her. He had been, everyone knew, since fourth grade. So he was waifish; some might even say delicate; he was still loyal. So he displayed affinity for the theater and was said to write poetry; he was, especially in comparison with Lindsay, steady, solid. In the end no one blamed him. He had warned her, we heard, and we believed this immediately. Of course he would have. Jealousy is a rock that stands against the river, even if, in the end, it becomes powerless, softened, condemned to wear the marks of her hands forever.

Perhaps if anything, we should blame love. For it was in love that David Sullivan took his child in his arms for the first time, salmon-pink and swaddled piscine, and said the words that would mark him for this job: "my little Guppy." And it was out of love that Maxine, a marine biologist, agreed to travel from her native New Orleans with a woman who loved space and felt the sky was the largest ocean you could stand at the edge of; it was the same emotion that drove Shatara to build her lover an ocean on the plains. And isn't it love that always knots the line, that snags and drifts, an undertow that sweeps us from the best of our intentions? Isn't it love that sends us, despite our better judgment, towards the swell and rush and then over the edge, spinning first with exhilaration through the air before smashing upon the rocks below?

You can't expect a seventeen-year-old girl to know about the inevitability of gravity. Even if you try, you cannot yank her out of the dive. Besides, it was already too late. By the time the sign was hung, the paint dry and the paper down, by the time Tropiquarium had opened for business, she was already as good as gone. And we, one by one, were quickly inching toward our own swan dives.

* * *

Hard to say what led the first of us into the humid-soft murmur of the aquarium store—just a need to put an end to the not-knowing? A Svengali-induced daze from those freakish colors? What makes an entire town shuffle, one by one, with some timidity and not a few looks over the shoulder, into the unknown? Whatever the reason, we trod into those captive seas willingly and without provocation to hear that burbling water, feel the low hum of generators and filters, and expose our northern skin to the violet, the emerald, the aqua-blue lights of the tanks.

Perhaps the impulse went deeper than we guessed that day. Maybe it wasn't simple curiosity at all or our need *to be the first inside* and then to tell all, a circle of wide eyes around us. Maybe, and this would attest to the way it possessed us those following months, maybe some deeper, more primal need was awakened. Something that drew on centuries of living landlocked under an endless sky, that touched a place as deep as those layers beneath the Missoula glacier where geologists have uncovered broken shells and fish fossils. Maybe that purple glow in the space above the paper had leaked into us like some long lost sense of salt and sand and nudged the coral of our dry bones alive. Maybe we'd been hoping for an ocean all along.

Many claimed to have been the first to visit Tropiquarium, but the first *customer*, the first of us who actually bought tank and filter and pump and filled it with purple anemones and brain coral, tiger shrimp, a blue and yellow tang, and a stunning French angelfish, was indisputably Lindsay Hammond herself. She used every cent she'd earned painting the place to do it, sending her mother immediately back into St. John's Hospital with heart palpitations. At first we thought it was out of pity that Dr. Hebermeyer offered Lindsay the job painting the new podiatry clinic, but after Mrs. Hammond's transformation and the doctor's own aquatic purchase, we understood it differently.

After a night at the hospital, Mrs. Hammond stayed home from work to rest. Then, on the seventh day, she rose from the couch in front of the tank, flushed her diet pills down the toilet, quit her job, subsequently breaking off that messy attachment with Frank "the Liar" McIntyre, and, with Lindsay's help, started the catering business she'd talked about before the divorce. The following Sunday evening she invited everyone over to sample her specialties, and, we knew, to view the tank. If it was Dr. Hebermeyer who later validated such extravagance, the Hammond women first showed us the possibility of *the home ocean.*

There in the living room, in the space where the entertainment center and TV had once stood, purred a ninety-gallon octagonal tank. The lights in the room had been dimmed, so that the reef of coral glowed in SweeTart colors, and the tang floated in serene hues, and the shrimp bumbled, happy red sprites over mint-green rocks. And there, suspended in the delicate pastel fizz, like a smudge of blackened gold, a half-polished gem the size of a large man's hand, swam the angelfish, its black dorsal a plume flowing from its regal, sloping face, its flukes moving in a slow, hypnotic rhythm even the swaying anemone seemed to follow. We gathered around, motionless, its yellow-ringed eye looking back at us, considering our glass-stretched faces and our dull clothes with a kind of humored scorn. And perhaps we would have stood there all night, waiting for it to move and release us from its arrestingly intelligent gaze, had Mrs. Hammond not opened the kitchen doors and released an aroma so thick with spice our knees wavered and we could not resist any morsel she held before us.

People still talk about the food we ate at the Hammonds': the eggplant, crabmeat and hot pepper gumbo laced with coconut shavings and coriander, the flash-fried oysters nestled between black and white truffles and watercress, the crawfish ravioli, the pan-seared red snapper in an artichoke and saffron *pico de gallo.* Our mouths still water, if somewhat guiltily, when we think on the platter of pomegranates, mangoes, and fresh pineapple, the tiny dishes of crème brulee, the white chocolate bread pudding in warmed rum anglaise. Such tastes we had never before experienced, spices that tangoed on our tongues and sweets that left us whirling and giddy. Our northern blood surged and shivered in feverish delight; we tittered like young lovers, all of us, licking our fingers and inching close, aroused in the pale pink glow of the tank. If an aquarium could stir such culinary passion from a woman who'd starved herself on Diet Coke and celery for three years, what, we dared wonder, would it bring the rest of us? What latent ardors might surface in us?

We were a little afraid, it's true, especially the next morning when we awoke, spent and heavy with the rich food, half the women in the town now pregnant. But when it was known that Dr. Hebermeyer, a man who did not go in for frivolity, a doctor who opposed the incongruity of golf courses in the high desert and who drove a ten-year-old Volvo and sent his children not to the private Rocky Mountain Christian but to Capitol High, that *he* had just maxed out his Platinum Visa on a two-hundred gallon tank for his home and was rounding up funds for a thousand-gallon job for St. John's children's wing, we shrugged off caution and followed suit. Madly.

Because it was no longer enough just to *visit* Tropiquarium, to wander for a too-brief lunch hour among the maze of waving sea-plants, stunned dumb for the rest of the day by their luxuriant rhythm of bend and curl in a fluorescent fizz. It was not enough to witness the feeding frenzy of piranha or watch patiently the dark caves for the elusive damselfish to appear just as Maxine doused the lights for the night; not enough to breathe a few lungfuls of the algae-rich air or to dampen our dry skin smooth again before returning to the drought-dizzy world outside. We had tasted; now we hungered. And not for a pet, not for a dull-eyed, gape-mouthed goldfish with its plastic castle and colored pebble floor. Not even for some twenty-gallon tank stocked with cheap tetras and the token silver-dollar Angel. No. Only hundred-gallon saltwater setups would satisfy our aquatic lust, only special-ordered seahorse and baby shark, reefs spiked with sea urchins and plush with anemone, peopled with grunts, blennies, gobies, and butter hamlets. The floors of our tanks must sprout garden eels and hide peacock flounder, our walls crawl with red-spotted shrimp, starfish, sea cucumbers. It was oceans under glass or nothing.

We sunk our savings, the rich and the struggling alike, into aquariums. Margot Stubbs sold her Mustang to finance a tank full of copper-banded butterflyfish; the Kents put a second mortgage on their home, knocked out their bedroom wall and had Shatara custom build a tank that could support a whole school of stoplight parrotfish. Even Father Stewart finally relented to the sisters' pleas for a tank in the convent, and then it was not long before he had taken up collection to build an aquarium in the narthex; thereby, he proclaimed one Sunday morning after retelling the five loaves and three fishes story, every time we entered the cathedral, would we be reminded of Christ's miracles.

Despite the Father's attempts at sanctifying our new obsession, however, in a month Tropiquarium had become more addictive than any adult entertainment shop, more indulgent than any casino or brothel, and more frequented than any bar. Maxine, the marine biologist, was our guru, Shatara our architect, and the once-overlooked Guppy, a boy of enviable standing. No longer did we cower awed and small in its fantastic galaxy; we strode into the store like junkies on a mission, wild-eyed after that new shipment of tangs, doubling our orders of brine shrimp daily.

When the fire season started up, we barely noticed, our eyes so verdant with phytoplankton, our minds snapping with measurements of salinity, alkalinity, and evaporative loss. The whole state could have burned to nothing, and we would not have noticed; we were busy hosting Hawaiian luaus and crawfish boils to show off our latest venomous Turkeyfish come in from China; we were taking Tango lessons and going home from work midday to nap at the foot of our tanks; we were singing karaoke to Don Ho, picking out "Margaritaville" on the guitar; we grew habañero peppers next to the kohlrabi. Mrs. Hammond—or LeiLani, as she was now called—could not cook enough.

If we didn't notice the friction between our guru and her architect, or that Guppy had stopped smiling as he used to, or that Lindsay kept falling off ladders and often sang to herself and had even started to wear skirts on occasion, it can also be pointed out that we didn't notice the tourists leave, or that when our children started school they covered their textbooks with drawings of seahorses and elkhorn coral and waves, or that no one in the town bothered to vote in the gubernatorial election as that was the day a special shipment of blackbarred soldierfish was to arrive from California. Our town was suddenly and blissfully lost at sea.

Only later did we realize the spores of destruction were already lodging in our waters, feeding on our obsessions, and multiplying.

* * *

Now that some time has passed, we take stabs guessing when it began, and most believe it must have already been set in motion at that first party LeiLani—still Mrs. Hammond then—threw. If we think hard, we can recall a certain restlessness Lindsay exhibited. She had flitted from group to group, hands fluttering, laughing a bit too loudly (and looking quite attractive, many remarked, grown-up, too, in the camel-brown slacks and embroidered blouse with bell sleeves, her shoulder-length hair still unkempt but stylishly so). Then, when Shatara and Maxine arrived, she suddenly stilled, retreated to watch like a damselfish behind fantail coral. People noticed that after she had greeted them, she did not speak another word to either of the two women, who, by everyone else, were treated as celebrities. Lindsay's eyes constantly roved, then darted down when she found whatever she sought, her sun-browned face flushing scarlet.

And remember how strange Guppy acted, we remind each other? How he, too, seemed agitated, darting back and forth from the women to Lindsay with that troubled expression so unlike him? As if he had to make a choice?

And then the toast! How could we have disregarded the portent of that toast?

It was after the Ahi tuna with Louisiana caviar tartar that Mrs. Hammond broke out the bottles of chilled White Zinfandel (wine was unfortunately not included in her epicurean revelation). She poured everyone a jelly glass and held up her own.

"To Tropiquarium!" she said. "Exactly what this town has always needed!"

"Hear, hear!" we all cried, raising our glasses to the two women standing beside the tank. "To Tropiquarium!"

Just as the sugary liquid hit our tongues, Shatara slipped her arm around Maxine's waist and pulled her into a quick but passionate kiss. There were gasps, and both Margot Stubbs and Penny Larson choked and spat their wine at Chuck Patterson's wide back. Father Stewart coughed and threw a stern, buggy eye around, but the rest of us were silent, the wine tweaking the back of our throats sharply, frozen in our still-smiling spots. Then, with a crash, Lindsay rushed from the room, some said with tears streaming, but most of us refuted that detail. Her sheet-white complexion testified to what we thought at the time, that the wine had made her sick, for she did not come back for the rest of the evening. Father Stewart even managed a "poor child," as he watched Mrs. Hammond clean up the glass and wine from the linoleum. Then the pecan-crusted Mahi-Mahi was served and someone spotted a speckled eel behind the coral in the Hammonds' tank, and the incident was forgotten. If we did notice, we didn't think much of Guppy's darkening expression before he, too, left a short while later, and we failed to assign any particular meaning to the way Maxine cut her eyes at Shatara several times that night.

For we had jumped, as Lindsay must have weeks before.

Later there were plenty of testimonies to the affair Lindsay began with Shatara. Chuck and Carey Patterson saw them several times by the river, though from the brothers' mid-stream vantage it looked innocent enough: two women trolling among the willow, pointing at geese, and stopping together to admire something in the shallows. And yet there had been a closeness between them, Carey recalled. Once he even thought he'd seen Shatara's hand slip up the girl's back and graze the loose strands beneath her ponytail. Jamie Wong said the two were regulars at his restaurant and drank pots of green tea beneath his tank of African ciclids until well after closing. Becky admitted they had breakfasted several times together, but she refused to further the gossip with details.

Hindsight-privileged, we've added up the darker proof: the recipes for Lindsay's mother's dishes that were unmistakably New Orleans influenced, although Mrs. Hammond, despite her adoption of a Hawaiian name, had about as much Southern blood as

Ole Knudsen; or the locket Shatara bought from Penny Larson that never appeared around Maxine's neck. Finally, that tank of Lindsay's, we realized, must have cost quite a bit more than two weeks' wages of painting work, no matter how well the women paid her. Maxine must have known about them long before the trip to Seattle. Guppy, too.

But to us, still in the dark, the Seattle trip seemed harmless. Maxine couldn't go, Guppy couldn't run the store by himself, and it was a long drive; the snows were coming. It was surely safer—and faster—for two to drive the truck and pick up the shipment of rocks and coral and new fish. And perhaps we were partly to blame; we would not wait for the usual monthly delivery. We had to have it all now; we'd pay extra. So Lindsay and Shatara made the trip together, and when they came back, like a bad tide, everything turned.

The day they were to leave, Barbara Simon-Davies came to town early, before the shop opened, and stood waiting for her coffee at the General Mercantile, where she overheard the teenagers arguing at the corner table.

"They're married, you know," Guppy said.

Lindsay, her back to Barbara, sat completely still.

"Had a ceremony and everything," the boy said. He tapped his fist against the bowl of his coffee spoon nervously. "In some states it's even legal."

"So you're an expert on marital law now?" Lindsay said, her voice a catfish barb. "You oughtta see if Frank needs another office bitch."

"I'm not the mistress at this table."

Lindsay sat back hard against the chair and looked away. "Why don't you go open your store, *fish boy*."

Guppy stood, then leaned over the table. "You are so predictable, you know that? So *typical*. And you'll never be any different."

"At least I'm doing something with my life."

"Painting *houses*? What happened to art school?"

Lindsay did not move, did not look at him, and Guppy straightened.

"Go, then," he said. "Seattle won't change anything. Cause no one's taking you out of here, Lindsay. No one."

We might have heard about this exchange earlier, but Barbara had other things on her mind. Her new yellow tang had been acting strange that morning, refusing to eat and gulping as if it couldn't breathe, and she'd rushed into town to consult Maxine. Her only thought as she grabbed her coffee and two sugar packets and hurried out to Tropiquarium was how fortunate it was that Maxine wasn't the one accompanying Shatara, abandoning the store and her sick tang for the weekend. Maxine would know what to do. She'd have some remedy on the shelf of medicines and vitamin supplements behind the counter.

Perhaps if Barbara had known that her yellow tang was the unsuspecting canary in the mines of our coming disaster, she might have stopped when Shatara passed her coming into the coffee shop to meet Lindsay. Maybe Barbara would have mentioned her fish, and Shatara, although not the marine biologist Maxine was, would have recognized the unmistakable symptoms of *ichthyophthirus* disease. Maybe then she wouldn't have left her partner to deal with the outbreak alone, and Maxine would not have come apart as she did; the epidemic might have even brought the couple closer together. Maybe none of the other plagues would have descended upon us.

But Barbara did not stop. She barely even said hello, and Shatara and Lindsay left for Seattle within an hour. Maxine and Guppy battled Ich alone.

Treating Barbara's yellow tang should not have been difficult. Ich is a common enough disease, and though eventually lethal, it is, at least in the early stages, treatable. Maxine was apologetic—for she had sold Barbara the infected fish—but not unduly worried. And yet, Barbara confided in us later, she *had* seemed somewhat distracted. When Guppy pulled the wrong medicine from the shelf, Maxine snapped, pushed past him and grabbed at the little vial herself. Then the color faded from her face, and she spun around, knocking the bottles to the floor as she searched through them.

"Didn't Bronson come just last week?" she turned to Guppy. "Didn't you sign the invoice? Didn't you *check* it?"

Guppy nodded. "It was all there," he said. "It was."

"Then where's the Ich treatment?" She shook the vial in his face. "This is for fin rot! Didn't you read the box?"

The boy looked at Barbara, then to the wrecked shelf, and when his eyes swam back to Maxine, they widened and filled with tears.

Maxine sighed and put her hand on his back, her voice soft, *motherly*, Barbara said. She sent the boy into the back and reached for the phone. But by then we were all waking up to lethargic fish who hovered on the bottom of the tank, gulping and anorexic, and before she could make her call, she was answering a dozen of ours, massaging her temple with her thin fingers as she tried to calm us. There had been a mix-up from her distributor, she said; the medicine wouldn't be here until tomorrow; in the meantime, freshwater baths and quarantine. She sent Barbara Simon-Davies home with the same instructions. But Barbara had forgotten to place a special order for a few more of those iridescent gobie-like beauties, and she started back inside then stopped. Maxine lay collapsed over the counter, her shoulders heaving with sobs. Backing out without a sound, Barbara went straight home, determined to nurse her tang back to health just for Maxine, to show the poor woman all her concern was not in vain.

If only the freshwater baths had worked. If only the snowstorm in the south hadn't delayed the distributor by another day. If only the fish had been quarantined sooner.

Two days later, white spots covering their gills and fins as if they had been sprinkled with a fine white sugar, a good number of our fish were dead. We filed to the shop bearing their pale bodies in sandwich bags. In the dark drone of the shop, Maxine consoled us, and Guppy went quietly around, taking the baggies from us with an embarrassed and somber expression.

Then suddenly the door banged open and laughter and light blared in on us. Carrying the first of the boxes from Seattle, keys held in her mouth, Shatara started in, Lindsay behind her.

They stopped, hushed by the crowd.

Shatara raised her eyebrows. "What's up?" she asked around the keys.

Still in shock, befuddled with grief, we looked to Maxine, and that's when we understood: she had not been crying over our Ich-infested fish as Barbara had with such reverence reported. The way Maxine drew herself up from comforting Sadie Parker and flashed her eyes at Lindsay, the scrape in her voice when she said the word, and how Shatara, still holding the box, shrank back against the door told us everything.

"Ich." It shot from Maxine's mouth like a gaff, lodging deep in her partner and her partner's lover, and taking all of us with it. "All of them," she said. And it was as if she were announcing the end of everything—not just the fifty-odd fish we'd lost—but the death of every fish, every reef, all waters forever poisoned.

Carefully, Shatara set down the box. She pulled the keys from her mouth, enclosing them in a tight fist, and licked her lips. She stepped away from Lindsay and turned to us like the accused before a jury. And maybe she saw the sharp need in our eyes to damn; maybe from this she gathered we knew everything, and her strange actions were a desperate attempt to win us back. She ripped into the box and began handing out the large, motley rocks.

"Not to replace your loss," she said in a skimming, hurried voice. She didn't dare look at Maxine, but set her eyes on Guppy instead, who stood in the store-room doorway, his arms full of dead fish. "But as a start. To reparations."

She was sincere, we recognize this now. She did not know that what she gave out was worse than Ich. She did not mean to take us all down with her. Because when Maxine, spine like a pylon, strode past her and out of the shop, Shatara ignored Lindsay's grasp and followed.

* * *

A resident of mountains knows danger lurks in the rocks—snake, mountain lion, bear. But those threats lie beyond our picture windows; they wait for us only in the world *out there*. These panes of ocean in our homes, they were our interior fantasies. We controlled them as we control the lights or the thermostat. As Father Stewart liked to quote, "Be fruitful and multiply, and replenish the earth and subdue it: and have dominion over the fish of the sea..." We were the designers of these worlds, their custodians; they lived for and because of us. Yes, Ich had shaken our faith somewhat, but it had not destroyed it. We were determined that night as we climbed into bed, having fed our remaining fish the antibiotics and treated their water with copper, that we could, in the end, control this parasite, too. It was preventable, we assured ourselves. With science, with devotion, we would gain the upper hand, and once again our aquabiota would thrive, the jeweled testaments of our power.

But beware the rocks, we should have remembered. Beware what hides within its pores. What waits silent and unseen within it as the rock descends to the floor of your tank. What waves its antenna about, tasting the fluid that has passed through the gills of unsuspecting residents. What slowly stretches its toothpick legs, arches its powerful fish-clubbing abdomen, and then, when all is silent—the aquarium beyond the glass and the fish-traveled waters within—when the lights have been doused and the fish settled down for the night, beware what emerges from the rock to feed.

Almost every one of us who took a rock from Shatara woke to a tank littered with the bones, fins, and gnawed heads of our fish. Still bleary with sleep, we gaped in disbelief, searched in horror the alleyways between the coral for a sign of our prized Achilles tang, for a straggling blenny, for just one surviving soldierfish. But all we found in that barren world was a small and unassuming stranger, too sated to retreat into its hole, crouching beside the rock as the scales of its victims floated around it.

Still in our pajamas, ignoring the snow that had blanketed the town overnight and continued to fall in freezing gusts, we marched to the aquarium store like the angry mob on Dr. Frankenstein. But the store was locked and dark inside. We did not wait around. In our pick-ups and Suburbans, we thundered up to Rimini.

Our convoy filled the driveway and spilled onto the main road for nearly half a mile. We jumped from the trucks before the engines had quit, stomped up to the house in our slippers, the heat of our rage impenetrable to the knee-deep drifts. Mounting the porch in one leap, we banged our fists against the door with shouts of lawsuits, of imprisonment, of revenge. We felt bloodthirsty and savage, attacked as we had been, our beauty, our pride, our very creation bashed against glass, paralyzed and powerless, then ripped apart by the tiny teeth of a coward—a *shrimp* of all creatures—who'd snuck out from a cave in the middle of the night. Someone was going to pay, by God! Someone was going to answer for what had been taken from us!

Then someone pointed out that the Tacoma was missing. Our cries died in our throats; our hearts stuttered and fell. No smoke came from the stovepipe. Through the front window, the place looked empty all right. Dark. There was no one home. For a while we milled around on the steps, in the yard, stuffing our hands, suddenly burning with cold, into our coat pockets, silent and somehow ashamed. The snow piled around us.

In painting, Lindsay often said, you can wash away a mistake. Jesso the whole blasted canvas white and fresh again, like thick blankets of snow and ice hiding a current, if you want. And maybe you'll forget what lies beneath. At least no one else will know. But there was no paint that could cover the misstrokes of that summer. And snow, however thick, does not erase the landscape here. It accentuates it, the valley along with the peak. The river continues whether we acknowledge it or not.

When we returned to our homes that afternoon, they, too, were dark. Empty and cold. The comforting hum of filter and pump choked off when the power quit. In all our tropical reverie, just as with the danger in the rock, we, Northern folk, had forgotten winter. Forgotten that, especially with early storms, power outages are as common as frostbite.

Perhaps we had been weakened, struck so suddenly by Ich and the mantis shrimp, that fighting back carried no hope. Perhaps the storm finally reminded us who we were. Or maybe, compared to Maxine's devastation, the end of such luxury seemed insignificant. For even those of us who could have jerry-rigged our tanks to run off the small generator in the basement let it be. We gathered with our families, pale descendents of the Dutch, Norwegian, and Irish, of sturdy stock, no strangers to defeat or to short days and long winters, and we huddled under bear rugs before our dark tanks. And as the hours passed and the snow fell, we watched the waters cool and leave our few surviving fish swimming slower and slower to drift finally to sleep, fall to the sand, then rise to float atop the icy surface. Night fell before we could witness the anemone's last wave, the sea cucumber's gasp of venom, or the octopus' convulsions. When dawn came, the last lush reefs had already grayed and hardened into bones.

All our oceans were dead when the snow stopped three days later, and we staggered, stiff and red-nosed, from our houses. Blinking in the blinding whiteness, we felt ourselves pulled across our lawns, beyond the quiet streets, and out into the covered wheat fields of the valley, looking for something. And there below us, through the blanched, silent world, the river ran in an eel-blue track to the sea.

Evolution of a Smart Girl

CASEY LEFANTE

He was the first one to look at you like that. Smoky, with a boyish grin. That's how he worked what he worked on a girl, but you didn't know that yet. He knew the way to a girl's heart was to make himself look like two things at once: the movie star she had inappropriate dreams about and the boy she caught frogs with when she was eight and developed an unrequited crush on when she was nine.

You never wore pink when you were growing up. You preferred blue jeans, T-shirts, dirty sneakers. You can't climb trees in dresses. Others told you how to be a girl, and you didn't trust them. You never believed that being a girl had anything to do with pink or princesses. Those were stereotypes. You knew, because you were smart, that being a girl meant more. To be a girl, you needed to know how to play the game: how to be coy, and cute, and tough as nails. All things at once.

When you were sixteen, you played flag football with the boys in your neighborhood. You liked dodging the assault, proving that girls can be quicker than boys. And on that day when you scraped your knee on your way to snatching a flag, you fell into him. And you looked up into his eyes, with pupils so big and black that they swallowed all of the brown, brown that matched his eyebrows, which were raised, and then his smile, that smile, a smirk so lopsided that all you could do was stare at it, begging it to stay directed at you, always.

* * *

Others told you to let the boys win at games, or not to play the games at all. But you played the games, and you showed them you were good. You showed them you were better, even. You were so good that they weren't even aware of the game. Only you: the tilt of your nose, the dark pools of your eyes, the curve where neck meets shoulder meets back. You were so good that these were the only things they could see, that they wanted to see. You made them crave you, and, at first, you didn't even know it.

* * *

You felt pressure, so much pressure, and you were sure it wasn't supposed to be like this, you were sure it was supposed to be different. It hurt too much; was it supposed to hurt? You realized that you'd stopped breathing, so you forced yourself to breathe in, breathe deeply, and all you smelled was the dinner that this first boy's mother was cooking, downstairs. Something with onions. You heard him above you, but he wasn't talking to you. You'd stopped talking a while ago. You wanted to readjust, you wanted to move, maybe stop, but you stayed. You hated yourself for being silent. You bit your lip, broke skin, tasted blood.

You thought it would be nicer.

You didn't think you'd smell onions.

But then, smart girl, you pushed into him. And the onions and sweat and blood filled you, but you pretended they didn't. You pretended you were somewhere else, diving in a bay, swimming deep past the breakers to a point you knew existed, and once you got there, you vowed never to leave, ever.

* * *

In school, they taught you that good girls wore skirts that reached past their knees. Good girls crossed their legs when they sat down. You weren't interested in being good, or even bad. You just wanted to be you. Things weren't black and white; you knew that because you were smart. All you needed to be was better than boys at the game. Good girls, smart girls, can surprise a boy with the sharp bite of teeth upon a neck, with the slow scratch of nails against a back. Scratches that start slow, slow, and then quicken, quicken, quicken, until they've made the sort of mark that stays with a boy, even when he's wilted into a grave man.

* * *

In a '97 Buick, your second boy's hands moved down your back. You still refer to him by his first and last name; he's that insignificant. Parked outside of school, just before lunch ended, you let the sun cast a hot eye on both of you as you lay there, restless. The hands traveled to the band of your plaid school skirt, and even though it wasn't hostile, it was clumsy, led by a boy who didn't really know what he wanted. All he knew was that he needed to prove his self-worth, and the way to self-worth was paved with sex, sex, sex. If he could please you, or believe he had pleased you, then, yes, he won.

This was the first time you pitied a boy. The first time you looked into a boy's eyes, at the little gold haloes right around his pupils, and thought, *God, I feel sorry for you.*

And yet, you let it happen. You let him worm his way through you, and you even shifted, even offered a cry so that he'd think he was doing well. And you saw yourself, and you saw him, and it was just parts, legs and arms and feet and hands, here and there, and you couldn't even tell whose was whose. And you saw yourself looking up at the Buick's gray roof, fabric sagging like a circus tent, and you thought, *When will this end, when will this end*, and you wondered, as this boy tried desperately to navigate you, why you didn't just get up.

* * *

College boys were different from high school boys. You figured this out in your first week as a freshman, dashing across campus with your arms full of books. Some girls only walked with purses or boys on their arms, but you always had your books, ready to read, and research, and learn at any moment. And the college boys, you learned, had experience and stories to tell. You didn't bother flirting with the ones your own age; you preferred the older ones, the ones who had just returned from semesters abroad, who knew foreign languages and the difference between Nice and nice. Educated boys. You flirted like it was a sport, and when they expected more, you lied to them, told them you had a boyfriend. You were good at setting boundaries.

Some girls rotted boys' teeth but not you. You made them work to figure you out, and whoever could stick with it the longest and sweat the most would win. You learned to pick boys like fruit, to weigh them and inspect for bruises. You turned them in your hands and studied the curves because, yes, some boys had curves. And there were times when you wanted the bruised ones, the ones who were so banged up that they didn't seem, on the surface, as though they could possibly be worth it. But you knew that once you removed the skin—once you cut deep, deep, deep—you'd find the good parts. Parts so good they could make a girl go stupid.

* * *

The third boy, your bruised boy, you met in the library. Or at the student union or across the quad. Somewhere. The thing about this one is that you can't remember the very first time you saw him. You met, and suddenly it was like he'd always been there. You don't even know why you ended up choosing him. Maybe it was because you couldn't have him.

When he paid attention to you, it was sometimes stifling. He was insecure, passive-aggressive and needy. You concocted imaginary fights with him, moments when you'd throw a glass of water in his face or kick him out of your car on an isolated highway. And yet, when he ignored you, you could think of nothing but him. You needed to see him give you the look that made your heart sink to the bottom of your feet and then rise, as if winged, up your body and into your head, dizzying you with want.

You liked to think that both of you knew exactly what you were doing. That you knew exactly why you were doing it. He was lonely and missed Her. He never told you Her name. All you knew was that She was never home, always working, never had time for him. And you, you knew that you were simply a replacement, a temporary elixir. You told yourself you were practicing on him, learning from him. You liked thinking that you knew you could leave this one at any time, just like you'd left the other two. And yet, you never did.

* * *

You didn't know what you were doing. Or did you? This, you knew, was the trick: don't let him know. Make him guess. Torture him with the puzzle of whether or not you are aware of your magic. Let him chase you as far as he can run; just don't get caught.

* * *

He came to your apartment every Wednesday night because that's when She taught a class across town. You used to eat chocolate that he brought home from the drugstore where he worked part-time between classes. Tiny squares of rich, brown sugar. The first bite was always the hardest, and you waited for your teeth to sink into it finally, to snap off a piece that would then sit in your mouth as you waited for it to melt.

He never let it melt. He just ate it, licked his fingers.

For a while, you wouldn't do it with him. He wanted to; he would tell you all the things he wanted to do to you, then apologize for wanting to do them. You rationed your self like candy, piece by piece, one at a time, and never too much at once. Every night, you gave him something else, until the night there was nothing else left to give.

At the time, in the moment, you were as sure of yourselves as any two people could be in a dark room, beneath sheets and sheets of black. It was the moments after then—the hours, the days, the ticks and tocks that carried you further and further from that moment—that you doubted. But at that moment, there was nothing but the two of you. And you, you were smart enough to know what it was.

Love and sex are two different things. You were always careful to remember that. Before you ever said the word, you had to make sure that you were the only one. You always paid careful attention to the moment when a boy first said it. You took note of where you were, what you wore, where he looked. If the two of you were horizontal, naked, and eyes closed, then you didn't believe the sentiment.

When this one said it, though, it didn't matter. You always believed it. You kept it under your pillow, safe and warm and close, close.

* * *

You practiced until you'd mastered the look: *foster/fear/fuck me.* All at once

* * *

His eyes were blue, so blue, and there were times when you wanted to swim right through them, straight into his brain, and then down, down to his chest, Chutes and Ladders, and into his shared heart. Some nights, you studied his face in the dark. You skimmed your fingertips across his forehead, dipped them down the cliffs of his closed eyes, brushed his eyelashes right, left, right, left. You memorized that. And you slipped down the slope of his nose to his mouth's narrow hills. And when you reached his neck, you wrapped your hand around it like a lover, or a killer. And you wondered, every time, if you could ever really conquer his body's terrain.

* * *

It ends. You see them one night, after it's over. Him and Her. You watch the littered dance floor from above, on the balcony with the yellow chairs. Drink in hand, you see the bodies sway, rub, slide, connect. You watch them weave, needle and thread, through the patchwork of mini dresses, knee-high boots, black leather. In, out, in, out, over and knot. She lays a hand on one of your bruised boy's hips (my hips, you think), her shoulders moving in ways you never knew shoulders could move. And heat fills you, and you try to remember that you don't care, that you know better, that you're smart, smart, smart. But then his eyes, arrows, catch you.

Snake Hill

BILL LOEHFELM

We came over the top of Snake Hill too fast and started our drop down the other side at the same speed. My father's giant old station wagon slalomed deep into the snaky curves like a fat skier in wet snow. The tires didn't screech, but they squeaked now and again. Streetlamps were few and far between. The trees were black shadows on both sides, the foliage dense and dark, close to the roadside. I tried to keep the headlights focused on the winding double yellow lines in front of me, keep those lines centered in the crossed beams of light. I hoped to hell that no one was coming up the hill in the opposite lane.

My brother snored over on the passenger side of the wagon's big bench seat, having passed out sometime in the first three minutes after we left the Haunted Café back on Bay Street. I hadn't seen him put back more than two or three drinks, less than half of what I'd had, and I got that sick, nervous feeling in my stomach that had been coming on more and more lately, the feeling that he was messing with more powerful stuff than booze. Pills, maybe. Powders. He hadn't, I noticed with a quick glance, despite my insistence and his assurances, fastened his seat belt. Couldn't even do that for me. I wanted to slam on the brakes and bounce his head off the dashboard, just to make a point. But I didn't do it. I kept riding the sharp, blind curves in the road. He shifted in his seat with the back-and-forth motion of the car.

Why, I wondered again, tightening my grip on the steering wheel, was I driving like a maniac to get us home by curfew when there was so much more to worry about? Because, I reminded myself, curfew was what our folks cared about. Curfew and the car. They wouldn't ask what Danny was getting into, because they didn't want to know, and I sure wouldn't tell. Wouldn't say anything about a seventeen-year-old with a grown-up hangover. They never did comment anymore, not after the past two years in our house. We'd had all the bad news we could handle.

I looked over at my brother again. His forehead was pressed against his window. I couldn't see his face, but I knew he always smiled in his sleep, the benefits of an empty conscience. Another quick check of the road and I glanced at the dashboard clock. One fifteen in the a.m. Well, we'd blown curfew. That was a lost cause. Seemed I was losing causes by the minute. More important now was the matter of getting down the hill. If I couldn't deliver us home on time, I could at least deliver us home in one piece. That plan hit the skids, literally, barely a moment after I had that thought.

I don't know if it was oil, or gravel, or the greasy entrails of something dead and left to rot, but coming out of an especially sharp turn, the back end of the station wagon fishtailed hard left, as if God had flicked the ass-end of the car with his finger. I didn't panic. I didn't overcorrect. I didn't make a sound. I held steady and hit the brakes.

The back left corner of the station wagon slammed into the guardrail, the back tires sliding and scratching on some roadside gravel. A deep thump pulsed through the car on impact, as if someone had whacked an empty pot with a spoon and we were inside the pot. It wasn't that loud, considering, but it lingered in my ears for an extra second nonetheless. The chassis bounced once or twice, and the car settled, still, on the side of the road like the collision had knocked the wind out of it. My brother groaned beside me. He touched his fingertips to his forehead. One eye was open, the other still closed. I guess he wanted to make sure the incident was worth the effort of opening both. I was glad he seemed okay. I grimaced in sympathy at the goose egg already rising over his right eye. Maybe that's why that left one had stayed closed.

"What the fuck, Kev?" he said. "We dead?"

"No," I said. "We're fine."

At least he knew we'd had an accident. He couldn't be that far gone.

He nodded as if I'd given him a lot of information to process. He squinted through the windshield with his one open eye, then turned and did the same out the back window. He was looking, I realized, for the other car.

"Just us," I said. I turned around too. A cloud of thin gray dust hung suspended in the ruby-red glow of the brake lights. I realized I still had the brake pedal pinned. "I tagged the guardrail coming out of a curve. Too much of a rush, I guess."

"I don't know why you give a fuck about curfew anymore," he said, turning to me, both eyes open now, bewilderment all over his face. He sniffed. "You're the only one who does."

"Who do you hang out with?" I asked.

"You."

"And who else?"

"No one, really," my brother said.

"And how do we get around?"

"In Dad's car."

"Ask me again why I care about curfew."

My brother scoffed: "Dad'll let you have the car whenever we hang out, especially because we hang out, whatever the fuck time we come home. What're you, dense?"

"And you're so wise on this how?"

Danny shrugged like the answer was so obvious he could barely speak it. "Dad thinks you look out for me. He thinks I'm safer when we're together. He wouldn't run the risk of separating us. Mom wouldn't let him."

"You saying you're not safer with me than you would be alone?" I swallowed hard. "Doing what you do these days?"

Danny turned one way in his seat and then the other, glancing around us. "Didn't you just wreck the car?"

"I didn't wreck it," I said. I didn't know what part of my commentary his crack about the car had been meant to criticize. "Just dinged it up at most."

I decided I should get a look at how bad before I tried continuing the drive home, or continuing my attempt at a conversation with my younger brother about his growing drug problem. Just in case it was worse than I thought, worse than it had sounded. The car, I mean.

I opened the door, cool night air rushing into the car. I realized I'd been sweating, the breeze running up the sleeves of my T-shirt. I took a deep breath. When I turned to hang out the door and look, the seat belt caught. Danny stifled a giggle. I popped the belt free and leaned out of the car.

"You smell gas?" Danny asked.

"No." So far, so good. I hadn't even thought of that. Gas tank was on that side too. I heard the flick of a lighter and smelled cigarette smoke. Glad he was so confident. But things seemed okay. The back tire wasn't flat. I could see the hubcap. No dents that I could see in the back quarter panel, at least in the faint wash of the dome light from inside the car.

"Light me one," I told Danny. Without turning, I reached my arm across the car for the cigarette. The lack of obvious damage had me feeling better, more and more confident that nothing was wrong that we couldn't play off as a parking lot accident and pin on some other idiot driver. Dad would grumble, but he'd forgive. And small dents he could pound out himself in the driveway. He was handy like that.

Danny slipped the cigarette into my fingers. I brought the smoke to my lips, tapped the brake pedal. The taillights ignited, a red burst off the back of the car washing over the wild green bushes and trunks of the trees. Still working, that was good. None of the telltale bright white gave away broken glass back there. Amazing, I thought, how bright those lights actually are. I tapped them again. And then I saw it. My throat went dry.

A shoe. One shoe.

A sneaker, really. A blue Ked, adult-sized. The cheap kind you see lined up in flimsy cardboard boxes along those long rows of shelves at the KMart or the Korvettes. Like old people wore. No big deal, I told myself, a shoe by the side of the road. Except this shoe stood on its heel, tilted a little to the left. I could see a bony, hairless, blue-veined ankle, the cuff of a pajama leg. An old person. Some poor, senile, old bastard who'd probably wandered away from one of the estates on the hill.

My throat closed, and my heart stopped, a fist reaching into my chest and squeezing my heart down to the size of a grape, strangling it.

Fuck me. I'd killed someone.

I heard Danny getting out of the car. Air exploded out of my chest, and my heart started again. I lunged for Danny, locking onto his forearm. He glanced down at my hand, not looking all that surprised I'd grabbed ahold of him.

"Get back in the car," I said.

"Lemme go," he said. "I gotta take a piss. Since we're apparently camping out here for the night."

"Get in the car." I did not want him seeing that body. And I didn't want anybody seeing us anywhere near it. I'd decided to run from the scene. I couldn't even remember making the decision. But I was totally sure of what I wanted to do.

"Dude, I gotta go," Danny said. "One sec."

"Wait till we get home."

"Who're you? Fucking Mom?"

"Someone could see us."

"I'll go back in the woods." He chuckled. "You already took care of the guardrail. Easy-peasy."

He tried to tug his arm free, half an effort because he expected me to let go. I didn't. He bristled, and for the first time since we'd stopped he looked a little angry.

"There's gotta be a car coming," I said, "either from ahead or behind us." We'd settled to a stop on the wrong side of the road, facing into oncoming traffic, our headlights burning bright down the side of the hill. It was mid-spring, the trees had only half their leaves. Our car was blatantly visible from every direction. Our voices probably carried far in the quiet night. The sound of the station wagon slamming the guardrail certainly had. People did live up here. They lived nearby over on Todt Hill and on Lighthouse Road too. The Hill people. Rich people. Rich people who didn't tolerate late-night, side-of-the-road bullshit, people who didn't come to see if you were all right, if there was anything they could do to help. They just called the cops, and went back to bed, and let the paid help deal with it. That could've happened already. The cops could be on their way up the hill as we sat there bickering like one of us had gotten more chocolate milk than the other at breakfast.

I didn't want to be dealt with. I wanted my brother back in the fucking car. And I wanted both of us home.

Danny settled on the edge of the front seat, one leg in and one leg out of the car, cigarette dangling from the corner of his mouth. He had his outside leg in the middle of the road. "What the fuck?" He reached under his seat, moving his hand around under it. "We don't have any beers left in here?"

I thought I saw headlights break through the trees below.

"We're in a hurry," I said, trying to keep my voice light and failing. "Remember?"

I watched my brother for a reaction to my bullshit. Could I have made it any more obvious that there was something at the back of the car I didn't want him to see? I hoped my guilt and horror, not only over what I had done by accident but what I was now doing on purpose, amplified my fears, like that remorse-ridden lunatic in "The Tell-Tale Heart." I realized gratefully that Danny had most likely never read the story. I also realized I was glad and relieved he was high and therefore, if not easily led, at least leadable.

That thought made me feel like shit. It made me sick.

"We're going," I said, my voice a croak. "Now."

I braked as I put the car in drive, using the sideview mirror to look into the cloud of red light and exhaust behind us. I saw the second foot as we inched away from the shoulder. Though it tilted away from the first foot at the toes, the heels were nearly touching, the feet therefore making a V shape, like feet did when their owner was flat on his back. On the soles I could see the Rice Krispies patterns in the waxy, honey-colored rubber. Or maybe I was imagining that last part. Our grandfather had worn those same shoes in the last years of his life. Before he died after two long, long years of stomach cancer, calling out for morphine till the bitter end.

* * *

Back in brightly lit Eltingville, streetlights and porch lights everywhere, I parked the car a few houses down from ours. It annoyed the neighbors to no end, seeing my father's beat-to-hell, twelve-year-old, 1977 gray behemoth of an Impala wagon parked in "their" parking spot.

Back in the day, long before us, before he'd even met our mother, our father had been a brawler, and Danny and I desperately wanted, just once, to see him throw down on the neighbors we liked least. Like the 'roided-out dude from my high school who washed his Monte Carlo SS twice a week, shirtless and cranking shitty club music, like the whole island was his personal health club/coke den/dancehall. Or the old guy who lived alone on mental disability checks and never drove and so sat behind his living room curtains all day, even when the kids on the block were at school, the guy waiting for some Wiffle ball or street hockey ball to bounce onto his pristine lawn so he could crank the window and threaten to call the cops. Or, more specifically, his son, the cop, whom we never saw, not once. But it never happened. Dad didn't fight anymore. At least not over parking spaces and certainly not over the wiseassery of his silly sons.

After I turned off the engine, I sat behind the wheel for a few moments, a few breaths, willing myself to leave what I'd seen and done on the hill up there. I silently swore never to take that short cut again, curfew be damned. I had a brief, ridiculous thought that if we did get busted for hitting someone back on the hill, that we, that I, could somehow blame my father. If he hadn't been so anal about the curfew, I would never have been in such a hurry. That particular bizarre assemblage of necessary moments that led to my killing someone would never have coalesced, and I would never have hit that person now lying there dead by the side of the road. My face got hot. Of all the rotten fucking luck. How many things had to go wrong for that person to be in that spot at that moment when the rear end of the Impala came smashing into him? If I'd tried to hit that person I never, ever could have done it. Not even head-on. What was that goddamn idiot doing wandering along a pitch-black road in the middle of the night? It had never entered my mind that there might be someone even more careless than me on that road. Certainly not someone I couldn't see coming. My head started to hurt. I had to stop thinking about it. Why was it so hot inside the car? I opened the door and stepped out into the street. Danny was already around the back of the car.

"Holy shit," I heard him say. It was an observation, not a weary summation of the night's adventures. That scared me. "Damn," he said.

A dent, probably. Maybe some torn-away piece of clothing. Blood, most likely. Worse, possibly. Body parts. I continued around the back of the car and saw what had arrested Danny's attention. The entire back bumper of the station wagon was missing. Gone. Shorn clean off when I'd fishtailed the Impala into the guardrail. And now lying by the side of the road at the scene of the accident. Could you trace a bumper back to the car from which it came? You could certainly get make and model and year. You could go around to body shops asking who'd come in for a replacement bumper for a '77 Impala station wagon. You could tell all your cop friends to keep an eye out for cars missing their rear bumpers. And then I realized no cop would even have to do that much work to find out what car had hit that dead person. Because, I realized, that bumper was lying there with the license plate still attached. I almost laughed. I'd killed someone, fled the accident, and left the license plate at the scene. I was too dumb to be a character in a Poe story. What had Danny said about our dad trusting me to look out for him? Talk about misplaced trust. I thought for a moment about walking into the house, waking him, and spilling everything, putting everything in his hands. But I didn't want this on him, and I didn't really want him to handle it. I just wanted it to go away. Getting him involved wouldn't make that happen. Now was not the time for wishful thinking.

Danny had a fistful of hair at the top of his head. He was staring at the back of the station wagon. "Wow. I betcha that's hard to do. Dad's gonna fucking freak."

"We gotta go back," I said.

"We?"

"Yes, we," I said. "I'm gonna need your help."

"Dude, I'm tired. How heavy can a bumper be, right? Toss it in the back. We'll hit the body shop in the morning. I'm still suspended. I've got the time. I'll take it in."

"You don't have a license," I said. "You're not allowed to drive."

Danny laughed. "That's your best argument?"

"I need you to look for the bumper," I said. "I'm gonna be driving in the dark."

"Wait till morning."

"Dad's gonna walk right past here on his way to the train. He's gonna see it."

"Then let's move the car around the corner."

"Then how do we explain getting home without it?"

"Bus?"

"Fuck! Danny! C'mon!" I kicked at the space where the bumper had been. "Help me out here."

Danny started laughing. I could've strangled him right there in the gutter. He'd played me right into a temper tantrum. He'd been doing it since we were little kids. I had a flash of us as eighty-year-old men, standing in this same street, me screaming at him, and him laughing. It would never end. He'd been willing to go back to Snake Hill from the moment I'd first asked. I should've known better. As if there had ever been a time when he'd rather go home and go to bed than traipse off on another adventure, no matter how minor. Well, this one wasn't as minor as he thought, but I saw no need to make him the wiser.

He walked to the passenger-side door, tried the handle, and found it locked. "We gonna go, or what?" He couldn't stop smiling. "I ain't got all night."

The words *accessory after the fact* scrolled across my brain. I tried to console myself with the fact that no cop, no court on earth, would believe Danny's denial that he knew nothing about the body. How would he defend himself? *Well, your honor, I was on the nod from a head full of backroom crank.* I told myself that in protecting myself I was protecting him too. And my father, whose name was on the registration attached to the wagon's license plate. Really, I was protecting the whole family by returning to the scene of the crime and cleaning it up.

I climbed into the driver's seat and started the car. *Maybe you should have thought about protecting the family,* a faint voice in the back of my head told me, *before you took Snake Hill at twice the advisable speed while six drinks deep on a weeknight.*

It's too late, I argued back as I pulled us away from the curb, *to do anything about those choices now*. I took us back the way we came, the wide residential streets of our neighborhood narrowing into the older, winding commercial corridors of Amboy Road with its short canvas awnings hanging over the bricked storefronts, every building hugging the thin strip of sidewalk dividing it from the road. Coming around the curves, which I took slowly, it looked impossible to step out of the nail salon or the deli or the driving school and not walk right into oncoming traffic. At intersections, I lingered too long at green lights, petrified of committing some violation.

The streets we followed back onto Richmond Road were only one lane each way and usually bustled, jam-packed with traffic in both directions, but at that late hour the streets were dead. We saw not a soul. And that fact only made me sure that Danny and I couldn't have looked more suspicious being out and about at that hour. Riding around in our damaged car couldn't help our image much. And should we get pulled over, how would we explain ourselves? Or the lack of a rear bumper, which was a great excuse to light us up in the first place. I wanted desperately to speed, to push our errand to its end. The knots in my stomach pulled tighter as we moved away from the homes and businesses and the road darkened.

We found the foot of Snake Hill and started our slow climb. I hoped we wouldn't encounter some version of my earlier, idiot self, careening down the hill road out of control at top speed.

"Think of it like this," Danny said. "Could've been worse. What if that guardrail wasn't there? Most of Snake Hill doesn't have any. We could've gone spinning off into the trees. Into God knows what else. What's the drop-off like over there?"

"I don't know."

"How steep you think it is?"

"I don't know that, either."

"Right," Danny said. "And now we don't have to."

"We should probably start looking for the bumper soon." I slowed our progress to a crawl, barely enough for forward motion, and decided I'd move as far as I could onto the narrow shoulder should someone come up behind us. Danny kept a steady watch on the roadside. He was humoring me, as we still had a couple hundred yards to go before we came anywhere near where the collision had been. I was grateful. I needed him to be quiet so I could think. I needed to decide how much to tell him.

One of Danny's qualities that I most envied was his refusal to judge. I wondered if it was cynicism, optimism, or apathy that left him shrugging off every atrocity and most acts of kindness that he witnessed on the news or saw in the papers. He'd always viewed most of the world from a peaceful distance, and that was even before he found the drugs. Maybe that was what he liked about them. Maybe they made that distance deeper or safer or made it feel permanent and right. Maybe that distance got harder to maintain as he grew older. Or maybe it was Grandpa's death, or what it did to our mother, the way it stoked her hot tears and her raging temper, that made him want his boat to drift even farther from shore. The agony in our house certainly made the fight look futile, even I could see that, and I believed in heaven.

As we both peered into the roadside shadows, I found myself wishing I had left Danny home. Not that he would've stayed there if I'd told him to. He'd never have let me back out into the night alone.

I heard a sharp "A-ha" from Danny and turned to see him pointing dead ahead through the windshield. And there, in the middle of the road, in all its slightly tarnished glory, was the Impala's bumper. Intact and lying there like so much chrome road kill.

"Nicely done," I said, pulling the car over to the side of the road.

There wasn't much of a shoulder, and half the wagon hung out into the traffic lane. We'd have fair warning about on-coming traffic from either direction, though, and the later it got, the smaller our chances of encountering another driver, anyway.

I threw the car into park, hit the hazards, and jumped out the door. I glanced into the woods, searching for the shoes in the weak glow of the Impala's dome light. I didn't see them, but I knew that didn't mean they weren't out there or that Danny wasn't going to see them. Unless, of course, they'd never been there to begin with, something I could convince myself was true if I worked at it hard enough. I'd prefer having had a hallucination to the reality that I'd killed someone.

I heard a groan. A faint, B-movie zombie groan.

There was no way. The old man I'd hit had to be dead. I'd hit him with an out-of-control, two-thousand-pound automobile. Christ, I'd never considered the alternative. A fucking miracle.

Danny was out of the car, looking at me over the roof and waiting for instructions. I didn't think he'd heard the groan in the woods. Maybe I hadn't either. Then I heard it again.

"Fuck." I hung my head.

"Fuck what?" Danny said. "The bumper's right here on the shoulder. We're golden. Let's dump it in the car and get the hell outta here."

Another groan.

"Did you hear that?" Danny asked.

"It's nothing," I said. "Some animal in the woods."

Danny laughed. "This is Staten Island, for Chrissakes. Animal in the woods, like this is fucking upstate or something? Gimme a break. Somebody's out there."

We heard a faint rustling in the leaves. Faint enough that it could have been the wind.

"Fuck this," Danny said. He went back to the car, pulled open the passenger-side door. He reached under the seat and pulled out a gun from underneath it. A small black pistol. I was shocked to see it.

"What the fuck is that?"

"It's a Pez dispenser. What's it fucking look like?"

"Where did you get that?"

"I had it for a while. This dude at school bet me on the Jets game and didn't have the cash. What's it matter? You never saw it."

He walked around the back of the car, peering into the dark woods. He stepped to the edge of the trees, to where I'd taken out the guardrail with the car, the gun held loosely at his side. "Yo! Fucknuts! You ain't scarin' nobody."

Enough of this, I thought. I jogged over to the bumper, grabbed one end, started dragging it toward the car, the metal grinding on the asphalt. "Help me with this, Danny. Put the gun away. It's somebody's old dog or something. Open the back of the car."

But Danny ignored me. He was staring into the dark woods, his head tilted to one side like a puppy that didn't understand a command. I stopped halfway to the car, bent over, panting, cradling one end of the bumper in my hands. I listened for what it was Danny heard. I heard it too. The old man's voice, a feeble attempt at words. Gibberish.

Danny turned to me. "There's somebody out there," he said, quieter this time, no aggression or defiance in his tone. "What the fuck?"

I set the bumper back down on the pavement. "I need your help. Me. Over here."

Danny looked at me for a long moment; then he started into the woods, picking his way over the dead fallen branches and through the underbrush, sloughing his way across the carpet of dead leaves.

"Goddamnit, Danny."

I looked at the bumper at my feet, looked into the woods, where Danny was now a slow-moving shadow among the trees. He'd gone right by the spot where I knew the old man was lying. Danny was probably still drunk, I reminded myself. And still high, as well.

The battered gray hulk of the station wagon sat silent by the side of the road, the pulsing hazard lights making the car look like a UFO awaiting liftoff.

I wasn't a horrible person. I thought the guy was dead. I didn't see any benefit to anyone in confessing that I'd killed him. I'd get in trouble, as would Danny, who got in plenty without my help. I felt bad for the old man, bad for his family. He had people who loved him, though not enough to keep him from staggering along a dark road in the middle of the night. But why should two families suffer? It sucked that people had lost their grandpa because I was a terrible drunk driver. Was it any worse than going by cancer? Any worse than a slow, awful death that traumatized your kid so bad that she traumatized her own? And why should my parents, one of whom had just lost her parent, lose their sons over the same accident, if they didn't have to? Nothing I did would bring him back to life.

But all that was moot now, I thought, because the old fucker wasn't dead.

I left the bumper where I'd dropped it and moved into the woods, making my way toward the shadow I knew was Danny. It got easier to find him when his disembodied face appeared in the golden glow of his lighter. He watched me the entire time I made my way to him. We'd ended up several yards deep in the woods. I'd thought the old man had been closer to the road. Then I figured it out. He'd crawled. Danny let the flame go out.

"Shit gets hot," Danny said. "Did you know about this? Is that why you were all fucking freaked?"

I said nothing. Hands on my knees, I bent over the old man, listening to his raspy breathing. How could he not be dead? I'd hit him with a fishtailing station wagon, flipping him over a guardrail. And yes, I'd left him there, broken and bleeding. Danny hit the lighter again.

The old man had gray eyes. They stared straight up. They stared past me and Danny, up into the night sky, maybe searching through the branches overhead for the stars. Maybe he saw something or someone coming for him. It did not appear that he saw me or my brother standing over him. I thought about how sad it would be if in his head, the last feeble circuits were firing and what he saw as the famed white light at the end of the tunnel was in reality just Danny's lighter, glowing there in the dark like the lantern on the ferryman's boat. No one would even look for him until the early morning. He wore thin blue pajamas and a ragged maroon robe that was thrown open, the top soaked dark purple with blood. His chest was caved in like someone had dropped a safe—or a station wagon—on him.

"This is a fucking mess," Danny said.

It was. The old man had misused the last of his strength crawling deeper into the woods and away from any chance of somebody seeing him in time to save him.

"We did this with the car, didn't we?" Danny asked. "You saw him, you knew he was here." He shook his head. "We gotta take care of him."

"Danny, listen. Look at him. He's got minutes left, tops. What're we gonna do? Drive all the way down the hill and find a pay phone somewhere? Nose-diving down this hill started all this. We gonna knock on doors up here on the hill? How do we explain how we found him? It ain't that tough to figure out he got hit by a car."

"I can't believe what I'm hearing. I never knew you could think like this." He let the lighter go out. "What if he doesn't have minutes left, what if it's hours? He's hung on this long."

"I can't tell you what to do," I said. Fuck it. "We can carry him to the car maybe. You wanna take care of him, we'll take care of him."

Danny hit the lighter again. "That wasn't what I meant by take care of him." He held the gun out to me. "This is."

"Jesus, Danny. Are you serious? I don't think that's the right idea."

"You leave him here dying in the woods. Now you're squeamish? Look at the guy. We'd be doing him a favor." The lighter went out. "Remember how Grandpa hung on and hung on, for weeks, months after they gave him only days? You want that for this poor bastard? For his family? I wish somebody had come for Grandpa with a gun."

I looked back to the road, at the squat gray mass of the car. Its flashing lights seemed to mark the seconds passing us by, silently beating the time like a lit-up heart. We were really pushing our luck. Another car would come over the hill sooner or later. I appreciated my brother making a moral argument on my behalf, giving me an ethical parachute. He meant well. I was the good brother, after all, the one who, till tonight at least, concerned himself with such things. But if morals, or ethics, or right and wrong were really my worries, I'd never have left the old man there in the first place. I was learning fast what I really cared about. From the moment I saw him handing it my way in the lighter's glow, I'd had only one real concern about the gun.

"You misunderstood me," I said. "Somebody's gonna hear that gunshot. We can't have that."

We stood there in the dark, the old man at our feet, his weak scratchy breaths growing further apart. I had the power to end it, his life, the whole fucked-up episode I'd gotten myself and my brother into. All I had to do was accept the power and not leave all our fates, as predictable as they might be considering where we lived, to other hands.

"Go back to the car," I said. "I'll meet you there in a minute."

"Fuck that."

"We can't leave him. We can't shoot him. Go. I'll take care of it."

"I got this," he said, kneeling down in the dead leaves. "You go back to the car. I'm much, much better at living with ugly shit than you are."

I kneeled across from him, speaking to him over the dying man. "Because it's only now that it's getting ugly?"

Danny crouched there, hands on his thighs, waiting, giving me time to make my case.

"You close and cover his mouth," I said. "And I'll pinch his nose shut. We'll carry it together. We'll never talk about it. Ever. That's my best offer."

"He's barely even here," Danny said, moving. "This shouldn't take long."

It didn't.

By the time Danny was halfway through his third whispered Hail Mary, the old man was dead. I hadn't thought to use the time to pray. And then we were done, and everything would be like it had been from the beginning, an accident.

We stood, brushed the twigs and dead leaves from our pants, and crept out of the woods. We didn't speak. Danny helped me load the bumper into the back of the station wagon. It barely fit. As we drove home across the island, Danny helped me work up a story for our folks to explain what had happened—to the car. It was the only thing we talked about.

This Game Do That to You

NICHOLAS MAINIERI

The baseball shine under the lights, and this run through your head as the pitch on its way: full count but you don't want no walk. A walk don't get you out of A ball. You swing, but the pitch disappear. Just gone. The catcher block it in the dirt, leap to his feet, tag you out. Game over. This the only night with a crowd—dollar-beer night—and they howling at you walking off the field. The fuck they at the rest of the week?

Already the guys got the music playing in the clubhouse. Wish for something good just one time. Maybe a dude from your own Chicago hood, like Common. He got something to say at least. Swear to God, Single-A make it hard to remember you even like baseball at all. Had fifty stolen out your locker the first week of summer. You can't find out who took it. The Latinos don't know English. The white dudes think you crazy. Like one day Ronnie look over from his locker and point at the five-point star inked on your forearm and ask what it is, so you tell him it's Vice Lords. And he ask what that is, "Like a gang or something?" How to tell him Greg made you get the tattoo when you was thirteen just so you could walk home from school? Greg is Vice Lords. Not you. But your brother always looking out. How to tell Ronnie that? You can't.

Tonight you get on the bus to drive all the way to Grand Rapids for a day game tomorrow, so you sit and untie your spikes and start packing. Ronnie lean over from his locker and smile. He think he all smart because he played in college, and he been here a few years since. "Jones," he say, "you ever seen a slider like that before?"

"Fuck no," you say.

"Don't throw no bitch sliders like that in high school, do they?"

"Already said no."

"Dude's gonna be a big-leaguer before long. Nasty shit."

Maybe so. But you know all that mean—better be able to hit that shit if you want to be a big-leaguer. You eighteen already, and no dummy. The clubhouse empty out and you sit thinking. Seem like you can't get a goddamn hit no more. Leroy the clubbie drag his vacuum into the room. Leroy got a gray beard and red face. Always a chew in his cheek.

"Not your fault tonight, big fella," Leroy say. "Blame the fucking scout that signed you." Then he start up his vacuum.

* * *

The bus rumble out in the lot. Skip sit up front reading over the box score. Don't need to look to know it say Jones, 0 for 4. Skip got to be thinking about the new center fielder. The club signed him now the college season ended. Short white dude, but the motherfucker can run. You better hit, or they'll call up his ass before they do you.

Only seat left on the bus is near the back, next to Mordecai. Been everywhere, they say. Played for everybody. Now all the way back down in Single-fucking-A, and he don't hang up his spikes. Mordecai look like an old teacher or something, wearing his glasses and reading a book.

He nod at you. "Come sit down beside me, and hear my sad story. I'm shot in the breast, and I know I must die."

You heard crazy shit like that before out his mouth. "Whatever you say, teacher man."

He crack a smile at that one. "Just something I was reading." He wave the book, and the cover say something about a drum.

Close your eyes after a while. Greg waiting here like he do sometimes, pulling you out on the porch at the start of summer, before you leave home to join the club. He point at the ink on your arm, and then he lift up his shirt, point at his own five-point star. "Don't fuck this up," he say. "Remember what back here for you. What ain't. Don't fuck this up. You remember."

Mordecai wake you, tapping your leg. Ask him, "We there?"

He nod at the window. "I didn't want you to miss this."

The black trees going by, the sky going orange. "Miss what?"

"Have you ever seen the sun come up before?"

"You woke me up for this?"

Mordecai just smile.

* * *

Hot as hell today. Mosquitoes. Nobody going to be in the crowd for a midweek day game either. Check the lineup after batting practice. Sure enough, Skip got the other center fielder, Morgan, in there. Swallow down what you feel. Know you'll get another chance.

You jog to the outfield to do some running, and all the pitchers out there cluster around something on the warning track. You go check it out. Ronnie stand in the middle of them, using a fungo bat to draw in the gravel. He trace a big circle, four feet around it, a tail, and a head with a smiley face. All the pitchers laugh.

"Fuck's that?" you say.

Ronnie shrug. "Rain turtle."

"Huh?"

He spread his arms and look up. "Rain turtle makes it rain."

You shake your head, smile. A rainout might be nice, but the sky blue as ever.

"You got a lot to learn, Jones," Ronnie say, laughing.

Do your sprints in the grass and get your legs warm. When you finish, all the pitchers gone back to the dugout or into the bullpen, but Mordecai come from somewhere and stand looking at the rain turtle like it something to think about. Then he use his spikes to sweep through the gravel and erase it. He do it until the whole rain turtle gone. Now he look at the sky like he nervous. Still no clouds. Yell at him, "What you doing, teacher man?" But Mordecai just go to the bullpen. He don't even turn around.

* * *

Into the seventh inning, still no score. Zero, zero. Skip yell for you from the end of the dugout. He cough out a dark clump of sunflower seeds and point at Morgan in the on-deck circle. "Get your bat," Skip say. "They bring in a lefty, you're gonna hit."

You wait with your stick and helmet and watch their pitcher. Breathing hard, wiping his forehead between pitches. He fall behind three and one but get a pop- up on the next pitch. Two out. All the same their manager come out to the mound and bring in the lefty. Skip call Morgan back, and you stroll to the on-deck circle. The umpire shout when the lefty make his last warm-up.

Kick at the chalk and dig in. Remember. Don't fuck this up.

The lefty surprise you by coming inside with the first pitch. Turn away and the ball hit you in the back. Don't hurt bad—sting a bit—but the catcher jump up like you about to charge the mound. Just jog to first.

"That a kid," the base coach say, coming over close to talk quiet. "Two out. Get in scoring position."

Take your lead. Expect the throw over. Dive back to the base, and the first baseman slap you hard as he can on the helmet with the tag. Get up, don't worry over no bush-league motherfucker like him. Take your lead again and break soon as the pitcher lift his foot. Your spikes pounding in the clay—you can always do this. Glance, see the catcher climbing out his stance. Slide hard feet first, the clay burn through your pants, and you pop up and stand as the throw get here.

On the next pitch, your hitter poke one through the right side of the infield. This is automatic. Got to score. Going around third, your favorite feeling in the world. Like running downhill. Like you never run this fast ever. Like you and Greg is kids again and you running just because. A Stony Island sidewalk and the Chicago sun. Home plate come into view, and you don't think about pro ball or getting called up or nothing.

You know the right fielder going to come up throwing by the way the catcher block the plate. He raise his glove and tense, and you feel the throw out there on its way. Dive around the catcher and slap home plate just before he tag you on the feet. No crowd to boo. No sound but your breath. Get up and stand in the clay under the sun, safe at home.

When you jog to center for the bottom half of the inning, Mordecai come out the bullpen and wink as he pass. Scoreboard say 1–0. Ain't going to last, you think. Mordecai got two pitches. Slow and slower.

He go full count on the lead-off man, and the dude foul off pitch after pitch. When Mordecai let go the ball, you lean to right field, anticipate. But the bottom just fall out the pitch like Mordecai yank on a string tied to the baseball, and the batter whiff, strike out. Mordecai do the next hitter the same way, and the third batter roll over the first pitch he see and dribble it in front of the plate. Mordecai field it himself and throw him out. Just like that. End of the seventh and you still up.

Mordecai sit at the end of the bench in the dugout. Already sweating, a towel around his shoulders. Got his elbows on his knees, and he stare out at the grass. He just smile, maybe happy there wasn't no rainout.

Team go down one-two-three in the top of the eighth. Back out to center.

Their lead-off man launch Mordecai's first pitch about a thousand miles. It just hang in the air forever till you can't see it no more. You don't even move, and the game all tied up. The next batter yank a pitch down the right-field line for a triple. Mordecai fall behind the third hitter three and one. Lean with the next pitch and now break for the gap in right center almost before you hear the crack of the bat. Glance once at the ball—so high up there—to figure where it might land, put your head down, run. The wind whistle. You push, running and running and feeling the ball up there. You and it. Don't fuck this up, Greg say. Don't fuck this up. Stop on the warning track and turn and block the sun with your glove and the baseball almost right on top of you and you catch it. Like that.

Take the baseball from your glove and raise your arm. The runner tagged and just walk home. The go-ahead run. Too far away to do anything about it. Everything so far. You feel like you do in the clubhouse after games. All by yourself.

The next hitter crush the first pitch he see from Mordecai. Gone. Make you hold your breath till it land. Mordecai just stand on the mound, hands on his hips, hanging his head. Simple, man. This game do that to you.

The dugout keep silent in the top half of the ninth. Go down one-two-three again. No fight. Game over. The dugout about empty, but Mordecai still sitting at the end of the bench, elbows on his knees, staring at the cement under his spikes.

* * *

Got the music playing again. Even on the road they do. But Skip stick his head in and yell to turn that shit down. Somebody do, and now when it go quiet, Skip call Mordecai over to the office. You don't watch Mordecai cross the floor. Least you try. Maybe everyone try. Get up and go to the shower and take your time. The water beating on you. You want to tell Mordecai something. Maybe say thanks for the sunrise. Shake your head. Stupid.

When you come out the shower, a book waits for you on your seat. Look around the room. Mordecai already gone. Ronnie just shrug, sitting at his locker. He laugh a bit and say, "At least the old dude don't have to come back tomorrow for another day game."

Don't answer. Just sit down. You wonder if Ronnie ever liked this game. Maybe when he a boy he did. Somebody creep over to the music now and turn it back up. Same shit. Maybe Ronnie just been here too long. Decide, right now, you don't ever want to draw no rain turtles. Flip through the pages of Mordecai's book. Put it to your ear and listen to them whir. Start to finish. Like that. Put it in your bag. You picture how Mordecai erased the rain turtle earlier, and you know he had something different to say from everybody else. But what of that? The game got no room for him. What can he do now? You don't know. Maybe go be a teacher. Coach high school someplace.

You take up your spikes. Black leather with the metal cleats. See the orange clay in the creases. Like they all just one thing, the clay and the leather. Tomorrow, you get to wear the shoes again. You can remember that.

All There Is

CRAIG T. MCWHORTER

If I thought in terms of enemies, you would be one.

I have been avoiding you because I'm here, in Provincetown, on vacation, and you represent far too great of a reality to allow me to vacate. Turning from you in the streets and on the beach, I do not want to speak to you. I do not know what I would say, how anyone could possibly say the right thing in such a situation.

And yet, there you are, walking toward me on the beach, three days after I first saw you, as utterly unavoidable as the greenhead flies whose sole intention in life seems to be to bite my skin. Of course you are here because nearly every scene of this particular drama sits among the men on this beach.

The sweat gathers at the rim of my cap, and I slip it off to let the breeze cross the bald skin on my head. And, in the distance, you still approach, much smaller than my raised cap so that if I lowered it you would disappear. Magic. The cap returns to my head. You are still there. And when you are so large that my hat no longer makes you disappear, when my staring might be noticeable, I turn and stare out to the ocean instead, waiting for you to pass. But it is so long before you cross my line of vision that I wonder, "Where did he go?," and turn back to my right only to find that you have stopped, that you are standing mere feet from my blanket, and that you are smiling and shielding your eyes with your hand in a mock salute, all because you know the friend, TJ, at my side.

You squat near his feet, just to my right, and the two of you acknowledge that you've seen each other at the guest house where apparently you're both staying. As I've avoided you this past week, your eyes avoid me. They travel from the sand encasing the tops of your toes to TJ's crotch and perhaps his eyes.

Despite being naked, I feel invulnerable. I'm surrounded by an invisible force field of martyrdom. I have been wronged.

Eventually, our proximity requires that we acknowledge the situation, but I refuse to go first.

And so you ask, almost state, "You're Tim, aren't you?"

It is brave, I think, to look at me sideways and acknowledge with one question, who I am and what you did to me.

The answer is yes. I'm Tim. You know, the man whose partner you fucked, here, on this same beach last summer while I was safely returned to Boston, summer over, back at work. It was my house where you must have shared coffee with him, my bed in which you must have slept with him. I was the one on the other end of the phone hearing explanations from Scott that he'd "made a new friend," that the two of you had gone to a movie, that you'd had dinner at Lorraine's. Were you there for any of those phone conversations? Waiting in the room while he spoke, perhaps admiring walls I painted, idly fingering door pulls I attached, perhaps impatient that he hang up with me so that he would come to bed with you? I have seen you there so many times in my mind that you are now a part of the furnishings, seated in the corner chair shredded by the cats until it looks like Angora, standing next to the abstract painting we bought at the flea market in Wellfleet. I've never even seen you in that house, and yet, I can no longer picture it without you.

Sometimes I think that house was why I fell in love with Scott. We'd been on the beach, a first date if "Maybe I'll see you later at the beach" counts as making a date. Then, with my bike stuck in the back of his car, we went back to that house. I watched the bubbles in my water navigate the ice cubes in my glass while he played the messages on his machine, not minding if I heard his life speaking at him from the black plastic box next to the phone, a Who's Who of "Hey Scott"s. I thought, this man has nothing to hide; no one could hide anything in this perfect little house. And when we had sex, most of the water still in my glass on the bedside table, his eyes confirmed my suspicions. He did not look away. He had nothing to hide. And so I stayed that night, and the next, and the next until my own apartment was just an overpriced closet and his friends started making jokes about lesbians and U-Hauls.

I loved the sounds of Commercial Street that drifted in through the front windows: the soft whir of bike tires and the occasional ting, ting of a bell mounted on the handle bars like we did when we were kids, "girrrl" groups of men and women headed into town for a tea dance or older couples who stopped at the picket fence and pointed out the lupine and peonies, the trolley and its drivers who slowed around the bend and then announced to the tourists, "Provincetown as we know it today began off to the left at Long Point lighthouse." They always said the exact same thing at the exact same place. I loved that the house was so filled with sun that no matter what time of day, I could lie on the couch with a book and pretend to read, bathed head to toe in light, enough light for him, me and the cats. I loved coming home from the beach sticky with salt and sweat and not being able to decide whether I wanted a cold beer or a hot shower first. Each seemed to be reduced to an absolute sensual purity by context and contrast, the ultimate clean, the ultimate refreshment. And at night, the ultimate sleep, curled around Scott, hugging his back into my chest, one knee-pillow spanning between our legs.

He was always there that first summer, intrinsic to my contentment as if he were a wizard casting spells and mixing up the sounds that thrilled my ears or seducing the sunlight into his house to keep me warm. He got up every day at seven even though he was on vacation. I followed shortly thereafter, and we sat on the front stoop and drank coffee with the crossword between us. Nearly every day, we played tennis, went to the beach, cooked and then walked from one end of town to the other seeing the same paintings in the same galleries, the same people on the streets. And I never got bored. I waited for the restlessness, for the desire to prowl bars and beach for new men, to stay out late drinking and sleep late into the hot part of the day while he did the crossword alone. But then, late into the summer, waking from a nap, cat purring on my chest, I realized, This is all there is, all I want.

* * *

TJ invites you to join us for lunch, the sexual potential between the two of you is obvious. Annoying. The three of us, TJ in the middle, all naked and munching on deli sandwiches brought from town along with the towels, bottles of water and suntan lotion in our backpacks.

I'm halfway through humus with roasted red peppers on a baguette, and these are the things I've thought since you slept with Scott. I thought about burning the book you wrote, a gift you signed to him, that I had read before I knew. Somehow, I thought, you would feel the heat, like pins stuck into the padded body of a Voodoo doll. Onto the pyre, I would add every picture of me and him and the contents of a drawer filled with relationship memorabilia, cards and letters all signed with his initials in a heart, and thus I would voo doo him too. I thought, maybe this would make it not hurt anymore.

I thought about finding your e-mail address and then spamming you with an infinite chain of vitriol. I hate you. I hate you. I hate you.

I thought about catching you in a crosswalk, cluelessly ambling across an intersection in front of my car, and how maybe the indentation of your face in my windshield, your body on my car's hood, would remove from my mind the equally graphic image of you with him having sex on this beach.

I'm done with my Cape Cod chips, and when you mention how hot it is, I nod in agreement. These are the places I've been since you slept with him.

For a while, I still lived with him in Boston, even after Scott had told me about you, and I walked the streets of the South End at night so I didn't have to be near him. The wizard had lost his powers. All the eccentricities I'd once thought so charming, seemed suddenly obvious for what they were, deep insecurities.

Each step against the brick sidewalk compacted the anger and hurt within me. I imagined every narrow side street to be a canyon, the rows of townhouses its steep stone walls. The curves of bow fronts and bays, the layers of red brick became the strata of a geological record. I wanted to record my own petroglyphs on those walls, stick figures of you and Scott on the beach, being swallowed by an enormous tidal wave, eaten by sharks, hunted by bands of warriors riding stick-figure ponies with smooth oval bellies and horizontal tails trailing behind like hyphens.

My mind reached out to passing strangers and said, He cheated on me. He's not the person you think he is. He's not spiritual, and gentle, and honest. He cheats, and he lies, and he uses people. I wanted them to hate him too.

I have sat in my new home, and watched TV, endless reruns of *Roseanne*, fundraising specials for PBS like *1000 years of Les Mis* and *Songs You Never Knew Andrew Lloyd Webber Wrote.* I did that for a long time. Sometimes I even cried during the Andrew Lloyd Webber specials.

I've been in a bar in Cambridge dancing shirtless with a man who exploded with muscle and power. The first man to touch desire within me since Scott, and we were on our second date. He was drunk when he arrived.

The only two dancing, we were also the only two shirtless, and he pulled me close, angling his head toward my chest, tongue extended to my nipple. I backed up. I said no again and again, and each rejection of his tongue pushed him to lap up beer instead. He became more insistent, his mouth ever nearer my nipple until I pushed him away.

With the other, with Scott, I did not say no to any excess, even when I knew it was killing us. He always got what he wanted. The third summer, I sat on this same beach drowning in the cum of men we had picked up together, our new routine, but threeways with him were like having sex with two strangers. I sat and watched my life become ephemeral. Who was this man who seemed to know no other goal than the next dick? When had he left me behind? Was he any different, any more sober, than the man who now wanted to lick my chest, who could no longer dance or speak he was so drunk?

So I kept saying no despite the temptation of clarity and of his mouth hard, suckling and needy on my nipple. I thought of my voice leaning to the arc of his ear and saying "bite it" above the drone of music and how the sting of his teeth edging into my flesh and cutting through the soft focus of my recent life could only mean one thing, he wanted me, here, now, in front of all these people. But only here and now, and I kept saying no because he seemed too much like Scott, too high on temporary. Another bottle, another dick, another nipple. It was all the same; they were all the same. I left when he started stumbling around me in circles, calling me a bitch.

Out the cab window I could still see the flashing lights of the dance floor through the transom windows above the doors, and they reminded me of car wrecks or crime scenes in TV movies.

I have been in a closet of a bedroom in the Fenway where five of us struggled to undress in the small spaces around the mattress. Five strangers lit vaguely by the light of a desk lamp shining into a corner while digital fish wandered across a computer screen dodging bubbles. A collection of unfamiliar shadows, white flashes of teeth and rolled eyeballs, four men who had followed one from a nearby bar like rats following the Pied Piper. I only learned some of their names on the walk over, and then we were all naked, and I watched as the bodies coupled and tripled and invaded each other. It was all slick with lube, frantic and intoxicating. Slick like condoms and AIDs didn't exist. For a moment it was like my life with Scott had never existed, and I plunged again and again into the bodies as they were offered. Four strangers. Four unknown sexual histories. Four different opportunities for infection. I came last and left first.

Crossing the bridge on the way to my car, I looked into the reeds of the Fenway beyond and knew that they were full of men and that many of those men were doing the same things I'd just done. We were all taking the same risks. We were all the same.

I'd thought I was safe with Scott, safe from disease and pied pipers. Safe from myself. Safe from loneliness.

On this beach with TJ, we talked about all the sex going on in the dunes behind us, all the sex in the reeds and the bathrooms and the bars. "We're all the same," he said. "We all want the same thing. We want not to feel lonely." And I thought, I just want to forget.

*   *   *

It is very hot, and after lunch, the three of us walk to the water that the Florida boys all insist is too cold for swimming. When the waves rise above my knees, I dive out toward Plymouth, and the relief is immediate. The contact of water on skin is more tangible for the temperature difference like a crisp apple, sour and sweet at once, and I stay under, stretching out my arms then forcing them back through the water, pulling me deeper, farther from the shore, an anemone undulating beneath the surface. When I come up for a breath you are next to me, you have followed me, and we turn and look together at TJ who is still wading along the shore. Quietly, we tread water and watch the traffic along the beach, somehow removed from it, so that all I hear is the gentle splash of our hands at the surface of the water and the loudspeaker from a whale-watch boat passing a half a mile off the coast. Then you dive back under, the white skin on your ass flashing and disappearing into the almost black ripples.

The three of us stand where the water reaches our waists, lifts and pulls at our flaccid penises inches below the surface. We talk about books that TJ hasn't read, both of us recommending them to him. We talk about faculty we both know, conferences we've both attended or will attend. It scares me that we have things in common other than Scott. But I like it too, like talking to you.

When the water finally feels cold rather than soothing, we all three head back to the beach.

All day, below the surface of our conversation, my mind rebels against the situation. When do I get up and kick sand in his face? When do I scream? When do I demand retribution? Why the fuck am I being nice to someone I've dreamed about hitting with my car? But I'm also taking inventory, not cruising, just assessing. I remember his dick being bigger, his body tighter. He's definitely put on some weight.

The thing is, you were supposed to be mine. I was the one who said how cute you were all summer as you walked past and smiled. I liked your trimmed goatee and cluster of dark whiskers circling your mouth. I liked your smooth, flat chest, the way your surfer shorts rode low on your hips so that from the front I could imagine glimpses of the dark hair spreading immediately below the waistline. And we had you together, the first time.

You were part of that third summer of three ways. I assumed while we three were together, that you were mine. That you were there because of me, and that for Scott, it was just another way of being with me.

But even then, I must have known. The following week, after watching Scott stare all day at a man two blankets over, I finally said to him, "Could we just go home and have sex. Just you and me." We did, and for two days it was like it had been that first summer: ultimate. For a while, we stopped making each other feel alone. Then I went back to Boston, and he went after you, and there was nothing for a very long time.

Later, he would tell me that you were a way of hurting me, that he saw how I desired you and wanted to take that, my desire even, and make it his own. He wanted to prove to me or to himself that he was good enough. Now, I look at you making plans to meet TJ later in the afternoon for a "drink," and I think, good enough for what?

We both watch TJ go, and I realize that it is not being wronged that has protected me all afternoon, but TJ's presence, like a padded glove cushioning the emotional blow of your fist in my gut. Suddenly, mouth dry, heart pounding, I look across the blanket gap where TJ used to be, and say, "I'm glad you came here. I'm glad you talked to me." I don't know why, but it's true. The emotional blow is more than just pain or anger.

You say, "You know that I didn't mean for it to happen."

I know that's true as well. You let it happen. Scott's the one who meant for it to happen. When he wants something, he gets it. I used to admire that about him. Then you tell me that he wanted a relationship with you. He flew out to see you in Chicago, and I think of him on that plane, doing the crossword in the in-flight magazine, sitting alone but imagining that he wouldn't have to be that way any more, the way I made him feel. At least you told him no.

You pause and, staring down at the pattern of your towel, say, "I'm sorry."

I sit with that for a while, like ice cream that you don't want to eat but you don't want to melt. Finally, I say, "He isn't." And then, when you don't respond, "I really hate him." You only nod.

Shortly later, you leave, chasing men back into dunes, and I cross over those dunes to the lake of a tidal pool that separates the beach from the roads and houses of Provincetown several hundred yards beyond. Part of me wishes you were still here, walking beside me, probably because our afternoon together seemed so pregnant with dramatic potential and I had the lead role as chief martyr. Partly because I liked you, liked talking to you.

The tide has started on its way out, and the water tugs at my legs below the knees, threatening to pull my feet from beneath me. Horseshoe crabs lose their tenuous hold to the sand and float with the tide, riding it like hang gliders. I am headed for the love canal, a break in the head-high reeds, just where the tidal pool is deepest, that winds and cleaves its way through the grasses back toward town. When I reach the entrance, the current, forced to travel in a narrower channel, is much stronger, and it beats against my chest and then against my thighs as I ascend an invisible sand hill below.

The course of the canal is serpentine, hair-pin curves and an ever narrowing path, and as I round each corner, I expect to see men coupled together, hands and mouths working overtime. I half expect to see you and wonder what would happen if I did. Would I join you like Scott must have, like I wanted to for so long? Would I feel better if I did? Instead, I see more rushing water, and floating crabs, and after one corner, a long black eel that swims across my path and mimics the shape of its larger geography. Along its backside a ribbon of a fin flutters rhythmically before the eel disappears into the reeds in front of my feet.

When those same reeds begin to touch my shoulders on either side and the canal has become more of a crack, I stop and turn around, facing the unseen dunes and beach beyond. A yellow bi-wing plane laden with tourists flies overhead, and its shadow momentarily darkens the green of the reeds before disappearing behind the dune.

The water now pushes at my back, urging me forward. I let it take me, and I do not fight or dive, but float along with the current head first, the rocks and algae zipping along beneath me, the path becoming wider again before me. At each curve, I bend my body to follow the water, imagining that I too have fins that guide me like sails. And it's so easy, this tumbling, this giving in to kinetic energy, this gentle, twisting float out to sea. It consumes me, and I think, This is all there is.

The love canal ends; its mouth opens to the larger, less defined tidal pool. In that pool, I stand sideways to the current, forcing a hole in its flow where the water must divide and curl around my front and back before rejoining itself. My back is to town, and before me, the one, single dune which defines Herring Cove Beach stretches left and right toward distant lighthouses. Men walk along the top, carrying backpacks, some with their towels wrapped around their waists like sarongs. Sand kicks up behind their feet and filters the late afternoon sunlight. The boys are heading back to town, to tea dances and cocktail parties. They will line up along the curb of Commercial Street waiting for tables at Gallerani's, or cluster in front of Spiritus eating pizza, cruising one another. They will walk the length of town seeing all the same paintings in all the same galleries and smiling at all the same people.

You are somewhere in that crowd, will be somewhere in town tonight, and I replay the day, hearing again and again your apology. I say now what I should have said then.

Thank you.

Counting Deer

KYLE MOX

It was the day before deer season. Through the passenger window of his father's rusted-out truck, Jacob watched the slide-show images click by as they left Carl's Grocery: a parking lot full of other rusted trucks, fading storefronts on Main Street, frame houses with browning lawns and small, cement porches. Scenes from a Midwestern autumn. Men in flannel shirts raking leaves, children in light jackets playing two-hand touch football in the street, grain trucks leaving the elevator, emptied for the last time of the year.

The old Ford felt as if it left the ground as it sped up over the viaduct that marked the northern border of Potterville. Jacob's father ground the gears and swore at the dashboard. A combine tractor trundled along on the road ahead of them, slowing traffic.

"Fuckin' great," his father said. Jacob felt a small creep of embarrassment at his father's profanity. He also felt a small surge of pride. Swearing was prohibited in front his mother and women in general. Swearing was one guilty pleasure the two of them could enjoy together as men.

"Wonder how long this will keep up," Jacob said. He had never uttered that sentence before, but it was the sort of idle thing he had heard men say down at his father's bar. It could be used in reference to rain, a losing team, a sliding economy, a bad song on the juke. Men preferred to use words that were like good trousers, broken-in and fit for any situation.

"That's one of Wright's," his father said. "They're probably going all the way to the damn county line."

The green monster chugged slowly ahead, nearly blocking out traffic in the oncoming lane as well. Jacob noticed dark clouds lurking at the horizon.

"Is it going to rain tomorrow?" Jacob asked.

"It always rains on opening day," his father said. Plaintive country music whispered in between their conversation. Jacob knew enough not to ask if they were going to stay home in the morning. Come hell or high water, they were going hunting. "Screw this," his father said. He gunned the engine and peeled off the blacktop onto a side road.

Little waves of chatterbumps shook the truck as it flew down the dirt road. Jacob assumed his father was just blowing off some frustration. The ice cream and hamburger thawing in the back probably weren't even on his mind. His father yanked down the overhead shade, pulled a Winston from a wrinkled pack, and plucked a lighter from a stack of folded receipts jammed between the dash and the window. The dashboard looked like a pile of trash, littered with pens, loose screws, scrawled notes, and instruction manuals, along with weeks of junk mail, but Jacob knew this dashboard served as his father's office. Somewhere in there hid the accounting book for the bar. His father steered with his knee as he cupped his hands to light the cigarette, never letting up on the gas. The truck rattled like an open box of hammers. The sun had lowered beneath the trees, and the air had taken on an amber glow.

"Where are we going?" Jacob asked. They were headed away from home.

"Up the road a bit," his father said. "I want to do some scouting."

Jacob groaned inwardly and turned back towards the window. He wanted to get home, eat dinner, and play guitar in his room. Scouting could mean another hour of driving around. It was bad enough they had to get up at the crack of dawn.

The truck slowed to a crawl. Ditch weeds drummed against the doors as they pulled to the side of the road.

"Look there," his father said. Through light branches of windbreak poplars, Jacob could see a small cluster of tawny forms on the far side of an empty field. Cornstalk whiskers stuck up through the dark soil. "Looks like about five, eight does."

His father turned off the radio, and they sat for slow minutes, watching the deer feed in the distance. Dusk began to fall around them, and small stars began to blink on in the gloom overhead. Jacob felt his pulse ebbing in his throat. Time ground to a halt.

After a small grunt, his father cut the headlights back on, put the truck in gear, and pulled away. Across the field, heads lifted from their grazing, and the deer bounded off into the woods.

About a mile later, his father stopped the truck on a short bridge. He reached down and pulled loose a small searchlight from the assortment of tools beneath the seat. He handed his son the cord. Jacob jammed the plug into the cigarette lighter.

With a tiny click, his father sent a beam of light like a column of ice out through the dusk into the soybean fields on either side of the creek. He swept the light slowly along the tree line, like cops Jacob had seen in old gangster movies searching for escaped prisoners.

"There!"

Jacob looked up. A tight cluster of luminous dots littered the faraway gloom, like lightning bugs frozen mid-flight. A few blinked off and back on.

"Must be twenty, thirty of 'em out there," his father said. He continued to hold the light on the herd. The herd continued to stare back at the light. "I figure you can sit out there on the ridge line late tomorrow, if you don't get a buck in the morning."

"Okay," Jacob said. His father clicked off the searchlight.

"But I've been scouting up at that crossover on Cady's farm, and there's been a load of tracks by there the last few days."

"Yeah, you told me," Jacob said.

"Don't worry, though," his father continued, "I'll be opposite corner from you, far enough back to watch you and take anything that crosses over the creek into the orchard." His father charged on with his battle plan. They had spent the last three weeks going step by step over Jacob's first hunt, and even though his father exuded all the confidence of General Patton, the boy could tell that his father was still worried.

"I think we'll go up to that other bridge on Milsap," his father said, "and see if there's any action."

"Dad," Jacob began.

"What? You in a hurry? You got a hot date?" He paused, as if expecting an answer. "Don't you want to get a buck tomorrow? I told you, it's all about preparation."

"We've got ice cream in the back. Mom's waiting for the meat."

Jacob knew he walked a tricky line with his father. He had to muster passable enthusiasm at appropriate times, but not too much, because his father often criticized too much visible excitement. It spooked the deer.

His father put the light back under the seat and drove off. He was obviously vexed at having to run errands on the night before deer season. Jacob couldn't figure out what the big deal was. Whether you got it on the first day or the last day, a dead deer was a dead deer.

"The only way to get a monster buck is to get him first thing," his father said. "I can't have you falling asleep out there, or daydreaming or anything. They spook after opening day. You got to be on top of it."

"Will do," Jacob said. His father turned down several more roads, zigzagging home, following a route that led by his various hunting spots. As they finally turned down their own road, Jacob could feel his guitar in his hands. He'd been working on some songs from the new Metallica album, trying to get the solos up to speed. His fingers flitted on his thigh, his right hand strummed the door handle. About two miles from home, his father turned the truck onto a tractor path hidden between the roadside trees.

"We've got time for one more," he said. The truck bumped down the path like a rusty mechanical bull, springs squeaking in protest. His father scanned the tree lines with the searchlight. Nothing.

"Well, I guess they're all resting up for tomorrow," he said. He turned off the light and made an awkward three-point turn, churning mud up the sides of the truck. Once they had reversed direction, Jacob's father paused to light another Winston.

"Dad," Jacob said. "Can I drive home?"

His father put the shifter in neutral and sucked at his cigarette.

Jacob knew he was pushing his luck here. "You know, I'm taking driver's ed this summer, and like you always say, it's all about preparation."

"Is that so?" Jacob knew his father hated falling into his own traps.

"Yeah."

"Well," his father said. He let the seconds tick by. "Let's get a jump on it. C'mon." As his father got out and circled the nose of the truck, Jacob slid over behind the wheel.

As they lurched forward, Jacob could feel the truck shaking beneath him like a living thing, the wheel sliding and vibrating in his hand. The hood dipped and thrust up like a ship in a storm.

"Easy, son," his father said. "Take it slow. This is rough ground." With one last thrust of power, the beast leapt from the mud-filled rut and out onto the road. "Turn, dammit, turn!"

Jacob jumped on the brake with both feet and cranked the wheel to avoid charging into the opposite ditch. The truck spun gravel as it skidded, shivered, and stalled. Both men let out a heavy breath.

"Sorry, Dad." Jacob waited for the hammer to fall.

His father let out a stream of smoke. Improbably, he laughed. "You just got excited, that's all. It's understandable, with such a fine piece of machinery here."

Jacob had to laugh.

"Start it up and take us home," his father said.

Jacob pressed the clutch and turned the ignition, and the engine rolled back to life. He held the truck at a steady twenty, afraid to shift gears, and kept his eyes glued to the dirt directly in front of the truck. Moths danced in the headlights.

"Dad?"

"What?"

"Can I change the radio?" This request was unprecedented. Jacob knew he probably had a better shot of bumming a cigarette. A man's radio was a sacred thing. Then again, so was his truck. Out of the corner of his eye, Jacob saw his father turn, slightly, as if in shock. Just as quickly, his posture relaxed.

"You're the driver," his father said.

Jacob tore his eyes from the road to steal a glance at his father, who just lit another cigarette, as if this were any other day. Jacob reached out with one careful hand and turned the knob. He felt his way through squeals and static until he heard heavy guitar.

In a moment of audacity, he even turned up the volume. After a three-count, his father turned it back down.

"I bet you can't wait, huh? Out cruising around with your buddies, blaring this crap loud enough to make your ears bleed, drag racing, shotgunning six-packs, jumping tracks."

"I haven't thought about it much," Jacob lied.

"My ass," his father said. "I'll tell you this, though: it'll be a cold day in hell before you take my truck out. I can good-God-damn-guarantee you that."

It'll be a cold day in hell before I'm caught dead in this truck, Jacob thought. The Ford was more rust than body; Jacob called it "Diarrhea" behind his father's back. It smelled like old smoke and used-up motor oil.

Jacob reached out to the stick shift and ground it into third gear. The speedometer crept up to thirty-five. Time sped up. Trees blurred by on either side. The wheel shivered in his hands as they flew over ridges of chatterbumps. Yes, Jacob could see himself blaring his music and drag racing through town. Except he would have a real car, something low and mean, with bright wheels and a dual exhaust. He would wax it every Saturday, and there would be no smoking or eating in the car. It would be his new home. On those wheels, time would fly by even faster, and before Jacob knew it, he would turn onto the highway and not let off the gas until he got to Chicago. Or St. Louis. Or New Orleans. Three shirts, two pairs of jeans, and his Fender. He'd never spend another spring picking rocks after the tiller, another summer washing out the coolers in the bar, another year chained to a school desk while life clicked by through the window.

"You've got the hang of this, son," his father said.

Jacob grinned in the dark. He knew he didn't feel like hunting tomorrow, but he also knew it was important to the old man. It seemed a small sacrifice to make, if the bastard was happy for one day out of the year. They had moments like this, at least. Jacob looked down. The needle crept towards forty-five, and the engine whined, running too hard in third gear.

"Careful, Jacob," his father said. "You're going too fast."

A tawny blur reflecting light in a dark eye. A loud slap like a board on water. A gut-thumping impact. The engine shivered and died.

Jacob stood in the road, looking down at the doe as she slowly writhed in the dirt. Her branch-like legs twisted in impossible directions, and blood pooled from her muzzle.

"Goddammit!"

The doe's body rose and fell in heavy gasps. Small specks of dirt stuck to her wet, black eye.

"Look at this!" his father shouted.

Jacob felt frozen in place, unwilling to look at the deer as she died but unable to turn away. The doe gasped wetly.

"Jake, you wrecked this bumper, but good," his father said.

Jacob turned slowly towards the truck. The left headlight had gone dark, and a small dent wrinkled the corner panel of the truck. Tufts of hair stuck in the grill. "I'm . . . sorry." Jacob wasn't sure what he was apologizing for. His legs began to quiver just above his knees.

His father ran his hand over his head, dislodging strands of thinning hair. He let out a long breath. "It's okay," he said. "It's okay, son. You couldn't help it."

Jacob clenched his fists to stop them from shaking.

"You couldn't help it," his father repeated. "You have to be careful out here. Not so fast. Be alert."

"I'm sorry, Dad, I . . ." Jacob turned back to the doe. Her twisted legs quivered, scratching quietly in the gravel. Blood continued to drip from her mouth and nose. "Dad, we can't just leave her here."

"Son, it's just a little doe, not even worth our trouble. Probably not even seventy pounds."

"But she's still alive," Jacob said. He heard his father's boot swivel in the gravel.

"Won't be for long," his father said. "Here, give me a hand." He reached down and grabbed one of the doe's legs. Jacob stood mute. "Come on, boy."

Jacob reached down and grasped a leg. The doe's fur was moist, and pieces of gravel dug into Jacob's palm. He could feel the warmth of her blood beneath her skin. Jacob had never touched a live deer before.

They dragged the doe to the edge of the road, halfway into the weeds. When Jacob let go of her leg, she released a small gasp.

"Good enough," his father said. "Let's go."

Jacob crossed in front of the truck, his shadow blurring over the body. He felt pressure in the corners of his eyes, bit his lip, tried to hold it together. He climbed into the truck, and his father took off before he could even shut the door.

A piercing guitar solo cried over a heavy backbeat.

His father turned off the radio.

"Dad, please," Jacob said.

"I'm tired of that shit."

"No, the deer. We have to do something." Jacob tried to keep his voice flat. Men did not beg. Men did not plead.

"What do you want to do, Jacob, take it to the vet? You going to bring it home, keep it in your room?"

"We should put it down," Jacob said. He had never uttered that sentence before, but it was the sort of resolute thing he had heard in old Western movies and war stories. "We need to put it out of its misery."

"Your heart's in the right place, son, but I wouldn't worry about it," his father said. "It's already dead, and if not, it will be before we can get back"

Jacob knew different. He had seen the look in the doe's eye. She could see him, smell him, but she was trapped in a broken cage of a body. Time had stopped for her.

The ghost-shadows of trees blurred by as Jacob chewed his lip, fighting down his tears with pain. His father smoked in silence. Their mailbox approached in the glare of the crippled headlights.

A lurking sense of doom crept at the edge of Jacob's mind, a premonition that some horrible event would soon take place. He had felt this velvet fear many times before, lying in bed, listening to the far-off trains rolling through town like a phantom herd of buffalo. At those moments, lying between waking and dreaming, Jacob felt the ceiling press down on him, felt his body grow and shrink, the room expand to an infinite plain of darkness. Jacob felt cold and lonely at those times, as if he were on the surface of the moon. But it had always been his secret, and it always happened when he was alone. He had no name for it, but this old sense of dread licked at him now, more powerful than it had ever been.

Jacob felt like he was standing at the edge of something very high, above something far away and unseen.

The truck eased into the driveway, and the engine knocked several times before falling quiet. Jacob shivered in his seat. His father got out and pulled the groceries from the bed. As he stepped up to the front door, he looked back at Jacob. His father held a quizzical expression that bordered on concern. Jacob opened the door and got out of the truck on shaky feet.

Inside, the TV laughed in the living room, and his mother's cooking filled the house with warm, moist air. His father kicked off his dirty boots while holding the groceries out to each side.

"Where've you boys been?" his mother asked. She stood in the kitchen doorway, hands on her hips, affecting a mock-serious scowl. She knew full well where they had been. It was the day before deer season.

"Here you are," his father said. He handed off the groceries and headed into the kitchen.

"Why, thank you, Joe," his mother said. "What's that? No thank you, I can put these up myself." She shot Jacob a sly wink.

Jacob stood, rooted in the doorway. Now that he was safe at home, he felt better, but still blank.

"What's wrong, Jacob?"

"We hit a deer."

His mother dropped the groceries on the counter and rushed up to him. "Oh my god," she said. "Are you okay?"

"I guess so," Jacob said. His mother pulled him tightly towards her and rubbed the back of his head. Jacob noticed, anew, that he was taller than she was. He pulled away from her embrace. Confusion crossed her face, quickly, like a hawk's shadow. She let him go and turned back to the kitchen. Jacob followed without taking off his boots. In the kitchen, his father foraged in the refrigerator.

"Joe, are you okay?" his mother asked.

His father stood up with a can of beer in his hand. "I'm fine," he said. "Why?"

"Jacob said you hit a deer on the way home."

Jacob's father shot a quick look at him over his mother's shoulder. Men did not confess to women. "It was just a little doe. No bigger than a dog. The truck's fine." He cracked the beer and took an audible slurp.

"My god, where was it?"

"Up the road about three miles."

His mother seemed satisfied in her investigation. His father turned to leave.

"Dad," Jacob said. "Can we go back?"

His father turned. A pot bubbled on the stove, filling the kitchen with the rich smell of oregano and cooking tomatoes. His mother banged a frying pan down on the range and pulled the plastic wrap from the hamburger.

"Why?"

"She wasn't dead," Jacob said. Doom crept just out of sight. Jacob knew they must make amends.

"It's dead by now. Trust me."

Again came a moment Jacob had seen in a Western movie: two men facing each other, unblinking, waiting for the other to move. His mother stirred her sauce slowly, watching them without looking up.

"All right, hotshot," his father said. "You don't trust your old man? Let's do this before you start crying about it. Get your goddamn gun."

His mother slammed down her spoon. "Joseph! Don't you talk like that to your son, not in this house."

His father banged his beer can down in retort. "I'm sorry; we're leaving." He walked back towards the front door. "We're going to look at a dead deer for a while, and then, maybe, just maybe, we can actually sit down to eat."

* * *

In the truck, Jacob's father handed the rifle across the seat to Jacob, who put it between his legs. His father put the bolt in his vest pocket and handed Jacob a single six-millimeter shell. Neither of them felt the need to explain their actions. The extracted bolt was for safety. The single shell would support their supposed intent.

"If we get stopped for poaching, I'm going to let them throw the book at you," his father said. "Never mind it's illegal to discharge a firearm on a public road."

The trip slipped along in silence. When they reached the spot, his father stopped the truck. Jacob looked at his father, trying to show resolve while hiding his fear and anger. He stepped down as his father cut the engine.

The doe was gone.

This was the place—Jacob could see the truck's skid marks. He bent down, easing his weight on the rifle. A small patch of blood had congealed into mud. There were no other marks in the dirt.

"She's gone," Jacob said.

"I see that," his father said.

Jacob knew she couldn't have run off. He had seen her broken legs pawing the air like a beetle on its back. Her chest had heaved painfully, her ribcage likely crushed. But yet, the doe was gone.

"Impossible," Jacob said.

"Coyotes or dogs, maybe dragged her into the brush. Or someone probably took her," his father said. "Rednecks, trash, goat people. They'll eat road kill."

"But . . ." Jacob couldn't argue with what he saw. The shell grew hot in his palm. A firm push of wind bent the trees on either side of them, rustling the last few dead leaves of autumn. Heavy drops of rain began to slowly beat the dusty ground and rapped on the truck.

"Well, that's that," his father said.

Jacob felt a surge of anger in his chest, and his tongue tasted of metal. He knew his father was responsible for this, somehow. Jacob was trying to set things right, but the old man wouldn't let him. Jacob felt coiled and tight as he crouched in the dirt.

"Don't worry, son," his father said. "You'll get yours tomorrow. A monster buck, not some piddley-ass doe." He pulled the rifle from his son's hand.

Jacob surged to his feet. His hands felt heavy and sharp, his face hot. "Why? Why do you care so much?" Jacob jabbed with his finger. "Who gives a shit? You don't need to kill them. And you don't have to enjoy it so fucking much."

His father's hand shot out like a snake and cracked Jacob across the cheek.

"Remember who you're talking to, boy."

Jacob's hand went up to his face. His father glared, ready for action.

"You're stupid," Jacob went on. His hand sliced the air. "Stupid, and ignorant, and..."

Jacob lost control of his words and began to cry.

* * *

They did not speak on the ride home, or at all for the rest of the night. His father just picked up his beer from where he had left it on the counter and went to watch TV, tracking mud across the carpet. Jacob's mother knew enough to let his carelessness go. The house filled with quiet electricity, as if the thunderclouds outside had settled in the attic.

Jacob felt as if he had stepped through a door that had locked behind him. He avoided the dinner table and went to his room to play guitar. The music wouldn't come. His fingers felt dead, and the notes whined horribly in his headphones. He raged on the strings, shredding his pick. Jacob wanted to crank the amp as loud as it would go and blare a wall of senseless noise. He would battle the thunder, scare the doom away, frighten his world back into place.

But if he did, Jacob knew the guitar would be gone by morning, and he would never play in the house again. He shut off the amp and threw the guitar on his bed. Rain drummed on the roof, keeping cold silence away like a warm blanket. Jacob lay down on his bed next to his guitar and fell asleep.

* * *

Hours later, he awoke to his mother's voice. She had been stroking his forehead.

"Jacob?"

Jacob pretended to sleep.

"I don't know what happened out there, but I'm sure it'll be okay by tomorrow." She started humming quietly and kept stroking his forehead. The rain had settled into a steady pattern on the roof. "I know you're upset with him," she said. "You're just too much alike, I think."

"Never," Jacob said. He rolled onto his side, away from his mother. She reached out to rub his back lightly. After a few moments, she began singing to him, as she had when he was a young boy.

I see the moon, the moon sees me,

Jacob felt himself drifting back into sleep, back into time. On those nights when his dark fears kept him awake, his mother had always appeared in his doorway. He had never cried out, but somehow, she knew. His mother would sit with him, as she did now, stroking his hair, singing away those invisible fears.

down through the leaves of the old oak tree,

Jacob had thought he could fight back his dread by making right his wrongs. But still, something pressed down on him, like deep water, and he couldn't push it aside. It wasn't just the doe—he knew that.

please let the light that shines on me,

Jacob could not bargain with his fear, could not reason with it. Here, at home with his mother singing to him, he knew he could not atone for his sins or even the scales. The dark thing in Jacob's mind moved about as it pleased and took what it would. It gobbled up innocent children and laughed at the righteous, walked with both the wicked and the good. It slept with the mother and the child and hid in a corner of the woods. It lurked on the other side of the door. Jacob knew it was there, and he waited.

shine on the one I love.

A July Story

K.L. OWENS

Iron red, linseed-cured, and caked in salt, in a place where the mercury never crept much above fifty Fahrenheit, the two-room house chose to keep its back to the sea. A wise choice, given the facing of the windows and the predilections of the wind. Still, in other Julys, Kitten had stood naked between ancient trees or buried his toes in sun-warm sand. In this new July, he donned the buckskin jacket from the peg by the door, used wool socks for gloves, and swaddled his head in a gaily-patterned scarf given to him by a gray-haired marm in some other July on some other island. Shivering on a shore made of black cobblestones--waves did not break, but clattered and rumbled--Kitten watched a bazaar of common murres bob on the wind and wondered which side of what ocean the house had selected this time.

The sky grew orange, pinkish blue, then muted violet and freckled with stars while Kitten enjoyed being outside. His nose was numb, his eyes watered small icicles whipped up by the wind, and his stomach gurgled, but Kitten kept his back to the house just as the house kept its back to the sea. How long had it been this time? Was there a town nearby? Would they have good things to eat?

Kitten dug a socked hand beneath his scarf, shoving at the coarse licks of hair that itched his neck. He'd yet to see a mirror. He removed one sock and blew on his fingers to keep them warm, dug under the scarf again, yanked. The hair could just be seen in the fading light. Gray now, perhaps even white, but still black near the tip. The wind snatched the hair from his fingers. Kitten didn't watch it go. There never had been, never would be, anyone to care about his hair, and besides, had nature been allowed its usual way with him, Kitten's hair would be like spider silk, lining the bottom of a pine box.

Gray hair led to golden hair, green eyes, and Kitten found himself thinking about Angelica Wilson, the young schoolteacher he'd fancied in his youth. Angelica was kind to Kitten on his fifteenth birthday, his last day in the world. She'd lent him the few coins he needed to purchase the bestiary he'd been eyeing on the bookseller's cart, and she'd given his baby sister, Mousie, a sweet. The bestiary was like the scarf: one of the few items the house had let him keep. Kitten suspected it had something to do with their being gifts.

Kitten glanced back at the house. Angelica Wilson would be dead now. Like Mousie. Like Mum and Father and the mates who, on the afternoon of his fifteenth birthday, dared him to go inside the strange red house. For the first few decades, Kitten liked to imagine that Angelica had married one of his mates, that Mousie found herself an upstanding young man and bore children of her own. He would pretend a child he passed in a July street was his nephew or niece. But these stories grew cold as a century turned and time marched on without him. Everyone Kitten once loved was dead. He should be, too.

Facing the sea once more, he spoke aloud. "My name is Kitten Blankenship." The wind would hear his usual prayer. "My parents were Margaret Hudson and Roger Blankenship, and I had a sister, Marcella. I was born in Yorkshire in 1853. And I would like to be free of the house now, please."

The bazaar of murres rose as one body at the echo of his voice and made, bleating, for a rock formation that rose from the sea. Their departure drew Kitten's eye to distant electric lights. From their sparseness and height, he picked out the perimeter of a small town. Kitten smiled but remained sitting on the cobblestone beach. A waning half-moon sagged low on the horizon, and he'd found a hollow in the rock face, its entrance swollen with small bones and matted fur. He didn't like to venture into the towns on his first night out of the house. Better to marvel at the natural world in a new place, enjoying his discoveries and regretting all he'd never been allowed to learn. The bones and fur, for instance. Kitten couldn't even say what they probably were; he didn't know where he was or what lived there, what sorts of animals nested in rock hollows on stony beaches. The bestiary might tell him but probably not. Kitten was sixteen or seventeen when he learned to tell stories to himself.

Hunger drove him back to the house. Some Julys, he slept outside. Even if no better shelter were available and he had to huddle against the house's oxide-colored walls, he'd never forsaken the mercy of a July. Not this time, though. This new place too cold, its wind too harsh and its town too far, so Kitten grudgingly pulled open the door that scraped loud on dry grass and reentered his prison.

On the table: a loaf of sweet bread, its crust steaming in the chill, an apple with reddening green skin, a smallish hunk of orangish cheese, a pot of hot water with lemon, and none of it there when he'd stepped outside. A July news bill told him the year was 1912 before Kitten stopped trying to catch the house in the act of providing his food. And 1946, a radio said, before he accepted the house was smarter than he was. Food simply appeared, three squares, when he had his back turned. The fare was never complex, but what Kitten appreciated more was the secret of its appearance that the house kept from him. He didn't want to see a hallway extend from a wall gone soft as clay, couldn't stomach the thought of the house reaching into other empty spaces to steal for him.

More often than not, Kitten dreamed of meat. A roast Cornish hen dripping in juice, sizzling belly of pork, a fat slice of ham. In his meat dreams, there was tea, too, and butter and jam for the bread, tall tin tumblers of fresh milk, lemony crumpets with a bit of clotted cream, peppermint sticks. Tonight's humble meal, he pretended was a fast for July Eve. Tomorrow, he would go into the town. He would learn the year, see what new marvels the passage of time had wrought, and find the good food. He would gorge himself on it, carry it in baskets wherever he went, and never share a morsel of it with the house.

The socks limited his dexterity, and Kitten's hands grew numb while he ate. Finished, he rose and stood before the lone small cabinet by the window. Shivering, with his hands tucked in his armpits, he said, "Gloves," then counted to ten, and opened the cabinet. Only the sewing kit there on the shelf. Only ever the sewing kit, full of needles and thimbles, but lacking thread. The expectant smile he'd worn since the house touched down, the front door opened, and he knew it was July, faded from Kitten's face. He could feel the knot in his throat. It made him sound like he was whimpering when he said, "Please? I'm cold."

The door to the second room, the hated room, the one that could expand and contract, reach through space and push beyond time, creaked open, then swung itself shut again. In the cabinet, the sewing kit skittered.

"No," Kitten moaned. "It's July. Please?"

The eldritch door opened and slammed, opened and slammed while Kitten squeezed shut his eyes and wrapped his arms about his head. Sometimes the house got angry with him, and it would tilt on its unnatural axis, befriending gravity to send him sprawling through the door. There, in the house's warped second room, roamed all of Kitten's lost time. All the months and years he should have aged but didn't, so long as he spent them wandering through the house's unmeasurable, self-contained maze. It was July, though, and Kitten had been let outside. The door shut itself once more, made a sound like the clicking of a lock, and when Kitten opened his eyes, a blanket rested on the back of the table's only chair, and the wood-burning stove crackled to life.

Kitten sniffled and wormed the socks back over his hands, readjusted his head scarf, wrapped the blanket around his shoulders, and settled down with his bestiary in front of the stove. Hours later, when the moon's light grayed the barren front room, a muffled sound drew Kitten back from the edges of sleep. He squinted at the new shadow beside the door. When he made it out, he sighed.

"Bicycle," he said. "Thank you."

* * *

Tucked into the basket on the bicycle were fleece-lined gloves and a wad of ten-dollar bills. The house provided. Its reach extended beyond closed doors and down long hallways, into empty rooms, abandoned atriums, and untrod stairwells. It connected to all forgotten and vacant places, into sealed-up voids and architectural blanks. The second room with its closed door was in perpetual communion with all the world's closed doors so that its pets might never escape. Kitten, like others before him and more sure to come, attempted, in his younger Julys, to leave the house behind. To run, hitchhike, beg clemency, seek asylum in a new city, a new building somewhere far from where the house touched down. All of them, the house's pets, hundreds of miles and weeks away, thinking themselves free, had once opened a closed door, crossed the threshold, and found themselves back inside the house.

Call it a cuckoo building. A spat-up space. Its learning curve was slow, recursive. It knew not what it did, only what it needed. A damned, demanding thing. Like a child. It killed its first pet, not out of malice, but for lack of knowing when its pet needed feeding. First a starving pet, moaning low, then a rotting pet, full of stink. So the house chose to return to its first pet's home, to use its hidden geometries to slip the bones through unoccupied walls. It put its pet back where it found him. Like a child.

Learning to mistrust doors, other pets ran away, not to other places, but to other sides, determining death preferable to the house's love. The house hurt but did not know how it came to hurt. It knew that it was broken, that some part of it was torn, ripped from its moorings and made sick inside. It could not form ideas; its communication was nonverbal, crudely symbolic, like a child's. It shook the sewing kit at its pets, but they did not know what to do.

The pets railed and left, came back and left again, came back and killed themselves. The house hurt. It kept them alive well past their times, its brokenness wronging them, too, from the inside out. It waited for one to come who could mend the tear, who knew the proper use of needle and thread.

Kitten stayed. He was the oldest. He no longer tried to leave. He paled when the sewing kit appeared, screamed at the walls and wept. *I don't know what you want me to do*, he said. *Tell me what to do, and I'll do it.* The house heard him, wished it knew. Kitten would do it, the house knew, if he could. He would mend the tear, sew them both up, house and pet, seal them up safe and together forever, the house and its Kitten.

* * *

Highway 101 graced the coastal Oregon town for two and a half miles before hair-pinning back along a picturesque but desolate shore. The people there prided themselves on their cows, and Kitten had his fill of cheese and burgers, ice cream and taffy and smoked jerky. He fished pale shells and marbleized rocks from the waves, explored junk shops, rented a kite from a beach shack and spent an afternoon flying it, huddled in the town's small library, filling his mind and his eyes with history he'd never lived. He learned that the century had turned again, not just a century, but a millennium this time, and Kitten thought that this must make him unique among men, but there was no one to tell, none who would believe.

Sometime in the town's past, a train ran through it. When the train stopped running, the town planted a caboose at the dead line-switch. The day Kitten discovered he was experiencing a new millennium, he took to pacing the rusting tracks until, five paces from the caboose, he saw a tie catch the light, and he knelt to look. Keys, a few dozen of them, from tiny gold ones meant for padlocks to thick silver ones made for deadbolts, were nailed to that tie and that tie only, and Kitten crouched low, finally sitting on the ground to run his fingers over the keys and wonder a new wonder.

"You know what they're there for?"

Kitten looked up into the face of a young girl. She had long, black hair, like Mousie's. Kitten had seen her more often than anyone else in the town; he suspected she was the daughter of one of the waitresses at the town's breakfast diner.

"You've been following me, haven't you?" he asked.

The little girl shrugged. "Maybe. You want to know about those keys, though?"

Kitten nodded. The girl smiled, plopped down beside him in the dirt, put both small hands on the tie as though she could touch all of the keys at once if she tried hard enough.

"I think they're very beautiful," she said. "All the colors and shapes and the different ways people nail them." She looked up to see if Kitten shared her feelings on this matter and, apparently not finding what she sought in his expression, lifted one skinny shoulder. "Anyway," she went on, "my mom says people treat these old train tracks like a wishing well, but opposite-like. These keys, they're for locks that people can't open. To places they've lost or can't go back to or that aren't there anymore. So they nail the keys here so the places won't be forgotten."

Kitten wished he had a key. He hadn't taken a key to the house in Yorkshire with him that day. He'd only meant to be gone with his mates for an afternoon, meant to go home to his birthday dinner before the sun set, and he thought how out of place his old key would look next to all of these modern ones. He exhaled, slow and shuddery, and said, "That's pretty."

"Pretty sad," the girl said. "I'm Lana. And yeah, I've been following you. I follow all the travelers. Not much happens here except new people coming and going." She seemed to have lost interest in the keys, having instead pulled a wad of mismatched yarn and string from her pocket, and she sat, trying to untangle the hopeless knot. She didn't look up from this project when she asked for Kitten's name, but when he replied, she dropped the pile of threads in her lap. "A boy named Kitten? You aren't BSing me, are you?"

"I don't know what BSing means."

"It means,"—Lana leaned in close, whispering—"bullshitting." She giggled, but Kitten still looked confused, so she rolled her eyes and said, "It means I think you're making things up. Where are you from, anyway?"

"A long way away," Kitten said.

"Like how far?"

"Like England," Kitten said, surprised at himself for mimicking her speech. But she reminded him so much of Mousie, it felt like playing one of their old games.

"Oh," Lana said, drawing out the word. "I get it. We talked about England in social studies last year. Mrs. Mullen said you still speak English there, but it's sort of a different type of English from here." She nodded, satisfied with her own explanation. "Where're you staying?"

"Outside of town," Kitten said, gesturing vaguely in the direction of where the house had come down. He didn't like thinking about the house while talking to Lana. "On the beach."

"In a motel?" Lana asked. "Or like camping?"

"Like camping."

Lana wrinkled her nose. "My mom took me camping once. I hated it. There weren't toilets, and I couldn't shower. Do you get to shower at your campsite? You smell like you get to shower. You're not one of those weird people who refuse to have jobs and jump trains and camp all the time because of politics, are you, Mr. Kitten?"

"I …" Kitten cocked his head, tried to figure out what the girl meant, but couldn't. He'd have to see if the library had any books on such subjects. It was embarrassing to know less about the world than a young girl, so he gave her a mischievous grin and said, "Well, what do you think?"

She crossed her arms, looked him up and down, left and right, then shook her head. "No," she decided. "You're not a weirdo. Even if you are camping on the beach, and your clothes are funny."

"Funny how?" Kitten asked.

"Old funny."

"I'm an old man."

"How old?"

"Would you believe me if I said I'm a hundred and sixty?"

"No!" Lana laughed. "How could you be that old and not be dead?"

"Maybe I should be dead," Kitten said, and he looked down at the keys. They caught the light, reflected it, dazzled his eyes, and before he could stop himself, he said, "Maybe I have a secret house with hidden rooms and endless hallways, and when I get lost inside it, time stops passing for me. Maybe I'm trapped there, and I only get to come out for one month every couple of years, and when I go back, the house erases my years. Maybe that's what's happened to me."

The sound of Lana's laughter broke the keys' spell, and Kitten's eyes got wide with the realization of what he'd said. A thing he'd never said to another, but even as Lana mocked him, he couldn't deny that telling someone, speaking it aloud, had felt good.

"Okay, *now* you're BSing me," Lana said. "You're funny, Mr. Kitten. I like that."

Something very close to them made a musical, chirping sound, and Lana pulled a flat, black phone from her pocket, poked it and frowned at it, then announced she had to go. She mounted the blue bicycle she'd left leaning against the side of the caboose and rode away, pink streamers fluttering from her handlebars.

Kitten remained on the tracks, feeling the cool shapes of the keys, thinking about what Lana had said about them, feeling clean and light from his confession.

* * *

Lana cropped up again and again. When Kitten least expected her, she'd slide into his booth at the Cow Belle Café and steal his fried potatoes, or flop down into the seat next to him at the library's long table and ask what he was reading, or find him on the beach and start skipping stones if the sea was still or drawing in the sand with a stick if the waves were high. She asked him questions about himself, sometimes, but mostly she talked to him about her own life. About the boys and girls at her school and who liked who and how nobody liked her, not like that. About her mom and her mom's new boyfriend, who drove a big Mack truck and smelled all the time of beer and cigars. About video games and the Internet and how her mom wouldn't let her use certain sites. She used Kitten to rehearse her arguments about why she should be allowed to wear makeup (Susie Dilligner did) or shave her legs (the swim team girls did) or have her own Facebook account (she was going to be in middle school this year, after all, and did her mom want her to be unpopular forever?).

And Kitten listened, asked questions in return, offered what little advice he had to give, and imagined that Lana was a new millennium's Mousie. He told Lana about Mousie and about how his mum had given five babies back to God before his surviving sister was born. About how her name was Marcella, but she was Mum's Miracle, and if he was Kitten, then she was his Mousie. When Lana asked, instead of his story about Mousie marrying one of his mates, he told Lana the truth: that he'd sent Mousie back home from the market on his fifteenth birthday and gone to meet up with his mates, and he entered the house on a dare. And he never saw Mousie or Mum or Father again. And when Lana's phone summoned her home and Kitten went back to the iron-red house, he thought about all of the Julys he'd passed alone, wondering if he could call Lana his friend.

A column of names, places, and objects decorated the inside of the house's front door. Kitten started it in the beginning of his tenure in the house, when he hadn't an inkling of how or why he was there or what would happen to him the longer he stayed. It was his list of remembrances and desires, started with 'Mum and Father and Mousie,' followed by 'Angelica Wilson' and the names of his mates. It got vaguer from there on out. It included things like 'mutton' and 'my good shoes' and 'a real bed.' In more practical moments, he'd included the dates from the two times the whole world had gone to war and a sort of genealogical tree he updated every time he learned about a new member of the royal family. The notation 'John the dog' helped him recall a shaggy, gray puppy that had followed him through a 1970s July. The hound bayed piteously when the house made its departure; Kitten wept at the decision to leave John in the world. If he hadn't, maybe he'd still have a dog-friend, maybe he wouldn't need the passing fancy of a little girl.

Nonetheless, one day he gave Lana two dollars and asked her to buy him a permanent black marker from the drugstore. She asked why he wouldn't do it himself, and he told her that the house wouldn't let him keep anything that wasn't a gift. She said she didn't believe it but came out with the marker tied up in a red ribbon. To the painted, carved, and penciled-in list, he used the marker to add the name 'Lana.'

One day, Kitten didn't go into town. He talked aloud, telling himself lies about wanting to explore the parts of the coast people didn't inhabit, to see the animals and contemplate the black waves of the sea and its cobblestones. The truth gnawed at him. July was winding down, a week left at best, and he needed to distance himself from Lana. She occupied his thoughts when he returned to huddle by the woodstove at night. He'd recall games and jokes he'd shared with Mousie and wonder whether Lana would like them or if they were too old. He'd flip the pages of his bestiary in the slim stove light, looking for neat tidbits to share with her. And though he wasn't ungrateful, he wondered if it had been a mistake to make a friend. One hundred and fifty years he'd missed his family, his friends, and the time made the missing fade. He hadn't had to miss anyone new and suspected it would hurt all over again, like he'd never missed anyone before, because already it hurt to think about how, once the house left, he wouldn't get to see Lana again. The house hadn't chosen the same place twice, not since Kitten had been with it, but even if it picked this part of Oregon again, another century might have passed, and Lana would be dead, the railroad tie rotten, its keys sunk into hard-packed gray earth.

Kitten didn't go to town the next day, either. He rode his bicycle in the opposite direction instead and delighted in finding the factory the people had built for their cows. He spent the day going on the guided tours, learning about the making of cheese and ice cream and watching the cattle grazing in a pen so huge, Kitten felt he'd traded seas of water for seas of beef. He tasted free samples of ten different kinds of cheese, tiny spoonfuls of thirty-six flavors of ice cream, sampled snippets of jerky, and watched children crank a machine that left smiling cow faces stamped into their pennies. With a bloated belly and a smile on his face, Kitten rode back to the house, where a pink bicycle streamer fluttered in the grass by the front door.

By the time he found Lana, pouting over a cup of hot cocoa in the Cow Belle Café, the cold on Kitten's skin seemed like a side effect of the cold in his belly. He didn't know what to say. He didn't want to admit to the house that he'd told Lana the truth about it, so he ordered a cup of coffee and sat across from her, enduring her scowls, waiting for them to turn into words. Lana's silence continued until Kitten suggested they go sit on the boardwalk across the street. There, Lana admitted she thought Kitten had left without telling her goodbye, so she biked along the beach, looking for his camp. She demanded an explanation for his two-day absence, and when Kitten said he'd only wanted to see what was in the other direction, Lana sneered and said it was only the Tillamook factory, that she'd been on a field trip there every year she'd been in school, and she never wanted to eat another piece of cheese in her life (a statement she undermined the next day when she helped herself to half of Kitten's grilled cheese sandwich). She also admitted to finding the house, which had never been there before, and she wanted an explanation for its appearance. She refused to believe it wasn't his, an edge in her voice when she recounted his tale of a moving, mysterious building capable of swallowing time and life. But Kitten couldn't humor her. He kept seeing the pink streamer from her bike curling in the grass and getting a feeling like he was sweating inside when he thought about her pushing at the door or standing on tip-toe to peer in a window. He pointed to a jagged rock formation.

"Look, Lana," he said. "Look at all the murres."

Squinting at the ocean, Lana nodded. "Did you know that a group of murres is called a fragrance?" she asked. "I know you like words and information and stuff."

"A fragrance? My bestiary says they're called a bazaar," he said. "A fragrance. Like the fragrance of myrrh. I like that. I think I like that one better. I'm going to miss you, Lana."

"You are leaving, then."

"Soon," Kitten said.

"How soon?"

"Soon."

"And will the house go with you?" she asked. "If I go back there, after you're gone, that house'll be gone, too, won't it? You weren't lying to me or making up stories. I felt it, when I was there. This strange feeling. The same feeling I got the first time I saw you. I didn't go in. Just so you know."

"Don't," Kitten said. "Don't you ever go in. Promise me, Lana. Promise me you won't ever go into a strange house by yourself."

But Lana didn't promise. Wouldn't promise, talked instead until the sun slipped low in the sky. She pulled her wad of yarn and string from her pocket and picked at it while she talked about wanting to leave Rockaway, Oregon. How she thought she never would, and how her mom didn't seem to care, and how Kitten had become a better friend in a few weeks than anyone she'd known in her whole life. Kitten patted Lana's back and stroked her black hair while she sniffled a young girl's sniffles and despaired of her future. He told her she'd leave Rockaway one day, that she just had to be patient, and she'd grow up strong and smart and beautiful, move away to a big city, and live a brilliant, exciting life. But Lana only bit her lip and thanked him for trying. When her phone chirped, she got on her bicycle and rode off without saying goodbye.

The sewing kit scrabbled at the walls of the cabinet throughout the night, flinging itself at the cabinet door, keeping Kitten awake. He got up, once, opened the cabinet, removed the kit, walked it through the crisp night air to the overhang, used all of his might to throw it into the Pacific, and waited for a splash he'd never hear above the waves. By the time he got back inside, the kit was back in the cabinet, and the cabinet dripped saltwater from its corners.

Four more days. Four more days of hot food and the sight of people, being in the world, and Lana's company. The girl acted subdued. On the fifth day, Kitten woke to the knowledge that this was the last of July. That he'd go back to the house that night and not emerge again for decades untold, and for the first time in years, he found himself wondering if he could outwit the house. Perhaps he could live on the beach, camp like he'd told Lana he did. Find a job, save money, build a house of his own, one he wanted, one without doors. Yet even as he thought these things, he knew it was useless. Who would hire a gray-haired man with no experience in any trade, who barely understood what a computer did, who'd never once spoken on a telephone? If he'd learned anything from Lana, it was how ill-fitted he was for this new millennium or it for him. His thoughts opposed themselves. Maybe he'd never come out of the house again. He never understood why it let him out some Julys but not others. Maybe it was to keep him human, to keep him sane. So maybe the real way to end it would be never to come out, to fall deep, deep inside, to go mad with the house, become its soul.

Kitten took the rest of the money to town with him. He'd spent some time looking around the house for some token to give to Lana, but the only thing that seemed appropriate was the bestiary, and Kitten couldn't bring himself to part with that. Instead, he treated Lana to a big waffle breakfast and ice cream for lunch and bought her a knapsack she coveted from a shop on Main Street. He assumed he'd return to the house once Lana's mum called her home. He hadn't expected it to be so early. Midafternoon when she jumped up from the railroad tie where they'd sat to contemplate the keys together one last time, she said something about a dentist appointment. She'd begged her mom not to make her go, to change the appointment to a different time or day. She hugged Kitten long and hard until his neck ached, and he hugged her back, broken-hearted to see her go.

He ate one last meal at the Cow Belle Café before walking his bicycle through the main street of town, saying silent goodbyes to Rockaway, Oregon. Kitten rode slowly, looking at the coast but not seeing it, thinking instead of all the places he'd been, the places the house had taken him: the tip of Florida where no one would look him in the eye; a deserted Italian shore where he hardly saw another living thing; the coast of North Carolina, where he'd met John the dog; a frozen lake where the inhabitants didn't speak any language he knew but who gave him salted fish and a hard, flavorless bread in exchange for his coins. Only the sight of the Tillamook factory shook Kitten from his memories and, confounded, he pointed his bicycle in the other direction. He rode back and forth, seeking the house without finding it, secretly hoping it had gone on without him, suspicious of that thought from the outset. He sought the overhang and the forked rock formation instead, the one always smelling of murres, and when he found them, he dropped his bicycle to the ground and stumbled forward, sobbing before he even knew what he saw.

Pushed-down grass marked the footprint of the house. Empty ocean shore echoed the sound of waves rattling the stones. He found the hollow in a rock full of fur and bones and then a blue bicycle with pink streamers on its handlebars lying in the weeds.

* * *

Lana is nineteen by her own clock and twenty-eight by the world's the first time the house lets her leave. She experiences an acute sensation whenever she remembers her initial hours in that warped and damaged place. How she opened the knapsack Kitten had bought her, the one she stuffed full of all the things her ten-year-old mind thought she'd need to hide out there and run away with Kitten. How she found the knapsack empty and was convinced she'd freeze or starve, because she hadn't believed Kitten when he'd told her the house would provide.

She still trembles a bit when the second door opens, and the floor shakes and groans, and tilts sideways, giving her a glimpse of a plain, unfurnished room that unfolds, unfurls into a growing black spiral, finding depth, seeking distance, Euclidean geometry stretching itself thin before it sucks her through. It has happened so many times now she's lost count and isn't as terrified as the first time she got lost in the house's secret, shifting maze.

The sewing kit bothered her a lot those first few years. It pounded, scraped and battered the cabinet and might as well have been battering the inside of her skull. She doesn't remember when she fished the knot of tangled thread from her pocket, when she set the knot next to the kit and watched, tears pouring down her face and a bad feeling in her stomach, while the two objects danced. Lana only knows that this is a recent development, this sense of what she needs to do.

The July air is warm when she steps out of the house. She doesn't know where she is and hardly thinks it matters. Lana doesn't wait. She walks to the nearest town as soon as she picks it out and finds a craft store. She spends all of the money she has, save the price of a hot meal, on yarn and twine and embroidery thread; then she goes back to the house.

It is excited. It knows that she knows. Atonal, piping music plays from behind the second door. The sewing kit jigs on the table, spins in circles and hops up and down, its needles sharp and shining, ready to be used.

"Shut up," Lana snaps. "I figured it out, no thanks to you. Have some patience."

She finds the marker she bought for Kitten when she was ten. It still has a red ribbon tied around it, though the ribbon has faded and split. Lana cries a little bit, thinking about it. She wonders if she'll be able to find Kitten again, if it's as simple as she thinks and the house will be fixed and she will be free. She tries to remember being ten and what it was she'd been thinking. She goes to the front door, runs her fingers down the list Kitten made. She's read it so many times she can recite it by heart. Then she kneels, lowers herself to her elbows so she can reach the door's bottommost edge, uncaps the marker, and makes her first and only addition right beneath her own name.

Kitten, she writes.

Feed the Head

DAVID PARKER, JR.

We keep track of time, even though there is no sunset or sunrise this far underground. There is only night here, hellish, hot and humid, but our foreman Pedro Alavar marks the hours carefully, using his wrist watch or the small clock in the rescue chamber. "Mario," he says to me as he stands in the eerie light of electric lamps with his bare chest and dirt-streaked face. "It is time to feed Don Cortez his supper."

A murmuring rises up from the men hunkered along the benches and scattered across the concrete floor where they hover in small groups above electric torches in order to play cards or say their rosaries together in desperate, rhythmic chants. Dinner time. The last supper. Some of us voted not to share rations with Don Cortez. After all, there was so little food, and now we have reached the very last of it. But we are a democracy in the chamber. Ten men voted to let Don Cortez starve, but twelve men voted to feed him. "I will do it," I reply.

"Good man," Pedro Alavar says to me.

Above us, the droning. The grinding of drills in the rock. The sound of angels. They are still trying to rescue us, and that keeps us going. On the surface, seven hundred meters above, they have not given up. Numerous crews and steel drill bits are churning through the rock, hunting for us. The grinding sound works its way into our dreams. It creates a hollow sound in our brains and the distant vibrations transfer from rock to bone as we try to sleep in this stifling heat. The question is, how long will they hunt? Fourteen days and nights we have been trapped according to the clock. No one above even knows if we're still alive. Our emergency rations were supposed to have run out seven days ago. The only sound more horrible than the drilling in the rock would be silence. At one point or another, we have all woken up from a dead sleep screaming because we thought we heard it stop.

Pedro Alavar divides the last of the food and water from the plastic pouches. He has worked a miracle by making it last this long, but even the loaves and the fishes reached an end eventually. We are all very skinny already; it won't take long for the hunger to drain us of what's left. I take the pittance allotted to Don Cortez and head to the tunnel. I always feed him before I feed myself. I want the men to think there is some strength in me.

"Mario," a voice says, and I turn to see that Miguel has addressed me. Miguel is devout, and he leads the men in prayers three times daily at an altar he has built in the sturdy section of the tunnel. He voted to let Don Cortez starve and counseled that it was for the greater good. I also voted to let Don Cortez starve. "God bless you," he says to me.

"And you," I reply. Then I step outside the concrete walls of the rescue chamber and into the tunnels. I feel sure that at least ten men secretly hope that I do not return to claim that last pitiful meal that awaits me there in the chamber. But I will return. I always do. I'm like the alley cat behind the butcher's shop.

Before the collapse, Don Cortez was just a man called Hector. He worked the same shift as me, but he worked with Grupo Nueve. The rest of his group was killed directly beneath the collapse. He said they could hear the whistling of the wood, but it was too late. My group was able to reach the safety chamber. Grupo Seis was able to escape, or so we believe. They were closer to the surface when the tunnel collapsed.

Now, poor Hector. Don Cortez. Trapped in the rubble. We have honored him for his sacrifice, and now I bring him this last meal. My belly grumbles as I creep around the bend in the tunnel, listening to the drone of drills in the rock, listening for the groan of tunnel wall or the whistle of wood beams. When the rock begins to go, it shifts its weight and squeezes all the air from the wood. The wood whistles before it snaps and brings the ceiling down with it. The tunnel is still very dangerous where Don Cortez lies buried. Much of the support is gone.

This tunnel still fills me with something like terror, but so does everything. Words like safe and unsafe have lost their meaning for me. I walk like a cat, soft and careful, until I come around the bend with my electric torch, and there he is. A head. His face glows pale amid the dark slumber of rock where he lies trapped. A head, and nothing more. As if he were a pale growth, like a tumor conjured from the beauty of the rock. We have laid a blanket beneath his cheek so he can sleep and propped a book open so he can read in the torchlight. The works of Pablo Neruda. He digests them one page at a time. When someone is brave enough to visit, they turn to the next page. "There you are," the head says from its perch.

"I bring your supper."

"Jose was here today."

"He was? He didn't tell me."

"He gave me two pages."

"That's excellent." I'm surprised by the twinge of jealousy that shoots through me. I know that men are free to come see the head. There's no reason to be jealous. But still, there's this feeling.

"He also killed a girl when he was young."

"What?"

"He was angry, and he shoved her off a high ledge on the mountain. People thought she fell. Jose has never told anyone that he killed her. He was nine years old."

"Are you serious?"

"He told me in strictest confidence."

"Why are you telling me?"

"What am I, some kind of priest? I didn't ask for his confession."

"The food is finished. This is the last of it."

"Listen," he says. "The drills are getting close."

"I know. I can't sleep anymore."

"Come," says the head. "Feed me."

I sit carefully next to Don Cortez and uncover the small portion of food: a spoonful of instant potatoes and two bites of precooked beef from the emergency rations. For dessert, there is a specially-formulated vitamin with the very last of the water to wash it down. "Will you turn the page?" he asks.

"Of course." I turn the page to a new poem and watch the head chew thoughtfully on his beef as the drills drone in the distance. A cascade of dirt falls from the loose rock ceiling and sends my pulse soaring, but I don't even flinch anymore. It takes a while, but a man can grow accustomed to anything, even his own grave.

* * *

I will be the first to admit that I did not handle things well in the beginning. When the mine collapsed, so did my nerves. Even in the best of days, I've always been wary of these crawlspaces of earth and rock, of mineral and iron-ore. I trained myself not to think about the thousands of tons of earth poised above me, ready to crush me into pulp and soot with the slightest shrug. I was a miner, like my father. There was no choosing. There was nothing to chose from. I had a wife, a son, a job in the mine. Ten days on, three days off. I put my boots on, left my village once a week, and went to work in these deep holes.

Then the ceilings came down with a boom and rumble like thunder and the horrible sound of rock rending itself apart. I went to pieces. I don't even remember it all; it was a blind panic. My body was in hot revolt, beyond control, and even the space between my molecules was charged with terror. The universe collapsed upon me, and I wept. I thrashed. The men held me down roughly, as they were trained to do. I was a danger to us all in a state like that. Finally, I cowered beneath the bench in the rescue chamber and groaned like a man who'd been gutshot.

Now I am the feeder. Years from now, when people read the biographer's tale of our account, there will be the heroes such as our leader Pedro Alavar, the devout such as Miguel Castanero, and the pitiable such as Don Cortez, the poor head.

Then there will be me, little more than a glorified alley cat. Part of me thinks it will be fine if we never escape from here. Then my shame might lie buried in this rock forever.

This is foolish, I know. Who would die for shame?

"Mario!" Luis shouts as I arrive back in the tunnels near the shelter. "Listen!"

Luis was a dynamite man, but now he is our designated poet. He and the men stand excitedly in the tunnel, their skin glowing in the lamplight. They look like skinny cavemen with their bushy hair and new beards, with their slick sheens of sweat from the wretched heat and bad air. They crouch and scurry. They cock their heads to listen to the vibrating rock and sniff the air. One of the drills seems to be very close. Pedro Alavar tries to herd them back into the rescue chamber. "Back!" Pedro Alavar shouts. "Everyone back. We don't know what else might collapse."

Finally, all the men retreat to the crowded concrete chamber to wait anxiously. Daniel, the biographer, makes furious notes in his yellow foreman's pad. The poet Luis grabs his own pen and gnaws on the back end of it as he stares at the scrum of men crowded around the chamber door. Perhaps he is already dreaming of a victory poem. A poem about ascending into stars and sky and cool, clean air. I look around at the poet, the biographer, the devout. In this democracy of doom, everyone has been elected to their roles. Everyone has his special contribution.

Finally, we hear a drill break through the roof of the tunnel nearby. A small collapsing of rock and the sound of swirling steel blades. A cheer goes up from the men. "Hurrah!"

"Hurrah!"

Up on the surface of the earth, the driver must have realized that he broke into open space. The drill bit grinds through open air from ceiling to floor, for five feet, and the driver stops the machine. It's a seventeen centimeter bit, the size of a skinny man's thigh, but it gleams like a gem in this quivering half-light of headlamps and electric torches as the men scramble back out into the tunnel. Even I must admit that those long, glimmering blades bring a certain hope. Maybe there is a way back to the surface after all.

"Quick," says Pedro Alavar. "Get me the note."

They have written a note that reads, "22 souls in the safety chamber. 1 man trapped in rubble. We are well and await your rescue." They fold it carefully and tape it to the drill bit using heavy insulation tape. The bit is hot from churning through rock, and it burns their hands, but Pedro Alavar doesn't stop. We can't afford to lose this chance. When the note is attached, he bangs on the gleaming steel drill bit with a hammer. Can they hear that all the way at the surface? We're more than seven hundred meters down. That is a long way for sound to travel, even through metal. He bangs and bangs.

After a time, the drill bit begins to move, back up into the earth, back into that dark hole from whence it came. It retreats toward the surface, and we all stand silently, peering carefully up into that black hole.

* * *

You are heroes, the letter from my wife says. The whole nation watches. The whole world.

"What do you think of that?" I ask Don Cortez as I drop a bite of potted meat on a cracker into his mouth and watch him chew thoughtfully. A stench has begun to grow from the rocks around the head. I'm sure it's partly his excrement, being delivered somewhere into that pile of rubble, and something else too. Some kind of rot. It's a horrible smell but strangely comforting once you have settled into it. There's something organic in it.

We hunker together in the torch light and shuffle through letters that have arrived from above. "Did you know that Raoul gave his wife syphilis?" the head asks.

"Why do you tell me these things?"

"He has two filthy girlfriends in the city and a wife and kids at home in his village."

"The men still confess to you?"

"The men crawl here to unburden themselves. Like I'm a toilet. Here, would you like to shit in my mouth too?"

"No," I reply. "Eat your crackers."

"They think their sins will die here in the tunnel with me."

"No one else will die in this tunnel," I say. "We are heroes after all."

"Of course," the head replies. "Our bravery is known around the world."

I steal a glance at him. Does he know about my moments of defeat? Has someone told him? Do they ridicule me behind my back? The head has become a popular destination among the men, a subterranean pilgrimage, our very own miracle like the grotto at Lourdes where the Virgin Mary appeared. I feel strangely proud of this fact, and strangely possessive. I have already asked Pedro Alavar to ensure that all the men seek my blessing before they travel to the head. "For the sake of safety," I told him. "Only I know all the weak spots in the tunnel, and so many people wish to see him." Now I will be doubly careful.

When we first found the head moaning in the dark, it was hard to believe he was even real. His entire body was trapped in the rubble, but somehow he wasn't crushed to death. How was it even possible? At first we tried to dig him out, but the rock was loose here, and we had no supports. It was a suicide mission. At night, I still listen for sounds of further collapse, and every day I half-expect to walk up and find the rest of Don Cortez buried in a tunnel sealed with rubble. But every day it is not, and I continue to creep in. It began as my penance but now is something more.

We sit here and listen to the groan and pop of the shifting rock. He and I watch cascades of dust fall from the wretched, low ceiling, and I read to him from the letters and newspapers, following his favorite sports scores and basking in my own closeness to the head.

* * *

Our family, friends and lovers have gathered at the mine. Hundreds of them. Maybe more. They have built a tent city around the mine entrance, and it grows bigger every day. Supporters come from everywhere. They are on the news, and reporters flock around like pigeons. Our families send letters that arrive in a small blue capsule that comes down through the hole. The capsule also brings food, water, medicine, books, newspapers and dominos. The men have begun to call the capsule, "The Dove." It brings olive leaves from distant shores.

It also brings surprises, such as when Raoul discovers that both his girlfriends and his wife are gathered above. "I hope you are rescued," the wife writes, "so I may beat you with a hammer when you come back home."

Now all the men fear the same punishment. Who knows how many wives and girlfriends are gathered at the top, wearing matching T-shirts with their loved one's face emblazoned on the front. Perhaps the authorities have to keep them straight. Who's here for Raoul? All the ladies here for Raoul please step this way. Are these kids with you? Okay. Okay, now who's here for Luis? Luis? Okay, yes, ladies, please step right over here.

This is the only time I have ever felt superior for not having a girlfriend from the camp village or from the city in the valley. Even my wife used to tease me and say no other woman would have me, but now I am glad there is only one for me. My situation might be complicated, being trapped seven hundred meters beneath the surface of the earth, but my correspondence is simple.

The blue Dove arrives in the hole once more, and everyone looks to it with some trepidation. What news from above? Now that we have food, water, and the world's attention, we have settled into an uneasy waiting game. We know we won't starve to death, but still our bodies shrivel in the rock dust and darkness. Our spirits atrophy even as we pray around Miguel's hand-built altar. How long can we actually live like this? How much can they really do to save us? No one has been rescued from this depth before, not ever. In the heat, men begin to snap and growl like dogs.

Pedro Alavar opens the Dove and discovers a small video camera sent by the state news service. He holds it in his hand for a moment and then looks up. "This is magnificent," he says. "We shall show the world our strength and our faces. If they know our faces, they will keep digging."

"Here," Raoul says. "Let me hold the camera, and you can speak to the people."

"Very good," Pedro Alavar says. He takes a seat so he can sit up straight, and then addresses the camera. "You can see we have grown thin, and we face many challenges, but we are strong, and we are with the people." He goes on for a short while about the conditions of things and then concludes with, "God bless you all."

Then Raoul takes the camera on a wandering tour of the facility, and you can see why he has so many girlfriends as he laughs and charms the camera, almost like he's flirting. He introduces the men and flips the camera around so he can speak directly to the lens. "This is our poet," Raoul says as he sticks the camera in Luis's face and then spins the lens around to address himself. "He is a master of words. He used to be a master of dynamite, but he has been converted, like the prostitute who reclaims her virginity when she is wed to Jesus. Aren't you like a young virgin now, Luis?"

"What on earth are you talking about?"

"He even had a book of Neruda once," Raoul tells the camera in a conspiratorial tone, "but we gave that book to Don Cortez. The poor head. Perhaps you will meet him too if you are lucky. But first I will show you the latrine and the chapel. We have built a grand society."

At first, Raoul seems friendly and funny, but soon he starts to seem frantic as he talks to the camera, almost as if he were confiding in the machine, as if it were his one true friend. "The others would like to eat me," he says. "Well, they can eat this," and he suddenly aims the camera at his own exposed cock which dangles limp as he swings it around with dramatic sweeps of his hips.

That's when Pedro Alavar finally says, "All right, Raoul. It's time to turn the camera off."

Thank god for Pedro Alavar. It takes three men to separate Raoul from the machine and calm him, and he demands that we send the video exactly as is. "That is for my wife!" Raoul cries out. "Juanita, I love you!"

* * *

The next day, after we have returned the camera to the surface, the Dove arrives again. This time it is full of pills. Prescription tubes full of Xanax. "This will help," is all the note says.

* * *

Soon, most of the men lie around in a pharmaceutically-enhanced tranquility, with their eyes half-open as they play cards on the floor, chant the rosary and listen to the sounds of the drills. Bigger drills now. Big enough to drop a pipe or pull a whole man up to the surface. Giant drills chewing through the earth, coming to get us, droning on and on, sending vibrations from rock to bone. The recurring nightmare has changed now, and one by one the men wake screaming and dreaming that the drill has come through the ceiling and ripped them to shreds.

Miguel the devout passes close by me, and he hisses, "This is your fault."

"What's my fault?" I reply.

"Your precious head is a curse upon us all. A sorcery."

"Don't be ridiculous."

Miguel hisses at me, loud enough for even the dazed men to look up, and then he slinks off toward his homemade altar in the safe part of the tunnels.

Luis and I just look at each other. Then I escort him in the opposite direction to feed Don Cortez and turn the page for him. "Ah, look, the poet has come," Don Cortez says when he sees us crawling toward him through the narrow tunnel. "To what do I owe this honor?"

"I have something for you," Luis says.

"Letters?" the head asks. "Or better yet, the sports page?"

"I have something even better," Luis says. "I have written a poem about you, Don Cortez."

"Oh god, no," the head says.

"Would you like to hear it?"

"Please, no. I can't take any more poetry. I'm sure it is a beautiful work, but you must save it for the angels. How did the Rangers do against Colo-Colo?"

I'm about to tease the head for being so curt, but I can see from the bruise-blue color creeping up the edges of his face that he is not well. He flinches from pains, and his stench has grown stronger. "Are you hungry?" I ask.

"No."

"They say the drill is very close. We will be home soon."

"That's wonderful," the head says.

* * *

When we arrive back near the rescue chamber, all the men stand excitedly in the tunnel once again with their matted hair and rangy limbs glowing in the lamplight. The big drill is beginning to get close. It's following the path of a previous drill, bearing down through the smaller hole. Large quantities of rock and earth have begun to fall from the smaller hole now, landing in the tunnel, as the big drill presses down from above. Finally, the men have work to do. Real work. Moving earth. They're so excited they sing as they organize into twenty-four-hour shifts to haul rock from beneath the hole and keep the tunnel clear. The work is grueling, especially for sun-starved men who have lost half their body mass from being trapped underground for weeks and weeks. Vitamin-deficient men with skin fungi and bleeding gums. Heat-pressed men with bloodshot eyes and wheezing chests. They grunt, and curse, and sing as they move the rock with hand trucks and low-slung, motorized haulers. "Go!" Pedro Alavar shouts as the next shift streams out of the chamber to take their turn beneath the hole.

Finally, the whole ceiling trembles and groans. Pedro Alavar brings the team back into the chamber to wait as the big drill grinds and chews its way through the last meters of rock and erupts into the tunnel like the sword of San Miguel striking from heaven. No one says a word this time, but some of the men weep openly as the giant steel bit slowly stops spinning and gleams wicked in the half light.

It takes six more days to line the escape route with safety tubing and to cast a concrete landing pad here at the base of the hole. Six days of anxiety, adrenaline and nerves. Six days of men snapping at each other and almost coming to blows. Now that they can clearly see the exit route, the minutes spent in the tunnel have become even more torturous. It would be a curious tragedy if we clawed each other to death just moments before we were to be rescued.

"Men!" Pedro Alavar begs. "Hold yourselves together. We are so close."

But for the first time, I see real mutiny in the glittering eyes that look back at him, and it fills me with dread and excitement at the same time. We have been waiting, and waiting, and waiting, and now finally something is going to happen. Something real.

But then something else happens: a man arrives. He has been squeezed into a long, narrow pod and lowered seven hundred meters to where we stand waiting. He looks like an astronaut stepping out of his capsule. He wears a safety suit and harness, boots, a mask with visor and respirator, a helmet with a built-in lamp. He seems huge as he crouches in the tunnel and reaches out to grip Pedro Alavar's extended hand. "We meet at last," he says.

The men look ragged compared to this astronaut, and they stand about and leer at him with eyes gleaming and teeth shining out of their filthy faces. They look like they might eat him, even Miguel as he shouts, "God will save the devout!"

Pedro Alavar keeps a great poise about him as he shakes the astronaut's hand. "Welcome, brother," he says.

* * *

I race to Don Cortez, almost reckless as I crawl and slip through the wreckage of the collapse. "Don Cortez!" I say as I come around the bend and enter the small glow of his lamp. "We are saved!"

But the head does not answer. Fear presses up into my throat, like coal slurry filling a canal. "Don Cortez?" I choke. But I already know. Even from here, I can see that the life has left him. The head has died in the night. Or in the day. I don't know which it is any more. He is almost the color of the rock, and if I didn't know that he was there, I might not even notice his motionless shape lost amid that mound of rubble. The head is misshapen now too. It appears a rock must have fallen from the ceiling and smashed him.

I crawl over, into the stench, and hover above the lifeless form. It is hideous. The blood has turned black beneath the skin, and a gash hangs open where the rock must have struck him, revealing the cracked bone of his skull. The rocks are caked in blood. His lips and tongue are swollen. The pale moons of eyeballs glimmer from behind the half-shut lids. The miracle of the head has ended. And of course it has. What did I think, that I would somehow remain the keeper of the head? That I would carry it out of here in a box and feed it in the village square? That I would travel with it across the country and let people bow before it like some kind of sacred relic?

Now I will be the miracle. We all will. We'll rise from this hole into the clean air and sunlight and a million people will embrace us. We will be the living returned from the realm of the dead. We will slowly become men again and regain our proper names and roles, even you, Don Cortez. You will be a man called Hector once again, buried in a cemetery on the hillside, and no one but I will dream of you sleeping in the rocks like this, keeping all our secrets.

I close the book of Neruda. I turn off his small lamp. I crawl back through the wreckage and leave the head alone in the dark.

Mr. Bird

DENISE PATRICK

Mr. Bird woke to the chill of another day without his beloved Milla. He sat up slowly, wincing at the various aches and twinges that were still with him while she was not. He smelled coffee and thought his mind was playing tricks on him again. He heard the shuffle of her slippers in the hallway outside the bedroom door, heard her call "Bird?" just as he slammed shut the door of his truck before driving into town. Fifty years couldn't be turned off like a light bulb, his sister Imogene said.

Mr. Bird looked over at the worn black suit weighing down the flimsy hanger on the closet door. Who'd come in and put that out, he wondered? In the ten days since death had taken Milla, he had endured constant intrusions on his private grief, including the arrival of inedible cakes that sat hardening on his kitchen counters, the cold calculations of a young funeral director, and heart-crushing comments like, "I know you must find comfort in all the years y'all had together." There was no comfort in any of that.

There was a soft knock on his bedroom door, and for a moment Mr. Bird didn't move. He wasn't sure it was real.

"Papa?" It was his grandson's croaky, almost-man voice. "Can I come in? I fixed your coffee."

"Come on in, boy." The old man raised his slumped shoulders. He glanced down at his nearly coal-black hands and realized that he was gripping the edge of the mattress. He loosened his fingers and sighed as Luke came in.

The boy almost tiptoed in, as if he were afraid he might disturb something. Maybe he was afraid, Mr. Bird thought; Milla had died in this room. But what a shame that a place where Luke had been so loved would frighten him now!

The boy had picked up Milla's house chores so surely, so naturally, that his brewed coffee smelled just like Milla's.

"Here you go," Luke said, giving his grandfather a trembly smile.

As Mr. Bird sipped and looked into his grandson's olive-skinned face, the boy's young eyes were Milla's eyes. "How you holding up?" Mr. Bird asked, keenly aware that he wouldn't know how to answer the question himself. He patted the covers next to him, and Luke sat down.

"I miss her," Luke said. He looked up at the black suit too, and then let his gaze roam around the room. "It's like she's not really gone."

"I feel the same." Mr. Bird gulped the hot coffee wishing for the first time that he was a different type of man, one who could explain things like loving and dying without scaring the daylights out of the boy. Instead, he drained the mug and looked out of the window at the few pines left on the hill in the distance. The trees seemed gray, like the January sky.

"Why didn't my mother come right away?" Luke asked abruptly. "Ma Milla was her own mother. Aren't you supposed to come right away when something happens to your mother?"

Mr. Bird didn't say the first thing that came to his mind: *Because your mother never grew up. You were a mistake, and she's still making mistakes.*

"She had some things to take care of; that's all. She'll be here in time for the service today."

Luke clucked, just like Milla used to. "She doesn't act like anybody's mother or daughter," he grumbled.

"She's your mother; respect her," Mr. Bird said. Luke shook his head but didn't answer back.

"Now go on, take this cup back, and you get dressed. You polish those shoes?"

"Yes, sir."

"Extra shine, like I showed you?"

"Yes, sir."

"Good. Take your lanky self out of here. I haveta put some clothes on these old bones." When Mr. Bird stood up, Luke looked him directly in the eyes. Mr. Bird stepped back, startled.

"When did you get so tall?" He meant to say this to himself.

Luke grinned. "I'm almost thirteen, Papa."

"I believe that's twelve and change, mister." Mr. Bird tugged a handful of the boy's curly brown hair.

"Okay, okay!" Luke ducked away, pausing at the door. His playfulness was gone, and the grin had faded. "Just, just don't call yourself old. Okay?"

Mr. Bird nodded, then moved to the tiny washroom next to the closet, the one he'd added for Milla. He splashed cold water onto his face before looking in the mirror. Old eyes looked back at him, faded old brown eyes perched over a sharp nose. He carefully brushed down the thin white hair on either side of his head and smoothed his stiff moustache before going back to the dresser to get clean socks.

Someone, probably his sister, had tucked one of the neatly folded funeral programs beneath a vase of wilting flowers. Milla's face smiled up at him from a black and white photo she'd taken in her last years of teaching. He blinked at the solemn caption printed below it.

Camilla Bates Hall. Sunrise, October 16, 1912. Sunset, January 11, 1982.

"Forgive her," he heard Milla saying to him. "Even after my sunset, can't you forgive her?"

Tears stung Mr. Bird's eyes and carried him back to another place, back to Milla.

* * *

It was September, but the night was clear, and the sky was filled with bright stars. Milla lay in the warmth of his arms as a cool breeze passed over them. They were stunned by the blessing they'd finally received after years of effort: Milla's golden face glowed with new motherhood. Mr. Bird held her against his heart, filled with the sureness that she would always feel firm and substantial, a natural part of him like the hair on his head or the hands that he used to cradle her breasts.

"Birdwell?"

"Hmmm?" he mumbled in contentment, closing his eyes.

"One day we won't be here like this."

"What you sayin,' Milla? We've got long lives to live! We're gonna name our baby girl Althea, like your mama, and we're gonna see her grown to be as pretty and smart as you are!"

"But Bird, darling, one day our baby girl will be out in the world. We have to make sure she can stand on her own. Make sure she knows, no matter what, that she's the one thing we love best."

Mr. Bird had opened his eyes in surprise to look down at his wife. She was crying.

* * *

Luke appeared just as Mr. Bird snapped his red suspenders into place. He didn't remember the suit trousers fitting so loose the last time he'd worn them. The crisp white shirt he wore itched him. Milla knew exactly how much starch to use. Mr. Bird sighed.

"Papa? I can't get this tie," the boy said.

Mr. Bird snorted and frowned.

"I did try!" Luke responded.

"Come here," Mr. Bird said, spinning Luke around. "Look. One end shorter …"

"I know! And then over …"

"But not like that! This way."

"Ohhh. Wait! And *then* over, right?"

Mr. Bird stepped back. "Right."

The sound of a car and crunching gravel made Luke bolt toward the living room. Mr. Bird followed in slow motion, leaving the bedroom for the first time this morning. His entire house felt unfamiliar to him, like he was walking through a dream.

"Auntie Imogene!" Luke said. "I thought you were my mother."

Mr. Bird watched his sister raise her arched eyebrows. Still vain at seventy-five, Milla would have said.

"I certainly am not your mother. Althea isn't here already? Well, where is she?"

The rapid-fire questions didn't allow for any answers, and Mr. Bird was glad.

"Did you have breakfast, Luke? Birdwell, have you eaten? I swear you have dropped ten pounds in the last week!" She hustled in with a huge purse and several grocery bags, stopping to peck her brother on the cheek.

"I know this is all too much, and you're not yourself," she whispered. "You go sit, and I'm gonna make you a little snack." She looked over her shoulder. "Luke!" she bellowed, "can't you help Auntie with these bags? I've got banana bread in here for you."

Mr. Bird felt relief in his sister's presence. She, alone, could anchor him in the present. He obeyed her orders, thankful once again that his wife and sister had gotten along like gangbusters and thankful that Milla had not been a woman who issued orders.

He took a seat in the armchair near the front window. A dozen houseplants of different sizes and shapes were clustered around the end table, all with tags that said "Sympathy" and scrawled names. He didn't bother to squint so he could read them. He blinked at the freshly dusted tabletop. Imogene's hand had been there, he knew. Some kind of clay plate with Luke's five-year-old handprint lay next to one of Milla's fancy Lladro figurines. Behind the porcelain dancing girl was a small silver frame.

He thought of Milla's photograph on the program, but this one was in color. And it wasn't his wife, but a snaggle-toothed child with two fat plaits tied up with red bows, and the same round cheeks her mother had. Althea.

* * *

Milla met him at the door with the news on that hot day thirteen years ago. As he hit the front step, he saw heat rising in waves from the swollen wood. She was standing in the shadows just inside the screen door, her small lips as taut as the silver-threaded black mane pulled up from her temples. Her smooth forearms were folded under her breasts, and there was a strawberry smudge streaked across her stiff white apron. She must have been making jam. He kicked off his heavy boots and stepped inside.

"Milla," he said, leaning to greet her with a kiss. She didn't move in toward him like she usually did, but he sensed her straining to get words out.

"Whatever is wrong with you?" he asked.

"Birdwell, there's a letter from Althea there on the sideboard. She's . . ." Milla turned her face from his and frowned into the setting sun as if it hurt her eyes.

"She's in the family way, Bird."

He was stunned, like the time when he was a boy and a horse had thrown him and knocked his breath right out. He reached for Milla and his arm felt heavy. When his hand touched his wife's shoulder, she shivered.

"I can't believe it," Milla whispered, pulling away from him. "Lord, Bird! I should never have let her go up to New York. She would've been closer at a state school, and . . ."

"We couldn't keep a child like Thea under our thumb," Mr. Bird interrupted, trying to make sense of what he heard.

Althea had never been easy. A smart, almost brilliant, child, she was never content with what *was*, always searching for something more, something better. And after all their struggles raising her on a country teacher's and a farmer's income, Tuskegee hadn't been "good enough." No black college would do, she told them, dashing Milla's dream of family tradition. Althea wanted to prove something. She wanted to compete on the same playing level with those who considered themselves "superior." Nowhere but Columbia University was good enough. Nowhere else could she prove beyond question all that she could accomplish.

Mr. Bird's anger rose slowly. He wanted to blame the big city, too, but deep down he'd known when Althea left that no matter how hard they loved her, there was already a mighty distance between them and their only child. Should he drive up to get her? Go and find the boy—the man? Insist that they marry? No, he thought. No.

In obvious distress, Milla wandered out to the back porch. Mr. Bird followed her there, and the two of them stood a moment staring across the pasture at pecan trees older than their daughter, heavy with nuts.

"What happened, Milla?" he asked. "Did she say?"

His wife shook her head without turning.

"Then it had to be her own choosing, to give up the only thing a woman's got," he said. "Goddammit, Milla! She chose."

"She says she's only taking off next semester and the summer; then she's going back to school."

"And what about the baby?" Mr. Bird asked. Milla finally looked at him, and he saw hurt and humiliation spread across her face.

"She said she made a mistake, and she waited too late to correct it."

"Mistake?" Mr. Bird wasn't sure he believed that, but Milla gently urged him not to press Althea when she came home withdrawn and close-mouthed about her circumstances. It was only after the birth in the back bedroom that they suspected that Luke's father was white. The way Althea didn't even want to hold him shocked Mr. Bird, and she didn't even bother to name him. Milla did that.

By the time Althea went back to college, it didn't matter to Mr. Bird that she maintained a scholarship and graduated with honors or that she went on to get other fancy degrees and even prestigious jobs, most recently with the federal state department.

Somehow over the years, as he had watched Luke grow and prosper under his roof, Mr. Bird's heart did something funny. His heart replaced the daughter he no longer understood with the grandson that he adored. For Milla's sake, Mr. Bird always treated his daughter with cordial respect. But now that Milla was gone, he wasn't sure what Althea meant to him.

* * *

Another car was pulling into the driveway, and Mr. Bird looked away from the table, the figurine and the picture. Of course, Althea had to rent a car for the hour or so drive from the Shreveport airport. It was a sensible little compact thing. Mr. Bird felt himself tense up as he blinked at his daughter's familiar silhouette. That could easily be a young Milla behind the wheel. Althea didn't get out. She just sat there as if the three years between her last visit and this one were a tall barbed-wire fence.

"Is it her? Is it?" Luke rushed in to peer out of the window.

At the same moment, Mr. Bird saw Althea look toward them. He couldn't read her expression through the windshield. He had thought she might not even show up. And now that she had, he wondered anew if he had somehow failed her. Was it he who had driven her away? Had he let her think she was a disappointment? Had he pushed her out of Luke's life when he could have tried harder to bring them together? She opened the car door, and Mr. Bird pried himself up out of the chair.

He felt heavy-hearted, ashamed that in Milla's lifetime he had not been generous enough to make the moves to heal his daughter or to heal himself.

"Finally she's here," Luke said. "Better last minute than not at all. I guess we're supposed to be grateful that she bothered to come to her own mother's funeral."

"She wasn't even in the country, son," Mr. Bird heard himself saying. "You know her job sends her all over the world. She came as soon as she could." He added with a murmur to himself, "I believe she must have done her best."

Luke jerked his head around to stare at his grandfather.

Mr. Bird realized that whatever he said, whatever he did today, the boy would take as scripture. "She did her best," Mr. Bird said again, in a firmer tone.

Luke came up next to him and grabbed his hand. What a firm grip the boy already had, Mr. Bird thought. He listened to Imogene humming that old hymn "Just As I Am" in his kitchen and heard his daughter's heels tapping up the steps and across the porch.

She knocked on the door of the house where she'd spent seventeen years growing up.

"Come on in," Mr. Bird said.

And when Althea stepped across the threshold, Mr. Bird looked into his daughter's face and saw no anger or coldness, but exhaustion and grief. She swayed a little, her eyes flickering toward Luke, then back to her father.

"Daddy," she whispered, "I'm, I'm so sorry."

Mr. Bird extended an arm toward her, spying over her shoulder the little girl in the old photo. He hadn't hugged his daughter in years. Still clutching Luke, he wrapped his other arm around Althea and pulled her face against his heart.

The Elevation

APRIL BLEVINS PEJIC

It was a Friday evening, and I sat on the floor of my cubicle putting on my knee pads and gloves for the long crawl home from work. At that time, I was a customer service rep for Columbia Power and Light, which basically meant I harassed people on the phone about paying their bills. I didn't enjoy it, but no one enjoyed much of anything before The Elevation, and the job allowed me to pay my own power bill, which at least provided a modicum of satisfaction. That had been a particularly rough day as I'd had to send out no fewer than twenty-two delinquency notices and cut power to four different customers, all of whom had called in to complain, but what the hell was I supposed to do about it?

So that night, I was in a foul mood and really looking forward to the dinner and bottle of wine that I knew Casey had waiting for me. I knew Casey had it waiting for me because she knew I was still ticked off at her about last week when she came home from work, stripped off her knee pads and gloves, and said she'd quit her job. Just like that. No more administrative work for Casey. No discussion, no warning, just a declaration of facts, shouted at an ear-splitting volume.

I crawled to the elevator and then crawled through the lobby, exhausted from my day and brooding about our dwindling finances. I stopped in the lobby to readjust the straps on my bag so it wouldn't start flapping against my back on the long crawl home. As I was about to push through the front door, the most incredible thing caught my eye.

In the glare from the streetlights outside the front windows, I saw a woman, just an ordinary woman by the look of her, doing the most extraordinary thing. She seemed to be moving down the sidewalk completely erect. Then I saw another person and another person, and as I stuck my head through the door, I realized I was the only one still on my hands and knees. Most of them seemed trepidatious, carefully placing a foot in front of them, testing it to see if it would bear their weight before swinging the other to the front. Some people held on to trees, others on to benches and walls for support, but they were doing so while fully erect on two legs.

I scampered to the phone behind the reception desk. Casey answered on the second ring. "Have you looked out the window?" I asked. "Can you see what people are doing?" I was near breathless with excitement.

"I know!" she said and giggled. "I haven't had this much fun in years."

"Are you doing it too?" I tried to picture her in our apartment, holding on to the back of the couch while she stumbled on her legs.

"Of course I am." She laughed. "Aren't you?"

"Well, sure," I said. I hated lying, but I couldn't let her have this on me too. "I'll be home in just a bit." I hung up the phone and crawled to the front windows. The people in the streets were laughing and singing as they moved about, clasping hands then letting them go again only to grab the hand of the next stranger passing by.

I watched for several minutes before I tried to stand myself. More and more people spilled into the streets, all up on two legs. Some stood hugging each other, some spun in circles, dizzying circles, round and round and round again, while others ambled back and forth on the same length of street.

I sat upright on my knees and pushed with my hands against the brick facade until I came to a squatting position with my feet underneath me. Muscles in my legs twitched and burned as I inched to standing. I locked my knees in place and tried to let go of the wall, wavered a bit, then stabilized. I couldn't believe how easy it was, really. Then I looked around me. The streetlights somehow looked softer, enchanted even, from this height. The stars were brighter, the greenery more verdant; even people were more attractive.

"Ha! I'm doing it," I yelled to no one in particular. "I'm really doing it!"

* * *

When I finally made it home, Casey was making pancakes and hopping back and forth from one foot to the other. She squealed in this delightful little way as she stood in front of the hot plate, which she had taken off the floor and propped up on a stack of books. As she poured batter, I realized for the first time how tall she was, how muscular her arms and shoulders were in comparison to her legs.

"Can you believe I'm cooking way up here?" she said. "And I'm not even kneeling on a stool or anything." She giggled again and bounced on her toes.

"I feel wobbly," I said. "Do you feel off-balance?"

She shook her head. "I want to call these sans-stool pancakes," she said, "but that sounds gross. How about freedom pancakes?" She handed me a plate, and I ate while standing. I wanted to still be angry. I wanted to scream at her in the way that had become normal in the last week and a half, but seeing her erect like that deflated my rage. Her dark hair seemed shinier; her skin seemed a healthier shade than the pallor in my memory. And I hoped that this new perception wasn't actually dependent on the height from which objects were viewed.

We spent the rest of the evening exploring our new legs and standing on every object in our apartment that we thought would hold our weight. We danced on the buffet. We jumped on the bed. We made obstacle courses of chairs and desks, the console television, and the upright piano so that we could travel from one side of the apartment to the other without touching the floor. We made love standing against the living room wall.

The next morning we half expected the world to have reverted to crawling again. The night before was so magical that we couldn't believe it would last. But sure enough, we got out of bed on our feet. News reports from across the globe flashed on our TV screen. It seemed that everyone in the world, collectively, at the same time, stood up, and I couldn't help wondering if I was the last man on Earth to crawl. Of course we didn't know what to call it at first. The media selected and rejected several terms: bipeding sounded too boring, upright-crawling too attached to the past, full-legged plod too clumsy. This, this new thing we were doing, was graceful and was described by one medical expert from the Cleveland Clinic as "the greatest societal elevation in the history of man." Pretty soon, everyone was calling it The Elevation and the associated action, walking.

For the first forty-eight hours of The Elevation we mostly just got used to our legs and feet and the way the ground felt beneath them. Where the tops of our feet were rough and calloused from being dragged across floors and streets, the bottoms were shiny and pink, and we delighted in the way concrete warmed them, tile cooled them, grass and carpet tickled them. We shucked our knee pads to allow for better ambulation. We moved from the walls out into the open, our arms free of the chore of keeping our faces out of the dirt. We were no longer forced to use our hands for balance on long journeys; we could now use them in any way we chose. We were quite self-congratulatory about the whole thing, like we'd somehow done something to deserve this new freedom of movement and happier disposition, and we held daily parades to showcase the things we could now do while walking.

The first parades were largely celebrations of the simple things we could now do on the move. Some people ate fried turkey legs, or oranges, or bean salad while walking down the street. Others drank coffee or beer, smoked cigarettes, or talked on their cell phones, things that would have been impossible to do while crawling. Others carried boxes of their favorite things and lifted them above their heads triumphantly. One man made an entire suit out of old knee pads and gloves, which were now largely useless. Casey made ankle bracelets from little bells that tinkled when she stepped. Though I relished the spectacle and being a part of it, I was most happy that my life of crawling to work and crawling back home to nurse my lagging sense of self-worth seemed behind me, a distant nightmare that I couldn't believe I ever actually participated in.

As the weeks wore on, the parades became more and more elaborate. People brought out instruments, choreographed dances, waved banners and batons. Casey sewed a costume of red, orange and yellow silk that looked like dancing flames when she walked.

"You need something," she said one day as she added another silk panel to her fire suit.

"What do you mean?" I asked.

"You need to be more festive," she said. "You know, make a banner or play the kazoo or something."

I'd been so enraptured by what everyone else was doing that I hadn't bothered putting any effort into my own appearance. "I think you're right." I thought about how wonderful this whole thing really was: how beautiful people were now, how lovely the parades of their talents, how great the sun felt on my face now that it wasn't angled toward the ground, how positivity electrified every particle. "Do you have a large black Sharpie?" I asked.

"Look in the drawer in the kitchen," she said.

I rustled through the books of matches, forgotten pens and rusty scissors until I finally found it. I took off my T-shirt and wrote Y-E-S! in giant black letters across the front. I put my T-shirt back on and went into the den.

"What do you think?" I asked.

She looked up from her sewing and cocked her head to the side in that way she does when she considers something carefully. "Yes?" she said.

"Yeah, I tried to think of the most positive word in the world." Saying it out loud made it sound silly. "You know, I just don't think we were nearly as positive or said yes nearly enough before The Elevation."

She smiled and nodded her head. "Yes," she said, "I love it."

* * *

A few days later, the residents of Columbia paraded for twenty-four hours straight. The plan was to walk to Manchec and then back again, but all the people from the county joined us along the way, and once we reached Manchec, all the Manchurians joined us as well. It just seemed silly to turn around and go home, so we kept on going and going with more people joining our ranks until the entire population of the United States marched in a snaking mass. We saw reports on our cell phones that people around the world were doing the same thing, India, Japan, even in Luxembourg, everyone walking and exploring en masse. Our arm and shoulder muscles softened, while our legs became larger, sturdier and tauter. We felt rooted in our new Elevation, and joviality kept us walking through our fatigue. When we were just too pooped to continue, we slept on the sides of the road under the most brilliant stars. It was a truly magical time in our history, but it seems all magic fades.

As the months passed and our feet grew calloused, the walking parade had become less an exploration of freedom and wonder and more and more a thing of obligation. We seemed to be walking not because we could and were excited about it, but because that's what we'd been doing for so long that we weren't sure what else to do with ourselves. Many people who ran low on cash began carrying The Sedants on their shoulders or piggy back. I'm not sure if The Sedants just tired more quickly than the rest of us or if they just enjoyed a more elevated view of the world, but it had become as commonplace to see people stacked two high as it had to see people carrying instruments or banners. No one seemed to mind the extra weight since The Sedants paid for the service, which allowed everyone to keep going.

On one particularly beautiful day, Casey nudged me and pointed at a man crawling in the ditch. His head was bald, his shoulders bowed as he struggled to keep up. "Why is he doing that?" she asked.

I had no idea. "Maybe he's crazy," I said. "I see a guy selling funnel cakes over there. Want one?"

Casey shook her head then trotted over to the man. "Sir, are you okay?"

He didn't stop crawling but turned his head in her direction. "I seem to have broken my leg," he said. Sure enough, his tibia jutted at the most awkward angle. It was the first time I recalled seeing anyone injured since The Elevation.

"Terrible luck, friend," I said. "That looks quite painful."

"Um hmm," he said. "It really is. I was carrying a Sedant, and the damn thing just snapped." The man said something else, but I couldn't hear him as the crowd swept us past him.

Casey kept looking over her shoulder trying to catch sight of him again. "We should do something." We were already a quarter of a mile ahead of him, and the gap was widening quickly.

"What can we possibly do?" I said. "Carry him? Please. I'll tell you what I'm going to do; I'm going to get a funnel cake." I pointed to a cart on the side of the road where a small crowd gathered around the aroma of fresh fried dough. I salivated.

Casey sighed. "It just doesn't seem right."

I hugged her to me as we continued walking. I didn't want that man's unfortunate injury to ruin her enjoyment of our progress. I pulled a twenty out of my pocket and bought us each a funnel cake smothered in drifts of powdered sugar.

We stood next to the cart to enjoy our treat. Grease soaked through the paper plate and glued powdered sugar to my fingertips. I sucked the sticky sweetness from my fingers and smiled at Casey who had a fine dusting of sugar on her lips. "See," I said, "everything is great."

Casey cocked her head to the side and glared at me. "I just can't get that man out of my head."

"But you have to admit that sweet fried dough is an incredible diversion." I shook the excess sugar from the front of my shirt. "Ready to go?"

Casey nodded and tossed the rest of her funnel cake in the garbage.

* * *

About twenty miles down the road, we witnessed several other wretches gathered beneath a large tree. They each held a piece of ripped-up banner that they must have been carrying together during the first days of the parade. One person's sign said *Hammer Toe*; another had written *Ankle Sprain*, yet another *Bunion*.

While I did feel quite bad for all those who had given up and sat down with their little signs, I was preoccupied with another problem: Casey and I were down to our last thirty dollars. Casey looked forlornly at the seated crippled, as I tried to devise a plan for keeping us fed, and that old anger that had settled so deeply inside me so many months ago began to creep back into my thoughts. A bottle of water for each of us and a shared chocolate bar cost us six dollars. We could do that exactly four more meals. If Casey hadn't quit her job when she did, she would have earned an additional $1,200, which would be in our account right now. I didn't want Casey or myself to fall ill due to malnourishment, which Casey said was the reigning hypothesis among medical professionals as to what exactly was up with all the injured sitting on the side of the road, but she had put us in a jam. And, of course, the responsibility of picking up the slack fell on me.

"Well," I said, "I think I might have to take on a Sedant."

Casey looked at me hard with that head-tilt of concentration. "I don't think that's a good idea," she said. I noticed then how the red and orange silks of her flame costume had faded so that her movement now more closely resembled a match-in-the-wind flicker.

"Remember when you impulsively quit your job? Yeah, well that had long-term consequences, i.e., we don't have any money now." I pointed to a woman sitting cross-legged on the side of the road holding a hand-lettered placard that said *Plantar Fasciitis*. "I don't see too many other options if we want to keep ourselves elevated."

"We could stop," Casey said.

"You can't be serious. Stop and do what?"

Casey sighed. "Whatever we want. Look around. Have you noticed that no one is playing instruments or dancing anymore?"

I hadn't noticed, but the crowd was much quieter; in fact, the seated or crawling lame had even stopped asking for help from passersby. They just held their signs without even making eye contact. Some of them lay on the ground sleeping. "Maybe everyone just needs a little nap," I said, nodding to the sleeping throngs. "Maybe they all just up and decided to quit, too."

Casey grabbed my arm. "Don't be a jerk."

"Ouch, what?"

"Are you serious right now?" Casey's voice was getting higher and higher, which meant she was either about to scream at me or stop talking to me completely. "Take a nap? I had no idea you could be such an insensitive baboon."

"All I'm trying to say is that some of us, i.e., me, have to pick up the slack for others who don't feel like carrying their weight, i.e., you, when you quit your job and also all those poor bastards lying around over there."

"Those are people, you ass."

"They aren't like me. Or you." I pointed at the left side of the road where many of the seated and sleeping had gathered. "Just read the signs: *Corns, Torn ACL, Dislocated Patella, Lisfranc Fracture, Fatigue, Depression*. They have problems. We don't, except that we need some cash to keep going."

Casey's nostrils flared in a way that let me know she didn't agree with me and was actually quite angry. "Have you even been reading the news on your phone, or were you just playing stupid games all this time?"

I didn't want to admit it, but I had been engrossed in a serious game of Words with a friend since we'd left St. Louis. I grunted in a way that wasn't affirmative or negative and hoped for the best.

"Don't talk to me for at least two miles," she said, and pushed ahead of the family of four we had been following since Dayton. Fine with me. I decided it would be prudent to use this quiet time to bone up on my current events so as to have plenty of ammunition when she started talking to me again and pulled up the latest headlines on my phone. Experts Say Injuries Due to Malnourishment. Malnourishment Related to Income. Is Carrying a Sedant Dangerous?: Experts Weigh In. CDC Says Injuries Not Related to Malnourishment but to Carrying The Sedants. Call for Removal of Lazy Tramps Cluttering Up View on Roadways. Eat the Sedants? Why Cannibalism Seems Like A Viable Option. Civil War Declared Pretty Much Everywhere but the United States and Canada. I clicked on the last one:

> As most of the world descends into chaos with the most brutal fighting we have ever experienced due to our ability to use our hands while mobilized in combat, the American and Canadian populations continue walking.

Sources say the Americans continue in what one person described as "the most pathetic parade in history" because they are all trying to get to the head of the line, but experts agree there is actually no head. Samson Fippers, the Congressional Head of Line Formation, said in an interview late Thursday night, "It's really the damnedest thing—if you look at satellite images of the country, there is no line! It's become an amorphous blob." Fippers said his office is working tirelessly to straighten things out, but noted that it was a pretty tough job since he was walking in the blob himself.

Experts say that Canadians are not experiencing the same problems of perspective that Americans seem to be suffering. When asked why Canadians weren't fighting like the rest of the world, Prime Minister Stephen Harper laughed until he hyperventilated. Once Harper caught his breath, he finally said between giggles, "Because Canadians are too nice. In fact, we don't have sociological problems in Canada."

* * *

Holy god. What was going on in the world? I pushed ahead to join Casey. "Umm, what the crap is happening?"

"Yeah, I know, right?" She seemed scared. "Remember when The Elevation first happened, and we were all just so happy to be up on our own feet and able to go anywhere we wanted carrying anything we wanted? And people were so nice to each other? We were even a more attractive population."

I looked down and noticed my exclamation point had smudged and mostly rubbed off so that my YES T-shirt now seemed less declarative and more plaintive. "I don't know what to do," I said.

"Look over there," Casey said and pointed to a group of the injured sitting beneath a clump of oak trees. They held cardboard and paper signs that said *Charcot Joint, Ingrown Toenail, Generalized Pain, Hunger, Depression.*

"Yeah," I said.

"We could go help them," she said.

"Oh, and what exactly are we going to help them with? Our last twenty-four bucks?"

"Yes. And we can build tree houses so everyone has a place to rest and recover, and we can plant a garden that will feed us all, and . . . "

"You're insane! So we'll just go babysit those grown-ass people until they die or suck us dry? That's a great idea." I couldn't believe the idiocy coming out of Casey's mouth. Maybe she was sick too. "Look, I'm going to get a Sedant and carry him to Denver, and then we'll be set for a while." I kissed the back of her neck. "I'm starting to worry about you."

Casey rubbed her palm on her forehead. "Don't you see? That's exactly what those people did."

"You can't actually know that for certain," I said.

"I do know that none of their problems are terminal," she said. "If we help them recover, then they will be healthy enough to help us with the work of creating our very own new town, right over there in those trees."

"Oh, really," I said. What the fuck? She had clearly lost it.

"Yes, and I will call it Elevationland." Casey smiled when she said this, and it was the first time I remembered seeing her smile since I gave her that harmonica back in Cleveland. It was clearly time for definitive action if I was going to save Casey from holding a sign that said *Crazy*.

"Okay, you go sit over there with them." I handed her all the money in my pocket. "Buy yourself some good hearty meals and just rest."

She looked bewildered as I kissed her goodbye. "You aren't staying with me?"

"I'll be back in just a few days, a week tops." I hated lying to her, but I couldn't be responsible for her and myself too if she wouldn't help me. "Just stay right over there, and dear god, don't make a sign." I kissed her again and left before I got choked up, which I knew I would.

A few blocks down I found a Sedant who needed a ride. I got a few dollars' advance from him for water, loaded him on my back and started toward Denver. He was a lot to bear, but his weight was nothing compared to the empty feeling I had now that Casey wasn't with me. I took off at a trot and ran and ran. If I concentrated on the movement of my body, the jolt as my feet hit the ground, the weight of this Sedant, the pain when he pulled my hair a little too hard, then I stopped worrying about Casey and feeling so lonely.

The next day I did the same thing, ran and ran and ran with that fat man on my back. After lunch, I put him up on my shoulders and, though I couldn't run with him like that, it eased the load on my aching joints. I ran sixty-four miles in five days, and I realized I was spending on food and water exactly what this man was paying me. If I was going to get ahead, I would need to start eating less and running more since I was being paid per mile. I tried not to think about Casey's flame suit dancing in the early Elevation parades. I tried not to think about the fun we had that first night on our feet, and in a weird way, the trying not to think kept me going through the worst days of fatigue. On Tuesday of the third week, the Sedant wanted to stop at a roadside restaurant advertising The Best Country Fried Steak West of Austin, TX. While he went inside to eat, I poked around the back of the restaurant until I found a water hose. I drank until I felt full, which technically was stealing, but I was getting pretty desperate. I'd been gone for nearly three weeks and had only managed to save $16.88. The Sedant came out looking quite sated and more than a little sleepy, and when he jumped on my back, I felt a pop and an electric surge from my spine all the way down my left leg. I ignored the burning throb as best I could. I took off at a canter, and just as I merged in with the other walkers, a pain from deep in my nerves seemed to swallow me up from the inside. I fell to the ground and landed hard on my face.

"What is wrong with you?" the Sedant said. "I'm docking your pay for dropping me."

I tried to stand, but the pain was so intense that I couldn't even get off my knees. "Please help me," I said and reached for the man's hand, but he recoiled from my touch.

"You're fired," he said and walked away.

After several hours of lying prostrate with the most agonizing affliction I had ever experienced, I was finally able to commando crawl to the side of the road so that I at least wasn't being stepped on anymore. I couldn't believe the pain, which wavered between a scream in my nerves and a shriek in my bones but never dissipated enough for me to get up again. I tried not to feel sorry for myself or make eye contact with any of the people rushing past me. I collected some of the trash littering the dirt where I sat and took the Sharpie marker from my pocket. I used my best penmanship so maybe someone in the crowd would read my signs and take me seriously. I staggered the signs in a circle around me and hoped they would look like a story instead of excuses:

Broken Back.

Missing Casey.

Please.

Take Me To Elevationland.

Someone There Cares For Me.

Oh Lazarus

RACHAEL PERALEZ

I had exactly four Pall Malls left when Leroy asked to bum one. I told him that I had them timed perfectly so I could smoke one every two hours while we hooked animal carcasses on the side of the road in service to the great state of Mississippi. Didn't he love Mississippi, with its sweetgums and good catfishing? We had, after all, broken her laws with our insatiable appetite for amphetamines and marijuana and crack cocaine. Big black Leroy told me to shut my stupid mouth and give him a goddamned cigarette. Stop talking for once in my life. I obliged both requests. You see, Leroy had a pretty short temper and possessed all the strength of a very pissed-off Philistine. At least the Old Testament Philistines. I figured having my face intact was worth one cigarette and my very temporary silence. When I handed him the cigarette, he tapped it against his palm and wrinkled his nose.

"You say you used to be a preacher, huh?"

"Yeeeah, but I can't save you, Leroy," I told him as I jabbed my sticker into a dead raccoon. Its ring tail flapped as I lifted it up like a puppet and bobbed it in front of Leroy singing "Jesus loves me, this I know, for the Bible tells me so." I pranced around until a warden came over and told Leroy to stop provoking Reverend Balls Deep. This time it was Leroy who obliged because my temper wasn't all that placid either, and sometimes I'd go into some holy rages. One such rage landed me here, picking up carcasses and eating overcooked canned spinach in a prison chow hall. At least they let me out to walk along the highway and see the red tails and look at everyone's trash.

* * *

I wrote some of my best sermons after I had pumped a little cold into my veins. Sometimes, I would strut up to the pulpit feeling like my chest had opened up and the golden light of the Most Holy Lamb had filled it to bursting with His word. My flock would walk up to me to shake my wet hand and look at me the way a cow looks at a new gate after those most inspired sermons. I just hugged necks, and gripped hands, and told them I'd pray for them. Then I would get into my Volvo and follow one of the members to his little home and eat chicken salad with pools of opaque liquid shimmering on top, while some dog stared at us through the screen door. I would make a few jokes, say a few prayers.

By the end of lunch usually I was coming down. I kept seeing that big buffalo-headed deceiver in every corner. Just flashes of his grin. My gums itched. I was a Baptist minister so I couldn't ask for a beer to soften my heartbeat. Always made me think of that joke about how you keep a Baptist from drinking all your beer on a fishing trip is to invite another Baptist along. And all I wanted was a Benzo and cold Coors.

When my giggling got too nervous and the conversation turned to the devil, I knew it was time to haul ass out of there. I ran over everything in my path on the way home. Squirrels never thought I was serious and just dillied in the road, chasing each other in these tight little circles until I heard at least one of them thump around in my undercarriage. I liked it. I liked it because I knew I could come back later under the pretense of being that soft-hearted preacher who picked up dead animals and buried them. I had a secret though. I just loved their pearly bones. I could make them live better, purer, clean as wool that's been washed by the blood. I would take them home and clean them, stripping away their skin and flesh and setting their carcasses out in a neat row on my back porch for the maggots to clean and the sun to bleach.

I had a Great Dane skeleton too. I kept the smallest tail vertebrae on a chain around my neck. Such a beautiful animal. Tall and lean, it would gallop across my yard, glossy muscles bunching and sliding across those heavy bones. The dog belonged to my neighbor, Jacob, who asked me if I had seen Moses when he didn't come home for his dog bed and kibble.

"Nooo. Not today," I said. "Where you think he ran off to?"

Jacob leaned against the horsewire fence and stared at the woods across the road. "No telling."

I had to bury Moses. Let the beetles do the work, otherwise I'd have flies coming from the ends of the earth. I was pretty used to the smell by that time, but that's a damn big dog to just leave rotting on your back porch. When the meat had finally been eaten, I set the bones in cold water and scrubbed them with a toothbrush. I was putting things in their right place. In their purest, pearl-white form. God himself never had a prettier collection of souls.

* * *

I guess I been partaking a little heavily the Sunday the sheriff came and hauled me off the jail. I had stayed up for three nights plunging the same needle into the veins on the tops of my feet over and over and trimming passages out of Isaiah with a pair of nail scissors. I was alone. There was always speculation as to why I was alone. Especially from the Methodists. The truth is I guess I never had but one sexual thought in my entire life, and that was when Lazarus rose from the grave in the Bible. I had a picture Bible growing up that my daddy had gotten me from some salesman with crooked fencepost teeth at the Zondervan's book store. I guess I was about six. He kept hitching at his crotch and saying how *rich* the drawings were. So Daddy got it for me and explained about how I couldn't draw in the pages on the ride home because it was still the Bible and did I understand? But I wasn't really listening because I had found my love. Lazarus. Oh Lazarus. He was holding Jesus' hand and the gauzy wrapping hung off his handsome face. Martha and Mary were gripping Jesus' robes and weeping, and I was so happy that I started flipping around the pages so Daddy wouldn't know that I loved a dead man.

I took that Bible back to my room and looked at Lazarus again under the dusty antique lamp I begged my momma for at a flea market. He had tears streaming down his face into his dark beard. Jesus looked so pleased. I got my first erection.

I had that brightness in me that Sunday morning. I was nearly weeping from the fullness of The Word when I saw Carol Jennings and Laura Miller in the back pew tittering and flipping through a magazine. They were the dark spot in the corner. I rubbed the smooth rabbit skull I kept in my pocket and cleared my throat into the mic. They went on snatching the pages back and forth and sighing wetly. The congregation was dead silent. Electricity ticked behind my eyes and threaded through my brain. I tore my sermon in half and pushed my shoulder into the pulpit stand until it collapsed and the sanctuary filled with the howl of feedback. I yanked at my tie and strode down the aisle toward them. Harlots harlots harlots harlots harlots. When I finally got to the back pew I snatched the magazine away from Carol's trembling hands.

"This is a house of worship. This is a house of God."

She was crying, and I had my thumb pressed against the hard little knot on her throat and kept pressing when I felt strong deacon hands pulling me away. They pushed their weight into me until I felt the rough carpet against my face. My rabbit skull splintered in my pocket, and I was sure that it was actually my spine cracking.

Well, the sheriff came and found three eightballs in my car. They also searched my house and found my collections and three more grams of crystal, a little less than an eighth of dope and twenty-five Benzos. So I went to trial, and then I went to jail because as much as I taught them about forgiveness, no one wanted to post my bond. I guess I did try to strangle a thirteen-year-old girl.

* * *

They finally started loading us into the van after we had dumped our bags into the flatbed behind the sheriff's truck. The warden chained Big Leroy to me and ducked our heads before we hopped into the vans like shackled circus elephants. On the ride back, I leaned over to Leroy and whispered to the side of his head that I took something from the road. Leroy told me to shut up, that I was going to get everyone on lockdown. I shook my pants leg, and a vile odor puffed into the air around us.

"Oh Jesus, Leroy. Leroy's cutting them over here. I call this cruel and unusual punishment. Jesus Lord. I've got to say a prayer for you, son. You got a demon in your asshole."

The van burst into raucous laughter, and Angel kicked the seat behind us. Chains rattled, and the warden hollered at us to settle down. I reached into the cuff of my pants leg and resituated the dead ground rattler I had found all flattened under an empty Dr Thunder box. I could feel some kind of sticky ooze matting my leg hair together. Another one for my collection. Another one to show my love real sacrifice. Real pretty. Real nice.

* * *

It happened like this on the first day I came to the pen. The day I first saw my love. After they brought me into the general population from the holding cell, they shoved some clean sheets at me and prodded me towards my cell. I had been clean for a few weeks, and everything seemed muddy. I had my Bible, and I was ready to pay my penance with some Ahab, who had killed a kid when he blew up his meth lab just to make a little biker blue. My mind slogged as I ticked through verses and parables. The fluorescent lights hummed above me, and I looked down at the V of the flip flops cutting between my socked toes.

When I finally reached my cell and walked inside, he was not King Ahab who sat there but my beloved Lazarus. He was thin and had the same sharpness about his dark, wild-eyed features as my children's Bible version. But he was so, so alive. Too much guts and moving bits and wet-mouthed speech. I came in and began making my bunk. I learned his named was Graham, and he was excited to have a preacher here with him. Maybe I could help him learn to be better. Because he had accidentally killed his girlfriend's boy child or girl child when he was high on junk, and left the gas on, and then took off to get some more, more, more. He started crying then and lifted his hair away from his face to show me where his girlfriend had come home and tried to tear out his eye when she found her baby dead and him asleep in the front yard. I put my hand on top of his head and called him my son like some pedo priest. He was disgustingly warm.

I read to him every night from the Bible because he said he never was real smart with books or church. Sometimes Herman from across the way would scream in his sleep and wake up everyone on the block. If you listened hard enough, you could hear Angel whisper to him in Spanish until the night went silent again. Graham would ask me if there was such a thing as haints, and I would tell him that the Bible tells us we go right to Him or to that lake of fire.

"Aren't such things as haints. Go back to sleep, son."

I concocted my plan to make Graham mine one morning when I got up before him to arrange my little collection of polished bones under the edge of my blanket. Graham never called me Reverend Balls Deep like everyone else despite my collection and the need to belt out in the communal showers: "Give me oil in my lamp, keep it burning burning burning."

He was sleeping so soundly that his chest barely rose, and his hand curled next to his nose. I watched him until he began to writhe under his blankets and wondered how hard it would be to give someone a lobotomy. Too hard. Pillow to the face? Graham was too young, too full of come. Too risky. I ruminated for weeks. All the while Graham kept talking, and moving, and leaking fluids like the rest of humanity. It finally came to me when we were out picking up dead animals and Leroy hollered like a lost calf and dashed to the warden screaming snake.

"It's a goddamned snake."

The warden laughed at him and told him to get back to work. The snake was probably scareder of his hollering and stomping than he was of it. It came to me then. I would poison Graham, just enough to make him cool and still. I could have really used some tweak.

* * *

Now I had my snake and just had to get it past the guards. I pinched the head off the rest of the body and let the length of the snake slap the floor. I tensed and looked around. Leroy stared out of the window and ignored me, yanking his hands as I shifted around. I clutched the head in my hands and figured it would be easiest to just hold it in my fist. The guards rarely paid Reverend Balls Deep any mind. I was crazy but harmless. I got the snake head in without any trouble. I usually held the animals I wanted in my mouth until I got to my cell where I retched them into my hand and admired them. I figured a snake head might be a little too risky. The guards didn't even look as they were unlocking my cuffs. It was a little too easy.

When I got to my cell, Graham was sitting on his bunk with the porno mag he traded a guard a horse contact for. I was so excited, I just stood on one foot rolling the snake head around between my fingers until he looked up from the sweat-moistened *Hustler*.

"Heey, Graham." I grinned and made all my nice teeth show.

"Hey, Reverend." He looked back at the pages of the mounds of fecund flesh flopping all over one another in a slick pile. I crawled into my bunk and hid the head under my pillow until night came.

* * *

That night I made Graham my Lazarus. I sat cross-legged in the bunk above him and counted his breaths. I was at 18,127 when I decided that number seemed holy enough and slid down beside him clutching the snake head by its jaws. His tender little wrist lay there full of lacy veins carrying blood back to his steady heart. I traced his forehead and felt the warm pulse of blood in my loins. I pried the snake's jaws open and tapped his wrist with such care. Graham's eyes fluttered under his lids. I couldn't move. He breathed sulfurous sweet on my face, and I did it. I plunged the fang into his wrist and pressed the head as hard as I could. Graham came to swinging and caught my front teeth. He flung blood from his knuckles and jumped clean out of bed.

"Son son son you were having a nightmare," I pleaded.

The snake head had bounced away into a dark corner somewhere. Graham caught his breath and looked at his wrist.

"Godalmighty it hurts."

I sat down on the floor. "Well yeah. You whacked my teeth pretty good."

"I feel kind of sick, Preacher."

I got him back to his bunk and bandaged his wrist with some Scotch tape and toilet paper. I waited until his breathing became uneven and he began moaning a girl's name over and over again. I hopped off my bunk and slid in bed beside him. He was sweating and begging to either Amanda or Jennifer for a cool drink of water. I petted him and told him he was going to be just fine. Soon he was going to walk from that old grave because he was a friend of Jesus. Just a little glass, Lord. That's all I need.

"I want to go home, Preacher."

"You're on your way, son. I'm right here with you." I held his hand, and pulled the white sheets over him, and tucked them around him. His dark eyes flicked around the room. They were wild and confused. He grabbed at my uniform and pressed his face against my chest. My Lazarus draped in white. In his most perfect form.

Elegy

CAROLYN RANU

You were not Larry in Luling, Louisiana. You were not yet ours in that woman's living room. We sat on the couch while you stood by the back door, ears folded against your head like birdwings. The racetrack had named you Fair Dinkum Mate, which was hard to say in one breath although the woman tried. Come here, Fair Dink, she said and slapped her thigh. Here boy, she said, wanting to show you off to us. But you stayed by the back door, not caring if we picked you. Her teenage son stood opposite me in the distance beyond the stucco archway that opened into the kitchen. He leaned against the counter eating a bowl of cereal in the dark. I watched him watch you. The woman told me earlier on the phone that you had grown fond of him. He liked to take you out in the back yard to run circles. He'd slap your rump. You'd chase him, your tongue sloppy. When the boy's spoon tapped his bowl, your ears pricked up and then folded in again.

Larry? I tried.

We had joked about one day owning a dog and naming him Larry. We joked in the different apartments while sitting on the futon, the windows open to the bars and to the busy street and to the library where the homeless man killed himself on the steps, the sanitation workers hosing blood off the cement in the morning. In all these petless places, William and I thought it would be funny to have a dog and name him Larry. Perhaps we didn't know what to do with our desire. We made light of it by turning the dog we couldn't have into something amusing, into a Larry. But when I called you Larry that night of your adoption, it didn't feel like a joke.

Larry, I tried again, holding out my hand. Come see.

One of the apartment buildings, the one across from the library, harbored a resident cat we'd coax through our front door. She was cream and orange and meant to kill the mice that crawled in the empty spaces between the walls. We probably could have heard the mice scurry any time of day if we listened, but it was at night with the lights off and with the hope for sleep that we tuned in to the scratch of their frantic movements behind the plaster. Don't feed her, the landlord warned us about the cat, or she won't be hungry enough to do her job. She liked the windowsill in our living room the best. She'd perch there in immobile contemplation, her tail hanging down in a hook. She was the kind of cat that when she meowed, she meowed without making a noise. Her mouth yawned open when she rubbed her head against my hand, and her eyes squinched. She seemed to be saying something. What's the matter? William would say when he caught me looking out the window and petting the cat, and I'd say, Nothing. I'd say, Why do you ask?

* * *

Oh, Larry, that woman and her son, the Luling backyard, it's strange to think you have memories that precede me. The peripheral passing of chain link as you ran happy circles, the crabgrass coming up at you, the boy's sneakered feet. Even when you're lying in your bed under the oleander, I wonder what you see that I don't from my place on the stoop. He's digging his own grave, I tell people about the nest you've excavated in the mulch and mud under the tree. They often stop on the sidewalk when they see you. Those who live on the block say, Hey Larry, and sometimes you'll look up. Their leashed dogs bark, and strain, and stick their noses between the fence posts with an eagerness that is uncomfortable for everybody.

There's the girl who walks around the neighborhood with a pet rat perched on her shoulders. I'll talk to her and not know the rat is there until it peeks out from her curtain of hair, a whiskered nose emerging from one side, a pale tail flicking down the other. I know your dog, she told me the first time we met. She and her dad pass our house every morning on their way to school. She thinks you look like a deer. She thinks that when you curl up under the oleander, you look dead. Well, I tell her, he is cadaverously calm.

William wants to plant a sago palm in your spot under the tree because it's the only empty place left in the yard, and when William gets nervous he likes to plant things. The pipes rumble beneath the kitchen floor, and I'll know he's out front with his pants rolled up at the cuff, hosing new elephant ears and nursing caladiums. I can even tell from the sound when he slides his thumb over the nozzle to scatter the spray.

* * *

You seemed happy enough when we first brought you to the house. We developed rituals, the morning walk to the coffee shop, a run along the levee. We learned to pet only your head because the rest of you would shed clumps of white hair that gathered in the bedroom corners. Luca, the neighbor, worried you were coming down from amphetamines and horse steroids from the racetrack. Look, he said one afternoon, gesturing to you splayed on the sidewalk. Your long mouth was slack, your tongue lolling onto the cement and your brown eyes, deep pools always, especially impenetrable that day, glazed open but seeing nothing. He's stuck in a K-hole, Luca said. It's withdrawal. But I told him no, you were meditative, dreamy. It's the dog equivalent of walking with your head down, I said. How you learn to walk with your head down, private worlds unfolding inside but outside nothing. A girl walks with her head down and bumps into people. Oops, I often hear myself say to strangers, sorry.

My mother worried how you would react to the first baby. She read news reports about dogs mauling infants. She thought you could confuse a baby for a rabbit. What about his predatory instinct, she asked me. Do you think it just goes away? But when we pulled to the curb with the new baby in the car, you only lifted your head and then harrumphed back down into the dirt.

It's not like we paid an outrageous amount of attention to you before, so I don't think you felt neglected with the new family arrangement. I think you felt relieved not to have to try anymore.

When we rolled the wind-up swing into one room, you got up and moved into another. You barked more often to be let out. Who can blame him? William and I would say to Luca, although secretly we missed the way you used to stand in the middle of the action, if we had a party or were just unloading the dishwasher, and you would remain there stoically in the way, not asking to be a part but not leaving either.

Sometimes I think all Larry needs to be human is a pair of arms, William told me one morning in bed, the baby thank god still asleep in his crib. The sun was throwing rectangles of light around the room that would fade and reform with each passing cloud. We could hear you lapping water in the kitchen and the clang of your rabies tag hitting against your heart tag hitting against your name tag when you lowered your long neck to drink from the bowl. I think I see Larry in every animal, William said.

And then there was the night at the coffee shop when William fed you ice cubes to make the baby laugh. The way you held your head up to snap at the cubes, made you look like you were talking.

I would understand if you confused the arrival of the twins with the men who added the extra room, a real nursery this time, to the back of our house. The construction was hard on both of us, your stomach groaning with coiled anxiety and mine fat with babies. The men were in and out of the house, knocking down walls and tracking plaster dust on long sheets of paper they had rolled out to protect the wood floors. You walked the edges of rooms, and sniffed the handles of hammers, and then skittered away when one of their hands reached down to pet you.

The house was getting bigger, but your world was shrinking. The men tramped past your oleander, back and forth from the door to their truck that played a loud, untuned radio station. They opened windows to air out the dust. Curtains billowed toward you, and doors slammed in secret drafts, all the noise and movement your private terror, your constant pant. You found a small space between the refrigerator and the kitchen cabinet to curl up and hide. You willed yourself to be small, almost invisible, a penny someone had dropped, a Cheerio never swept up.

Even outside, and I know you'll claim this was an accident but there are no accidents, life guns a person toward one end through direct or indirect means, you know that, Larry, even outside, leashless in Audubon Park where people flock on nice days with blankets and rollerblades, even there where the laugh therapy group sits cross-legged under the giant oak tree laughing and rocking, rocking and laughing, even there, you found tragedy on the edge of an algae-slicked pond you mistook for grass. I heard the splash and knew it was you before I turned away from the stroller and looked. A boy approaching from the opposite direction also stopped. Together we watched the water ripple out in little backwards waves that disrupted the green scrim you had disappeared beneath. He's okay, I think I told the boy, although I did wonder if you could swim. I could never count on survival instincts with you. We held our breath until you surfaced, stiff legs first like a drowned mule. You bobbed, and righted yourself, and clambered up the bank. You sludged back onto shore. Well, okay, let's get on with it, you basically told me. You had cut your back leg in the resurfacing, a slice on your thin skin that trailed a line of blood on the sidewalk so that we had to stop and make a tourniquet with a baby wipe.

Once home, I put the babies—there were three of them now—in their beds for a nap and crawled into my own. I could hear the murmuring of the neighbor eating lunch with a Dutch friend in her back yard, the clanking of her knife against her plate. They were talking about cancer. You know, the one said, it literally eats your brain. It's horrible, she said, and I imagined, as she said this, the delicate way she had of pushing her food onto her fork with her knife. Later, when I went into the kitchen for a glass of water, I found you again between refrigerator and counter, licking, licking, your tongue flat and deliberate; you had licked the baby wipe off the wound and refused to let the blood scab. Your mouth and legs were stained red.

Larry, I said, we've got to put a stop to this.

But we didn't stop.

Stitched and returned to your bed under the oleander, you still caused trouble. The veterinarian had gone on about your teeth, about periodontal disease, its abscessation and sub-gingival calculus, the way a tooth can rot from the inside out. I listened and nodded. There's a lot of pressure to love you at the veterinarian's office. Ned, the vet, sells a self-produced record of songs about dogs by the cash register. He and his golden retriever are on the cover of the album, all bare feet and mandolin. When we walk into the office, the receptionists *ooh* and *ahh* over you and call you Old Man and stroke the length of your body with manicured hands that you lean into, traitor. They ask me if you've been eating. They ask me if you're feeling well, as though I have access to your thoughts and would know, as though anyone could know how another felt. And I do love you, but I refuse to make a display of my affection for them. I also refused to pay to have your teeth cleaned, which seems undignified and extravagant for a dog, who should be nose deep in the dirt, rolling legs up on the grass. So the day I stood behind Ned in the grocery store line I became uncomfortable. I tried not to talk about you—there are other interests in this world—but the woman in front of us had a cart full of food, and the conversation went on until it narrowed into you, your teeth, my guilt. I admitted how your breath does smell like a fish factory. If his breath is bad, Ned told me, it's because his teeth are rotting. Make the appointment, he urged. It's the reasonable thing to do.

But when have we ever been reasonable, Larry? I know you hate the vet. You make me use the leash to pull you out of the van. You resist me all the way up the stairs and through the door. All you want from life is to stop and smell where other dogs have peed, and I pull you away from even that pleasure because I can only stand and wait for so long. Better to let you walk without tether. I started leaving the leash at home, trusting you to follow me to the coffee shop. I let you cross busy streets unfettered, much to the alarm of William and other pedestrians. I even started leaving the front gate open in case you wanted to escape your oleander nest for a stroll.

Once you snuck out and followed me and the kids to the grocery store without our knowing. We returned home to an open gate, an empty yard. Mom, how many times have I told you to close the gate? my oldest son scolded me. A man who read your phone tag left a message saying he was standing with you outside the automatic doors and then another message saying he was loading you into his car and taking you to his house to play with his dogs until he heard from me. The kids scrambled out of the van when they saw you in his huge, fenced-in yard. Is that Larry? one asked. There you were, a dog among dogs, a pack running heedless from the front yard to the back yard to the front again, running so fast your hind legs flew out beneath you when you banked for the turn. I didn't want to bring you home.

Later that week, the vet receptionist called to book your teeth cleaning appointment. She asked if she was talking to Larry's mom, and I said no, you're speaking to Larry's owner.

* * *

I know you know what I was up to. You had already started to bleed when I walked out the door that night. To meet a friend for a drink, I had told William and the kids. I bent down and took your leg in my hand. I thought maybe you had cut yourself on the thorns of the bougainvillea. Larry's bleeding, I called to William through the screen door, and he said he'd take a look, and so I left. It was a licked smear of red. It was nothing. And around midnight, when my cell started to ring, I didn't answer. I'm allowed to have drinks with my friend, I thought. I'm allowed, I thought, even though we all knew my friend was more than a friend. When the phone continued to ring, I turned it off because I knew. Just like that, I knew it was all over.

I drove home without the radio playing, always playing, but not that night. You didn't lift your head when I pulled up to the curb or when I clanged the front gate closed. The house was dark; you were curled under the oleander, listless except for your tongue licking your mouth, licking your leg. It was not you that I saw in the dark but the movement of your tongue flattening out around your leg. Larry, I tried. I knelt and held out my hand. Come see, I said. You shifted the position of your head in the dirt, revealing a dark pool of blood. Your nose was dry, your legs licked red. Where have you been? William yelled out from behind the screen door. I couldn't see him either, only the darker outline of a body in dark doorway. I've been calling you and calling you for the van, and where have you been? he asked, although I think he knew too. I looked at your mouth. The inside pus had festered and oozed out and split open your gums. He's been bleeding all night, William said. I couldn't take him to the vet, he said. I was calling you for the van. All I wanted was the van, he said.

And there I was kneeling beside you, petting you, the whole length of you, and oh, Larry, it doesn't have to be like this. You've killed him, William says from behind the screen. Mulch hangs from your lips, clotted up in lumps of your blood, and Larry, it doesn't have to be like this. You've killed our dog, William is saying from the door, and I want to tell you that there are other ways to be happy. I saw wild parrots rise from the ground the other day. They lifted up all at once, as though blades of grass were ascending. I thought to tell you about it, Larry.

The Ones Who Don't Say They Love You

MAURICE RUFFIN

You on the sidewalk out front of the convenience store. The sun beat down like it do every morning. The street cleaner pass by spraying lemonade-smelling water. It get your tennis shoes, shoes that's coming loose at the heel, so your socks get wet, too. Soapy water drip down the curb. Not like this street stay clean long.

Mr. Jellnik round the corner like he being dogged. He ain't much to look at. They never is. He like the other men who come down for foot-fixing conventions and brain-fixing conventions. He got a fat neck and skin like old peaches. His wallet fat too; that all you care about.

Jellnik eye you from crotch to mouth. He pull out a pack. He smoke. You pull one from the pack and light yours with his.

"Why are you the only one out here this morning?" He cover his eyes half way. The sun glare off the Mississippi River Bridge like I SEE YOU BOY.

"I'm the onliest one you need," you say.

"True enough."

The other tappers already off to work, probably almost done with the men they left with. They left you with the tip box. The box is for your protection. You wear bottle caps on your soles and dance so people think you and the others are cymbal monkeys.

A police car roll up the street. The lights flash *blue white blue*, but the car don't slow down even though the cop lean over to get a eyeful of your faces. Jellnik's butt cheeks tense up. You could tell him don't sweat it, but you like seeing him squirm. If you didn't like seeing him squirm, you would tell him cops never arrest Johns, especially not Johns from Ida-fucking-ho. What you do probably make the cops puke. It's easy to lock up dudes for shooting dudes. That's good business. Putting a junior high slut in jail is bad business. If they hear all about what you do, people stop coming to town. You all starve then.

The stoplight turn green. The police car pull off. Jellnik's ass relax. You don't really need to tap to stay out of jail. But if you don't fake it, what else you got?

* * *

Jellnik the only one who buy you food after he do his business. Now, you sore inside and out, but you starving, too. The queenie cook behind the counter flipping pancakes. Maybe the pancake take your mind off zhow rough Jellnik handle you.

Jellnik's toast and runny eggs come out first. He squirt ketchup all over. He gulp coffee, get a refill, gulp that, too. He don't give you none. Your stomach growl. When you bring food to the corner, the other tappers take most of it, leave you the scrap. Most days you don't eat till you go home. But today you hungry. What the shit is the holdup? The queenie cook went in back and your pancake sitting on the cold side of the grill like a Frisbee that just stop spinning.

Jellnik been here all week. The first day he show up, he take Pink and Quincy first, one in the morning and the other round lunch. He come back for you after noontime rocking up the street with hair stuck to his forehead. After he take a piece of you, he never buy what Pink and Quincy selling again. That's a plus on top of the money. It's the only time you won out when they around. You too dark, and your hair ain't wavy and good like Pink hair. But now you can laugh inside when you see them, but don't laugh out loud. They punch you if you smile.

Jellnik break out a roll of cash. He put down two twenty-dollar bills. One for the food and one for you. Twenty won't cover the food, so that'll come out of what you earn.

"When I leave tonight," Jellnik say, "I want you to come with me."

He pour sugar in his coffee. His finger got ketchup on it that he don't see. He stir his coffee with that finger.

"I'll get you a plane ticket, and I have a storage unit you can stay in until we find you something more appropriate."

"Man," you say, "I ain't going to nobody Idaho."

"Listen to me," he say. "You can do better than this place. It's not safe for you."

"Nobody mess with me 'round here," you say.

He put a hand on your face where you bruised from when Pink hit you the other day. You like to flinch away, but you don't 'cause his hand feel warm.

"You don't know anything," Jellnik say. "I've been visiting New Orleans for over twenty years. You think you're one of the first boys to stand on that corner? What do you think happened to the boys who were there before you?"

You could tell Jellnik about Pink's brother, Simmy, who went puff like match smoke last month. Simmy was the first one you met when you came out here. He looked out for you, but now he gone. You know he ain't go to no Idaho.

"Why you care about what happen to me?" you ask.

"Just be back at the corner around 6 p.m. with your personal belongings. I'll be in a gray sport utility vehicle."

When Jellnik get up, the stool squeal like it being stabbed. Your pancake black and crusty still dying on that grill.

The queenie cook wearing mascara and hoop earrings, so you know he a full-on Mary. He flip the pancake to your plate. He smack the plate down. Sound like it crack, but it don't. He shake his head at you like he better than you. You want to jump over the counter and stomp his face on the grill. Or make him suck your junk. You want to make him say your name like he mean it. But he grown. He break you in five pieces, if you try. You be on the wrong end like always.

The pancake darker than you. You don't touch it.

You snatch all the money and run. The cook yell after you, but those just words.

* * *

Lorraine don't have no legs. When you go into the house with a box of chicken and biscuits, she back early from the casino downtown. She in her spot in front of the TV. You bought toilet paper and chocolate milk, too. She don't look up. She eating a bag of orange puffs. Her lips orange. She keep them puffs on her lap so the little kids won't get none. None of you like to get close to her. She grab too hard.

You go to the kitchen and put the chicken down. You yell out the back door for the little boys rolling in the grass by the flat-tire pickup truck. The boys are foster boys like you. Lorraine get a check every two weeks for keeping y'all. You don't get any because she call it rent. She take rent to the casino. If she win, she don't tell you.

"You better find your own," she always say. But she eat what you bring home. Her cut she call it.

You go back to the kitchen. You open the box and a roach in it. The little boys come in the back door, screaming and smacking each other. You can't let them see that roach because then they won't eat. You don't have money to buy more, and the little bit of chicken you brought ain't enough for them anyway. You pop the bug in your mouth.

Jellnik's storage shed must be pretty big. A big man wouldn't have a small shed. A big man would have a shed big enough to do cartwheels in. His condo in the French Quarter is small. But everything in the French Quarter small. If everything was big, it would be the French Dollar. When he put you in position, you stare out the window. There a tree outside with heart-shaped leaves. You count those leaves. You never get past fifteen. In all the times you done business with Jellnik, he never say he love you. That's the only reason you listen to him at all. The other ones always love you.

* * *

You don't want to see Pink and Quincy at the corner, but they tap dancing extra fast. They trying to ring the last little bit of pocket change out of the tourists before it get dark. The cops won't take you in for hustling Johns, but they don't stand for curfew-breakers.

It don't look right for tappers to be on the street after dark. What don't look right is bad for business. Bottle caps scraping concrete make you sick like you ate a crateful of bottle caps. You wonder where Jellnik at. It's after time. You wonder if you feel better when he come around.

"Where you been at?" Quincy say.

"Not making any, I bet," Pink say. "Ain't never got his shit together, this baby here."

You tell them to suck a horse, and they howl.

"You a salty little bitch today," Pink say. "You slow?"

You tell them you ain't slow. You tell them you about to get paid. You tell them you leaving with Jellnik as soon as he get here.

"Humpty Dumpty?" Quincy frown.

"That man ain't bringing you nowheres, boy," Pink say.

A gray SUV down the block. It look like it going to turn before it make it to you. You stop looking.

Quincy pinch your shoulder. "You're serious, ain't you, baby?"

"He coming for me," you say.

"I bet you twenty he ain't," Pink say.

Pink wrestle you and snatch your last from your pocket. It's only a five. Pink say that'll do until you get more. You tell him you ain't lost yet. Pink say he good for the night and leave with your five.

You only have one bottle cap for your shoe, but you going to pass some time tapping. Make some change to buy a cold drink because your mouth taste like funk. You dance until that cap break loose and roll into the gutter.

Something flash. A police car creep your way. The lights blink slow, but the car speed up. You can't see the cop driving, but hands in cuffs press on the back seat glass. Jellnik's face behind those hands.

You step in the street like you going to follow. But you don't.

Reasons for Concern Regarding My Girlfriend of Five Days, Monica Garza

JOHN TAIT

That she cursed twice in the first full sentence she spoke to me, even though she was trying to pacify me after my accident with her uninsured younger brother. That she also drives uninsured and seems to view this as a lifestyle choice. That she is twenty-four, and I am thirty-nine. That she has tattoos: two visible, one partly visible, unknown invisible. That in that first meeting, after her uninsured brother's truck crushed my Corolla's right front bumper in the *Sac N' Save* parking lot, and after he next tried to drive off before I blocked him in, and after he then swore and threatened for fifteen minutes before getting on his cell phone, Monica appeared and actually tried to convince me not to call the police. That she succeeded. That after she and I talked for another half hour, I decided to forget the matter entirely, even though between my divorce settlement and credit card debt, I'll have trouble paying the repair myself.

That she asked me out first, and to my surprise, pleasure and suspicion, said she'd enjoyed our conversation and I seemed nice, then asked if I wanted to see a movie. That she made the first move four hours later, at a picnic table up on the levee along the artificial lake, or at least nuzzled me in the evening chill when the conversation fell off and gave a series of soft, impatient sighs until I kissed her.

That she seems more impressed than she should that I am an adjunct professor of English at the local college. That she probably thinks I'm wealthier than I am. That she refers to her job in the Walmart auto center as a career. That her determination to work slavishly to support her doltish brother's education seems less admirable to me than misguided. That she wears shorter skirts and larger earrings and is better looking than any woman I've dated since high school. That she's less educated than any woman I've dated since high school.

That for two hours from the time I dropped her off that night to the time I climbed into my bed, nearly forgetting to take off my shoes, I couldn't form a single, coherent thought.

Notable Insecurities at the Two-Week Mark with New Girlfriend, Monica Garza

Because I am so white and so lame at times when I'm with her that I feel like Lawrence freaking Welk. Because I know she humors my attempts to be cool, like when I asked yesterday about a song on her radio, "Is that *banda* or *grupera*?" and she said wryly that it was neither, then changed channels. Because my best friend is named Doug, who is an actuary who is married to another actuary, and they live with two yellow labs in a gated community called Idle Pines, and Monica's best friend Analeticia is a manicurist who dates a guy I think is named Puppet who drives a chopped Civic with "*Chingalo!*" in gothic script on the back windshield, and both Analeticia and Puppet stared at me with stony incomprehension the only time we met. Because whenever I talk politics, art, literature or the intricacies of human behavior with Monica, while she appears to understand fully, she seems utterly uninterested and just watches me with an amused, indulgent look like I'm a precocious child. Because when I finally convinced her to read chapters from my latest unpublished novel, she at first declined to comment, then said mildly that my characters seemed to have much free time, and they spent a lot of it staring into the rain and agonizing over decisions they would never make or staring into the rain and contemplating actions they would never take.

Because, though I thanked her for her feedback, kissed her forehead and made a show of noting her comments on my draft, I actually felt hurt and misunderstood.

Because when I force myself to be brutally honest, I can't for the life of me see why someone like Monica Garza would want to go out with someone like me.

Because I question my own motives. Because I worried for an hour the other night, while preparing for my postcolonial lit seminar, that I view Monica, with her Mestizo cheekbones and glossy black hair, as some objectified, exotic "other" to colonize with my white maleness. Because I have imagined, more than once, running into my ex and have pictured in exquisite slo-mo her every grimace and twitch at seeing me with a pretty girl fifteen years younger, before remembering that she would probably laugh. Because I have both fretted about running into neighbors, colleagues or students while with Monica and secretly hoped that we are observed, discussed.

Because for the first time I can remember, the physical relationship has advanced faster than I feel comfortable. Because after our first time making love Monica interrogated me about what I liked and didn't like, then gave her own preferences, after which I said I usually liked to discover such things naturally, to which she said that it was just as natural to talk about them, to which I said that her way took away from the spontaneity, to which she said that my way guaranteed that one or both of us would never enjoy activities that the other was perfectly willing to join in just because we'd never bothered to ask, to which I had no real response.

Because she likes to go out dancing and I like to stay in reading. Because I speak softly and hear poorly and she talks so loudly it makes my ears ring but can hear my neighbor's cat jump on the sill outside the bedroom window to watch us. Because she walks faster than me, drags me by my shirtfront into mall stores with gaudy signs and loud music where she buys her short skirts and large earrings. Because most of what sustains our relationship so far is what we find amusing or incomprehensible about each other, her snickering at my alphabetized New American Film collection and morning Tai Chi, me marveling at her girlish little charm bracelets and industrial-sized overnight makeup bag.

Because she grew up speaking a language I can barely form a sentence in. Because she can have a phone conversation with her cousin, and I can hear my name spoken twice but have no idea what she is saying about me.

Because I never care about any of these things while I'm with her, but only afterward, alone, late, pouring a glass of milk at my open fridge.

Troubling Revelations Regarding Monica Garza, My Girlfriend of a Month And a Half

The fact that, an hour before what I will refer to as our "big talk," at my place following our weekend away in Austin, she admitted that she flirted with me that first day mainly in hopes I wouldn't call the police on her uninsured brother, and I laughed a lot because I'd suspected as much, then laughed less because I hadn't really wanted to believe it. The fact that, immediately before the "big talk," while continuing a debate on whether I am either a cautious or a crappy driver, a clip of a girl crying beside a burnt house came on the TV news, and Monica's demeanor changed, and she sat up straight in bed then told me, with grave expression and moist eyes, that she had some "important things" to tell me.

The fact that the first thing she told me was how she ran away at sixteen and became an exotic dancer in San Antonio, a story I tried to receive with the unflappable understanding of a man of the world. The fact that she went on to describe how, during the stripping years, she dated a dealer and became "half-addicted" to methamphetamine and contracted one of the "not-so-bad" hepatitises, which I also tried to hear with cool equanimity. The fact that she next went on to tell me how at eighteen she was incarcerated in Wilson County Jail for fifteen months for kiting checks while involved with another man, who is now dead, details which I tried, less successfully, to shrug off, distracted by the quiet, persistent voice that repeated, in case I'd forgotten, that SHE WAS IN JAIL.

The fact that, after our big talk, as I watched her sob and tell me that I wouldn't think the same of her anymore, she looked so miserable, and I was still so dazed that I told her that everyone does things they regret, that I certainly had, even stealing a Christmas tree from a department store once while on acid back in college, and that we could only hope to learn from our mistakes. The fact that, as I said these words, I hated how much I sounded like some ineffectual youth counselor. The fact that, after she kissed me and went home, I absently took my wallet from the dresser and counted the cash, a moot action since I couldn't remember how much I'd had before, and was so filled with self-reproach after that I threw said wallet hard against said dresser.

Reasons I Shouldn't Call My Quasi-Girlfriend of Nearly Two Months, Monica Garza

Because I haven't called for over a week following our "big talk," with a resulting build-up of anticipatory dread for the moment when I do. Because, there was honestly some ambiguity about who would call whom. Because even in the message she left today, asking if I wanted to come out clubbing with her and Analeticia this Friday, though she tried to seem casual, the way her voice hitched at the end sounded so tentative and anxious that it made me feel the same.

Because my parents are visiting from Kansas City this weekend, and though our relationship has of late matured into a fellowship of adult equals who respect each others' life decisions, and though Mom and Dad have managed to adapt admirably to America's changing culture, I can't be sure what effect the combination of Monica's youth, ethnicity, social class, wardrobe, legal history, bodily decoration and vocabulary might have on them. Because I get so mad that I would even care, at almost forty, about the above that I feel like inviting Monica over anyway, which another part of me recognizes is an immature and dangerous rebellious impulse, much like the one that led me fifteen months ago to go out for drinks with a woman I knew had a crush on me just because my wife had made some belittling remarks, though the marriage-ending tryst that followed was pretty much my own dumb fault. Because I just got a new cell phone and haven't transferred all my old numbers yet. Because I would actually think of the previous issue as an excuse not to call someone.

Probable Reasons Why Monica Garza, The Girl I Was Until Recently Involved With, Hasn't Called Me

Because when she last appeared, at two-thirty on Friday night / Saturday morning, dropped off by best friend Analeticia after their night of clubbing, and she hammered on my door, waking my parents on the foldout in the front room, I didn't answer until she'd wailed my name and shouted in a voice both playful and severe that I was a dick and better take what was coming to me. Because when I did answer, I told Monica that we should talk some other time. Because when she then laughed and started to walk away, swaying on her high heels, then wheeled back to call me a coward and hypocrite, I acted like I didn't understand. Because when she suddenly darted inside my apartment, then lost her balance on the slippery hardwood and fell and only then looked up to see my parents in their plaid pajamas and smiled at them with heartbreakingly hopeful timidity, Monica received back a look I could call arctic. Because, in my parents' defense, one of the reasons for their reaction might have been that, as Monica fell, her skirt rose the small distance necessary to show she wasn't wearing underwear. Because, instead of helping, I stood over her and felt an irrational fear that she might grab or grope me in view of my parents. Because, when she rose and I introduced her, we all noticed that the hand she waved in greeting before stuffing it hastily into her purse held the same panties she should have been wearing. Because I then called a cab for her. Because when I led her outside and she stood, facing away, shivering and sniffling, I didn't touch her or speak until her cab arrived, just paid the driver, then went back inside where my parents waited, their faces stricken and very pale.

Feelings I Must Fight in the Wake of My Split(?) from Monica Garza

A malaise that makes it hard to focus on what I should: my teaching, my writing, my income tax preparation. A tiresome funk I can only alleviate by writing long, self-involved lists. A compulsion to go to Walmart and walk the aisles, approaching the auto center with dread and hope until I glimpse her, maybe over by the spark plugs, and flee. A painful awareness that never before in my life has a pretty girl banged on my door and wailed my name in the middle of the night, and it's unlikely this will ever happen again.

A dread that, by losing Monica, I've lost my one late opportunity to become a person who continues to grow and change along with a growing and changing world rather than shutting myself fearfully away with the rest of the people like me. A naive optimism, fueled by well-intentioned movies and TV shows, that we Americans can overcome all barriers between us and embrace each other based on our shared humanity. A recognition that even though the above is a crock, it shouldn't be. The worry that I am more concerned with what others think of me than with my own happiness, a fact that makes me wish I was miles from every other human being, maybe on some unpopulated island or at least archipelago, though when I imagine myself in that desolate place it seems only natural to add a companion, leading to fantasies (about M. G.) that are both pleasant and troubling.

Consolations to Remain Mindful of Post-Monica G.

That a year from now I will be dating a woman more age, ethnicity and background appropriate, a librarian, journalist or real estate agent who wears long skirts and small earrings, a relationship I will find pleasant, comfortable, comprehensible. That a year from now, if I do see Monica Garza, maybe at the mall, clinging to the arm of her young, tattooed *novio*, I won't be as torn up by that image as I am now. That I shouldn't be expected, at nearly forty, to undergo changes I am unequipped to make. That, though our brief time together is over, at least the pleasures I remember are mine to store fondly in my memories. That even though the preceding is a crock, it really shouldn't be.

Questions I Wish I Had Been Able to Ask Monica Garza, the Woman I Can No Longer Quite Believe I Dated for A While Last Year

What did she come to talk about that night, drunk and banging on my door?

Why did she say I was a coward and hypocrite, or at least did she think I was those things in ways I don't already know I am?

What was it like to run away at sixteen and be alone in the city?

What was it like to be in jail at eighteen?

What dreams does one give up to work at the Walmart auto center to support an uninsured, doltish younger brother?

Did she hope that, if we continued dating, I would help her financially?

If not, did she hope I would help her in some other way?

If not, why did she want to be with me?

Could she understand that, the more I think on it, those revelations about her past didn't bother me so much for what they said about her as much as for how they contributed to my larger worry that she lived in a different world than mine -- not just a different culture or different neighborhood, but a place I could never inhabit, a place from which somebody, looking over, might find someone like me quaint, dull, complacent, undeservedly protected?

What is she doing right now, while I write this?

Where is she now?

If, just suppose, Monica, I was passing by the Walmart auto center with my cart of groceries and was to run into you, maybe over by the spark plugs, and was to overcome my impulse to flee, and we were to talk, maybe laugh at what happened between us last year, how would you look at me now and what would you see and what might we talk about with the honesty possible in the brief moments allowed for such things?

And would I be able to handle it as I waved then walked away, feeling you watching me, steering my grocery cart through the aspirin and diaper displays back toward the checkout?

The Mason Jar

JESSICA VIADA

Ultimately, it became an issue of practicality. Ana could no longer relegate her thoughts about Evan to the moments just before she slipped into sleep at night or to the spaces between her eyelashes when she blinked away her dreams in the morning. For weeks now, the thoughts followed her out of bed, dripped down the back of her neck in the shower, hummed in her ears with the whirring of the hairdryer. They disturbed her during meetings at work, invisible gnats that she swatted at while taking notes on her yellow legal pad. At the gym, they manifested themselves on the treadmill despite her efforts to stomp them out each time her foot met the belt. Thoughts of Evan's fingers, Evan's mouth, Evan's breath chattered incessantly, until Ana thought she would scream.

"Are you okay?" her sister, Iris, asked over dinner at Ana's house. The pasta that Ana had cooked for them was soggy, and Ana watched Iris push around limp pieces of penne with her fork. "You seem a little distracted."

"I'm fine," Ana responded, pushing her plate aside. "Just overworked." She lifted the bottle of merlot from the center of the table.

"Have you talked to Evan lately?" Iris asked as the wine spilled into her glass.

"We haven't spoken in a while."

"Do you want to talk about it?"

Ana sighed. Iris had listened dutifully in the days after Evan left. She made tea, brought Kleenex, followed Ana's circling thoughts with patience that was uncharacteristic but not limitless. "I'm tired of talking about it. He'll come around."

Later, after Iris had gone home, the thoughts returned as Ana cleaned her kitchen. Evan's disarming smile, Evan's cheek against her neck. She wiped them away from the burners of the stove and the countertop but noticed that they had also gathered in the cold tomato sauce. Ana rinsed them down the sink and turned on the garbage disposal. That's it, Ana thought, *enough*. She downed the rest of her wine, threw open one of the kitchen cupboards, and pulled out a clean Mason jar. Then she grabbed a long-handled wooden spoon, marched into her bedroom, and shut the door.

When Ana emerged, the Mason jar she carried was heavy with thick liquid that looked like molasses and gleamed under the kitchen lights. The wooden spoon that Ana held in her other hand was slick with saliva. Her hand trembled lightly as she placed the spoon in the sink. Tiny beads of perspiration had formed along her hairline, and Ana wiped them away. She set the jar squarely on one of the countertop's red clay tiles and cut a circle of white cheese cloth. She secured the cloth over the jar's opening with a rubber band, washed the spoon, and went to bed.

In the morning, Ana awoke with a terrible ache in her chest. She felt bruised and tender. Yet in spite of the pain, Ana felt strangely calm. She watched the summer sunlight play upon the corner of her bedspread. The house was still, and Ana wondered whether it had ever been so quiet. In the shower that morning, Ana examined her chest. The hollow between her breasts seemed slightly deeper than usual, though the skin was pink and smooth. Gently, she pressed two fingers to the space and cried out in pain. She wrapped herself in a soft blue robe and shook two aspirin from the bottle in the medicine cabinet. Her bare feet made small patting sounds on her way to the kitchen to pour herself a glass of water.

The Mason jar twinkled on the counter in the early morning light. Its rich, dark content was the same color as Ana's wet hair, black with amber edges. The jar was hot, as if it had just emerged from the dishwasher. Ana set her glass down next to the jar and put her nose to the cheese cloth. The smell was dense and sweet. It reminded her of something she used to eat as a child. She was tempted to lift the cheese cloth and run her finger along the inside edge: just a taste. Instead, she opened a drawer and pulled out a white index card and a black marker. She wrote Evan's name carefully, adding elegant flourishes to the curves of the E, the open arms of the V. Ana propped the card against the jar and poured herself a bowl of cereal, lingering over the counter as she ate. She picked up the phone and dialed Evan's number. His voice on the recording sounded impatient and rough, nothing like the soft voice in her ear that she craved.

"*You've reached Evan. I'm not available. Please leave a message.*"

"Hi, Evan, I, I have something for you. If you want to stop by and pick it up, that would be great. Thanks, bye."

She placed the phone back into its receiver and continued getting ready for work.

At the office that day, Ana was able to concentrate for the first time in weeks. The tension that she usually carried in her shoulder blades melted away, and she conducted her meetings with clarity and focus. During lunch, one of her colleagues commented that she seemed well-rested. Later, at the gym, Ana felt lighter. It was as if she were almost floating over the treadmill instead of pounding its track. She ran seven miles, a new record, and even toward the end when her lungs started to burn, Ana's mind remained still, almost detached. She decided it was the perfect time to try yoga again. The low lights and soft music in the yoga studio heightened the quietness Ana felt, and as she followed the instructor's movements, she was pleased to discover that the thoughts that had been consuming her were not hiding in their usual places. In a forward fold, she saw that they were not nestled between her toes. Nor did they fall from the crease behind her knee during warrior pose. They did not even trickle down her arms when she lifted her body into a backbend.

When she returned home that evening, Ana found Iris in the kitchen examining the jar.

"So you're not even calling before you come over now?" Ana asked.

"I left a message. Check your phone," her sister answered. She bent over the jar. "What is this?"

"It's for Evan. Leave it alone."

"Is he coming by?"

"Yes."

"Did you talk to him?" Iris looked at her sister and raised one eyebrow.

"I left a message."

"Oh Ana," Iris sighed. "Let it go."

As she turned to face Ana, Iris's elbow struck the jar, knocking it sideways. The rubber band popped off the top, and the thick black liquid pushed past the cheese cloth and oozed over the counter. A fine steam rose from its surface and a syrupy smell filled the kitchen.

"Iris!" Ana shrieked. She rushed over and set the jar upright. She shoved her sister away and snatched a spoon from the drawer. The spoon made scraping noises against the countertop as Ana scooped up the syrup.

"I'm sorry!" Iris cried. "Here, let me help." She reached for the sponge in Ana's sink.

Ana impatiently tapped the neck of the spoon against the glass as she shook syrup back into the jar. "That's fine, Iris. You've done enough."

Iris ignored her sister and began wiping the black liquid from the counter. Some of it stuck to her fingers, and Iris brought her hand to her face and sniffed.

"It smells good," Iris said. "Are you trying to lure him back with dessert?"

Before Ana could answer, Iris stuck her fingers in her mouth. Her eyes widened. "Oh my God," she whispered. "Ana, what is this? It's amazing."

"Is it?" Ana asked. She brought the spoon under the light to examine the syrup more carefully. The liquid had a reddish tinge and tiny crystals gleamed through the syrup like stars. She placed the spoon on her tongue and closed her mouth around the liquid. It tasted silky, dissolving on her tongue like butter. It was sweet but not overwhelming or rich as Ana would have expected from the consistency of the syrup. She swallowed, and her entire body flooded with warmth. Ana closed her eyes and imagined the long tongues of hummingbirds lapping nectar from orange trumpet-shaped blossoms. This is what they must taste, she thought.

"Seriously, Ana," Iris said. "If Evan could taste this, he wouldn't be able to get enough."

"I know," Ana replied, opening her eyes.

"Should we put a lid over it, so it can't spill anymore?"

"No, it needs to breathe."

* * *

Over the next couple of days, the calm detachment inside of Ana did not diminish. She left two more messages for Evan to come and get what she had waiting for him. Her tone was casual but composed, and she was pleased that there was not much emotion connected to her request. In her newfound stillness, Ana decided to attend to things she had been neglecting. She tied back her hair and cleaned the house as she had never done before. She wiped the dust from the top of the refrigerator and shook crumbs from the toaster over the sink. She scrubbed the floors with a stiff brush and cleaned the windows from the outside. When she finished, the house smelled fresh and new. She ran a damp paper towel over the sides of the jar, which was still warm under her fingertips. Ana thought about taking another taste, but Iris called and invited her to the beach.

It was the first time Ana had been to the beach in weeks. She let the wind curl the ends of her hair and waded out into the cold sea with Iris. She splashed water upwards into the blue cloudless sky and watched light catch on the drops above her head. Next to Iris on the shore, Ana sifted warm sand through her fingers and listened to the breeze. She watched grains of salt drying on the tiny hairs along her arm, and she licked them off her sun-soaked skin. When she returned home in the evening, she checked her messages but heard nothing from Evan. She still felt confident that he would come around eventually, so she showered and drifted off to sleep with the memory of the ocean current.

In the middle of the night, Ana awoke choking. A dense haze filled the bedroom. Ana briefly wondered if her house was on fire but realized that she did not smell smoke. What she did smell was a sticky sweetness permeating the air. She stumbled out of bed and down the hall. When Ana flipped on the kitchen light, the haze was almost impenetrable. It obscured the clock on the microwave and wrapped around the jar in muddy layers. The entire house reeked of syrup, and Ana gagged on the scent. She opened all of the windows and hurried back to bed, breathing through her covers to muffle the odor.

In the morning, Ana wondered whether she had been dreaming. The haze had vanished, and the smell had dissipated, but the windows were still open, and Ana noticed tiny reddish bubbles forming on the surface of the dark liquid. She called Evan, not bothering to cover the urgency in her voice when she again received his voicemail. Ana decided to keep the windows open while she was at work to avoid another incident.

After work, Ana met Iris at the gym and invited her sister over for dinner. The night was hot and dry, and the full moon shone brightly. As Ana fumbled for her keys on the doorstep, Iris spoke.

"Do you hear that?" she asked her sister.

"What?" Ana asked. She pulled her key out of her purse.

"That noise." Iris gestured to the door. "Did you leave something running?"

"No, I don't think so," Ana said. She put her ear to the door and heard a low humming on the other side. She frowned at her sister and opened the door. In the foyer, everything looked normal except for a small moth clinging to the wall. Ana shooed it away, and it fluttered through the open door to the porch light, beating its wings against the bare bulb.

"It's coming from the kitchen," Iris said.

The sound grew louder as the women approached the kitchen, and when Ana turned on the light, she stumbled backward. Brown, gray, and ivory-colored moths covered every surface. They fluttered upwards towards the light and pulsed their wings frantically. They clung to the microwave and to the hands of the open-faced clock above the doorway. They stuck to the surface of the refrigerator like magnets. They beat their wings against the stainless steel sink. Wide wings of furry sunset moths spread over the counter tiles like pot holders. Moonlight seeped through the window panes and between moth wings, and the moths flew in an erratic cloud over the Mason jar.

Iris screamed and sprinted to Ana's bathroom, slamming the door behind her. Ana took the dish towel hanging from the oven rack and batted the moths out of her way as she moved toward the jar. The smell was pungent, and hundreds of fruit flies had gathered and were hovering around and crawling over the edges of the cheese cloth. Ana gripped the jar with the towel and held it at arm's length as she placed it in the sink.

"Iris, get out here and help me," Ana called. She herded the moths to the kitchen windows. A minute later, Iris emerged from the bathroom wielding a can of insecticide. She covered her eyes and ran through the kitchen spraying. Several moths fell to the floor midflight and jerked their small bodies before dying. The others frantically moved toward the window, following the sweeping motions of Ana's towel. Iris moved to the sink, and Ana heard the shh-shh of the spray can as Iris attacked the fruit flies.

"Try not to get any in the jar," Ana called over her shoulder.

Twenty minutes later, when the last of the moths had been swept from the floor and the fruit flies were rinsed down the drain, Ana and Iris sat at the kitchen table. The Mason jar stood between them.

"Clearly," Iris said, "it is time to get rid of this."

"I think it'll be okay now. Maybe I'll put it in the refrigerator."

"Ana, you can't be serious," her sister said, rubbing her forehead. "Evan is not going to come get this. He doesn't want it. And even if he did, he couldn't eat it; it's rotting."

"It's not. It's fermenting."

"Oh, Jesus."

"I'll just give it one more day."

"Do what you want," Iris said, rising from the table. "Just don't call me the next time you have a home invasion. I'm exhausted; I'm going home."

Ana sat for a long time staring at the jar. The sweet scent rising from the syrup was sour around the edges, and the liquid was no longer warm to the touch. Her sister was right. Evan was not going to call back or come by her house. He was not interested in what she had for him. Maybe he didn't even want to know that she had anything for him. Ana felt a hard knot rise in her throat before she realized that tears were already spilling onto her cheeks. They fell furiously, making small puddles on the table. Why not? Why wouldn't he just taste it? She knew that if he would just allow himself one tiny mouthful, he would never want anything else.

She put her head down and let her sobs spread through the kitchen. They echoed off the walls, and she shuddered.

Finally, after what seemed like hours, her crying subsided. Her face was swollen. Exhausted and delirious with sorrow and frustration, Ana seized the jar in front of her, ripped away the cheese cloth, and drank. The dense liquid coated Ana's raw throat and soothed her aching stomach. When she had emptied the jar, Ana stood. She felt shaky and hot, as if she might be sick. The room spun and Ana wobbled to her bedroom. She collapsed on her bed into a dreamless black slumber.

When she woke the next morning, Ana felt warmth pulsing through her entire body. Her heart felt swollen in her chest. As the morning light filtered through her curtains, Ana felt hopeful. She felt that she could have everything she wanted, and Evan was no longer among those things. The world seemed boundless and Evan seemed a trivial part of all that lay ahead of her. Ana smiled and sat up, eager to start the day.

Salvation

JEN VIOLI

You listen to him start the joke for probably the hundredth time. You stopped counting last Lent around time seventy-five because your neon green Post-it note, the one you keep stuck beneath the Saint Agnes Parish office calendar, ran out of space on both sides for hatch marks.

"What's the difference between a liturgist and a terrorist?" he asks the couple in to plan their June wedding. All three sit at the conference table across from your desk, where *Reception* is written in faux gold on faux wood. Not your name, but what you are there for. To recept.

The couple says nothing.

You remember when you thought he was attractive, really something to take in. His zeal, his faith, his insistence on using all three names, Gerald Paul Andrews, convinced you that he must have plenty to share, even an extra moniker. Something to give you, who has only and ever just wanted some measure of love.

Now you watch Gerald waiting for something, wanting something.

The woman looks at the box-shaped purse on her lap. She touches the latch. The man says nothing but shrugs a little.

"You can negotiate with a terrorist," Gerald says.

Met with blank stares, he says, "It's funny because, as I'm sure you know, most liturgists are real sticklers." He says sticklers like he's getting stabbed or stabbing someone. Either way, someone's getting stickled.

He uses this joke to break the ice, to show that he's not like those other liturgists, that he's a traditionalist (don't even ask about Wagner and his pagan overtones) but open, modern. That he'll definitely suggest Bach's *Jesu, Joy of Man's Desiring*, but he's fine with a little John Michael Talbot, too. Progressive.

Most couples laugh, at least a little awkward giggle, but not these two.

The woman sits like a mannequin, except for a slight twitch in her nose.

The man shifts in his chair, and after Gerald's laughter at his own joke fades into silence, the man claps his hand on the woman's knee like they're hunting buddies, and finally says, to Gerald, "Okay, should we plan something?"

"Right," Gerald says, opening his thick binder, licking his index finger to turn the page. Once, this finger licking fell into your category called *Sexy*, but right now, it turns your stomach.

Soon Gerald's rattling off prelude and postlude possibilities, and the man is saying, "Yes, that'll work just fine."

What neither of them notices is that the woman is crying, tears in a slow stream, staining her navy silk shirt with black streaks.

You think of saying to her, *Let's get out of here. This place is poison. Let's go run naked in the woods and listen to all the Wagner we want and have martinis, dirty ones.*

But you don't. Despite what Gerald Paul Andrews thinks, you can't save someone else.

But what you realize, watching this woman's tears and feeling the flow of them loosen you like a branch long stuck in a dry riverbed, what makes you stand now, without explanation, taking your purse and leaving the peach-colored raincoat which you've never liked but Gerald said was really *smart*,

What you know with certainty as you walk away from his nasal voice and snorty laugh, into the air with hints of tulips, hoping that the weeping woman will come to her own clarity,

What carries you forward is the truth that becomes the recessional song you don't need approval for: that you can only save yourself.

So you do.

Trade Secrets

TAWNI WATERS

This ain't the story I want to tell. I want to tell you the one about the shiny armored knight and the princess with eyes the color of robins' eggs. She waits for him by the river, crying tears of blood. You know the one. There's dragons and witches and a few close calls, but in the end, everything turns out all right. They all live happily ever after in that story. They always do.

The story I got to tell you ain't like that. He wasn't exactly a knight, because of the fingers he lost in the factory accident and the way his nose was shaped like a blob of dough. He had yellow-brown, bulgy eyes that popped out like a frog and a freckly bald spot on his head.

And me? Well, my eyes are smaller than pennies and just as round. The same color too. The rest of me is blue-white, my skin so thin and pale the veins peek out behind it. My body is shaped like one of those party balloons the clowns twist up, round and lumpy. I got nice lips though. No one can fault me for my lips. That was why he asked me to marry him, on account of when he saw my lips all puckered up like a cherry and whistling, he had himself notions about kissing me right there on the spot. But Clement was the good kind of boy who doesn't kiss without a contract, so instead of smooching me, he proposed. I was twenty-two by then and hadn't got any offers to speak of. I didn't have room to be picky. Still, I was put off by the fingers and the mushy nose.

I was holding out for Marty Robbins. That's who I wanted to marry. That voice! Ain't you ever heard someone talk, and the sound sends shivers into your toes, like you're on one of those electric shaking honeymoon beds? That was what it was like for me when I first heard Marty Robbins sing about, out in the west Texas town of El Paso, I fell in love with a Mexican girl. That's the only part of the song I know; I ain't much for remembering. But I know the girl in the song is named Felina, and she holds him in her arms while he bleeds all over her and dies. Ain't that romantic? Go ahead and laugh if you want, but I liked that song, and I set my sights on marrying Marty. We were on a first name basis, me and Marty, at least inside my head. But turns out he died two days after Clement proposed, which left me with no other option but to go ahead and say "I do."

We live in a trailer on the east end of River's Edge, the end where all the trailers are, where the grass only grows in ugly clumps and the flowers always die because the soil ain't no good. I decorated it real nice though, with ceramic angels I painted myself and checkered curtains I got at the Dollar Store. Clement still works in the cement factory. Has ever since he can remember. Me, I work in the grocery down the road.

We've tried for a hundred years, it seems like, to have us a baby, but something in my belly ain't right for that. Five times, I've got a baby inside me, and five times, I've bled it out just about the day I bought the first pair of footy pajamas. That's enough to break your heart. An unborn baby dying ain't like when Gramma died because you don't get no nice grave to visit and put flowers on. Instead, you get an empty graveyard belly that aches and blood in your panties. Nobody will cry with you.

"You wasn't even showing for mercy's sake," they say when you tear up. Well, they don't say it, but you know they think it. And right away, after the doctors suck what's left of the baby from you with a vacuum, people want to take you out for steak and potatoes, like the whole thing is something to celebrate. You get to the point where you go around sobbing deep in your belly but smiling on your face. Even Clement won't cry with me no more. He says, "Don't tell me until you're sure next time."

So I ain't told him about this baby in my belly yet. She's been sleeping in there for two and a half months now, but I ain't gone to the doctor on account of if I think of myself as pregnant and get excited about it, it will jinx the baby, and she'll come bleeding down my legs. Like Groucho Marx used to say, I done kept this one under my hat or under my baggy old sweat shirt, if you wanna get literal about it, which you shouldn't, 'cause it's just an expression, but I know some people are picky about things like that, all crazy scared of telling lies, for fear of burning in hell. So call it what you will. Under my hat or under my sweater, this baby is hid clean away. I ain't bought any footy pajamas either. I think the footy pajamas are what curses the babies and makes them come out. I swear, every time I buy a pair, the next day, the baby dies inside me. Still, I can't help but get somewhat excited deep down where no one can see it. This baby is a girl, like I told you, and I'm guessing she's gonna have long piano-playing fingers like Clement's daddy. I can already hear her little voice, saying, "Momma, would you pour me some apple cider?" "Momma, read me a storybook."

Momma. Can you imagine that? Me, a momma? It gives me shivers up and down my spine to think about it. I'll go ahead and tell you I've named this one. Shashana. I found that in a book. Doesn't it have a nice ring? And I done made up my mind that when Shashana makes it three months, I'm gonna go to the doctor, and I'm gonna tell Clement. Maybe he'll buy nonalcoholic cider for us to celebrate with like he did that first time I had a young 'un in me.

"No champagne for you," he said. "Not while you're carrying my rug rat."

Maybe I'll take up knitting when Shashana has been alive in my belly three months. See, all the others have died before three months, so if this one makes it three months, it's home free. But I shouldn't talk no more about that. I'll jinx it.

You're probably wondering things like, what are my hobbies. So I'll tell you. My hobbies are collecting magazines and dancing the jitterbug. I know what you're saying. No one dances the jitterbug these days. But I do, just the same. One time, I entered a contest the radio station put on, and I won me a hundred dollars. I dance like a dream. And like I said, I collect magazines. Not for those banana nut brownie recipes or the stories about how to catch yourself a right nice man, on account of I already got one, but for the pictures of the girls.

Man, those girls. You look at the covers of those magazines, and you think, they can't be real, with their big old bosoms, and spidery little legs, and those faces. God above! Their faces are so pretty, they almost make you cry to look at them, staring out at you with those wide eyes, looking all lost and confused. They always look kinda dazed, don't they, like someone just walked by with a gun and stole their money and their coat, which is why they're standing there in half a dress with their peachy skin hanging out. Those pictures are so far away from my life, I can't even imagine that there are people out there who really look like that. But they do, because once in a while, one of those girls will come on the television and do an interview, and she looks just the same. Perfect.

There's this girl that comes by the store some days, always to buy raspberry donuts, and she looks almost that pretty. Not though, because her thighs are a little lumpy under her jeans, and she gets a zit on her forehead every now and then. Plus, in the place where her pinky should be, she's got a scarred nub that makes me wanna vomit every time I look at it. Still, my heart just pounds when she saunters right in through the front doors, and I watch her good, trying to find little signs that she ain't as perfect as she seems. That's how come I noticed about the cellulite on her thighs. It made me feel better when I seen that. I call her Medusa inside my head. That's from that story about the ugly witch lady with snakes for hair, and calling the girl that is my way of getting back at her for being so pretty. When she comes to my register and puts the donuts on the scanner, I think, "Oh, way to go Medusa. You'll be even uglier and fatter when you wake up tomorrow, you eat all of these." She always smiles at me with those pearly teeth, never mind what I'm thinking. I don't smile back though. Just ring up her stupid donuts and send her packing. Serves her right.

You want cellulite though, you oughta take a look at me. Man, I look like the cellulite fairy went after me with a baseball bat. I tried wrapping my legs in cellophane like they said in the magazines. But I just got hot and sweated a lot. Clement said I looked like cottage cheese in a baggie and laughed real hard. So that was the end of that.

I'm thinking about all this because right now, I'm stacking oranges high and mighty to the ceiling, and their bumpy skin reminds me of my thighs. I gotta say, I get some satisfaction from piling the oranges. You may think that it's a mindless job, but really, it's quite a bit of work, getting them to fit together just right. One false move, and the whole lot of them come tumbling down and go rolling away across the tile, tripping customers and making old ladies cry out with terror.

Once, when I was new at working in the supermarket, I mispiled the oranges, and down they fell. This old blue-haired woman with bald patches saw one of the fruits coming for her, and she put up such a fuss, nearly popped my eardrums, screaming about oh, my god, I'm allergic to cats, someone get this animal away from me. I learned my lesson right then and there, and ever since that day, I done taken a certain pride and care in stacking the oranges perfect, knowing that I'm doing my part to keep the shopping public safe from terror.

See, I take my job at the grocery real serious. I know that in the big scheme of things, maybe I'm not making a huge splash, like, say, Jackie O. or one of those magazine glamour girls. But I'm doing my part to make sure that society has its belly filled, and when you think about it, that's the most important thing in the whole world. Food. None of us could do much of anything else if we couldn't eat. I'm one of the basic building blocks in the American system. Like that fancy food pyramid the government puts out to let us know how not to get fat and die of heart attacks. You know the one. Bread and cereal is at the bottom. It's the most important thing, and it holds up everything else. Well, I'm the bread and cereal of our nation. Without me, the whole rest of the country would come tumbling down like a stack of mispiled oranges. So when I tie on my blue apron in the morning, I feel just as much pride as a policeman putting on his badge or a schoolteacher sliding on her glasses. Because my job is maybe the most important job of all.

The people here in River's Edge can count on me, and they know it. When they need their deli meat sliced perfect for a wedding shower or they need to know if aspirin is on aisle ten or eleven, they come looking for me. They don't waste their time with the other cashiers. They see I'm the one who knows my stuff. Also, I'm the one they ask if they need private stuff, like cream for hemorrhoids or birth control products. They know I won't go blabbing about it to the other customers. I give them service with a smile, but I don't waste their time with no chitchat. I cut to the chase, grin friendly-like, but not over-eager, say aspirin is in aisle ten. They appreciate my willingness to help and my respectfulness of their time. Time is money, people say, and I know that. I ain't one to waste people's precious minutes directing them to the wrong aisle or asking them how their son's soccer season is or isn't going. That ain't my business, far as I'm concerned.

Not all the cashiers are that way. Back in December, Ronny, one of them high school kids Mac hired, told some lady the aspirin was in aisle eleven. Boy, was that a big to-do. That's what caused the grief and questioning about which aisle the aspirin might be in. Ever since Ronny done that, no one in River's Edge has had any luck in finding the aspirin aisle without my help. I don't mind though, 'cause that's what I'm here for anyways. I get paid over five dollars an hour to do this job, and I intend to do it to the best of my ability.

The only girl I cannot give service with a smile is the one I told you about, the big old green-eyed, perfect girl who comes trouncing in here with her battered cowboy hat perched on her head, flouncing around, looking all pretty for everyone to gape at. Medusa. Her I cannot stand.

Which ain't a good thing at this moment, because she just walked through the door, and she's sashaying for me now, right when I'm finishing the orange pile. I turn my back a little so she can't see my face too good. Still, I watch her out of the corners of my eyes, to notice if she's growing a zit today or not. She must have an oil gland problem in her forehead, because pretty often, she'll get a pimple there. She pulls the cowboy hat low those days, but I still see it. Today, she does not have a pimple, which chaffs my hide.

"Excuse me," she says. She is standing right behind me. I can feel her hot breath on my neck, and it smells like onion rings. I can hear her smiling. Have you ever heard someone smile? You know, their voice is all lilty and perky, and you just get a notion to wring their necks, it's so irritating. That's how I feel with little miss perfect smiling and panting her reeky onion breath down my neck.

"Yeah?" I say.

"Can you tell me where the granola bars are?" she asks. Right away, I get to wondering. Is she going on a diet now, no more donuts, granola bars instead? Is that it? But I don't ask her those questions, because like I said, it ain't my way to waste people's time with chitchat, plus I just plain don't like Medusa, nor do I want to spend one more second smelling her bad breath.

"Aisle three," I say, "right next to Fruit Roll-Ups." I myself have a particular liking for Fruit Roll-Ups, especially the kind with rainbow colors in them. But she don't need to know that.

"Thanks," she says, and off she goes. I can hear her flouncing the same way I heard her smiling before. Geez, she gets on my nerves. I keep pretending to stack the oranges because I don't want to go elsewhere while she's in the store. If I do, chances are, I'll see her again. I've got my fill of Medusa for one day, thank you very much. So I just jostle the oranges around a bit to look like I'm still working, not the ones on the bottom because that would send the whole stack rolling, but the two or three on top because it's pretty safe to mess with those ones without creating havoc. I'm just about to call it safe and go off and find some shelves to stock when she flounces up behind me again, only this time I don't hear her flouncing. The first thing I hear is "EXCUSE ME!" loud like a sonic boom. I jump so high, I topple my whole stack of oranges, and down they go, rolling and dancing across the floor.

"Oh, that's a pisser!" I say, wheeling around to face her. "See what you made me do!" She looks all wide-eyed and shocked, and I'm pretty rankled that she can look so forlorn and pretty at the same time. When I'm forlorn, my forehead wrinkles up like a deflated balloon, and my eyes just disappear, but her, she looks like she's at some modeling shoot, and the camera guy is saying, "OK, Medusa, now look forlorn and shocked for me."

"I'm sorry," she says, and she bends over to help me pick the oranges up, only when she does, her cowboy hat goes flying, and aha, I see it, she does have a zit after all, right up there along her hairline. So that's why she wears that old Stetson. She reaches for the hat. But while she's reaching, an orange rolls right up under her high-heeled boot, and down she falls, flat on her butt. I gotta laugh at that.

"Serves you right," I say.

And you may think that's mean-spirited, or even downright nasty, for me to kick someone when they're down like that. But that ain't usually my nature. Just a while ago, I told this guy exactly where to find fresh honey, even though we don't carry none in our store. I gave him directions to the Foster's bee farm and everything. That's the kind of person I usually am. But Medusa gets under my skin.

"I didn't mean to mess you up," she's saying now, and she's got a little tear in her eye.

I feel like a first-class heel when I see that. "It's just I take some amount of pride in my orange stacking," I say by way of explaining myself.

"Yeah, well, I'll help you restack them," she says, and she's reaching for my hand.

I got no choice but to yank her to her feet. Her fingers are all soft and sweaty in mine, the way my goldfish feels when I catch him so I can wash his bowl. I try to discourage her from helping me with the oranges. I tell her it's kinda an art form, and I'd just as soon do it myself as have an amateur help me out, but she don't pay me any mind. Before I can tell her the part about me being sorta like that guy who painted the Sistine Chapel, and her being sorta like the pope who kept sticking his nose into the business and messing up the painting, she's stacking one orange on top of the other. She's stacking them crooked, but she's quick. I gotta give her credit for her quickness.

And pretty soon, like it or not, me and Medusa are a team, chasing oranges around together and piling them up. I show her all my trade secrets, how to stack the fruits perfect so they won't slip and ruin the whole project, how you got to move slow, not fast. She asks questions that most new grocery store workers don't think to ask, and I'm starting to suspect she has a natural talent.

She says, "What if there's an extra big navel, which way should you face it, up or down?" And, "Should you wipe off the fly spots before you put the orange in the stack?"

When the stack is halfway done, I go on and ask her about the granola bars, if she's gone and given up donuts for good, or if this is just a fluke. She says no it's not a fluke, she's put on ten pounds in six months, isn't that unbelievable?

I say, "I put on ten pounds in a week once. That's when I quit weighing myself."

I haven't had a conversation like this with a real grown up in years. After Daddy died, Momma moved off to a retirement resort in Arizona, without so much as a goodbye to her shameful, fatty daughter. Since then, Clement is mostly the only person I do any kind of talking with, besides, apples are over in the produce aisle, and feminine hygiene's aisle twelve. And come to think of it, even Clement don't like to talk much when he gets home from the factory, he's so dead dog tired. Weekends, he goes out with the boys for beers. So that leaves me having conversations with our beagle Frosty, but Frosty don't talk back, except to say, yip-yip, yap-yap, bark-bark-bark when he's hungry.

So talking to Medusa, whose real name turns out to be Melina, is like going out to the ice cream parlor and getting a whole mountain of ice cream. It's that big of a treat. I mean you should see us, stacking the oranges real precise, but laughing some too while we're going. She tells me a joke that goes like this.

"What do you call a fish without eyes? Fsh."

I laugh pretty hard at that; isn't that a good one?

So I tell her this one, since we're on the subject of critters missing important body parts. "What do you call a cow with no legs? Ground beef."

She giggles something awful, shrieks more to the point, like a fire engine or something. She's got a laugh so sharp, it cuts right into your brain. She snorts a lot too, like a big fat hog. Still, it feels nice having a good laugh with another human being.

I'm so busy having fun, I don't even notice the pain in my belly until it gets deep and strong. Feels like my guts are twisting together.

"Oh God," I sorta whisper.

I don't have to check my panties. I know there's blood in there without looking. I know that baby died right there inside me while I was laughing. I know that I'll spend the afternoon in the hospital knocked out while they suck out my baby with that vacuum. When the first baby died, the doctor didn't give me no anesthetic while he vacuumed me. I screamed like hellfire. One nurse I met says I shoulda sued him. It's common practice to give anesthetic for the vacuuming, but I didn't know that then. Anyways, every time since, they've given me some knockout medicine, so I know they will this time too.

When Melina sees that I stopped laughing, her peachy face gets all confused, and she says, "Something wrong?"

"Yeah," I say. "I'm bleeding out my baby now. I gotta go to the hospital."

She does something funny then, something that I think wraps chains around our hearts and ties us together forever. She starts to cry. Not big, you understand, just a few tears. But enough to make me feel like maybe someone else in this world thinks this baby inside me is worth crying over.

We walk out through the store hand in hand, both of us blubbering like little children. I don't even stop to tell Mac where I'm going. When we get outside, tiny puffs of snow are flurrying all around us, and the sun is invisible behind a swirl of gray storm clouds. Semis are honking down on the freeway, and someone's listening to heavy metal music in the apartments next door. But I only halfway notice all of that. Mostly, I'm seeing the face of this baby girl in my belly, maybe all wrapped around with pretty blond white curls, smiling up on some cloud in heaven with the angels, playing a harp with her piano fingers.

"I'm sick and tired of my babies running off to heaven," I tell Melina. "I wanna hold one of them sometime. Change their diaper once. You know, everyone gripes about the mustardy smell of fresh baby poop, but I'd give my heart and soul to smell it just one time."

Melina laughs and cries all at once. Her eyes are red and puffy, but those perfect teeth are wet with spit and smiling. As she walks along the slick pavement in those high heels of hers, I'm thinking she's gonna fall, but she never does. And I'm saying inside my head, gosh darn, she's prettier now than ever. I bet she'd dance a mean jitterbug.

Suddenly, I'm hot way down deep into the middle of my heart. This must be what love feels like, I think. I don't suppose I ever knew till just now what love was. I thought, in my own way, I loved Clement, maybe in a quiet way, not like the Marty Robbins song, but still real. But this thing I feel for Melina right now is like nothing I ever knew. I want to reach out and grab her, hold her head to my chest, tell her all my secrets. I wanna study the wrinkles on her hands. I wanna know what are her hobbies, what makes her tick. It's just pure and true what I'm feeling, looking at the way Melina's soft brown curls fall down over her eyes. It's like rainwater on a summer day. It takes away some of the pain of the baby dying inside me. My guts are all bunched up and twisted from Sashana dying, but they're all twisted up with love too.

Melina leads me to an old caramel-colored Buick and helps me into the back seat. "His name is Pedro," she says. "Lay down."

"Whose name is Pedro?" I ask, clutching at my belly.

"The car. I just thought you might want to know his name." She puts a checkered coat under my head for a pillow.

When she slides into the front seat, she reaches back and holds my dry, old, fat hand in one of her pretty ones, tells me it will all work out. She believes in fate, she says while we're driving. She believes she was brought to the grocery today for a reason. She believes we were meant to meet, maybe so we could just say goodbye to this baby together. But maybe so we could save it too. Don't give up just yet. She honks the horn real hard then, to make other cars get out of the way.

"Her name's Shashana," I say.

"Hang on, Shashana," Melina whispers.

Outside, cars are whizzing by us on the freeway, and I'm thinking, what in the world is happening to me? This baby inside me is dying.

But, God forgive me, even with the pain in my gut and the sadness of losing Sashana, I feel more alive right now than I ever thought I could.

Tear Sheets

MISSY WILKINSON

Decades ago, I moved into my great-uncle's old place in the 9th Ward's Bywater neighborhood. The rent was cheap, and the neighborhood, well, the neighborhood was *interesting*. The Industrial Canal and the river reined in a pastiche of well-kept shotgun houses and those on the verge of collapse, barely stitched together with kudzu vines and termite spit. At night, when the streets rang with river barge horns and occasional gunshots, I searched the classified ads halfheartedly for a job. I thumbed through the listings, past ads for porn theaters, massage parlors, strip clubs and nude models. *Why not?* I'd ask myself. Shackled with a fresh liberal arts degree, I could have used the mainline injection of cash that industry promised, but ultimately, another ad quickened my pulse and compelled me to action.

ARGUS WEEKLY HAS AN OPENING FOR AN EDITORIAL INTERN. INTERNS WILL WRITE ON DEADLINE AND FOR LONG-TERM PROJECTS.

My focus had been literature, not journalism, but writers are nothing if not champions of their own hopeless causes, so I edited my best scholarly papers down to clip size, typed up a resume, and mailed it in. Five days later I was called to interview. I was shocked. Maybe I was still demoralized after a door-to-door job hunt through the French Quarter that was equal parts sweaty and fruitless.

The managing editor peered at me over her reading glasses. A safety pin held the arm to the lenses. I should have seen this as a sign that the editorial staff was overworked: even a trip to the optometrist was a major undertaking. "Most of our interns are college students. You do know this is unpaid?"

"I just want the experience," I told her. *And the byline,* I thought but didn't say. *And the glory!*

"How many hours a week are you available?"

"How many do you want me?"

She hired me. Four months later, when she retired, I took her job. I credit this to good timing and a willingness to work myself to the bone. I covered home, fashion and beauty, which wasn't in my job description, but which the rest of the all-male staff was loathe to touch. To my surprise and the surprise of my co-workers, I flourished. I took up smoking and became fashionably thin. I subscribed to *Vogue*. I cultivated relationships with local boutique owners, designers, photographers and makeup artists. There weren't many. Our fashion community was diffuse to the point of invisibility. But it existed, and I saw potential. I saw myself as the galvanizing force that would unite all these elements and bring New Orleans to national prominence as a fashion mecca, a position commensurate with its undisputed status as a music mecca.

I was running on the high-octane fuel of a young woman with lots of ambition and very little love or money. A high-power editorial position seemed the ideal way to attract these good things.

I had a lot to learn. I have a lot to learn.

* * *

"Something like this." Corinne Claire, a model-cum-fashion-photographer, laid the latest issue of *Vogue* on my desk. It featured a cadaverous young model draped across a rooftop. In the background loomed the metallic, serrated edge of the skyline. The model wore yards and yards of frothy tulle. I wondered what local boutique carried a dress like that one, which cost as much as a small house in Chalmette.

"I love it. Let's do it," I told Corinne. Her real name was Sharon Carbo. I saw it when she filled out her independent contractor paperwork. But she had been a real model. A hair under six feet tall, blessed with the high cheekbones and thirty-four-inch hips the major markets demanded, she had walked Parisian runways and observed great photographers at work. She soaked it all up. Then she had a baby and moved back home to the suburbs of New Orleans.

Together we flipped through comp cards of local models that the talent agencies had sent us.

"Too short," Corinne sneered. "Too fat. Lips too thin. I know her. Her attitude's bad."

"This is what we have to work with." I gestured at the glossy stacks of short, smiling local girls. Girls who would never work in any major market, girls who were pretty but nothing special. Twelve years ago, I had been a girl with thwarted aspirations like theirs, with a similar card.

"The model can make or break the shoot," Corinne said. "I know a great girl in New York who'll work for the tear sheets."

"I don't have the budget to fly anybody in."

Corinne brushed her blonde, asymmetric bangs to the side. It was a very fashionable cut. I wondered whether I ought to cut my hair, even though I had been growing it out for two years.

"Well, use a local girl, then," she said. "However, please don't publish the photographs with my name. I have a reputation to uphold."

* * *

I told Lori about the interactions over drinks at the Fairmont Hotel bar. The owners were among our advertisers, and they had invited me to come by for a complimentary cocktail. Even during my down time, I had an eye on strengthening relationships with advertisers. And free drinks, of course, always.

"That's ridiculous," Lori said as she drained her pint of Abita. "Who does she think she is?"

"Corinne is a really good photographer. Probably the best the magazine has ever worked with."

"Still. Does she publish anywhere else? Has she ever shot for anybody big?"

"She does portfolio development for local models, mostly. She knows how to make them look tall. She uses a wide angle lens, I think."

"What a bitch."

I loved that about Lori, how she would instantly side with me and nurture her hatred for my nemeses until it exceeded my own. She even took it upon herself to research them, passing on unsavory nuggets that came her way via her extensive, city-wide gossip net. Lori would have made an excellent PR agent, but she was a waitress at a Metairie diner. With only a high school diploma from a public school in Denham Springs, where the Ku Klux Klan still held public rallies, Lori had neither the ambition nor the preparation for much more than waitressing.

"Scott's killing me, man. I just don't know what to do with him." She gazed searchingly at the mason jars of lemon wedges, dried star fruit and cinnamon sticks on the bar, as though one of them might house the shriveled ruins of her heart.

"You need to move on."

"I know he's seeing other chicks. I *know* he is. But I can't help it. I love the dude." Lori signaled to the bartender. He smiled at her. Lori smiled back. "That bartender thinks I'm easy. Look at his face."

"No, he doesn't," I protested weakly. But inwardly I agreed: he probably *did* think Lori was easy. Her body was soft, inviting, clad in inexpensive, revealing clothes. She had pretty blue Shelly Duvall eyes above a weak chin and a small mouth. She fell fast and too hard. She had called me her soul mate after two trips to the mall. And though I found her proclamation charming, I could see how, coupled with sex that came too easy and too drunk, a guy would turn tail and run. It was a shame. But it was how the world was.

"Scott said I was fat."

"Oh, my god. *I hate* that guy!" I was yelling. I tend to get too loud when I am excited. I have a strong diaphragm.

"Shush. Listen. He didn't say it just like that. He said I don't need any more of his protein shakes. He said Bree looked like she could use a few, and that was how he liked his women."

Bree was Lori's little sister, a scrawny high school senior. Protein shakes was how Scott referred to his semen. Another of his charming habits. "You're still blowing him?" I asked, too loud.

The bartender looked back at us. Lori blushed. When she blushed, her cheeks stayed pale, but her chest and neck turned bright red. "I slept at his house the other night. It was just going to be platonic, but I don't know … Then, afterwards, as he was falling asleep, he told me not to look in his bottom drawer."

"What, does he think he's Bluebeard or something?"

"No clue."

"Did you look?"

"Of course not! He was right there."

"Fuck Bluebeard."

"Fuck Corinne."

"Fuck them both." I slammed my glass down, like something had been resolved. In a way, it had, until the next night, when we would convene and bitch about something else and get drunk again.

* * *

Corinne and I pulled the dresses for the shoot from five boutiques the next day.

"Couldn't you get any Harold Clarke?" she asked.

Harold Clarke was a local designer who created fantastic gowns for celebrities and local richies to wear to bals masques. His gowns were the closest approximation to what Corinne had showed me in *Vogue*. When *Wheel of Fortune* filmed in town, Vanna White always wore Harold Clarke.

"I needed to feature these particular advertisers." Actually, I had left three messages at Harold Clarke's atelier. He hadn't called back.

Corinne sighed. "I'll see what I can do."

I ended up letting her select most of the gowns and accessories. Every time I held up a gown I liked, she'd make a face and say something vague, like, "Oh, that's interesting beading," or "Black and gold sequins. I think that's meant to be worn to a Saints game." So I stopped trying.

"By the way, I found a model," she said as we sorted through racks of plastic-swathed gowns. "She's short, though. Five foot seven."

I was five foot seven, but I tried not to look insulted. Truthfully, that *was* short for a model. Corinne produced a photo. The girl had fair skin, and clear green eyes, and gobs of red hair. She was pretty, but with all the makeup and the flattering lighting, it was impossible to tell what she really looked like. Still, I trusted Corinne's vision, and more than that, I didn't want to deal with her attitude. Nor did I want to continue combing the city for a model she wouldn't reject. I had enough deadlines to worry about already.

"Oh, good," Corinne cooed when I gave my approval. "The only thing is, she doesn't work for tear sheets."

After some quick calculations, I said, "I can spare a hundred dollars from the budget."

"That's a lot less than her usual day rate."

For print? I wondered. *In New Orleans? Even* Vogue *only pays its models two hundred dollars for an editorial.* Who did Corinne think she was putting on?

"One hundred is all we can pay," I repeated.

"Well, I'll pass that on to her."

The last store was a secondhand boutique where Uptown ladies brought last season's designer garments and lavish gowns worn once at Mardi Gras balls. While Corinne consulted with the owner, I dug around for a slinky dress. Something sexy, unlike the poofy confections of silk and peacock feathers and tulle she had pulled so far.

On the hanger, it didn't look like much. Just black and sparkly and drapy. I showed it to Corinne, but before she could make a dismissive remark, I pointed out the label. "It's a Harold Clarke."

"Perfect!" she breathed.

* * *

The model looked nothing like her head shot. She was five foot four if she was an inch, flat-chested, big-nosed and sullen. She stared at herself in the mirror, watching the stylist install curlers in her long, ratty hair, while I introduced myself and thanked her for coming.

"Is she really a model?" the makeup artist asked. We stood in the street as she smoked a cigarette and I fed my parking meter. "She looks about ten years old."

"I don't know what her deal is. The photographer recommended her."

"Yeah, that photographer kept trying to tell me how to do the makeup and getting in the way. I was like, Fine. You do it."

"I'm sorry." I resisted the urge to talk smack. That could wait until I was out of a volatile, professional situation, safe with Lori. "She's rather domineering."

"Who does she think she is? Stanley Kubrick?"

It took all my willpower to bite my tongue. "Want to see the dresses?"

"Ooh. Yes!" She tossed her cigarette into the gutter, and I showed off the gowns. They were beautiful, I had to admit. Corinne had chosen well.

* * *

The shoot went smoothly. It did not rain. We got our rooftop shot, but Corinne framed it against old New Orleans, the small red tile roofs and the St. Louis Cathedral's pricking spires, rather than the gleaming high-rise hotels of the Central Business District and Canal Street. I pointed out that this wasn't very similar to the *Vogue* editorial she had so admired.

"Well, we don't exactly have a New York-caliber skyline," she said, clicking photos of the model, who moved fluidly and professionally. I had seen enough novices to recognize the mark of a true model. So many girls seize up and go into rigid, pseudo-fashion posturing. But a good model is at home in her own skin. She opens herself and lets the camera see inside. That's what this ugly, short girl was doing with Corinne. Again, I wondered how Corinne had found her.

Corinne had more or less assumed the reins of art director, so all I needed to do was sit back and watch. I busied myself by ordering and fetching food, writing down the prices of the dresses, covering the bottoms of the high heels with duct tape so they wouldn't get scuffed. Corinne and the model seemed at ease with each other. They swept out of the elevator before I did, assuming that they were foremost and I would follow. I began to resent my loss of authority, and then I began to question myself for taking it that hard. Was I really so egotistical? Did I so relish being in control and calling the shots? Apparently, I did.

"What's your job here?" the model asked as I knelt on the floor, scraping stubborn tape off the bottom of a shoe. "Are you from the store?"

"No, I'm the editor," I told her curtly.

She didn't say anything to that, only admired herself in the mirror of the hotel room we were using as a changing room. She was wearing the Harold Clarke. "I love this dress," she murmured, running her hands down her narrow hips. She was too short for it. It puddled on the floor. "How much does it cost?"

"It should say on the tag."

She unzipped the dress and stepped out of it with a total lack of modesty. Her figure was not boyish as much as childish. Her breasts were small, with tiny, rosy nipples. She had shaved her pubic hair. At the time, this was uncommon, and I wondered at first if she had not physically matured, or if she perhaps had some hormonal imbalance. But looking closer, I saw faint stubble there, so I knew she had done this to herself. I realized I was staring and busied myself with a shoe. But she had noticed and gave me a queer, recognizing look.

"It doesn't have a tag." She dropped the dress at my feet. "Ask the boutique owner to hold it for me."

"Sure." I smiled at her. "It's a beautiful dress, isn't it?"

At that moment, I resolved to buy the dress if it fell within my limited means. But I suspected that neither of us could afford it. Even secondhand, the dress would cost thousands.

* * *

That night, Lori called me, sobbing. "It's pornography."

"What's pornography?"

"In Scott's drawer. I looked, and it's pornography. It's vile. It's horrible."

I wondered what had gotten into Lori. When had she become so conservative? Perhaps her Pentecostal upbringing was rearing its head.

"Lori, you can do so much better than Scott." I said it from my heart, and I meant it. But heartfelt words rarely saturate the barren ground they are meant to nurture. They just roll right off. Lori went on devising ways to win Scott back, though the concept of *back* was a dubious one, since he had never in their eight months of having sex called her his girlfriend.

I listened to her schemes, but mostly I thought about the dress. If I had a dress like that in my closet, I would be a different woman. A woman with new potential. A woman who expected black tie invitations and assembled her wardrobe accordingly. Such a woman was likelier to step into a glittering, expansive future than one who was ill-prepared, was she not?

The dress was still in my car. I told Lori I would call her right back. When I tried on the dress, I realized, with a sinking feeling, that sometimes more expensive things were genuinely better. My sturdy, middle-class upbringing had worked hard to blind me to this truth, but now it stared at me from my own mirror. The dress elongated my legs, brought out the slender definition of my arms. It gave me the illusion of possessing a figure I never really had. Too short and too plain to be a model. Too this, too that, while at the same time never enough. Until now.

* * *

"Isn't it beautiful?" the boutique owner said as she lifted the dress from its plastic wrapping. "I wore it once to a Mardi Gras ball. I sat at the king's table."

"How much is it?"

She looked up from the ledger she was balancing and fixed me with a shrewd eye. "For you?"

I liked this woman very much. Corinne had dismissed her shop because it traded in secondhand clothing ("*Used,*" Corinne had sniffed), but I knew that the owner was a designer herself who had done stints in Paris and New York and had returned to her hometown New Orleans for the only reason anyone ever returns to a city so scarred and tragic: sheer love.

"For me," I told her.

The owner gazed at the dress with misty, sentimental eyes, as though she were reminiscing over her daughter's senior photograph. Then her eyes became shrewd once more, calculating how substantial of a dowry such a daughter would require. "I paid thirty-four hundred dollars for this dress. It's listed here for twelve hundred."

She paused, an infinitely long pause during which time soared up into an arc and stopped there at its apex, hanging motionless for an incalculable moment. Then she spoke and time continued.

"For you, because you do so much for my store, for you, one twenty."

* * *

That night, Lori and I met over drinks and devised revenge plans for our enemies. She composed a pitch-perfect speech I could deliver to the model to inform her of my purchase. After all, I had told her I would ask the owner to hold the dress. I could not renege. I had my integrity to think of.

"So I'll say, 'Oh, I wanted to let you know I bought that dress. I wanted to save you a trip out there.'"

I honestly could not wait to make the call. The hatred I felt for the model only intensified with time, like a bad case of ringworm. Little things she had done during the shoot irked me more and more. The way she complained that the shoes hurt her feet and incessantly yawned in between sets. What reason did she have to be so tired? I was the one who had been busting ass to set the shoot up for the last few weeks.

"And then she'll say, 'But I told you I wanted that dress!'" For not having ever met the girl, Lori's impression was dead-on, a perfect blend of ennui and superiority.

"Look, if it makes you feel any better, it didn't look good on you in the first place. It was really tailored for a taller woman. It is a beautiful dress, but why pay twelve hundred bucks for something that doesn't flatter your body type? Anyway, after she saw it on me, the owner said the dress just seemed to be *made for me*—"

Lori was cracking up. "Oh my God. I'm dying. You have to deliver it just like that!"

"Then she cut the price because I've done so much to help out her business!"

"Seriously, can I listen in when you tell her this?"

"So you see, it's nothing personal. I just wanted to save you the trip. Also, I thought I'd save you the gas money. I know you're on a tight budget. I am the one who approved your paycheck, after all…"

"It just keeps getting better!" Lori crowed.

"And I've done a lot of local modeling in the past, and I know there isn't really any money in print, especially for a short woman in New Orleans…"

"Oh my God! You're a genius."

"So really, it wouldn't have been such a good idea for you to purchase a dress that was well out of your budget and not especially flattering. Some day, you'll thank me."

"I love this," Lori sighed.

"And I bet that day will be the first of the month, when you're actually able to pay your rent."

* * *

That night, Lori and I sneaked into Scott's apartment. While her forte was passive-aggressive speeches, I have always been more of the breaking-and-entering type. And the beauty is, rarely do I have to break. I have trespassed enough times to know there's always a sheet of loose plywood, an unlatched attic window, or a spare key in a potted plant. So we let ourselves into Scott's house with very little fuss, through an unlocked second floor window near a sturdy oak with low hanging branches that I climbed with no difficulty at all.

This was to be a reconnaissance mission, the first act in a drama that would unfold in acts for Scott, each more terrifying than the last. I wished first to threaten him (a brick through the window), then to humiliate him in public. The pornography collection would somehow play into this. How, I did not yet know.

"There it is." Lori shined her flashlight at the bottom drawer, loathe even to touch its handle.

I slid the drawer open. It was heavy with the weight of so many magazines. I thought for a moment back to those long afternoons spent unemployed in coffee shops, reading newspapers and nursing cups of house blend. How would things be different had I responded to an adult ad rather than *The Argus Weekly*'s?

It was a pointless thought, one that I put immediately out of my mind. I flipped through the stack of magazines; it was nothing I had not seen before. Fluffy coifs of pubic hair. Want ads posting pictures of genitalia, where you could send letters to the owner of the erect penis or size DD breasts and meet for anonymous sex. Or just masturbate to the image and the thought.

Except there was more, as there always is in tales of sin. Those magazines, it turns out, were a ruse. In the middle of the stack, not at the bottom or the top, where it would be too obvious, were Polaroid pictures of naked children. They were taken in a wood-paneled den where somebody had set up a wading pool on the linoleum floor. Rubber ducks and inflatable sea horses had been tossed aside, their siren song sung.

"See?" Lori's eyes were red and brimming. "I told you it was horrible."

Among the Polaroids was a picture of the model. I would not have recognized her if she had not been so cavalier about nudity during our shoot. She was on her knees, tilting her head at an angle very similar to the one she used in her headshot. One hand rested on a folding chair. It would have been better if she had been holding an oversized lollipop or teddy bear, something over-the-top to suggest she was simulating childhood rather than living it. I could not tell how old she had been when the photo was taken. I knew from her paperwork that she was eighteen now. But this photo could have been taken yesterday or three years ago. It was impossible to tell.

"Come on, let's get out of here," Lori whispered.

I carefully arranged all the materials the way Scott had left them. I let Lori out the front door, then locked the deadbolt behind her and climbed out the window. I fought the very strong desire to commit arson. Waiting for me on the lawn, Lori was in tears.

I hugged her awkwardly as we loped across the dark wet grass. I didn't think I could tell her whom I had seen in the photos. I hadn't quite processed that myself.

"The most horrible thing is, I still love him," she said, wiping her tears on her sleeve. "What kind of a sicko does that make me?"

* * *

The editorial was well received by the publisher, the editor-in-chief, and the art director.

"Who is this girl? I think she's the prettiest model we've ever featured," the editor told me as we inspected a proof of the cover.

"A friend of the photographer's."

"We definitely need to use her again. This is very good work." His eyes never wavered from her photograph.

* * *

I never did deliver my speech to the model, though I rehearsed it many times in my mind. I practiced speeches for Scott, interrogations that might help me uncover who she was, how long ago the photos had been taken, whether Corinne had had any hand in them. But I feared that, somehow, this would jeopardize my job. So I stayed silent. Lori eventually found a new guy to pine over, one who cheated but who at least did so with consenting adults. When I see Scott out at bars or in coffee shops, I greet him civilly. I hope he is getting help for his problem. I wonder why he even tempted Lori with knowledge of the forbidden drawer, and the only answer I can come up with is that he wanted her to find it so she would finally leave him alone. Or perhaps so that she would intervene.

I have decided not to concern myself with things that aren't my business. Maybe the model was of age in the photos; maybe she wasn't. All I know for certain is that New Orleans is very, very small and very, very deep. The more I learn about it, the less I understand it: the myriad secret societies that exist within its walls of crumbling brick and bargeboard, how dense and Byzantine the blood ties are, how easy it is to slip into a dark, powerful undercurrent, emerging on some unknown shore or not at all.

I still have the dress, and I am still waiting for the right occasion. Though it hasn't yet arrived, I am optimistic. More than that, I am prepared. I am becoming, day by day, the woman I want to be, a woman who expects good things to come her way. Who prepares her wardrobe accordingly.

Keyhole

LARRY WORMINGTON

Tracer rounds whiz by, their light reflected in the concertina wire just inches from my face. Flat on my back, I dig in my heels and inch forward. My body tenses, and I jerk sideways as the ground erupts to my right, covering me with chunks of dirt and debris. Deafened and tingling, I push on. It can't be much farther. God, please don't let it be much farther. I slide along, trying to stay as flat as possible, my Kevlar helmet pushing a line through the sand as I go. All I can focus on is my forward progress and the vice-grip I have on my M16.

My helmet hits something solid. Someone is up ahead but isn't moving. The ringing in my ears and the strobe effect of artillery make it hard to focus, like watching fireworks from the deep end of a swimming pool. I manage to pull myself up to the man's side. His voice is a broken record of panic.

"Can't do this. Can't do this. Can't do this."

It's Wallace, a small, freckled recruit from St. Louis they'd just dropped back to our platoon. His legs are moving, but the rest of him isn't. Tears slide down the sides of his camo-streaked face as he mutters and continues to squirm. The muzzle of his weapon is wrapped in razor wire, but he doesn't seem to notice.

"Wallace, your weapon's stuck."

He continues to struggle.

"Wallace."

He flinches and then looks at me through Coke-bottle lenses.

"What? I'm okay. I'm okay."

"The wire, Wallace. Here, let me help."

Bad idea. I wait for the next tracer flash and try to grab his rifle barrel as it and the nest of concertina swing back and forth. Just as I think I've got it, Wallace jerks the weapon downward, ripping my fingers open on the wire's many teeth.

"Damn, man, fucking watch it."

"I'm s-sorry,"

The artillery stops, and the field we're crossing lights up from a line of surrounding flood lamps. I shut my eyes and put my hand to my mouth, tasting the coppery sting of blood. Deep laughter and clapping make me forget about my shredded fingers. A few feet away, to the right of the live-fire training course, is the man I wish death upon several times a day, Staff Sergeant Pena. He stands in a pressed camouflage uniform, his chest puffed out and his tan arms crossed. He has a weasel grin, and his drill instructor cover is cocked back like a halo on his balding head. The rest of Kilo Company is at a position of attention behind him.

"Recruits, take a good look at these two," Pena says. "They're the ones that'll get you killed in real combat. Cole, you and your lover get your asses out of there. The shitters need cleaning." Still lying on my back, I crane my neck and glance behind me. Another few feet and I'd have made it.

"Fucking, Wallace," I whisper.

Pena and the other D.I.s have my number now. Up until this point, I'd kept a low profile. My dad told me, 'Keep your head down and don't volunteer for anything.' That was the formula for surviving Marine Corps boot camp. It was working, too. Now I'm a shit bird, and everything I do will be mocked and scrutinized.

To make matters worse, my little act of chivalry turns Wallace into my shadow. They place him in first squad, right behind me in platoon formations. He's also put on my fire team in training exercises and made my bunkmate, in the cot above me. I can't get away from him. I'm one-twenty soaking wet, a little slow, and somewhat uncoordinated, not the best candidate to *carry* someone else, mentally or physically. Staff Sergeant Pena and the other drill instructors even have a name for us: the Turtledoves.

"Where are my love birds?" Pena says. "Turtledoves, get up to my classroom now."

The classroom's an open space, about thirty by thirty, outside the drill instructor's duty hut in each training barracks at Marine Corps Recruiting Depot (MCRD), San Diego. In theory, it's a place of instruction, thus the name. In practice, it's a torture chamber, a place where D.I.s punish the guilty and innocent. On any given day, a drill instructor can be heard yelling: "You wanna fuckin' play, boys, we'll play. I got more games than Milton Bradley." Before I met Wallace, I wasn't summoned to class. Now, I was setting attendance records.

"Push-ups, boys, drop," Pena said. "Too fucking slow, get up. Now drop, on your backs. Sit ups. Sit ups. Too slow. Up. Bends and thrusts. Faster, faster. Too fucking slow. Stop. Drop. Push-ups, stop in the up position. Stay there. Wallace, I better not see your chest touch the deck. Down. Mountain climbers, get those knees up. Faster dammit. I got all-fucking-day, boys."

I piston my legs, push, jump, then do it all again. Sweat burns the cuts on my hand, and they sprout fresh blood spots through my bandages. I don't have time to care. I just make sure I do everything a little better, a little faster, than Wallace. It isn't that difficult. He just thrashes on the floor like a dying bug, trying to get his bony body into the right position for whatever Pena calls next. Each time he gets into a rhythm, Pena calls out a change. The wiry D.I. smiles the whole time, putting his head down when I look up, hiding his enjoyment beneath the brim of his Smokey Bear.

"Stop," Pena says. "Stand at attention. Lock your damn body, Wallace."

My heart thuds as I catch my breath with a closed mouth and a rigid body. Seconds tick by, and Pena stands there, flipping through a folder spread out on his training pulpit. I watch without appearing to, my peripheral vision skills vastly improved after the last two months of training. I see Wallace's name in bold type on the top of the folder.

"So, Timothy Wallace, how it is you've been dropped from training by three platoons and you still look like a skeleton?"

"Sir?" Wallace says.

"Did I tell you to fucking speak?" Pena asks. "Shut the hell up. It says here you've failed to qualify three times at the rifle range. Is that right? You can answer now."

"Yes, sir."

Pena approaches him, turning his back to me and leaning in close, as if he's about to tell Wallace a secret. Wallace swallows hard, lips trembling. The rest of the platoon sits at the end of their bunks, polishing boots while feigning inattention.

"Know what happens when you go UNK your fourth time?" Pena says.

Wallace opens his mouth, but nothing comes out.

"You go home," Pena says.

Wallace closes his eyes. Pena leans in even closer.

"That's why you're such a fuck-up, isn't it? You found yourself a way out. Well, there's nothing that says you have to go home in one piece."

Wallace's eyes are wide. Pena slaps him hard on the back and executes a perfect about-face. He's facing me now and looks surprised, like he forgot I was behind him. I'm a statue, my eyes locked on the far wall. He studies me, moving closer and closer, stopping only when he's pushed up against my right shoulder. His breath is hot on my ear.

"You didn't hear shit. Understand?"

I nod.

"If you give a fuck about him, Cole, you'll help him," he says.

I stare back at him.

"Get your fucking eyes off me, recruit," Pena says.

He snatches the folder off the podium. Taps warbles from the loudspeaker, and he dismisses us.

"Guide and squad leaders, square away this platoon. We leave for the rifle range at o-six-hundred tomorrow. All your shit better be ready."

The rifle range, known to west coast Marines as Edson Range, is located inside the largest Marine base in the United States, Camp Pendleton, California. To get there from MCRD San Diego, we take a half hour bus ride in silence. Although Pena and our junior D.I.s patrol the aisles frequently, I feel alive for the first time in months.

Each day in boot camp is like a week trapped in a cramped box with no food and no light. We see no one but our D.I.s and our fellow recruits, day in and day out. There are no phones, no television, and no news; the only contact with the outside world comes via letters from friends and family, delivered twice a week. If no one writes, you never get out of the box. But here, today, speeding down I-5, I remember the world. We pass Burger King, and flame-broiled aroma fills my nostrils. Girls with wavy hair drive by in gleaming sports cars, windows down and blouses aflutter. They smile and wave, driving me to arousal. Rows of empty phone booths outside a 7-11 beckon. I hear my girlfriend's voice and her laugh. I see her stretched out on a blanket, waiting for me. The ocean sparkles in the California sun, and I remember coconut-tan legs and long, blonde hair.

Pena yells the moment we go through Pendleton's main gate, reminding us what world we belong to.

"Recruits," Pena says, "welcome to Camp Pendleton. You are now surrounded by the largest population of Marines on the planet. In honor of this occasion, we're throwing you all a little party. In the gas chamber."

Wallace, my seatmate, groans. "Fourth time," he says.

I give a small nod, keeping my eyes on our handlers up front. I'm not looking forward to it, but anything Wallace could survive three times can't be all that bad.

A stump of a Marine takes us through the basics of bio-hazard protection. He speaks too loud and too fast, just like all the others. Without asking if we have questions, he hands us each a gas mask before dividing the platoon into pairs. Pena makes certain I stay with Wallace. After a short march across a parched field, we reach a cinderblock building. Yellow buckets filled with water and sponges are lined up by a huge metal door. With only a few small windows, the place looks like an above-ground bunker.

"Recruits," the instructor says, "this exercise will teach you to trust your gas mask if you're ever exposed to a biological or chemical attack. Put your gas mask on, then don and clear. You should have a tight seal and be breathing clean, filtered air. Once you've done this, turn to your buddy and make sure his mask is secure. When everyone is ready, we will enter the chamber in teams of two. It is important for each team to work together throughout the exercise. Stay with your partner at all times. He's your ticket out of my little house of horrors."

My mask gives me trouble right away. The straps are cinched too tight in the back, making it almost impossible to get over my head. Others are already entering the building, and I see that we might be the last group. I yank the straps.

"Relax," Wallace says. "Turn around, and I'll loosen the straps in the back. We'll get it."

His voice is muffled by his mask, yet calm. I look back, making sure it's really him. His mask is secure, and he's ready to go.

"Come on, face forward," he says. "I have to get it seated. There, all good."

He spins me back around.

"Now you have to clear it, like this," he says.

He does the move twice, pinching down the nose of the mask while exhaling, then inhaling while covering the circular filters on either side with his hands, to make the seal. I follow his lead, and the mask tightens around my face. I nod, and we walk inside.

Canisters of CS gas are already popped, fogging the inside of the dark chamber as we enter. Something is wrong. My hands and neck sting, and my eyes tear up.

"Recruits, jumping-jacks, counts of four, exercise," Pena says from a loudspeaker.

We start counting off, and I hack phlegm. Others around me are coughing as well. My eyes sting so bad I can't open them. All my exposed skin is on fire.

"Stop, recruits. That's good. Now, I want you all to remove your masks," Pena says.

The words make me laugh aloud. Remove our masks? Are you kidding?

"Now, recruits."

I shake my head then rip off the mask. The burning is everywhere now. I can't stop coughing, which makes me inhale even more CS gas.

"Don and clear your mask now," Pena says. "If you don't clear it, it won't work."

The coughing, burning, and oozing snot render me helpless. I fight with the mask and end up falling backward on the floor, kicking empty CS canisters as I go down. I fold into a ball and rip at my eyes, my mask forgotten.

"Cole, come on," Wallace says. "You gotta get that mask on."

I can't speak. Everything burns.

"Give me your hand, Cole," Wallace says.

I can't think. Wallace grabs me and pulls hard, bringing me to my feet. There's an opening, and he drags me toward it. We reach the door, and someone closes it. I can't see anything now.

"Please, Staff Sergeant, I need to get him out," Wallace says.

"Nope. He can't leave without a mask on," Pena says.

I can just make him out, his big arms crossed, his stance wide.

If I had a weapon, I'd empty it into him.

"Here, Cole. Take mine. I'll go back and get yours," Wallace says.

He slips the mask over my head as I sit on the floor, useless.

"Breathe in, now blow out," Wallace says. He then starts to cough.

Pena is laughing.

"Look at my little turtledoves, looking out for each other. Awwwww."

I sense the difference right away. I can't breathe without going into a coughing fit. I squint and see a small blur coming toward me.

"Cole, it's me," Wallace says. "Your mask is fucked, but I got it on. Let's get out of here."

Pena finally opens the door, and we stumble through, snot, saliva, and tears pouring out of us both. The sky never looked so blue.

We're given the afternoon to clean up, square away our temporary barracks, and recover from the gas exposure. With our drill instructors in a large Quonset hut next door, we're able to talk at a low whisper for the first time in weeks.

"Thanks for today."

"I owed you," Wallace says.

As I apply a fresh coat of polish to my mucus-covered boots, I finally ask what has been on my mind for weeks.

"Is what Pena said true? Are you trying to get out?"

"Fuck no. Getting out's the last thing I want."

"Really? No offense, but you don't exactly seem to be cut out for this stuff."

Wallace doesn't answer right away. He just pulls something from his footlocker and hands it to me.

"Maybe I'm not, but he was," Wallace says.

It's a weathered photo of a Marine in dress blues. The man in the picture resembles Wallace but is older and much larger. The inscription on the back reads: *Semper Fi, brother. -Tom*

"Your dad?"

"My brother. He died in Beirut when the barracks were bombed in eighty-three. I was fourteen."

"I'm sorry. So, you're following in his footsteps or something?"

"Or something," Wallace says.

He takes back the photo and removes his thick glasses.

"Those things keeping you from qualifying at the range?"

"No, I can see well enough. I get up there, and I just get so nervous. I can't control my breathing. Rounds go all over the place. Once I even shot the wrong target."

He smiles as he says this, and I realize I like him. Maybe I had all along. I picture him up there on the firing line, his brother's face bouncing through his head.

"Well, you'll get it this time, right?"

He just nods and wipes his spectacles with a green T-shirt.

It's ten a.m., day one, and I already hate marksmanship training. My legs are stiff from sitting in one place for two hours, aiming my empty M16 at a barrel as a shooting coach talks about sight alignment, sight picture, trigger squeeze, and breath control. Half the platoon wears eye patches on their non-shooting eyes. The result of being told they possess poor eye control in relation to target focus, a fancy way of saying they can't keep their off-eye closed when they shoot. Evidently, sight alignment is hard to achieve when both eyes are trying to achieve it simultaneously.

I sit for hours in a fixed position, dry-firing as my arms, legs, and ass fall asleep. I pull the trigger about a thousand times, looking forward to doing it for real.

* * *

The first shooting day arrives. I load my first clip and tap it on my helmet to settle the rounds evenly in the clip, just like I'd seen on TV. It's goofy, but it excites me. I'm about to fire an M16.

"Groups one through four, you're up first," Pena says. "Follow your shooting coaches to your assigned boxes at the two-hundred meter line. All other groups get down below the berm to pull targets."

I'm in group three, with Wallace and several others, so I head to the firing line. Since I'm the next to last shooter in my group, I sit back at the spotter box and watch. It's ugly at first, shooters not getting set before they fire or firing before the targets appear. Just a bunch of crazy eighteen-year-olds, stressed to the max and outfitted with loaded assault rifles.

My time comes, and I feel good. Everything comes back to me: the training, the breathing. It all feels natural. I finish at the two-hundred-meter line, hitting twenty-three out of a possible twenty-five bull's eyes. I'm rolling. On the three-hundred-meter line it's the same story, only this time I put all fifteen shots in the center. At the five-hundred-meter line, Staff Sergeant Pena and several shooting coaches start paying attention. I take ten shots from the prone position at five hundred meters, registering nine bulls out of ten. I finish my first full course run three points shy of perfect, something I'm sure few recruits have ever done.

For each good shot I made, Wallace makes an equally bad one. I watch him all afternoon, hands covering my face as he jerks, lurches, twitches, and coughs while squeezing off shots. I talk to him, saying whatever I can think of to calm him. At the five-hundred-meter line, he seems a little more relaxed, but the damage is done. Out of a possible two hundred fifty points, Wallace scores one hundred twenty-five. A recruit needs a minimum of one hundred ninety to qualify.

"That's why they call it a practice round, Wally," I say. "Don't sweat it. You have four more cracks at this."

The week changes everything for me. Pena stops his constant harassment and ridicule. He even asks me to help other recruits having range difficulties. Instead of spending hours down in the pits dragging targets, I stay up on the line and watch other shooters, offering advice. The man I wished dead is acting like a human being for a change, but I don't buy it. I'm just a big feather in his cap now, and I know it. Graduating a recruit that aces the rifle range, a feat only a handful of Marines have ever accomplished, would probably mean promotion. Still, gratitude and respect trump bullying and condescension every time.

Wallace continues to shoot abysmally low scores, once even dipping below one hundred. Pena lets me help him more and more. He even allows me up at the firing line, something range officials aren't happy about. The more I try to help though, the worse Wallace shoots. Tomorrow is Friday, qualification day, his last chance. I'm not feeling too good about it.

"Cole, go see Staff Sergeant Pena," a junior D.I. says.

I stop collecting spent casings on the firing line and head back to the squad bay.

Pena sits in the Quonset hut, his feet up on a desk. "From Cole to diamonds, right recruit?" he says.

"Yes, sir."

"You shot a two-forty-nine today. You going to get that last point for me tomorrow?"

"I'll get it, sir."

"Good man. I'm counting on it."

"Sir, about Wallace."

"Don't worry, Cole. It wasn't a real threat. I was just trying to motivate him. If he blows it tomorrow, he'll be home where he belongs by Monday, in one piece."

"Thank you, sir."

"Of course, now get back to the platoon."

For the big day, they pair the platoon members up again. Wallace and I are together, as usual. We get an early morning run as well, so the sun will be behind us the entire time. Wallace goes first. He's all nerves but seems to be keeping it together. I squeeze his shoulders and push him forward.

"Your brother's with you, man. I feel him. Go finish this."

He nods and approaches the line.

"Stop thinking, stop hesitating, and stop adjusting your glasses," I say. "Just aim and squeeze. Shut everything else out."

At the two-hundred-meter line, he looks calm and determined. He fires without hesitation. The difference in him is immediate. Shots that were misses all week turn into twos and threes. He finishes the first leg with a score north of one hundred for the first time all week.

I follow suit with a perfect score, and we head to the three-hundred-meter line.

More of the same there. Wallace is dialed in. Maybe it wasn't just hollow talk; maybe there is a ghost on his shoulder.

"You got a little edgy there at the end, Wall, but you're still good to go," I say. "You only need thirty-one points at five-hundred meters, and you have ten shots to get it. That's nothing."

I take his spot and feel a familiar calm. Everything slows down until Wallace and the other shooters melt away. A light breeze blows on my forearms, and the sunlight warms my back. Then there's nothing, just me, my weapon, and the target. I don't miss.

Wallace walks beside me, kicking empty brass and smiling as we approach our last firing position.

"Regardless of how this turns out, Cole, I want to thank you. You're the first friend I've had in four platoons of recruits."

I pat him on the back and nod, trying to remain focused. After all, I have a perfect game going.

"You know the drill," the range officer says. "Five-hundred-meter line: ten shots from the prone position at a body silhouette target, ten-minute time limit. Anything in the black gets you five points. This is where you earn your first Marine Corps badge. Shooters down and ready."

Wallace is all over the place from the start.

"Slow down," I say. "You're rushing your shots."

Six shots in and he has two fours, a three and three misses. Eleven points. He needs twenty more, which means four straight bulls. I cringe as he pulls the trigger on his seventh shot. When they raise the red lolly-pop indicating a bull's eye from down in the berm, I can't believe it. Wallace doesn't respond. He just waits for the marker to drop and fires again. The red marker rises again. When it drops, Wallace fires. The marker comes up a third time. To say I'm shocked would be an understatement. This guy hasn't hit more than two bulls all week, now he's popped three in a row. I hold my breath as Wallace squeezes off the last shot.

Nothing happens for almost a minute. The shooting coach at the line goes over to the range officer and asks him what's going on. He radios down to the berm and I hear a crackling response.

"No hole on the last shot. Shooter missed."

I watch as a white marker appears and is swung in a half-moon in front of the target, waving Wallace a miss for the last shot. He stands and stares down range, then looks back at me, his eyes full of tears.

"Next shooters, take your places," the range officer says.

Wallace walks past me to the spotter box then stumbles to his knees. I have no words for him and no time.

I get to the line needing to forget and dial it in. Nothing feels right though. I squirm around my mark, trying to find a comfortable shooting position. Four minutes pass before I take my first shot. Bull. Okay, just breathe. I take another shot. Bull. I stay in position and take five more shots, all bulls. Wallace's face fills my head. Try as I may, I can't push it away. Bull. My breathing hitches a little, but I still have enough rhythm to squeeze off another shot. Bull. Now I not only can see Wallace's face, but that of his brother. What will he tell his family when he goes back home?

Last shot, I pull the trigger.

I wait, but nothing happens. Rolling over on my back, I look up at the group gathered behind me, four range officers, several of my junior D.I.s, and Staff Sergeant Pena. They look down at me then back down range, confusion evident in their faces. The range C.O. is among the onlookers and he calls down to the berm.

"Stop fucking around," he says into the walkie. "This isn't funny. What? Are you serious? No way."

I get up and walk over, but I already know before the white marker appears down the line, waving from left to right. I missed my last shot. I walk over to Wallace and sit down. He doesn't even look up.

Ten minutes later, Pena pulls me aside, grinning.

"They just called up," he says. "The range officers pulled the target to verify your score. They found a keyhole shot. A fucking keyhole, can you believe it?"

"Sir, I don't understand," I say. "What's that?"

"A shot so close to a prior shot that it basically passes through the same hole. You did it, Cole. You scored a perfect two-fifty. All you have to do is go down to the range office and sign off on your card," he says.

With each dusty step, realization hits me. Wallace and I shot on the same target. The keyhole shot could just as easily be his. How the hell am I supposed to confirm it's mine? I turn around and head back to the line to find Wallace. I see him sitting on a bench, staring at his feet. Before I reach him, Pena stops me.

"What are you doing? I ordered you to go down and confirm your score."

"Sir, Wallace shot on that target too. He only needs one bull to qualify."

"You must be kidding. Look at him, Cole. He doesn't belong here. Plus, what are the chances that's his keyhole shot and not yours? Come on."

As he says this, another image of Wallace appears to me, one of caged terror that night in the razor wire. Countless others follow, ones of him stumbling, flailing, and falling, a stamp of fear ever-present.

I look over at Wallace who's watching us. Can he hear what we're saying? He waves, and then drops his head. A question occurs to me just then. Was his brother a good shot?

"Wallace," I call out. He doesn't move. "Wallace?"

He shifts, turning his back to me.

I do an about-face and head back down to the range office to sign off on my perfect score.

The Quiet Thing

CHE YEUN

With one semester left in college, I maxed out all of my credit cards. I filled out new credit forms with optimum information, but none of the remaining banks approved my applications. I would have signed up for a private loan, except I'd already made that mistake once. Once was all it took. Now I was stuck with forty percent interest. At the end of each month, the numbers ballooned. My punishment for being just another stupid, selfish, money-hungry girl in Seoul.

We sell girls like you, the collections agent liked to remind me. We pull gold fillings out of girls like you. We cut toes. We piss on girls like you.

I'm running away, I said.

He laughed. No you're not. You wanted that crocodile handbag. We made it possible for you to have it. Now you make our numbers right.

Eventually I registered for a student loan and used that money to pay off some debt. I waited for my parents to send my tuition fee. When it came through, I used it to pay off more debt. Any perfume or handbag with the tag and box, I sold it as well. I cleared out of the university dorms.

I moved into a ghost neighborhood. A forgotten tangle of alleyways in the heart of Seoul. I looked at one apartment, a studio unit with no gas supply, just some plastic windows, and I took it. My bathroom converted into a shower when I sat on the toilet and held the nozzle over my head. I set up a flimsy clothesline on the balcony, with nails and a handful of shoelaces from the discount store. I slept on the floor, in a pile of old blankets. The blankets weren't mine. They were dropped off at my door one day, probably by the nice old couple renting the place to me. The couple also found me a few shifts at a nearby supermarket.

* * *

When I got hungry I ordered Diet Coke and double-fried chicken. Somehow, no matter which shop I ordered from, the same delivery boy came around. I heard his voice and saw his face over and over again, without ever really getting to know anything about him.

I sold my cell phone with nationwide LTE and a sixteen megapixel camera. I didn't write down any of the numbers stored inside. I didn't transfer any of the pictures to my laptop. I sold my laptop.

With all lines of communication purged, I didn't have to lie to my family or beg and borrow from my friends. I pictured them asking everyone at church to pray for my safe return. All would continue to be good people without me. People who tried their best on tests, arrived at church on time, and never parked in the handicapped space. Good people, enlightened people. Too ashamed to be seen with a crocodile handbag. Not once tempted by the vanity of taking away the life and the skin of another one of God's creatures.

I could feel them worrying for me. The worry pulled at me like ant pheromones. That's all I was, an ant magnetized by its colony. I felt poisoned.

I said goodbye to their petty perfections. I would never have to face them anymore. After all, we shared a city with twenty-five million other people, a city built on the logic of numberless streets and looping subway lines. I unplugged myself from their Matrix.

But sometimes I had dreams of following them undetected. I drove with them to where they bought their groceries. In these dreams I helped them pick out clothes and sipped on creamy espresso while they cut their hair.

* * *

One morning I woke up with a tooth in my mouth. It didn't belong to me. I dropped it onto my hand, a small molar with the slopes of a mountain range. The next morning I spat out a sharp canine. My tongue felt sore where the tooth had pressed into me.

I walked to the 7-Eleven with the cash I'd made at the supermarket. I borrowed the cashier's phone to send a money wire to my loan agent.

The teeth stopped appearing.

* * *

There were days when all the cicadas in the city seemed to sound at once. I had once been told the species in Korea were abnormally shrill. A single cicada held up to the ear could turn a person deaf. But then there were inexplicable days when the cicadas collectively vanished. I couldn't hear the cries at all.

Not too far from my building was a golf range. I couldn't tell which alley would lead me there. But I could see the massive green net with a bulls-eye target on it. The red rings of the target were marked with fat numbers, indicating how far your pitch shot would have landed on a real course.

The golf range parking lot filled up every day with sleek foreign sedans. All morning and afternoon I heard the metallic thuk thuk thuk of golf clubs making contact. On a clear day I could even see the golf balls flying in an arc. I envied the housewives with nothing else to do, just killing time, refining their swings.

The previous tenant had left a flowerpot on the balcony, in the corner with the most daylight. Whatever had been growing inside was now pale and dead. I used it as an ashtray.

I hung up my supermarket uniform to dry only at night. I didn't want anyone walking by to look up at my laundry and know I was the supermarket girl. I sat beside my clothes, the chemical smell of cheap detergent surrounding me, and waited for my chicken delivery.

* * *

From the balcony I also observed my new neighbor, Nara. She lived in the apartment across the hall, had more friends than I knew were possible, and wore thigh-high leather boots even in the summer. Each boot zipped all the way up to the soft, plump bulge of her thigh. She walked weightlessly. Hair, make-up, pantyhose: everything about her looked expensive. Her fake blue contacts held and twisted light like gemstones.

Nara enjoyed vampire hours. She departed after dark and returned in the morning after a night out with her girls. It became a soothing routine for me to watch her with my cold leftover chicken on the balcony. When the cicadas started shrieking in the morning, and the streetlamps turned off one by one, Nara turned the corner and came home.

I watched her and listened to damp leaves brushing each other in the wind.

Once in a while, she stayed at home. Or she had visitors, a friend who would stay over for the night. Afterwards Nara walked her girlfriend out to the front steps of our apartment complex.

From bits and pieces of conversation, I gathered that her hangout was a place called Shampoo. It was a famous club catering to foreigners, and half-Koreans, and supermodels. The owner, Ricky, also operated several other venues. Ricky the kingpin, the Czar of Seoul. And no one was closer to him than Nara.

Eventually, every girl who came by wanted to pry about Ricky. Why wasn't he at the whisky bar last night? When does the whisky bar open tomorrow? Can you sneak me on the table booking list?

So how generous is he? a girl with warrior cheekbones asked her one day.

He's my boss, Nara replied.

Bullshit. I know all about your business with him, you little shit.

You know nothing. Zero point zero.

You fat fuck. So some nobody who doesn't exist fixed your tits and fixed your face? You were a fat, hairy fuck before he came along.

Nara kept still, slender arms crossed at her waist.

Cheekbones dropped her head to shake and tease her flat hair into a big poof once more. I'll see you on Tuesday, she said. She gathered her hair into a bun, then let it fall, and just like that they were smiling again.

* * *

I timed my chores to run into Nara in the narrow corridor between our homes. Sometimes I wasn't so sure that she hadn't planned to run into me.

Miss Kim, she called me, even though that wasn't my name. Do you have hot water?

She followed me into my unit with three plastic buckets stacked in her arms. We filled each one. I held my door open as she carried them back into her room. She walked slowly, no spills.

We kept running into each other at night and moving water together.

She was a courteous guest. She took her slippers off and lined them up neatly next to my shoes before coming in. She brought gifts. A bunch of grapes from the supermarket or samples of lotion from a department store. Once she handed me a real calla lily, slipped from a hotel lobby when no one was looking.

The flower had only one petal that wrapped into itself. The petal flared out like a white sail. I stuck the calla in the flowerpot while she ran some water for her shower.

You should just bathe here.

Miss Kim, I can't.

But the relief in her fake blue eyes told me she would.

For the first time I noticed the pink rims of her eyes. Inflammation on the verge of infection. A common look on Korean women who couldn't stop their cosmetic surgeries. They kept slicing their eyes wider and wider each time, until the eyelids couldn't shut properly when they tried to sleep. Half the women in Seoul walked around with saline drops to soothe the sting.

I didn't mind Nara's swollen tear ducts and eyelash glands. She was still graceful, the tips of her wet hair curling away from her shoulders. Even her breath smelled warm and sweet, like fresh bread on display at a bakery.

You look clean, Nara said, when she grew comfortable with me. Clean enough to be in college.

I started playing with loans.

Where are your parents?

Dead.

She nodded slowly.

I'd always thought she was my age like all the other club rats I knew. But from this close I realized she was much older, old enough to have a child to teach words to. Instead she just had a cold sunless room, like me. We have to take care of each other, she said. She reached out her hand, but before I could react, she let it fall on her lap. She folded the hem of her dress over and over again. We absolutely must take care of each other. That's what we're here for.

* * *

I showed her the molar and the canine I'd been storing in a paper cup. She shook the cup around to see better in the dim light. Has he taken a shit on your pillow yet? she asked.

Not yet.

You still have time.

I buried the teeth in the flowerpot, next to the yellowing calla. At night I shut my windows to keep out the breeze. Sometimes a noise woke me in the middle of the night. I bit down on my tongue. But it turned out to be a phone, or a floorboard, or a birdcall from outside that I'd never heard before.

* * *

I came home from work to find her waiting for me in the corridor. Next to her purse, on the floor, were shoeboxes full of coins. The boxes were so heavy she dragged and kicked them over the threshold. I dug my hands into the massive collection, five-hundred-won coins with identical engravings of a crane taking flight. She told me our mission was to comb through them all, until we found one marked with the year 1998. Only eight thousand of them had been minted that year. Now, each one was worth over a million in auction. There was a secondary list of other production years that were valuable for other reasons. A new alloy, an unexpected misprint.

We'll share everything we find, she said.

We stopped at different vending machines each day. Machines for colas, for coffee, for cigarettes. We checked for forgotten change in the trays. Sometimes we could afford to make a purchase ourselves and collect the coins they spat out. I looked forward to my shifts at the supermarket. After lunch and after closing, I went through the coins in every register.

It wasn't just the years that were different. Engraving tools seemed to change as well, which affected the thickness of lines and the milling of edges. Some coins felt heavier than others, depending on the compound used. They aged and wore down differently. Sometimes even the crane seemed slightly off to me, although Nara swore the crane had always been the same.

We sat on my blankets and looked through them together. Nara fell asleep first.

I didn't stop her. I wanted to hear her breathe and burble through dreams. I wanted to see her hair fan out on my pillow.

* * *

She never picked up her phone in front of me.

If Ricky ever comes looking, she said, we don't know each other. Remember that. You never knew me.

You're not allowed to have friends? I asked.

No, she said. Not anyone he doesn't already know.

Does Ricky know your hot water got cut off?

He used to in the past. Not anymore.

Why not?

Because I'm not a parasite. I settle my accounts.

But you must owe him a lot.

Nara looked at me. He and I will get past that, she said. Like human beings.

I wondered how much her eyes had cost Ricky. How much the rest of her had cost him. It would be enough money to change my life around, to make me a simple university student again. He could change every person he ever met, if he wanted to.

It's not just money, she continued. It's history. Many lifetimes. We've been brothers, sisters, parents to each other, over and over again. We keep meeting and giving and parting and meeting and giving. For thousands of years. Every fortuneteller says so.

Do you really believe that? I asked.

I've been blessed.

He's a very convenient solution for the rest of your life.

Don't think like that. People get punished for thinking like that.

Who would punish me?

It doesn't matter. We are all on this earth to take care of each other.

* * *

But she stopped taking care of Ricky. She went days without seeing him. The days turned into a week, two weeks. She stopped meeting up with her girlfriends from Shampoo.

She wouldn't answer calls, either. I heard her phone vibrating constantly, the low hum echoing through our thin walls.

All the while, Nara grew closer to me.

The first time I saw her without make-up, she showed me every surgery scar around her nose and eyelids. She recited the date and price of each of the scars. She took my hands and guided my fingertips along her jawline, the unnaturally sharp ridge, the numb spots indicating nerve damage.

Our first kiss happened after she traced her lower lip with my fingers this way. That was another numb spot, that lip, and all it could sense was hot or cold.

I could taste how lonely she was, and I knew that I was just as lonely for recognizing it.

* * *

Nara showed up at my door with a white envelope. The crisp edges told me it had never been used before. Inside were two paper talismans, black ink on imperial yellow paper. I couldn't decipher the frantic brushstrokes.

These will protect you, she told me. No one is hurting you until you pay everything back.

She slid one talisman inside my pillowcase and took the other one to the bathroom sink. She set it on fire with a lighter, collecting the ash in a glass. She filled the glass with hot water and stirred to separate the clumps. I was to drink the whole thing.

I washed down the burnt taste with some warm Diet Coke. She watched me with her big blue eyes.

This can't protect me, I said. This can't be enough.

Of course, it's enough. The fortuneteller grinds the ink himself.

How much did these cost?

She didn't answer. She squeezed my hand into hers. There was nothing for her to gain from me in return. But here she came, anyway. Wasn't that also a kind of fate?

Have you ever asked your fortuneteller about me? I couldn't help but ask her one day.

Yes.

What did he say?

He said we might be linked from the past. Or we might not be. He doesn't know yet.

Why not?

Well. He gets paid first, and then he finds out.

* * *

But I didn't want to pay a conman to tell me anything. Instead, I insisted we would find a 1998 coin together. That would also be a kind of fate. Nara wasn't convinced. She gave all kinds of statistics on probability to feed her doubt.

I didn't care. Not even about the coin. I just wanted her to feel with me like she did with Ricky, the weight of history anchoring us from somewhere far below.

Ricky could have all her other lifetimes. I just wanted this one.

I sold my pillow talisman to another cashier at the supermarket. I used the money to buy chicken feet, pig ears, and baby clams from the meat section. Back home I cut off one chicken toe and clipped off the tip of a pig ear. I crushed one baby clam to get a shard of its shell. I coated these foreign objects with my saliva, spat them out into my palm, and with them I knocked on Nara's door.

The loan agent came back, I said. They're trying to kill me. I woke up choking.

Where's the talisman?

It didn't work. It's gone.

Let me see your mouth. Are you bleeding?

I opened my mouth wide for her to look. I wanted her to see my cavities and gravel gray fillings. I wanted her to see I had nowhere else to go.

Nara set about cleaning my room of any trace of the intrusion. Materially and spiritually, the sanctity of my space had to be reclaimed. She brought over her plastic buckets and an old dishrag. Even the toilet was scrubbed, inside and outside. We stuffed my blankets and pillows into a suitcase and dragged it over to the cleaner's. She instructed the man to clean the suitcase as well.

We poured bleach all over my bathroom.

We bathed at the public bathhouse instead. We were naked, but there was so much steam and many other women in the bathhouse with us. We might as well have been in Shampoo, surrounded by a thousand other Rickys.

Without the silicone lenses her real irises were as hard and flat as beans. And without any make-up, the roundness of her naked face seemed bloated. I kept expecting her to take it off, like a mask, to reveal another face underneath.

She scrubbed me clean, almost raw.

There, she said. Not a trace left.

Now what? I asked.

Now you forget it ever happened.

Why wasn't there more? I wondered, but I knew it would be impolite to ask. I wanted her to make me sleep in her room, away from danger. To tell me to pray to my ancestors for protection. And then to teach me how to pray to them. How to cook broth and lay out the fruits on the altar.

Instead we packed up our toiletries and covered our bodies with clothes again.

* * *

One night a black Bentley cruised down the street. Slowly, like a whale, with its headlights off and windows rolled down. It stopped near our apartment entrance, blocking the entire alley. One arm popped out the driver's window with a lit cigarette between fingers. I knew Ricky was inside.

Nara met him on the steps of our building. In the darkness, the backs of her bare knees shone moon white.

You hate me, Ricky said. His voice carried upwards, with the pillar of smoke from his hand. I made you beautiful, he said. Now you want me gone.

You're a kid, she replied. A kid with a lot of money. You're a shark in a fishbowl.

Ricky tossed the cigarette. It hit a cement wall and rolled along the pavement without losing its spark.

But you're the one who wanted this. You wanted to be beautiful.

Right now I just want to be ugly. Ugly and incapable and quiet.

What are you talking about? You're beautiful. You always were.

Nara didn't say anything.

You're just lonely, he said. Beautiful people always are.

Nara crossed and uncrossed her arms. I wanted to see her break his heart. Instead she walked up to the car and tapped the side mirror.

Put your lights on, she said. You're not the mafia.

Ricky laughed. His hand reached out. He grabbed her by a leg, right in between her thighs. And she let him.

You can do the quiet thing with me, he said. We can smoke in bed and make each other sick and watch movies together.

Why would I do that?

Because it's fun. Ricky moved his hand up and down on her skin. It's not always a fight.

Nara didn't say anything.

She let him hold on to her leg. For a very long time, until the chicken delivery boy arrived in the alley. The boy pulled his scooter right up to kiss the Bentley, unafraid of how much a single scratch could cost him. He honked his horn in long stark notes. Ricky let go of Nara's leg and drove away.

She stayed outside by herself long after he'd gone. She ran her hands over the cotton fabric stretched across her flat stomach. It kept her calm, to touch her own beauty and know it was still there.

I am blessed, she said to herself. I am blessed I am blessed I am blessed.

* * *

As a child, I had once seen an orchid that looked like a bee. I'd thrown away the flower in confusion, in alarm, in anger. Its largest petal wasn't a petal at all but a heavy black bulb lipped with brown fur. The bulb had evolved into an exact reproduction of the shape, color, smell, and touch of its target. That's how the orchid survived, by fooling its pollinators into believing she was one of them.

Nara survived the same way. When she wanted to be beautiful, she went to Ricky. When she needed to feel ugly and incapable and quiet, she came to me. I helped her pretend her life also took place in a very small and very humiliating world.

But now that she was beautiful, she couldn't stop, no matter how ugly she had been before. How do you give beauty back? Who do you give it back to?

We couldn't live across the hall from each other forever.

She would have to move away, into a seaside condo behind wrought-iron gates, bare feet on tiles of imported marble. Sweeping her past into dark corners. Telling her new friends, over cool slices of sashimi at brunch, whatever new past she cared to invent. Ricky and his After Hours Empire would take care of it all.

When that happened, I would be left behind. By then I would have to buy another uniform for the supermarket to replace my fading one. This was our future.

Thankfully, I didn't have to wait too long for it. Nara and Ricky got back together.

But not without first readjusting some parts of Nara, widening her eyes and injecting experimental-yet-promising fat burners into her thighs.

For one week she went back and forth between her room and the hospital, busy with follow-up appointments. Ricky drove her around and brought her food.

For one week she dropped me the way she had dropped Ricky. I didn't have a phone to send or receive calls. Even if I had, it would have been silent.

* * *

She came over when the initial swelling in her face had reduced to green bruises. It was safe to wash herself properly again. Her eyelids were still puffy, but the stitches had come out, and I could tell the results would be exquisite. Soon her face, like the rest of her, would be as smooth as the inside of a seashell.

She showed up with her shoeboxes, a new sample of coins in circulation.

Let me explain, she said.

I knew I shouldn't let her in, but I did.

You keep what you find, I told her. And I keep mine.

Nara gave up after only a few handfuls. She reached for my pillow, and she let the post-operation medication knock her out without explaining anything.

The smell of metal gave me a headache. But I kept moving my fingers and eyes. I needed ten coins from 1998, ten out of eight thousand, to settle all of my accounts. Seventy-seven grams of copper and nickel.

I calculated how long it would take me to pay everything back if I didn't find any. No matter how many different ways I mixed the numbers, the answer stayed the same.

* * *

The Bentley dropped Nara off after all-nighters at Shampoo, when the black sky had turned into white clouds.

She always looked up at my balcony. I didn't budge from behind my laundry.

I stayed still next to the flowerpot, which had seen some rain but not enough to help the calla take root. Some weeds were sprouting. Slender leaves on thick stems. I tried to pull them out. The leaves broke off. Drops of white sap formed on the tip of the stems. I pulled the stems out as well and rubbed the sap between my fingers until it turned to chalk.

You're a weed, I whispered. We kill weeds like you.

Nara unlocked the entrance and walked inside.

In a few hours, the housewives would return to the golf range for lessons, and the thuk thuk thuk would begin again. For a while the neighborhood dogs would bark at the noise, trying to make it stop. It never stopped. Those dogs started up every morning, when just the previous day they had accepted the futility and retreated in silence.

You're a dog, I said out loud.

The barking stopped for a while, then resumed.

You're a dog, I repeated, louder.

I couldn't see them anywhere in the maze of alleyways and utility cables. But I wanted to make sure they could hear me over each other.

We ruin dogs like you, I said to them. We stole you from your mothers. Now we will make you wait all day for us, for nothing.

The barking ceased. All of it. I wondered if they had really understood me or if they just wanted me to shut up. Either way, I felt better. I didn't have to hear the dogs anymore. Just like that, a part of my life had changed.

I began with small changes like that.

I threw out the flowerpot.

I took down my makeshift clothesline and invested in a proper laundry rack.

When Nara knocked on my door, I ignored her.

In one short afternoon I figured out the alleys around me.

I even found my way to the golf range and went inside. I couldn't afford a membership, but I left with a business card.

I went to the 7-Eleven to borrow the cashier's phone again. This time I called my loan agent directly.

I told him I'd have all ten million by tomorrow.

Don't disappoint me, he said. I've had enough people disappointing me lately.

I waited for Nara one last time. But this time I didn't hide on my balcony. I waited on the steps of our apartment with two coins in my pocket, a 1997 and a 1999. I held them together for good luck. I waited in my darkest clothes to blend in with the night. When the Bentley drifted by, I would be invisible until it was too late.

The softest part of any car is the windshield, glass so soft that it's almost impossible to shatter. That was the part of the Bentley I had to make contact with. I had to land on my back if I didn't want permanent damage. No matter what, I had to clear the beam.

Then I would close my eyes for a while, to make them think they might have really hurt me. To overwhelm them with relief when I turned out to be fine.

I watched the Bentley roll down the alley. The headlights were off.

When the time came, I covered my head with my arms. I dove like an Olympian.

I hit the windshield and prayed it wouldn't shatter. I told myself I wasn't a human body hitting glass. I was a sugar cube stirred into hot coffee. I couldn't rupture. I couldn't break. I could only swirl and melt into smaller particles that grew faint and dissolved completely.

I bounced and rolled forever on the pavement. My head was still attached to my neck. A cement wall rushed towards me.

A door slammed. Ricky stood over me.

What the fuck are you doing? he shouted, looking straight into my eyes.

The neighborhood dogs started up again.

Ten million won, I heard myself say.

He threw his lighter at the cement wall near my head. The handful of blue plastic exploded.

I couldn't see Nara. Only the carved shape of Nara inside the car. She called out to Ricky. Just get her the money, she said.

I kept my eyes on Ricky. His dry lips. The small balcony three floors above him, and then the scattering of clouds above that.

Ten million won, I said again. Or we can wait for the cops.

Call the cops, Ricky said. Bring them. I'll make sure they take care of you.

It's nothing, Nara said. Just get the money, and we can go.

Someday she would feel embarrassed for sharing any part of herself with someone like me. Once the pity faded, she would deny I had ever existed. But in that moment she was afraid of me and what I was capable of. Her hands came together to cover her cold neck. It's nothing, she kept saying, but she couldn't even get out of the car.

FACULTY

excerpt from *A House Divided*
Inky Holler

FREDRICK BARTON

Aside from church, the only social gathering spot in the New Peterstown, Louisiana, of 1938 was Rufus Caine's Grocery and Feeds, the general store. After buying their supplies, area wives lingered to talk while the younger children played games like kick-the-can in the dirt parking lot and the older children engaged in adolescent boasting, horseplay, and flirting with the opposite sex.

The summer that Pruitt Caldwell lost his job when the local sawmill closed, he was forced to take his entire family into the cotton fields. Pruitt seethed with indignation at this demotion in his circumstances. But his children hated it less because their own work left them with money to spend on treats at the store. Pruitt's wife Osby bought such staples as flour, lard and sugar, but her children spent their pennies on gum, sweets and soft drinks. Wayne liked candied apples; James preferred Baby Ruth candy bars; Monroe and Franklin both bought a thick twist of black licorice for each day of the week.

Fourteen-year-old Jeff Caldwell contented himself with lemon drops, five for a penny, and otherwise mostly saved his money. The only other extravagance he allowed himself was a bottle of orange soda, which he didn't particularly care for but which he knew was the favorite of Mary Frances Branson. Jeff had developed a crush on brown-haired, blue-eyed Mary Frances, and he liked to curry her favor by offering to share his drink with her. On those Sundays when Mary Frances was at the store, he would pluck his soft drink from the galvanized wash tub filled with ice and water and toss his nickel into the cash basket. Then he would saunter out onto the porch as if his every move were not calculated. He would lean up against the porch rail on whichever side of the front steps Mary Frances had chosen to sit that day, take a swallow of the sweet orange drink and casually, as if he'd just thought of it, look over at Mary Frances and offer her a swallow, too. When she accepted, which she always did, he'd wipe the mouth of the bottle with his shirt tail and pass the drink to her. And she'd wipe the mouth of the bottle again on the hem of her dress before taking a sip. He wondered if she noticed that he never wiped the bottle when she passed it back to him.

Aside from the lemon drops and orange drink, Jeff saved his money assiduously. He turned his collection of pennies and nickels into dimes and quarters and eventually into dollar bills, all of which he kept rolled in a sock and hidden in a hole on the underside of his mattress. He did all this because he had a plan. When school started and his work in the cotton fields had ended, he wanted to take Mary Frances Branson to a Saturday-night movie in Alexandria, buy her some popcorn and a Coca-Cola and afterwards buy her a malted at the Rexall.

Jeff fantasized about every detail of his date. Since he wasn't old enough yet to drive legally, he would have to persuade his older brother Wayne to double-date with him in their father's rusted pickup. It would be crowded, the four of them in the cab together. But that was part of Jeff's plan, too. Mary Frances would have to ride in his lap, his arms wrapped securely around her waist so the jouncing of the truck over the rutted gravel road would not send her flying against the window or into the dash. Thus existed the exquisite possibility that an awaiting pothole would bounce her so violently that his hands, unavoidably and guiltlessly, would slide across her breasts. In pursuit of this plan, Jeff judiciously sought rapprochement with his older brother and tried to avoid their usual run-ins.

Meanwhile, Wayne had a plan of his own. He began to fine-tune it when he located Jeff's hiding place and discovered that Jeff had amassed an astonishing treasure of more than three dollars. Later, when Jeff broached the subject of a double date, Wayne agreed immediately and without his usual expression of surly suspicion. Instead, Wayne smiled lewdly and punched Jeff lightly on the arm. "I know what you're looking forward to, little brother. Four of us together in the cab, you get to squirm all the way to Alec with Mary Frances Branson on your lap. I wouldn't mind that treat myself. Specially if she don't wear panties 'cause it's too hot. Maybe I'll just drive down the road apiece and then let you get behind the wheel once we're out of sight of the house."

"I'm the one taking Mary Frances Branson, you understand," Jeff said, alarmed. "You gotta take somebody else. That's what a double date means. Two girls. One for each of us."

"You mean the two of us wouldn't be doubling up on Mary Frances?" Wayne said.

"No!" Jeff replied.

Wayne laughed out loud and punched Jeff again, still not hard. "You are so easy to rile. I'll take Becky Price. We'll have ourselves a good old time."

The whole plan seemed to be falling into place so effortlessly that Jeff didn't realize for a day or so after school began that he hadn't actually asked Mary Frances for a date. When he finally did so at afternoon recess during the second week of school, Mary Frances's reaction was so blasé that Jeff found it unsettling. "Oh, sure," she said without additional comment. Jeff stated the exact time two Saturday nights later, and Mary Frances responded, "That's fine." She didn't ask what movie he wanted to take her to or any other details, and in the absence of any stated interest on her part, Jeff quickly broke away from her and subsequently decided to avoid her at school until after they'd gone out.

On the Friday eight days before Jeff's date with Mary Frances, after school and after all the Caldwell boys had finished their chores, Jeff was sitting on the back porch steps reading a library copy of *Oliver Twist* when Wayne came to sit beside him. The sky was yellow and fading, and a blue-black line of thunderheads could be seen thumb-smudged on the horizon over the trees to the southwest. Jeff was still in work clothes, overalls and a T-shirt. He had removed his shoes and scratched absently at the tops of his feet as he read. Wayne was barefooted, too, and shirtless as well; his jeans were buttoned, but he hadn't buckled his belt. He had just come out from the washing shed where he'd cleaned up after working under Osby's direction in her vegetable garden. He mopped at himself with a towel as he sat down next to his brother.

"You planning on just playing bookworm all night?" Wayne asked Jeff.

Jeff shrugged and kept on reading. He was practically immune to Wayne's relentless verbal harassment. So Wayne draped his towel over Jeff's book.

"Stop that, dang it," Jeff said.

"I want to ask you something," Wayne said.

"What?" Jeff replied, handing the towel back to Wayne.

"Want to go out riding with us tonight?" Wayne said. "Bobby's got his daddy's truck. Me and Johnny are going with him over to Dry Prong. Their high school's got a sock hop in the gym this evening."

"I don't know," Jeff said. He was surprised to be included on such an outing and did not really want to go. Bobby and Johnny were Wayne's friends, not Jeff's. Johnny Davis was crazy as far as Jeff was concerned. And Bobby Sawyer would let Johnny egg him on into just about anything. The last thing Jeff wanted to do was have to break up some scrape Bobby and Johnny might get into with the Dry Prong boys. But he didn't want to say no straight out because he didn't want to queer his arrangement with Wayne for the next weekend. So he said, "I don't know anybody at Dry Prong."

"Aw, come on," Wayne implored. "Who's it gonna hurt? Maybe we'll just ride around awhile. But if we end up over at Dry Prong, maybe you'll meet you a girl you like even better than Mary Frances Branson."

Such a notion was preposterous, but Jeff finally agreed to go with them. "You better go on and wash up then," Wayne said. "Bobby will be by here in twenty minutes."

Every Saturday night Osby insisted that each of the Caldwells take a full hot bath in the galvanized tub in which she scrubbed the family laundry against a metal washboard. Saturday baths involved taking the wash tub into the kitchen where water was heated in a huge iron kettle on the stove. Bathing took almost the entire evening as the tub had to be emptied and refilled after the first three boys soaked and scrubbed.

On the days other than Saturday, washing was done in the shed and didn't involve either a bath or hot water. This kind of washing was practiced every other day in the warmer months, less often in winter. Following his usual routine, Jeff undressed and dipped a tin pail into the wash tub. He set the pail on a warped wooden table where a bar of soap lay, still tacky from being used by Wayne. Jeff studied the soap suspiciously, always concerned that Wayne might have done something foul with it which Wayne would later reveal for the purpose of humiliating Jeff. Jeff wet his hands in the pail and rubbed the soap briskly into a lather. Holding the soap in one hand and grasping the pail with the other, he stepped over to the hole in the middle of the floor which allowed the water to drain to the ground below. He rinsed both his hands and the soap bar itself, then soaped up the communal wash cloth, rubbed it vigorously against itself and rinsed it over the drain. Only then, with what he considered a clean bar of soap and a clean cloth, did he begin to wash himself, lathering with his hands and using the wet cloth to wipe away the soap. Afterwards, he dressed in clean clothes and went to wait with Wayne on the front porch.

Johnny was already in the truck when Bobby arrived, and Wayne immediately climbed into the cab, thumbing Jeff into the gritty bed in the back. Jeff was used to this common snub and barely took notice. It would have been crowded and uncomfortable had he tried to squeeze into the cab, and he wouldn't have had anything to say if either Johnny or Wayne rode with him in the back. So he was content to ride along with only his thoughts for company. The moon was just coming up, a huge orange disk that shone through the trees. The wind was cool and pleasant whipping through his wet hair, and life seemed delectably worthwhile as Jeff mused about bouncing along this same route a week hence with Mary Frances Branson perched on his lap. The moon would not be so large that night, he knew. But it would be exquisitely lovely; he was sure of it.

At State Highway 1, Bobby turned north. Jeff disliked this stretch of highway with its cutover land on either side. Stripped of its trees, the land absorbed more heat, and even though Bobby picked up speed on the pavement, Jeff could feel the temperature ratchet upwards, draining some of the pleasantness out of the night. When they reached the parish road into Dry Prong, Bobby passed it by; Jeff was thoroughly perplexed when Bobby eventually turned east off the highway rather than west. As the truck rattled out onto still another local gravel road, Jeff hammered on the rear window of the cab and yelled out, "Where we going?" The boys inside responded only with laughter, and Jeff pounded on the window and yelled out a second time, "I said, where we going?"

Wayne stuck his head out the window and yelled back, "You'll find out when we get there, won't you?"

Jeff shook his head in resignation and twisted around to sit again with his back against the cab, his right arm thrown up across the rail to steady himself as the truck bounced along. He knew he should have stayed at home. He might have finished his book. He made no more inquiries, denying Wayne and the others the pleasure of refusing to tell him what they were up to. He watched the central Louisiana landscape slide by on either side of the truck. The night was bright, and as they passed out of the ugly expanse of cutover, he could make out the star-shaped leaves of a row of sweet gums growing in the sluicy area just past the roadside ditch.

After fifteen minutes of riding through an area of scrub pine growing back from an earlier cut, Bobby turned onto a rutted drive that had never been graded. The truck slowed to less than ten miles per hour as the vegetation canopied over this dark lane. Through the night, carried on a breeze smelling of damp earth, night-blooming jasmine and muscadine, Jeff could suddenly hear the sound of music, the tinkling of piano keys and the low wailing notes of a saxophone. He stood up in the back of the truck to look over the top of the cab, almost losing his balance as a wheel slammed through a washout hole. "Where in the devil are we?" Jeff called out.

Wayne stuck his head out the window and said, "Sit down and shut up, or we're gonna make you get out and wait here for us in the dark until we get back."

Jeff spread his legs wide for balance and continued to peer over the top of the cab which Bobby steered left and right along the twisting, downhill lane. Jeff squinted in a vain effort to see beyond the reach of the truck's headlights, whose reflection off leaves and branches had the odd effect of making the truck seem enveloped in a closed green cave of vegetation. Jeff could smell slow-moving water; they were coming down to a bayou somewhere, or a lake perhaps. The music grew louder, and now Jeff could hear the murmur of voices.

Finally, the truck eased into a clearing, and its lights flashed across a building awash in the glow of a hundred kerosene lamps. A dozen vehicles of various kinds—lumber truck, a milk van, and a hearse, along with several pickups and black sedans—were parked haphazardly in front of an unpainted two-story wood building erected on pilings out over the water of a bayou. Steps from the front porch came down on land. At the foot of the steps someone had spread fresh wood shavings over a bed of gravel.

"What is this place?" Jeff asked as he climbed out of the bed and the other boys got out of the cab.

"Come on and find out," Bobby said, and they all started for the building. As they drew closer, Jeff could see in the flickering light people standing on the porch in small groups, mostly couples, some with their arms around one another. Inside, the music started up again, fast music with a hard beat, and some of the couples moved inside. It wasn't until Jeff started up the steps that he realized everybody on the porch was black. Some of the people were dressed like most every Negro he had ever seen, the men in loose cotton shirts and coveralls and the women in shapeless, loose-weave shifts. But many of them were dressed like no Negro he had ever seen, not even those prosperous, black-suited Negro preachers and funeral directors he had seen a time or two in Alexandria. Here many of the men wore shiny, striped suits and bright shirts with colorful ties. Most of the women wore clingy, satin dresses with plunging necklines. This was a place from outside Louisiana, from outside any world that Jeff had ever encountered.

Perhaps it was just the loud music which drowned out the sound, but Jeff felt as if all conversation had stopped and all eyes were following the four white boys. Tobacco smoke hung heavy in the air, and Jeff felt disoriented. No one had said a word to them, but Jeff felt distinctly alien. As the boys reached the level of the porch, a full-figured, red-haired black woman of forty or so came out from inside on the arm of a tall, thin black man wearing a wide-brimmed hat and smoking a cigarette in a long white holder. The woman wore a red lace dress with a flared bottom trimmed in black satin, black, ribbed nylons and open-toed shoes with very high heels. On her head she had a small black hat, like a skull cap with four points. Its veil reached down toward the arch of her eyebrows which were plucked to the width of a pencil lead.

"Oh, honey, now ain't that the truth," Jeff heard her say, and she laughed and patted her companion's arm. Then she noticed the four white boys and said to the man at her side after sizing them up, "Now looky what we got here." None of the boys made a response, and the lady in the red dress stepped over to them, leaving the thin man standing in the doorway. "You boys know where you are, now do you?" she asked, walking down the line of them, looking each one frankly in the face. Jeff had never known a black person to relate to a white person, even a white child, with such brazenness. Unable to meet her gaze, he looked down at his shoes.

"Red Ruby's," Johnny Davis said, and the lady in the red dress turned her eyes to him.

"Why I do believe some people use that name," she said, licking her lips and smiling.

"If this is Red Ruby's," Bobby Sawyer said, "then I guess we come to the right place."

"Oh, have you now, honey?" she said.

"I guess we have," Bobby replied.

"And what would be bringing you out to this dark place?" the lady in the red dress asked, and the man in the doorway behind her snickered and turned to say something to someone behind him. Almost immediately, he was joined by another Negro man, also dressed in a fancy suit. Both men stared at the lineup of white boys with unconcealed amusement. "What would be bringing you white boys out in this black night?" the lady in red asked, and both the men in the doorway guffawed. Not one of the boys had any idea what they were laughing about.

"We heard we could get some action here," Wayne said, and Jeff heard the slight quaver in his voice.

The lady in the red dress turned on her heel and moved directly in front of Wayne who stood at the end of the line. She cocked her weight onto one leg and rested her hand on her hip, lifting her opposite leg to brush against Wayne's ankle with her toes. "Now are you the leader of these boys?" she asked Wayne. "Are you the one they followed into this inky holler?"

"I guess," Wayne said. "It was my idea. But they all wanted to come."

Not me, Jeff thought. He had no idea what was going on.

"So you want some *ac*tion for all these boys," she said, emphasizing the first syllable of action. "Is that what you want, leader man?"

"I guess," Wayne said. "Yes."

The lady in the red dress turned again and walked down to where Jeff was standing. "Even for this baby?" she said to Wayne. "Even for this baby who probably ain't even got any hair . . . " She reached out and rubbed Jeff's face along his jaw line. " . . . on his chin?" The men behind her laughed loudly again.

"I'm fourteen," Jeff said, somewhat indignantly. "I shave sometimes. Over my lip."

"I'm sure you do, honey," the lady in red said, continuing to caress Jeff's face. Then she turned away and walked back to Wayne. "*Ac*tion ain't free, leader man; I'm sure you understand that."

"I got money," Wayne said.

"Good," the lady in red said. "And what about your fellas and my baby boy? Do they have money, too? For their *ac*tion?"

"I got money for all of us," Wayne said.

"Why, you all want to follow me then," the lady in red said, smiling broadly. She turned and moved toward the doorway, the boys falling in behind her single file. Jeff brought up the rear, perplexed about what was going on. He suspected Wayne was going to buy moonshine, and if so, Wayne had another think coming if he thought Jeff was going to drink any of it.

As the lady in red swept through the doorway, she said to the two men in the doorway, "These fine young white boys have come to Red Ruby's for some *ac*tion." The two black men seemed to think that was the funniest thing she had said all night.

The downstairs room at Red Ruby's was a dark sea of ripe humanity. The room was thick with cigarette smoke under which hung a smell of perfume and body odor and another smoky smell, sweet and green, that Jeff could not identify. It was very warm. The top-hinged shutters to all the windows were propped open with wooden slats, but little of the heavy outside air stirred inside. Showers of yellow light fell from kerosene lamps standing on every window ledge and splashed across the wooden tables set up around the edge of the room. Pools of red shimmered about the flickering candle in the center of each table and illuminated the litter of beer and liquor bottles and overflowing ashtrays. In the far corner of the room, four musicians, a pianist, a bass player, a drummer and a saxophonist, played their narcotic music as if in a trance.

The lady in red led them through a gyrating throng of dancers and up a staircase to the second floor. As they walked down a hall, the lady in red closed a door through which Jeff could hear a buzz of voices, men and women together. At the end of the hall, the lady in red showed them into a room with two sofas facing each other and two hard-backed chairs closing off the square. Here she told them to wait. She directed that Bobby, Johnny and Jeff sit down on one of the sofas and that Wayne accompany her back into the hall. Jeff could hear them talking in the hall, but he could not hear what they were saying. A few minutes later, Wayne returned and sat with the others.

"Y'all ever gonna tell me what the devil's going on?" Jeff inquired.

Bobby and Johnny snickered. Wayne said, "You ain't gonna have to wait no time at all to find out, little brother. So just hold your horses."

"Somebody else is about to hold his horse," Bobby said and laughed.

"If he's got himself a horse, that is," Johnny replied and socked Bobby in the arm.

Bobby winced and said, "Ow, Johnny, that hurt." He rubbed the spot where he'd been punched.

"Oh, don't be such a baby," Johnny responded, scowling, "or we won't let you have none neither. Will we, Wayne?"

"Shut up the both of you," Wayne said.

The lady in red opened the door and came back in. Trailing behind her were four young Negro women. All were older than the four white boys, but none was older than her early twenties; the two youngest appeared to be seventeen or eighteen. Each was dressed in a long, white cotton smock that hung just below her knees. The lady in red lined them up opposite the boys.

"Okay, girls," the lady in red ordered. "Show them what you got."

The girls lifted their smocks up around their necks. Underneath they were completely naked. Jeff was offended in a way. It was so indecent making the girls display themselves like this. But he couldn't take his eyes away. He looked at each of the girls in turn, at their breasts and at the tufts of black hair between their legs. Jeff knew exactly what was happening now. He had heard Wayne and the other boys talk about whorehouses, and he'd even imagined going to one, although never to one with Negro girls. But even when he'd imagined it, he'd never imagined this. He thought of just him and the whore in a room all alone. And the two of them getting undressed and her not minding that he touched her. His fantasies about visiting a whorehouse had always had a core element of romance. He would be nice, and she would find him special. But this was so raw he felt ashamed even as he became utterly aroused. He wondered if the girls could see that his pecker was standing up like a twenty-year-old pine.

"Turn around, girls," the lady in red ordered. "In case one of these boys is a rear-end man." She laughed. "Just remember, reverse *ac*tion costs twice as much." Jeff had no idea what she was talking about. The girls dropped their hands to gather the backs of the smocks and then turned around to face away from the boys. After a moment, the lady in red said, "Okay, y'all can turn around again. But keep your dresses up until you're chosen."

The girls faced forward, and Wayne said, "I'll take the yellow one." He pointed out the lightest skinned of the four women. Her hair was a reddish brown, and she had freckles all over her body. When Wayne pointed to her, she looked briefly at the lady in red who nodded slightly, and then she let her smock drop.

"I want the one with those big titties," Johnny said. She was the tallest and had the second darkest skin, and Jeff was glad Johnny picked her because Jeff wasn't really attracted to her thick-waisted, heavy-breasted body. She looked almost bored by the proceedings and dropped her dress immediately when Johnny pointed to her.

"Your turn now, Bobby," Wayne said.

"I don't know," Bobby said.

"Well ain't but two left," Johnny said. "Pick one of 'em and let's get on with it."

The two girls left were barely older than the boys. Both were slightly built. One had brown skin and medium-size breasts. Jeff liked her looks. She kept her eyes on the floor, and Jeff liked that about her. His heart went out to her. The other girl had the prettier face of the two, Jeff thought, and the pigtails into which she had braided her dark hair made her seem younger than she presumably was. But she hadn't any breasts at all to speak of, just a little puffiness on either side of her chest and two long puckerings of nipple. Her skin was so dark it was almost blue. She didn't meet anyone's gaze either, but she kept her eyes lifted and stared straight ahead of herself, and Jeff found himself somewhat intimidated by the fire in her eyes.

"You don't pick one right this second," Wayne said, "I ain't gonna pay for it."

"Okay," Bobby said. "I'll take that one." He pointed at the dark-skinned girl. Johnny snickered for some reason, and Bobby instantly said, "No, no, I guess I'll take that one," pointing out the other girl.

"Jeesum Petes," Wayne said.

"Well, I don't know which one to pick," Bobby said to Wayne. "You pick one for me."

"I don't give a dern which one you pick, Bobby. I ain't gonna do it to her; you are."

Bobby finally, uncertainly and unhappily, settled on the lighter-skinned girl, and the woman in red showed them to separate rooms. "You boys got yourselves thirty minutes of *ac*tion," she said, laughing. "Not that it should take any of you nearly that long." The room Jeff entered with the dark-skinned girl was tiny and bare, painted white to capture and hold the light. There was a lamp on the window ledge that held out the night and lit the room in flickering gold rings. Underneath the window was a hard-back wooden chair and next to that an iron single bed with open springs and a thin cotton mattress. There was no top sheet, and the bottom sheet was stained with gray and faintly yellowish splotches. On the chair, a tin bowl full of water sat next to a bar of soap and a folded yellow hand towel. There was nothing else in the room. "What's your name?" Jeff asked the dark-skinned girl. With her smock down and her pigtails bouncing against her neck she looked about twelve.

"Leila," she said. She sat at the head of the bed with her legs next to the chair.

"I'm Jeff." He sat at the foot of the bed. He did not know how to begin and wasn't sure he really wanted to. His erection had disappeared.

"I got to wash you," Leila said. "That's Miss Ruby's first rule."

"You don't have to," Jeff responded. "I already washed before I left home."

"I still got to wash you," Leila said. "Like I said, it's Miss Ruby's first rule."

"You don't even have a towel," he said. "That yellow thing there isn't barely bigger than a wash rag. And there isn't near enough water in that little bowl."

"I ain't got to wash nothing but your peter," Leila said. "But I got to wash that or we can't do nothing else." Jeff was astonished but said nothing. "Some mens likes the washing part."

"Well, what do you want me to do?" Jeff said. She still hadn't looked at him. "You know. About the washing."

"Well, you can just unbutton and poke it out if you want," Leila said.

"I guess I can wash it myself," Jeff said. "Maybe I ought to just do that."

"I don't know," Leila said. "I'm supposed to. Miss Ruby showed us the right way and all." Jeff was thoroughly uncomfortable, but he stood up and started to unbutton his fly. "You can take your britches all the way off, if you want," Leila said. "Some mens does that." Jeff stopped unbuttoning himself and looked at the girl. She was staring at the wall across from the bed. "I likes it better if you takes your britches all the way off."

Jeff continued to stare at her, but she refused to meet his gaze. "Why's that?" he asked, not sure he wanted to pull his pants off.

"I just likes it better," Leila said. "You can leave your drawers on if you want."

"What difference does it make?" Jeff said. Leila didn't answer. "I'll do it however you want, I guess, but I don't know what difference it makes." He sat back on the bed and started unlacing his shoes.

"If you just poke it out your pants," Leila said finally, "then I get hurt up some by the buttons." Jeff finished untying his shoes and took off his pants. "Those buttons feels mighty hard, when the mens gets to pounding."

"I won't hurt you," Jeff said.

"Yeah," Leila said.

"I promise," Jeff said. "If I start hurting you, you just tell me, and I'll stop."

"Yeah," Leila said. Jeff laid his pants across the bed's iron foot rail and sat back down. He was wearing just undershorts, his T-shirt and a dingy pair of white cotton socks. "Well," Leila said, "I guess you better come on. Miss Ruby don't like it taking longer than it should."

"We don't have to, I guess," Jeff said, surprising himself because, in fact, he did want to.

Finally Leila looked at him, her face immobile but her eyes wide pools of black fire. "What you mean, you don't want to do it now? I ain't done nuthin. I just told you to come and let's get started. That's all."

"I just thought maybe you didn't want to," Jeff said. "If it hurts you sometimes and all."

"I didn't say it hurt. Don't you go telling Miss Ruby I said that."

"Don't get riled up," Jeff said. "I'm not gonna tell Miss Ruby anything."

"I'm not riled up," Leila said. "Don't be saying *that* neither." Her eyes were glistening now, and she turned her face away from him back toward the wall across from the bed. "Now just come on down here and poke your thing out so I can wash it and we can get started."

Jeff got up and walked to the head of the bed. He stood in front of her and pulled himself through the fly in his boxers, and she washed him with the bar of soap, rinsed him with wet hands and then used the little towel to pat him dry. He was hard by the time she finished. Then she pulled her smock over her tiny breasts and up under her arms and lay down on her back in the middle of the bed. Jeff got on his knees between her legs, and she took him in her hand and guided him inside her. He looked into her face, but though her eyes were open, her gaze would not interlock with his. And so he began, rocking himself in and out of her. And she lay still beneath him, save once to open her legs wider. And he was determined to remain mindful of her concern about pounding, and he tried to go slow, but then he closed his eyes and lost himself. And he shuddered uncontrollably and disappeared into a vast blackness.

* * *

When Jeff opened his eyes, Leila was staring at him with hot black eyes that were no longer wet. He lowered his face to hers, meaning to kiss her lips, but she turned her head away and offered only her jaw which bulged and relaxed, bulged and relaxed as if she were chewing something. Jeff eased out of this waif-like Negro girl and fixed himself back in his drawers. He sat back on the end of the bed, saying nothing, and she lay as he had lain upon her, her head still turned to the side staring at the wall, immobile except for the pulsing bulge of muscle in her jaw. After a few minutes, there was a knock on the door, and Jeff could hear Miss Ruby's voice from the hall. "Time's up in there, baby." And then she laughed.

Jeff pulled his pants back on and laced up his shoes. He looked one last time at Leila who still lay unmoving on the bed. He wanted to say something to her, but he had no words. So he rose and left the room and closed the door gently behind him as if he were leaving her sleeping and taking care not to disturb her.

Jeff learned shortly later on the ride home that Wayne had used Jeff's savings to pay for three of their four encounters with Red Ruby's girls. The money he had planned to use for movie tickets and a shared malt with Mary Frances Branson was gone. He had no choice but to cancel their date. And he never attempted to schedule another one, for which he had no money anyway.

But the embarrassment he felt at having to face Mary Frances and the fury he felt toward Wayne were not the things that lingered longest in his memory. Mary Frances started dating and ultimately married a high school classmate. Jeff managed to get a college scholarship and seldom returned to New Peterstown after he left home. But he felt Leila's black eyes burning into him for the rest of his life.

excerpt from

The Scientist's Daughters

AMANDA BOYDEN

The murderer, Ruth Catherine Schmidt, born to a pair of normal Lutherans on the Eastern seaboard, goes rogue in her teens after being quote-unquote rescued by one Reverend Bobby Morganton. The reverend inducts Ruth the way he does all his initiates, schooling her in the ways of sucking cock and letting him watch her do the same to other initiates. He never—oh, how shall we say?—goes all the way with the girls until they quote-unquote marry him in a private ceremony, attended by their lord and savior and the full church congregation, at which point they all bear witness to Reverend Bobby doin' the deed.

Such an introduction to the higher powers is, for Ruth, just that, however. An introduction. She yearns for more discipline, for guiding principles that are holy rules, never meant to be broken. Part of her genetic makeup, you could say. Neither the reverend nor her parents are anywhere close to being up to the task of full-blown discipline.

In her freshman year at college in the Midwest, however, Ruth finds In His Glorious Image protesting on her very own campus. She has lusted for their fervor. She has craved their conviction. She joins and rises quickly through the ranks, organizing bake sales and lettering signs late into the night. She makes it her early mission to remove all Dr. Seuss from elementary schools, and while she's not wholly successful, she gets noticed by some of the leaders. IHGI gives her what she needs, a means of flagellating not only herself but the world around her too.

Over the years, Ruth has no reason to marry or procreate. She finds all she requires in the mores of IHGI. And over the years, Ruth grows ever more powerful and ever more armored. The years pass quickly. Think of a montage, of a character in a movie growing older in the course of a minute. Yeah, like that. Suddenly Ruth the Soldier has arrived. She knows what needs to be done, and she will sacrifice herself for the good of the nation, in the name of God, Amen.

A younger member of IHGI provides the gun. Forgive him, Lord, for he doesn't listen closely. He believes the gun he procures is intended for self-defense. Too bad for Thomas Henley. No Aquinas, he! He gets two years for rolling over on the lot of them and is killed in prison in his first twenty-four hours. God's henchmen are swift!

So back to the bitch. Ruth, in her montage of passing years, has grown more and more plain. She's grown so innocuous that she disappears into the background of St. Louis. She is pallid. She is insipid. And she is mighty, mighty powerful. It's her secret. She sucks on it every day like a piece of rock salt that never shrinks. She will take out demons by the dozens. She only needs to choose which ones. She only needs to point her almighty finger.

We've decided she chooses Leonard and his crew of two dozen, give or take, because of his failure to see her. She's walked his university campus for months, has sat next to him while he drinks tea and she's eaten bagels in The Bookish Café, has roamed his department's halls, making sure to coincide her walks with his. She's timed them. Leonard's walks, that is. His bowels are nothing if not regular. And he never sees her. He never ever looks at Ruth. Damn it, Leonard! Seriously. Not once does he lay eyes on her.

Her cause is true and just, Ruth decides: we are created in His image, she believes, not man's version of His image. And no, not for a single second does she perceive herself to be a hypocrite. Leonard studies God's doing while Ruth studies Leonard's manipulations of God's work.

Leonard, he is the one. Ruth decides it over apple juice and cereal with skim milk on a Tuesday morning. (Oh, that silly skim milk, that man-manipulated product.)

So she's got the gun. And she's invisible. She just needs to get Leonard and as many of his underlings as she's able into a single room at the same time. And yes, we know, it's impossible to understand Ruth by any real measure of the imagination, but she exists. She is what she is, same as us. Or, ahem, what we were. Verb tenses don't count nearly as much as you might think.

She stalks the halls and watches the administrative assistant. 'The black secretary' Ruth calls Arletta in her head. Ruth just waits till the black secretary leaves her station to take a look at the monthly calendar. Henry Birthday Pizza Party Lounge. Hell yeah! Big score for Ruth! WOOOO HOOOO!!

Apologies. We know. Respect for the upcoming dead and all that.

Ruth just walks into the building same as she has sixteen times before. Forty-something Ruth, a little out of shape but not bad. Mousy hair, no makeup save her cherry lip balm. Her pockets bulge with extra magazines. Ruth has shoved the gun itself down the back of her baggy pants to the point where the muzzle rubs between her butt cheeks. This strange factor turns Ruth into a woman on fire. Say it again: *on fire!* She enjoys the inconvenience, the pro*tru*sion. Walk around with a sense of power in your crack and feel what's possible!

Ruth has scoped out the faculty lounge already and just bides her time in the women's restroom. She sits in a stall and daydreams about her glory. The highest of IHGI don't know her plans, which is what Ruth has intended. They will reward her in death with every honor.

Arletta walks into the restroom and tries the door to Ruth's stall. Ruth freezes then says, "*Occupado*." We have no idea where she might have picked up Spanish. Or when. Although, come to think of it, that's the exact word Leonard's used his whole adult life in the can. Did she actually try to stalk him into the men's room? It'd be so out of character.

"Sorry," Arletta says and enters the stall next to Ruth's.

Ruth decides it's time to fulfill her destiny. The human meddling in God's domain shall be stopped.

Ruth leaves the stall and washes her hands. Her reflection in the mirror, she believes, is one of purity and light. She is in a state of absolution and grace. She's target-practiced with her Beretta 92FS, G series, for over a month. You could call her a deadeye. Lord Jesus, here comes your next wife! She loves her gun, not as much as God, but as much as she allows herself an inanimate object, with its beautiful lack of a manual safety. Her mighty, swift sword. She examines all its parts one last time.

In the stall, Arletta cocks her head. She's not sure what she hears. She's a woman of science rather than a truster of instincts, unfortunately, because her gut is definitely telling her something.

Ruth goes out and down the hallway with the Beretta in her hand. One door, two doors, three doors, four. The lounge, and her destiny, awaits behind number five. She can hear a smatter of laughter, voices, sinful people talking.

A balloon pops before Ruth reaches the doorway. She stops in her tracks for a split second before she realizes the source of the noise.

At the same time, Arletta enters the hallway behind Ruth, and for a moment she believes she sees a woman with a gun in her hand. She's gotta start getting more sleep, she tells herself.

Arletta rubs her eyes and walks with renewed energy. She's six months away from retirement, and Henry, her longtime paramour (although neither of them is married, she simply likes the word when thinking of Henry and his beautiful head of red hair) has agreed to let her take him out for his birthday on a very special date this evening. Pizza in the lounge is but a mere precursor. She has the best dinner reservation in the city, followed by caviar and a balcony jacuzzi in a hotel suite that cost her a week's salary. Extravagance, much like intuition, doesn't regularly factor into Arletta's day-to-day, but she loves Henry, has for the last twenty-seven years, and will till her dying moment. (We know this sucks, but it's a good thing, kinda. They'll be together. Swear.)

Ruth turns into the lounge and scans for the doctor. She recognizes the back of his head, steps forward, and puts the barrel of the gun in Leonard's hair. Leonard's last thought is, Who's touching me? Ruth fires.

Leonard's skull and blood and brains go showering across the room. We know. It's horrific. Beyond horrific. But try to think of it the way Leonard might have, in a naïve, scientifically romantic sort of way: his brain went out into the universe. He shared it with everybody in his final moment, the way he tried to way back when he was premed. Seriously, it's what Leonard would have thought right then if his brain were still functioning.

And rest assured, Leonard had no idea what happened. Like Cowboy said, we should all be so lucky. Leonard wasn't eating pizza, but he'd brought his tofu sandwich and salad, spinach this time, with him and was enjoying a plastic glass of red wine rather than his usual tea. He knew these people, and with whatever capacity for love Leonard might have had, he kinda loved them, and he certainly valued what they all did.

Twenty-two other professors, researchers, assistants, and graduate students fill the room, and they're so centered on the pizza boxes spread across the table that most don't react to the first gunshot. They're not looking. They're not paying attention. They mistake it for another balloon popping. They're geeks, after all. Who'd be shooting at them? Why would they even begin to think that a noise they heard in the middle of a birthday pizza party would be a pistol shot? One graduate student, to her observational credit, looks at the opposite wall, not understanding why it's raining pieces of insulation or something.

Ruth goes after birthday boy Henry next. His pointed paper hat makes him a ridiculously easy target. She aims and shoots, and down Henry goes. More people in the room look at Henry to see why he's fainted, or strangely falling on the floor, than they still do at the mousy stranger in their midst.

Arletta, however, still clicking down the hallway, has come to the skin-prickling realization that what she thought she saw was indeed correct, as abhorrent as it could be. She runs faster than she has in her heels and in her entire employment, turns into the lounge, and sees a short white woman shooting her colleagues, her friends, all of them now pressed into the corner. Where is Henry?

Arletta has one moment. Just one. And bless her soul through-and-through: she lunges at the small mouse woman. Arletta has a flash of a vision that she will tackle the shooter, but it doesn't happen. The little woman only stumbles and recoups on top of the pizza. The woman turns around. Arletta can't place the woman's face. Henry?

Ruth fires and hits Arletta in the throat. Arletta reaches out with flopping arms to the woman and fumbles with the woman's breast and her ear. Ruth fires again, and Arletta falls to the floor. She finds Henry there, under the table, with a dark hole in his cheek.

Arletta drags herself across the carpet. She thinks Henry's breathing. He is. She pulls her face up to his. They look into each other's eyes, upside-down. "Henry," she says. He blinks, or maybe she imagines he blinks.

Ruth fires the rest of her magazine into the corner, reloads, and fires again. A grad student screams. And fuck Ruth into hell, we say, because she understands, for the first time in her sheltered, miserable existence, what the expression 'fish in a barrel' actually means.

She shoots till all the ammo is gone. The room, when she's done, stinks of metallic blood and pepperoni.

She's ready to meet her maker.

Born With A Tooth

JOSEPH BOYDEN

My wolf hung at the trading post for two weeks until that new teacher up from Toronto bought him. My long-legged Timber with half a left ear. A local trapper snared and sold my wolf to Trading Post Charlie, who skinned him and pinned him on the wall next to the faded MasterCard sign. He was worth more than $250.

The teacher's been here less than a month, sent to us by the Education Authority at Christmastime so the rez kids can learn the Queen's English. They gave him a little house and a parka, and I think he's lonely like me and has got a lot to watch and learn. He knows nothing about a snowmobile, or guns, or the bush, or the insult and danger of looking in the eyes. I can tell by watching him. He's got a thin face, and he's tall and awkward. My face is round, and I can drive a snowmobile as good as Lucky Lachance.

The one and only Lucky Lachance is my uncle, gone for four days of every week. He knows something's wrong because lately he comes back from work saying, "Just because your name's Sue Born With A Tooth doesn't mean you have to stay on this reservation the rest of your life, Jesus fuck." He works for the Ontario Northland railway on the Polar Bear Express. His train runs from Cochrane to Moosonee, mostly taking tourists in summer and supplies in winter across Northern Ontario and up to our stomping ground on the bottom tip of James Bay. The tourists call it the wilderness, but Lucky Lachance calls it the asshole of Hudson Bay. He's French Canadian, and he's got a dirty mouth. His sister is my mother, and I think my father's most probably dead. My father came carrying my name with him from somewhere out west. He brought my name to this place of Blueboys, and Whiskeyjacks, and Wapachees, and Netmakers, and even in this place my name stands out. Eighteen years ago my mother sewed my father his first suit, and seventeen years ago he got her pregnant with me. All I know is he was full-blooded Cree and belonged to the Bear Clan. In grade four I learned that the name for French and Indian mixed is Metis. I always thought that around here that made me nothing special times two.

Lucky says I'm looking into my fucking womanhood, and if I want to see the world he'll get me a free train ticket to Cochrane. He says it's time to stop moping around. "If you're not in school, it's time to work," he says. But I don't want to leave Moose Factory. I can't imagine another place where in summer you have to canoe or take a motorboat or a water taxi to the mainland and in winter they plough a road across the ice so cars can come back and forth. My mother wants me to learn how to sew.

Trading Post Charlie might have wondered why I was around the store so often the two weeks the wolf was there. I didn't buy anything. Charlie's fifty and is comfortable around me and pointed out all the pictures of his grandkids under the glass countertop once, but I could see his wife was jealous, me coming every day to drink free coffee and smoke her husband's cigarettes. She figured my visits out, though. Charlie's wife sold my wolf to the teacher yesterday.

For fourteen days I just showed up in the morning, knocking snow off my boots and letting a steam of cold air in through the door. I tried to learn how to drink Charlie's coffee and tried to make Charlie tell me everything he knew about the wolf. I think Charlie probably did know it was the wolf I came for, but he wouldn't look me in the eye, or anyone else for that matter. He's OjiCree and too polite. He doesn't talk much, just sells milk and bread and shotgun shells to the locals, pelts and Indian crafts to summer tourists.

But Charlie finally began to talk when he saw I wasn't going anywhere. "The trapper got the wolf in a snare. That blizzard come up off the bay, and the trapper figures it was two or three days the wolf choked slow before the lines could be checked again. The trapper said he ended the choke with a bullet in the wolf's brain."

Later Charlie said, "It's the rare one that comes to the island and stays for long. Trapper'd seen the wolf's prints in the snow last winter. This winter too. He tracked him a while. Usually a pack comes across the ice for a night of following moose, but they never stay so close to humans long."

I imagined I could see the black wire mark when I ran my hand against his fur. He'd already started collecting dust.

My wolf was skinny but brave. He came to see me often that winter two years ago, disappeared before spring, then came back again the next freeze. I watched him and loved him.

I still can't sleep, my head wandering and thinking the wolf waits outside for me. There aren't too many reasons to go outside in the dark when it's minus forty and trees pop and crack in the cold. Tonight marks that night two winters ago.

I couldn't get comfortable in bed, so I pulled my parka and mukluks on and went outside. It was the cold that makes your fingers burn through mittens, and the moisture in your nose freeze, and your toes ache no matter how many pairs of socks you wear. I walked just to walk, south on our road, smelling the woodsmoke and watching sparks fly from neighbors' chimneys. I looked up at the black and tried to find Mars and Venus, the stars that don't twinkle. I was hoping to see the northern lights. I wanted to walk quiet like the ancestors because I could sense them behind rocks and perched in the scrub pines, watching me and judging me. But my feet crunched on the dry snow and echoed in my ears under my hat loud enough that I felt silly. If the ancestors had been around, I had scared them away.

When I got to the edge of Charles Island, I lit a smoke and looked out at the ice highway running across the bay to Moosonee's twinkling lights. That's when I first came across him. I heard his paws in the snow, so I took my toque off to hear him better. I walked home slowly and felt his eyes on my back, but it wasn't spooky, only like an old friend come back to visit. Even though my ears hurt, I kept my hat off because I knew he was there. He followed me home but didn't show his face till the next night. That's when I laid my trap. Lucky's friend had gutted a moose, and

I stole some innards and put them in a snowbank in our backyard. That next night I waited by the window for him, waited until past two. Then he appeared like a ghost or a shadow, slinking, lean, sniffing and jittery. I watched him drag my present into the bush.

* * *

Charlie tells me his name is Michael and he's only been teaching for two years. Lucky calls him a city slicker cocksucker and asks me what this guy thinks he can teach anyone. I follow this teacher to the trading post and coffee shop and post office. He never knows it. I wait for school to let out and follow to see where he lives. He walks along with his parka hood up, dragging his boots and humming.

I start thinking I want him to notice me, so I get bolder, crossing the street when he does and walking by him or taking a seat near him at Trapper's Restaurant and only ordering a coffee. He looks at me; I look away. When he smiles at me, I walk away.

* * *

It was three months, close to the ice breakup that first winter, when my wolf finally trusted me enough to stay in sight when I came outside. All winter I'd watched from the living-room window after Mom and Lucky had gone to their beds. At first I tried luring him with pieces of chicken or whitefish. I'd sit on the back step with my hand outstretched, waiting. But he wouldn't leave the shadows. So I'd arrange the scraps in a circle and go inside to my window perch and watch him slink across the yard. He knew I was there but wouldn't look up. He grew fuller and less jumpy. The night he finally ate from my hand, I knew something was going special.

* * *

Michael comes up to me at the coffee shop today and asks if he can sit by me. I say, "Okay," so he sits directly across the table and asks questions.

"Why don't I see you at the high school?" he says. I just shrug. He'll learn soon enough. Most of the rez kids make it to grade nine. That's when the government says it's legal to leave school behind. And that's when a lot of us know it's right. He asks me what my name is, and I tell him I'm Sue Born With A Tooth. He stares at my eyes, and I want to ask him if he's trying to insult me, but that would be rude. He's got little whiskers, and his skin is very white, and the fur on his hanging parka hood frames his jaw nicely. He says my hair is long, and black, and pretty, and I tell him I have to go. I leave change on the table and walk outside.

"Can we have coffee again?" he asks, following me out.

"I guess," I say.

"When?" he asks. "Tomorrow?"

"I guess," I say.

* * *

On the night he first touched me, I had no meat to offer the wolf, just a bone and gristle. But he was lonely, and I was too. It was the act of offering, and the middle of a long night, and each of us growing used to one another. I held the bone in my bare hand and felt the moisture on my fingers freeze to a throb. I walked to the middle of the yard. He was in the shadows but slowly walked up when I stretched out my hand. He padded slow and tense from his hiding place and raised the fur on his neck. It made him look bigger and mean, and he kept walking out as I stood slumped and relaxed but wanting to explode inside.

He stopped a couple meters from me. I thought that would be as close as he'd come, but I kept my stare focused on the snow by his feet. He walked closer, till his nose twitched by my hand. He flattened his ears back, and I looked at the left one, ragged and bitten or shot half off. I felt his eyes on mine, so I looked too. Yellow eyes. Harvest moons. He smiled at me with his black lips and opened his mouth, and the white teeth gently took the bone. He turned around and trotted slowly back to the edge of the bush, then turned his head to me before disappearing.

I often wondered where he went all day, whether he was safe or if his visits put him in danger. I wanted to ask Lucky about the hunters on the island. I wanted to know if they knew about my stray. No one ever talked about any wolf tracks near their door in the mornings after a new snowfall. But still, I worried for him.

*   *   *

My mother talks so little that there are people in Moose Factory who believe she doesn't know how. She works with her sewing machine out of the house. She's very small and very smart. You can see it in her shiny black eyes. "*C'est dommage.* It is too bad there is so much of your father in you," she tells me. "Unable to sleep at night, always wanting to dance with the ghosts." I wonder how much she actually sees and how much she knows to sense. I've watched her sew for hours, and the day comes that I will stitch too, but for now I get everything I need from a few coins in Lucky's money jar.

Michael asks me out to drink coffee most days after his teaching and continues staring at my eyes. I want to tell him that I don't think I really like coffee after all and that we should go to his house and smoke cigarettes instead. Lucky saw us and teases me at home.

"Sue hangs out with the city fuck. The skinny cocksucker thinks he's going to get some French and Indian ass at the same time, eh? He thinks the Metis like to mate, eh?" His words make me run to my room. But Lucky always knocks gently and tells me he is sorry. He says, "Metis means that you are stuck in the middle, Sue."

Whenever he says that, I know he's going to finish his talk. He reminds me that Indians consider me a Frenchie, and whites look at me like I'm Indian. But I imagine I don't feel different from most of the rez kids. Maybe I'm lonelier. My best friend has a husband and a baby now, and another friend moved to Thunder Bay. Tonight Lucky says he is not here enough to watch out for me, and I should be careful with the city boys.

*   *   *

Michael has him somewhere in his house. I want to sit by Michael's stove and look at him. Michael talks a lot when we go out to the coffee shop. He tells me about Toronto, the woman mayor, the Canadian National Exhibition, the men who sleep on heating grates in the middle of the winter underneath huge glass buildings. He tells me about his little brother and parents. Michael asks if he can come over to my house for dinner. He says he's writing a paper on the Aboriginals of Northern Ontario. But I can hear Lucky saying, "Do you want another potato, cocksucker?" so I say I'll go to Michael's house instead.

It's a small cottage on Ministik Road, outside the rez boundary, just a clapboard living room and a kitchen with dried flowers on the tiny table and a wood-burning stove. I help him carry wood in, and we leave our coats and boots by the stove. He cooks dinner and fumbles with the plates while setting the table. He talks a lot, asks a lot of questions about me and Moose Factory. I tell him my daddy was a full-blood Wolf Clan Cree. That he worked in the bush and was the son of a hunter. I lie and tell Michael my father was killed while hunting. I don't know why I say this. I look down at the floor, then at the walls. I don't see him.

After dinner we sit on the sofa and listen to music, drinking beer.

"You're not the most talkative person," Michael says. "Aren't there things you want to know about me?" He leans closer and takes my hand in his. It's sweaty.

"Do you have a girlfriend in Toronto?" I ask.

"No," he says. "There's a woman I like, but ..." and I stop his talk with a little kiss.

Lucky would be angry if he knew I was alone with Michael in his house. But Lucky's on the train tonight, somewhere near the Soo.

I want to tell this one about the other. About how close we were by the second winter. How he'd come up to me in the middle of the night almost as friendly as a dog and take gifts from my hand, then go back to the edge of the bush to eat. He wouldn't let me touch him, didn't want the smell of human on his fur.

I want to tell Michael about that time when the ice was beginning to break up on the bay and even snowmobilers weren't crossing any more. It was late, and I offered him a strip of venison. He walked up and ignored my hand. Instead he nuzzled me hard between my legs. He could smell my blood. I felt his hot breath and tongue against my jeans for just a moment.

Michael looks awkward pulling out the sofa bed. "If I had known I'd be living like this," he says, "I'd have shipped my futon up with me." He's holding onto me and unbuttoning my shirt. I want to know what a futon is, but I lie back and let him struggle with my jeans.

I can feel his tongue and his breath in the dark. He's come back to me, nipping and licking, tasting me. He slides up, and I can feel the hair of his chest on my belly, on my breasts. He is hard against me and pushes inside for my first time, his shoulder across my neck. The white flash of pain is his smile and dark lips. He nudges my legs wider. I bite his ear, and he yelps, and I can feel him release inside of me.

Michael mumbles and half talks in his sleep, so I quietly get up and pull my clothes on. The stove's gone out, and I can see my breath, so I squeak the stove door open and fill it with wood. I leave and walk down Ankerite Road, listening to my boots crunch in the snow and trees moan in the cold. Tonight it's so dark and empty, I wonder if anything is alive.

* * *

The days are getting longer again. Michael and I don't go out for coffee much any more. People in town started talking, asking why a teacher and a seventeen-year-old half-Indian girl were hanging out so much. Michael ran into Lucky and thought he was a big bearded lumberjack come to chop him down. Lucky says he didn't say a word to him. Just looked. When we do meet for coffee, this teacher doesn't look at my eyes anymore, just mumbles into his cup and watches out the window, then kisses my cheek and leaves. I wanted to tell him he was the first, but I can't now.

Sunny days leave the ice highway slushy and dangerous to cross. I only asked Michael about my wolf one time, a little while ago. I tried to sound casual and like I didn't care, but my voice came out squeaky and tense.

"That pelt, the damaged one?" he said. "I sent it out on the mail plane to my woman friend in Toronto. She loves northern stuff."

I try not to think of my wolf any more, sent to hang in that woman's house.

* * *

Michael calls me today after the first canoe race of the year, the one from Moose Factory to Moosonee celebrating the spring. He asks me to meet him at the usual place.

"I'm leaving, back to Toronto," he says as I stare out the window at the bay and people on the ferry dock. The trees will bud soon. He lights a smoke. "I thought I might want to renew my contract and stay through the summer. But I've got business to take care of back in the city." He smiles. A casual smile. "Besides I hear the blackflies drive you crazy in the spring. Don't worry, though. I'll write. Maybe you can visit me sometime."

He always talks too much. I light a smoke and look him in the eyes. He looks back for a second, then looks down and plays with his cigarette pack. I stare at him till he gets up and leaves.

* * *

The last night he visited me a few months back, I knew my wolf could smell the evil in the air. He was jumpy, and his yellow eyes looked dull. I was tired and didn't want to get out of my warm bed. But I knew he was there, looking up at my window from his shadows at the tree line. I knew he wanted to see me. There was no food to offer so I poured him a bowl of milk and went outside. He sneaked up to me, then looked over his shoulder. He sniffed the saucer but let the milk freeze. I wondered what he had done all day, if he had caught a hare or run from his enemies. Half awake and not thinking, I reached out to scratch his torn ear. I lazily ran my fingers over his scruffy head and scratched his neck. Just as I realized what I was doing, he nipped at my hand and walked away, looking back over his shoulder at me until he disappeared into the dark. He had the smell on him.

* * *

I don't like coffee any more, but I still go to the coffee shop and drink it. When Michael left, Lucky said that the city fuck was worried the blackflies might chew his cock off if he stayed any longer.

My stomach's getting puffy, so I try not to smoke, but it's become a habit. It won't be long before Mom and Lucky notice. It won't be good. I'll have to tell them soon.

When it comes, the pain will be like that night with him. And worse. I will open my legs wide, and scream, and curse, and howl. Then the midwife will back away, muttering prayers and crying. My baby's grey furry head will enter this world. He will bare his white teeth and gnaw through our cord. He will look at me and smile with his black lips and yellow eyes. He will run off into the bush, and he will cross the ice highway.

Rider

BARB JOHNSON

After school, we ride around looking for cute guys. I would never use that phrase—cute guys—but Janie says it all the time. On the radio, a girl with a whispery voice is moaning, You're my man. You're my man. Janie says, Oh, turn it up! I love that song! Don't you love that song? Janie says this to the rearview mirror where our eyes meet. Sometimes she winks at me when she says things, and I get this falling feeling.

I am in love with Janie Lowell, but it's a secret kind of love, all trench coat and dark glasses.

When Janie asks me if I love the whispery song on the car's radio, I say, I do love that song, which is a lie like all the other lies I tell to keep my place in this car. I want to be near Janie, and that means saying what needs to be said. I don't say it with an exclamation point. I'm not that kind of girl.

I'm the kind of girl who wants Janie to kick all these other girls out of here and crawl in the back with me. I want to do moist things with her. I want her to want this, too. There's a wrong song in me that I haven't found a way to drown out, although I've tried. Am trying, right this minute, by singing along with the breathy voice on the radio.

At a red light, the other girls start in about the guys in the car ahead of us. They're all, Get this thing in gear, Janie! This is the sort of talk that causes Janie to panic and stall the car. It's a stick shift with an unpredictable clutch, the wrong vehicle for quick getaways. When Janie stalls the car, she just laughs. The other girls laugh, too. Oh, well, they say. We'll get 'em next time.

The other girls in this car, they want to be cheerleaders. They want to be voted best dressed. They get excited about the heinous parts of high school, like pep rallies, which are a kind of carpet bombing mission in a made-up war. Everything is strictly us or them, for or against. It doesn't pay to be on the wrong side of the field. Janie and the other girls don't seem to have to think about things like pep rallies. They like what they're supposed to like. They go where they're supposed to go.

Anytime we're all being marched to the gym, Janie and the other girls get all giggly and excited. I generally duck out to smoke a joint in the bathroom until all the rah-rah is over. The smell draws the loadies, and I sell them dime bags. Assemblies are good for business. While Janie is in the gym yelling with all her might for *victory, victory is our right!* I read my library copy of Walt Whitman. I used to have my own copy, but it fell apart. The one from the library is long overdue.

I don't worry about the library fines. The other girls don't worry about those sorts of things, either. They worry about what to wear to the party, if these shoes look right with this dress. I worry about the wrong song that plays inside me, the kind of problem that can't be fixed with the right accessories.

The wrong song is only in my head, so no one else can really hear it, I guess. The music doesn't go with what's in front of me, though. It's like listening to the soundtrack of *Godzilla* while watching *Bambi*, and it's starting to drive me crazy. I have decided to drown it out by filling my mind with other things, normal things, like how to keep the skin on my elbows soft by rubbing them with avocadoes, like how to worry about the shape of my eyebrows, like how to straighten the bunched fabric of tight pants pockets with the corner of a clothes hanger. I imagine that soon the noise of all these normal thoughts in my head will drown out the wrong song completely, and I will be free from thinking about kissing Janie Lowell.

While we drive around, I try to get Janie and the other girls into a conversation about the future. I wonder what comes next, what sort of plans normal girls make. I wonder what all I could do if I didn't have to spend every day watching myself, keeping track of where my hands are, minding my face when Janie and I meet at our lockers and she leans in and—*muah!*—kisses me the way all the girls are kissing all the girls this year.

No matter where I try to take it, though, every conversation in this car turns back on itself and heads toward the Opinion Poll. Today's Opinion Poll is meant for me. Isn't Charlie Derby cute? Don't you wish he'd break up with Diana and take you to Janie's party? The other girls' questions sound as though they were lifted from the same after-school movie as their worries.

Oh, Janie says about me and Charlie at the party, wouldn't that be great? Janie's mouth is beautiful. The words that come out of it are like a code or some other language that I can't understand.

Diana Derby, Janie goes on, making Diana *Mrs. Derby* with just her mind. That sounds dumb, doesn't it? She checks my opinion in the rearview mirror.

Maybe they'll name their kid Roller, I say. Or Kentucky. Janie studies my face. I can see she's right on the verge of saying, What? when the other girls start laughing. Roller Derby! Kentucky Derby! Get it? And when Janie does get it, she beams me a wink and a smile in the mirror, and I fall and fall.

I have no interest in Charlie Derby breaking up with his girlfriend. Last year, I had sex with him in his car behind the tool shed in the vast yard of our high school. More than once. Often, even. Charlie Derby? I thought he would drown out the wrong song.

* * *

For her birthday, Janie's having two parties. The real party, a dance with the guys from school, is tomorrow night. Tonight, it's just us girls, a slumber party, which is an extended version of driving around looking for cute guys, and thus will require a lot of lying. I have trouble knowing which lies are perfect and which ones will make people wonder about me. It's like those words in foreign languages: if you put the emphasis in the wrong place, you end up telling someone you like to lick pig noses when all you meant to say was, I love your new haircut.

Sitting on the carpet in Janie's living room, which is mostly covered in sleeping bags, someone suggests we play Truth or Dare, a little hazing ritual dressed up like a fun game. People want to know other people's secrets. They enjoy the shame of others. If I had any sense at all, I'd lie about having cramps and get out of here, but when I'm around Janie, all the sense just leaks out of me.

While everyone is warming up their killer instincts, Janie asks her mother a truth question. Janie's mother will tell her just about anything, which is why Janie hasn't shooed her away. Janie's question is this: Why did Uncle Steve move to San Francisco?

Your uncle's *like that*, Janie's mother says, putting her hand out, palm down, rocking it side to side. Everyone in San Francisco is *like that*.

No one needs to ask what *like that* means.

I look down in case Janie is going to look at me when her mother says this. In case the answer is meant for me. I feel myself blushing. Red cheeks are like a homing device for other people's bad intentions. I try to think if I have done anything to make Janie suspicious. I have been drinking; we all have. In theory, the drinking will loosen us up to play a mean-spirited game that no one would play sober. I have decided this is how life is: amping yourself up to do stuff no one wants to do but no one has the sense to call off, either. The reality when I'm drinking is that I forget to be someone else. I forget to mind my face. My hands *linger*.

Once Janie's mother leaves, it's too late for me to get out of here. Every movement now makes me either us or them, chickening out or not. The game goes pretty much the way I think it will. Girls asking sex questions, which, in the absence of boys, turns to daring one another to kiss for the camera. I watch them like a science project, how they arch their bodies as though they are porn stars in the video Janie stole from her father's stash and played for us one afternoon when her parents were out. Beautiful ragdolls whose mouths never fully close. Maybe that's how it's supposed to be. Maybe that's normal.

I hold the camera and egg the other girls on. If you're too quiet, the pack senses fear and turns on you. My immunity doesn't last, though. Just when it looks like everyone is losing interest in the game, someone dares me to make out with Janie. I don't know whether they have chosen Janie to be my partner because they sense something about me or whether it's because I have actually fooled them and they think making out with Janie is something

I definitely do not want to do. Just to be safe, I pretend that I am only pretending to be hesitant about touching Janie Lowell. I put my leg between her legs and pull her to me, sliding my hand under her shirt to cup her breast because being outrageous never looks like what it is: a small fire that burns off my actual feelings every minute of the day.

After this, we watch the video of ourselves, and the other girls analyze the hideous life their camera action suggests: two girls, no men, how sad, *ewww*.

Everyone my age talks about wanting to be different. The truth is, the only people who want to be different from everyone else are the ones who aren't. Being the same is a little luxury that lets you do whatever you want, to play at kissing girls, for instance, which is a thing now. I don't touch those kinds of girls. I don't let them touch me. Eventually, they will all go off with cute guys and do what they're supposed to do, and I will be left behind, the wrong song playing in me all the while.

Not long after the Truth-or-Dare video, I edge over to my sleeping bag and crawl in. I pretend to pass out, then lie there listening for clues. Does anyone think I am *like that*? According to the Opinion Poll, no one does. According to the Opinion Poll, I was a slut for sleeping with Charlie Derby, but there was still a good chance that I could beat Diana out in the competition to win his love. It exhausts me to think I might have to keep this up my whole life.

I have put my bag on the other side of the room from Janie's because I am through with pretending for the evening. In my own little corner, I doze off for real. I wake up just as Janie is crawling in with me. Like the Truth-or-Dare game, this looks like something it isn't. All around the room, girls are paired up in sleeping bags. Tomorrow night, one of these pairs will be what everyone is talking about at the party, and this will draw the boys out of their herd, sniffing. It's just a game. Even so, the wrong song starts up in me. When Janie fakes a slumber roll that lands her arm around my waist, I want to pull her fingers into my mouth, put my bare hands all over her. I want to do something that can't be undone. I want to go too far. For or against. I roll over to face Janie, whose mouth is right there, so close that my own mouth nearly collides with it.

She's wide awake, of course. I ask her if she wants some water, and then I slip out of the bag to get some for myself.

Stumbling through the dark of the unfamiliar house, I am only what I am. It may be that I am the kind of person who belongs in San Francisco, which is at least two thousand miles from here. On a map, it would be a simple line from one place to another, a shorter trip than the walk back to my sleeping bag will be. I could get there from here. Anyone could. The trick is knowing when to leave.

In Janie's kitchen, I fill a glass with water, which is something people in the movies do to calm down. I don't calm down. My heart goes on banging in my ears, like I'm running from flashing red lights instead of drinking water in the dim kitchen. It smells like cornbread in here, a few bright squares of it drying up in a pan on the table.

I wish I could sit at that table for the rest of my life, passing that happy yellow bread to a cute guy everyone agrees I was lucky to land. I wish I was that kind of girl. But I'm the kind of girl who notices the key rack that Janie's father made from an old "One Way" sign, the arrow pointing out the back door. Janie's key ring is a big red heart, the pointed end of which can be used as a weapon on someone who gets too close. Dangling from the heart is the key that fits in Janie's car, and I can't help but think about the two thousand miles I could drive in just a few days if I left right this minute.

Magic Boxes

JAMES KNUDSEN

I stand behind a tower of question marks. The words MAGIC BOXES $1 sparkle across the banner above my head. Though most of these boxes contain key rings with foreign car insignias, rhinestone collar pins, and ankle bracelets with tin hearts, the shoppers snap them up on the slim dream of finding something valuable.

The spiel that brings them jostling their shopping carts down the aisles of Dave's Discount World is not my own. Every thirty minutes I play a tape of an excited voice that says nothing about odds. These garish green boxes are "modern treasure chests; no one loses." Dollar bills are pointed at me from every direction. Then the tearing open begins.

"Oh, a key chain," says one. "Just my luck."

"You gave me the wrong box," says another, who's just found a circle pin. "I wanted the one *behind* this one."

I am fascinated by these reactions.

A tall young man in a soiled yellow jumpsuit methodically shakes every box on the counter. "This one has vibes," he says finally. He cannot bear the tension of opening his choice, so he hands it to a companion.

"Did your vibe tell you you was getting a Virgo bracelet?" the companion hoots.

"Lemme see that," says the tall one. With a whip-like gesture, he sails the bracelet over my head toward the escalator. This is the closest I've come to the events of a recent nightmare: a large group of disappointed customers storms the counter, and I'm knocked down in a hail of cheap jewelry.

In the two weeks I've worked here, I've yet to see anyone find one of the lavish prizes promised in the small Lucite display case that revolves at the end of the counter. I ask my supervisor if it wouldn't be good publicity to have at least one big winner, and he snickers, "As long as nobody wins, everybody thinks the odds are improving. It's like a slot machine."

Sometimes I wonder if there are any digital watches and diamond pendants in these boxes. Not that it matters; I'd just like to know if failure is guaranteed.

"I'll take three," a short black woman says as she rifles her smudged vinyl purse for the money. She hands me the crumpled bills and stands there.

"Go ahead and pick them," I say.

"No, I want you to pick them." She looks triumphant.

No one has asked me to do this before. Perhaps her strategy is that I know which boxes are loaded and will consciously or unconsciously select one for her. I could explain, but she is standing there holding her shopping bag open like a trick-or-treater. I quickly drop the three boxes nearest her end of the counter into the bag. I want her to see that no deliberation is involved; my choices are pure chance.

"Later," she says.

I watch her walk toward the door. Her cloth coat hangs in threads at the hem and her fur collar trails down her back like a ponytail. Must you be poor to be so reckless?

Later I realize that she's the first customer I've had who has not immediately torn into her box to determine the extent of her loss.

* * *

I've noticed that when it rains, people are more likely to buy magic boxes. They come straight to the counter, water dripping from their rainhats or shaking out their umbrellas as if they've planned this expedition. They stand clear of the counter, careful not to get the boxes wet, and give me elaborate instructions. "I want the box in the third row on the far left, the second from the bottom. The one with the smashed-down corner."

The results are always the same.

One woman gets a tie bar. "What is it?" she smiles. Perhaps she thinks it is something of great value; she's sure there are expensive things she's never heard of.

I demonstrate by scissoring my fingers over my tie.

Her smile fades slightly as she nods. "I guess I'll have to get me a tie." She stumbles off toward the housewares department. It's a rainy day; she just wanted a cheap thrill, and now she'll have to buy a tie, maybe a sportcoat.

This is a hell of a way to make a living, but it suits me. I need some money so I can move on. When I came here, I told the personnel manager that I was interested in a "retail career," but that was nonsense. It's taken me a long time to realize that I know more than I care to. I always wanted to get to the bottom of things, and I think I've finally made it. My cynicism is as pure as the gospel music that filters over from the record department.

* * *

Days pass, and the woman in the worn coat returns. She gives me a lovely smile and requests three more boxes. This time I grab them from the back and shoot them into her bag like a basketball player. She giggles.

When she is gone, I begin to wonder. She is the only customer who's ever returned for more. Even if they hide their disappointment by oohing over an ankle bracelet or mumbling how the Alfa-Romeo key chain was just what they needed, they don't come back. My job is a service in that way: there's a lesson to be learned.

But this woman is a mystery. Could it be that in one of the first three boxes she actually found a watch or diamond? I imagine her swinging the pendant in the dim sunlight of a dirty window.

A teenage girl drags a sheepish-looking boy over to the counter and commands him, "I want that diamond pendant." Her eyes follow the diamond in the Lucite case around and around.

The boy digs deep into the pocket of his blue jeans and fishes around. He has so little money, he doesn't need a wallet. The girl picks over the boxes, and when the dollar is forked over, she grabs one. Like a child at Christmas, she kneels down on the floor in front of the counter and tears it open. "You blew it," she says to the boy as she pulls out a string of beige plastic beads.

"Correction," says the boy. "*You* blew it. That's your Coke and fries."

The girl hands me the beads and says matter-of-factly, "I want my dollar back."

"Sorry." I point to the sign: All Sales Final.

"You didn't want me to win," the girl says petulantly.

"That has nothing to do with it," I say.

The girl ignores me, and I wonder whether she was referring to me or her boyfriend.

* * *

The woman in the worn coat is one of the first to enter the store when the doors are opened several days later. She looks wonderful, ecstatic. Her clothes are the same and yet different. Her fur collar has been pinned up, and she's clipped the threads that were dangling from her hem. Her purse gleams.

When she orders three more boxes, I pause for a moment to check: no diamond pendant around her neck, no digital watch on her wrist. This time I make an elaborate show of covering my eyes with my left hand. I put three boxes into her bag clumsily, then spread my fingers and peek at her. She is smiling broadly, rows of dull gold teeth. Will she never learn?

I run into my supervisor at lunch and take him aside. "Level with me," I say. "Are there any watches or pendants in those magic boxes?"

He looks at me nervously. "Why? Are the natives getting restless?"

"No. I'm just curious. I really don't care, and I don't think anyone else does either."

"Good, good." He seemed relieved. "There was at least one watch." He holds up his wrist and lets it flash under the cafeteria lights. "Like it?"

* * *

In the afternoon, I forget to play the tape. Sales fall dramatically. A little boy wearing a Superman T-shirt, with a bath towel tied around his neck for a cape, drags a gray-haired woman, probably his grandmother, over to the counter. "I want magic," he says.

The old woman frowns. Ridiculously, I expect her to answer, *So do I.* She unsnaps her shoulder bag and starts to reach in.

"You know," I say, startling myself, "we have magic tricks in our toy department."

The old woman brightens.

"I want this one," the boy says defiantly.

I look around for my supervisor and lean over the counter so that I'm almost face-to-face with the boy. "Listen, these boxes just have cheap junk in them. There's no magic."

The boy steps back and jams his thumb into his mouth. His words are garbled, but he is shouting, "I want one!"

I look at the old woman. She is tired and wants to go home. She has her wallet out now and hands me a dollar. The boy stands on tiptoe and takes down a box. He removes his towel cape and covers the box for privacy. He shrieks when he opens it, and I'm sure he's found a digital watch. "Neat!" he cries.

It is not a digital watch. It is another astrological bracelet. This one is Sagittarius and has a tiny half-man, half-horse shooting his bow skyward. He shows it to the old woman, and she nods. "Now we can go home. Thank the nice man."

This "thank-you" is a first. I have to laugh. As I leave work, my supervisor corners me. "I didn't hear the tape this afternoon. That hurts business, got it?"

* * *

In the morning, a cashier tells me that my supervisor is out sick. She winks theatrically. Does this mean that my supervisor really isn't sick or that I should *take advantage* of his absence? Before I consider what I'm doing, I borrow some real jewelry from the counter next to mine. I appear to be examining and straightening my merchandise like an old Pops in a general store, but I am actually adding a diamond pendant and a digital watch to two of the boxes. I put these boxes on the ledge slightly behind the counter next to the tape player.

As if in answer to my actions, I see the lady in the worn coat approaching through the front door. I take the two special boxes and add a third from the top of the pile. As always, she smiles when I put the boxes into her bag. After she leaves, I am amazed at what I've done; I turn on the tape, and it's business as usual.

The lady in the worn coat doesn't come back, and something about it disappoints me. It seems clear that she only came back out of some sense that the odds were improving. She was sure each time that her lucky day had arrived, and her persistence paid off. I feel guilty for my part in her foolishness. She's learned nothing.

A week passes. My supervisor tells me that the magic box concession is going to close soon. Public interest will fade. Like a carnival concession with a weighted wheel of fortune, it will have to move on. The Miami branch is waiting. There is an opening for me in the shoe department if I care to stay on at Discount World, but I don't.

When the lady in the worn coat returns, I hide my surprise. I start to pick up boxes for her, but she touches my hand. "None for me today."

I set them down. "You must have won something." I play dumb for the benefit of my supervisor who has been grumbling about missing stock.

The lady in the worn coat tilts her head and stares at me.

"You must have gotten a big surprise in one of your boxes," I explain.

"What? I know that stuff's junk in there. Having them around just makes me feel good."

"But you still have them?"

"Stacked right up on the kitchen table." She smiles. "A nice little wall."

"You should open them," I tell her. "You never know what you might find."

"Lord," she winks. "I'd give them away first. There's people that need that kind of stuff."

"But anything might be in them!"

"So?" She gives me a short salute. "Later."

Pappy

JOANNA LEAKE

Orlin stood by the bus stop, took one last drag on his last cigarette, then flicked it onto the sidewalk and crushed it out with the toe of his boot. Out of the corner of his eye he saw a woman pull up to the red light. She was blonde, her hair puffed up and fancy, sitting in her cream-colored Mercedes, looking at him with her mouth all pinched, like his cigarette smashed on the cement was a personal insult, like he had just ground ashes into the middle of her living room rug.

Orlin watched her drive away and half thought about following her, going right into her house, which he pictured as red brick and three stories high, and actually throwing his cigarette down in her living room, just to see the look on her face. And then maybe he would get her down on the carpet, stuff a sock in her mouth, roll her over, and do nasty things to her, get her thinking about something besides how much his cigarette had offended her. But he knew that wasn't about to happen, none of it.

He wasn't going anywhere because his Camaro had been sitting on the side of the interstate for three weeks with a boot on it, and four hundred dollars of parking tickets stuffed in the glove box, and a blown universal joint, and the gas tank on empty. So these days, anywhere he wanted to go, he was taking the bus, riding with every other pitiful loser in the city who didn't have a car.

And now he was waiting for the bus to go somewhere he didn't want to go, even though he'd been telling himself for a while he ought to. He'd put it off for too long. So when his mother called him this morning, getting him at the pay phone at the bar since his own phone was long gone, cut off weeks ago, and whining at him, her voice all weak and tragic but still able to cut into his brain like a siren and make him want to scream for mercy, he said he would go. He promised he'd go. He told her if she just wouldn't call him at the bar, or anywhere else for that matter, he'd go. Like it was her idea. Like he didn't know what he had to do.

He squinted down the street, looking for the bus. He thought about taking the watch out of his pocket, checking to see what time it was. But it didn't make any difference. The bus would come whenever it came, and he had to wait. He could feel his blood thumping inside his head and a flush of heat rising up, making his scalp prickle. He tried to take a deep breath. He wished he had another cigarette. Maybe that would help. He needed to calm down

The kids got onto the bus like a swarm of annoying bugs. They filled up the seats around him, tossing big, heavy book packs around, punching each other, laughing like idiots at nothing. They sprawled over the seats like syrup, settling in like it was some big party. They had music players plugged into their ears, and they slurped on cans of Coke and opened bags of potato chips and Cheetos. Orlin wanted to strangle them. It was bad enough to be on the bus, without them taking it over like it was their personal limo.

One kid, a tall boy almost Orlin's size but thinner, wearing what looked like size thirty sneakers, looked at him and then elbowed his friend and laughed. Orlin tried to think what could be funny. His jeans? His ZZ Top T-shirt? His hair slicked back in a pony tail? How could some kid in baggy pants with a pierced nose laugh at anybody? He seriously thought about going over and grabbing the kid by the neck, punching him for a while and then stuffing him through the window and shaking him, making him tell what he thought was so funny. That would be an excellent plan. Orlin kicked the floor. Until the bus driver stopped, and the cops came and carted him off to jail, and he had to spend the night in the holding tank waiting for a P.D. Or until his mother came, snuffly and miserable, holding on to a shredded-up piece of Kleenex like it was a life line, talking about what she'd had to do to make his bail. Or until that kid looked him right in the eye and told him what he had been laughing at.

The only thing to do was just sit there, look out the window, try to concentrate on something, anything except being in this bus, watching these kids smiling and eating junk food and moving to music he couldn't hear.

Orlin was starting to get that feeling. It was happening a lot. Like a big, invisible fist had punched a hole in his chest. It made it hard to breathe right and did something strange to his throat. If Pappy had been there, they would have been the ones laughing. Laughing at how those kids wanted to get laid but never could, how they thought they were such hot shit but didn't know dick. Talking about slamming them up against a wall somewhere and beating the shit out of them. Or maybe even doing it, the two of them kicking butt, then going to get a beer and laughing about it afterwards. If he was with Pappy, even if they had been riding a bus, it would have been OK. When Pappy was around, Orlin hadn't felt the heat in his face or heard his blood thumping. He had always been able to breathe before.

* * *

It was on the service road, between an auto body shop and a Chinese restaurant with a sign showing a fat dragon holding chopsticks. A squatty, blond building, Gulf Pines Manor. The minute he saw it, he knew the whole place was a lie. Orlin didn't see anything remotely like a pine tree, and they were miles from the Gulf. He knew from TV that manors were all in England and had butlers who opened doors, and brought people drinks on silver trays, and laid out clothes for them to wear the next day. Manors had things like moose heads and swords on the walls. Gulf Pines Manor was a piece of shit, and they could call it the White House or The Ponderosa or Disney-fucking-land and it wouldn't change a thing.

Orlin walked through the glass doors, which he had to open for himself since there wasn't one chance in hell that a butler or anybody else was going to do it for him. Inside reminded him of the emergency room, the times he'd been there to get stitched up or once when he OD'd on ludes and he started to fall down and jerk around like a puppet. It was the same weird, yellow light, and the same green, tile floor, and the same overweight lady behind the desk wearing a white uniform and looking like she would rather be anywhere else on earth than there. Orlin knew how she felt. It was like walking into a giant diaper pail. That mixed with another smell, something sour and dusty. It must have been some kind of old-age scent, because looking around, everyone he saw was old. Not just old, like how Santa Claus or that Kentucky Fried Chicken Colonel was old. These people were past ancient, dried up, ready to blow away, sitting slumped over in wheelchairs or wobbling by on creaky walkers. He never knew Pappy was trapped with all these old people. He thought Pappy would be in a place for people like him, young people who just accidentally got fucked up.

Smelling that smell and seeing those old people, Orlin thought about turning around and just walking out, but his feet felt stuck. He had imagined it different. Some place sunny, with flowers in big vases. He had thought there would be nurses, pretty ones, like Hooters girls only wearing nurses' clothes, and everyone would make a fuss over Pappy because they knew who he used to be. Nobody had told him it would be like this.

"Do you need help?" The lady behind the desk was peering over the counter.

Orlin made himself look her in the eyes. "I want to see Vernon Dees," he said. It sounded strange, hearing himself say it. He never called him Vernon. When they were both little, him just two years younger, his mother had watched him tagging along behind—it was to see a cat that had gotten run over on the highway he remembered—and she said, "He follows him around just like he was his Pappy." And that stuck. Orlin and Pappy.

The lady was flipping through pages on a beat-up clipboard. She had short, fat fingers stuffed into gold rings. "He's on the restricted list."

Orlin stared at her.

"It means family only," she told him.

"Yeah?" Orlin said. The place was one big lie, and she was lying too. Candy had been to visit Pappy, and she wasn't family, only his girlfriend, more like his ex-girlfriend now. He walked over to the counter, feeling like he could move his feet again, letting a smile he liked to think of as scary come across his face. "I'm his fucking brother."

* * *

He was waiting in something they called the Day Room, nothing more than a big, mostly empty space, with a TV set babbling up on the wall, and some tables with moth-eaten magazines on them, and a few blue plastic chairs scattered around. And, of course, more of the old people. They didn't seem to notice Orlin walking in or sitting down. Or more likely they just didn't give a shit, most of them sitting, staring at the TV or at each other or just into space, looking like some horror movie alien stole their brains and just left the empty shells there as some kind of bad decoration. Orlin thought they looked like lawn ornaments, only they were indoors. And ugly.

Ugly was the exact word Candy had used talking about Pappy, trying to make it seem like she was the one he ought to feel bad for. Everything was always about Candy. You never had a problem, only her. Poor Candy. So he was supposed to put his arm around her, and buy her drinks, and help her feel better because Pappy looked ugly now and couldn't take her places or fuck her or buy her things. She had said they had shaved one side of his head and that his eyes didn't look right anymore. She told him Pappy's hand was curled up so it looked like a claw and there was a tube stuck in his neck. Orlin closed his eyes. He didn't really believe Candy's bullshit, but still he tried to imagine it, to picture Pappy in his head so, in case it was true, seeing him in real life wouldn't be so bad. Now he was wondering if maybe Pappy looked old. Maybe it was something contagious you could get from being surrounded by old people on every side. Candy said Pappy couldn't really talk anymore. Orlin wondered if he might be hoping that at least that part of Candy's story was true.

Except he knew every other word out of her mouth was a lie. Pappy was bigger and smarter, but Orlin was the one who knew Candy. He knew how she could tilt her head to one side and look at you, the way her voice could get low and smoky, the feel of her finger as she ran it down your arm, maybe just careless or maybe wanting something more. And if you were drunk, or maybe racing on meth, or maybe just feeling bad because you got fired from the carwash, a shit job but a job just the same, and you owed Big Wally money for the weed he'd fronted you, and you wanted something that was yours for once, wanted somebody to want you, then Candy might start out telling you her troubles and end up climbing in the back seat of your Camaro and grabbing your zipper with her teeth. Then you forgot about all the bullshit, and for a while Candy turned into someone else.

Orlin heard a squeak of rubber wheels. It wasn't anybody, just an old lady, rolling herself to get closer to the TV, her hands pushing the wheelchair along, her nails painted bright red, which surprised Orlin. It was the first cheerful thing he'd seen.

She parked herself and pushed down some kind of hand brake to keep from rolling away. "Now why they want to watch this is beyond me." She pointed up at the TV where a man in chef's clothes was chopping up some mysterious looking vegetables and tossing them into a skillet. "It just reminds you of what real food used to taste like," she told Orlin.

Orlin shrugged. "Maybe it's some kind of torture," he said. "To try and drive you nuts."

The old lady smiled. "You think?"

Orlin smiled back. "Nobody's watching. Go on and change it." She was wearing wire glasses, and behind the lenses her eyes were blue. He reached over the table and handed her the remote.

She aimed it at the TV on the wall and clicked. The man kept on chopping his vegetables.

"Battery's dead, I guess," Orlin said.

"Who are you waiting for?" she asked him. "They're lucky you take the time to visit. Most of the families don't give two shits, you know. I'm guessing grandparents."

Orlin shook his head. "My brother," he said. "He got in an accident. The hospital kicked him out, and he ended up here."

"That's a bad deal." The old lady sighed. "It's sad for somebody young."

"It wasn't exactly an accident." Orlin wondered why he was telling her, but she was smiling at him, and her eyes looked kind, like she might listen. "Three guys beat him up. Out behind a motel after a party."

"At least it took three of them," she said.

"Damn right." He looked down at his hands. "I wasn't there. If I'd of been there to help him it never woulda happened."

The old lady snorted. "There's no way to know that. You might as well not speculate on what might have been."

Orlin looked at her out of the corner of his eye. One thing about being old, maybe it made you smart. Maybe she might know something about how the world worked, about how things got so fucked up. Maybe she might know how to unfuck things. Or at least know enough to understand. He thought of telling her about what happened at the Thrifty Inn. Or about the night before when Candy had called him, crying her eyes out, in a blind panic because she was pregnant, telling him it was his and acting like the whole thing was his fault, like it was something he had done to Pappy and to her out of meanness, like she was just a pure victim, like she hadn't come on to him that night, whining about how Pappy was ignoring her. And now it was his job to get the money for an abortion, or else she would have to tell Pappy, and then everything would hit the fan. And even though she knew for a fact that he was tapped out, that he was hustling to pay Big Wally back and didn't have two cents to spare, that didn't matter. Because of course nothing mattered to Candy except what she wanted at that exact minute. So at the motel, partying with Pappy, and Big Wally, and two of Big Wally's cousins from some piece of shit town in Alabama, he got the idea. They were watching a pay-per-view fight, one of those kick boxing things, and Orlin saw Pappy take off his watch, the big, gold Rolex he wore, with diamonds in the face and a dial the size of a hubcap. It was so easy, just to pick it up, put it in his pocket. And then later, when the cousins had taken off, and everyone was stoned, and the kickboxers were winding down, it was easy to tell Pappy that Big Wally took his watch. Nobody ever got the best of Pappy, not Pappy with his hard hands and big arms and mean tattoos. Orlin left, knowing Pappy would pound Big Wally into paste. He left thinking he could hock the watch and give Candy her money, and that everything would be OK. But of course that didn't happen. Big Wally's cousins came back looking for a set of keys. And then it all went to shit, and he never saw Pappy again, not when the ambulance came or in the hospital. And he never would see him, at least not like he used to be. Candy went to some Korean guy who got rid of the baby, and now she was dancing at one of his clubs. So wasn't that nice how it all worked out, for her at least.

Orlin put his hand in his pocket and touched the cool, smooth links of the Rolex.

He felt the big fist punch him in his chest and the heat prickle his scalp. He looked at the old lady, her blue eyes and her old face. He tried to breathe. "I got my brother's watch," he told her, pulling it out of his pocket. "I'm giving it back to him."

She looked at the watch, reached out to touch it with a wrinkled, red-tipped finger. "Sweet Jesus on a scooter," she said. "Don't be a butt-head. That's a Rolex. He's never gonna use it. People in here can't tell you what day it is, much less tell time."

Orlin sat in his blue chair after she rolled herself away. He watched the chef on TV and looked at the old people staring at nothing. The room was quiet, except for a man snoring by the window and the sound of the chef's knife hacking some kind of giant cabbage to shreds. And something else, something louder, the ragged gasps of breath that it took Orlin a while to recognize as his own.

The Son of Gilberto Writes Letter to Wife

M.O. WALSH

You say I'd be a good father, Susan. Fine.

Now I will tell you what you don't know.

We captured Bucky Carter. He was the fat kid who used to pound us. He smashed up our remote control racers a few years before, when me and Tommy Newman were like eight. Mine was *The Hornet.* Silver spring suspension, all that. Bucky Carter was a chunk, a bully to us back then, but eventually Tommy and I grew into him. We became surplus bandits, Tommy a military kid and me the son of a carny. We snuck cigarettes and jumped off roofs. Bucky Carter got fat, and we got tall. He never had any friends that I knew of.

Back on the day he broke our racers, Tommy Newman and I took the blood oath like kids do. We swore among other things to get sicko revenge. So, when the time came, we were armed. Nothing major. Throwing stars, brass knuckles, a blind-fold. All for like a dollar fifty at the surplus. We set up an ambush where Bucky crossed through Winston's Woods, near the train tracks, on the bike trail that runs between the old army base and what's now the *ZooCarnival.* Tommy rigged a clothesline between two trees so we could pull it tight when Bucky rode by. We plucked him right off his bike. Then we ran out from the woods like ninjas and stood on his belly.

Bucky said, *Hey guys, Heinrich, Tommy!* like an idiot, like he was happy to see us.

Tommy shook his nunchucks at him and said, *Look what you did to my hand!*

He opened his palm, and we could see where the clothesline had burned it, cut a thin line through the pad of his thumb and he was bleeding. He wrapped his hand with the blindfold. *You're going to be sorry you did that!* Tommy said and pulled Bucky up by his shirt.

Look at him, I said. *He's not sorry.*

That dildo don't know what he is, Tommy said.

Instead of the full-out assault we had planned, Bucky's capture was over before we knew it. No use for plans B through K, which included what to do if one of us went down. Call Tommy's cousin for back-up. The pay phone on Clark street. 546-0318. Code word Fatboy. I remember it all. But Bucky didn't put up a fight. Instead he looked at us gem-eyed, as if we had saved the day. I tied his hands with a whip. Then Tommy and I walked Bucky Carter and his bike, single file, down the train tracks and back to my house.

Tommy threw rocks at the passing trains, and the whole time, the whole stupid walk, Bucky talked about baseball cards. He was looking for a Ricky Henderson rookie: 1980 Topps, wood panel framing, Henderson playing for the A's, batting gloves in one hand, ready to steal second. I still have the card. Tommy told him to shut up about it, or else he would go KGB on his ass. At fourteen, his dad a sergeant, I imagine only Tommy knew what this meant.

We snuck into my garage and tied Bucky to a chair with some speaker wire, his hands behind his back. Then we wrapped his ankles with duct tape. Tommy Newman had vengeful designs, so we discussed our options. While he described what different tools in my garage might do to a person, I held each one of them in my hand like I was weighing it. Everything Tommy said. Hammer. Hacksaw. Wrench. Drill. Right in front of Bucky. And soon, a hammer to the face became our most eager idea.

But not the flat part, Tommy said, *the claw end.*

Bucky asked us what game we were playing.

This is no game, Jack! Tommy said, and I laughed. We gave Bucky a few titty-twisters, and then my father walked in. He was wearing a blue and white bath robe, searching for vodka in the deep freezer.

This is how I will always remember him. Thin. Shorn. His face like a pencil sketch. No matter the kind of man he was before this or what kind he may be now, and regardless of what you think writing this will do to my memory, this is how fathers will look to me. Robes, entering garages through kitchen doors, sleepwalker eyes, feet in slippers at 4:30 p.m., descending the stairs to where I stand.

He didn't even notice us.

Tommy said *Gilberto!*

Tommy hadn't seen my father in years. We were fourteen.

Gilberto the Brave.

My father.

Shit.

My father tamed the animals. Back when there was work, and shortly again in the future when there was work. But during this time, I can't even describe it. That's what I'm telling you. You wonder why we don't talk about it. Some big man, me. Sitting here in sweat pants, typing to you in the middle of night.

If nothing else, I can tell you my father was shredded meat. Gone five years from home at that point, he'd lost the proud belly of a tamer, the necessary mass to intimidate. Instead he'd become elbowed and sharp, deep scars purpling his chest like earthworms. Yet despite his wasted physique, his obvious thinness of bone, if it is a word, I still quoke beneath him. An absolute ghost in my house.

If you searched his name now, you would find Gilberto the Brave with his chest out, cracking his whip for the old travelling circus, his arm around the ringmaster himself. Gilberto the Master of Unwinnable Games. You would see newspaper clippings, a dark beard across his jaw like a chin strap. All there in his frozen past. But he had been five years gone at that point, *five years*, traveling the fairs, he said, and looking for work. Not even a syllable home. But when news spread that a local tycoon was starting up a new carnival, right there in Fluker where we lived, my father returned to us a stranger, dusty and eviscerated of soul.

But I have to be honest. It was my mother too, a tumor in her throat, living off government money and staying in bed. She barely had her voice even then and rang a bell when she needed me. So, we still lived in the same house he'd left us in, sure. But me and her like that, and he was supposed to just walk back in? Sleep in that bed? And we were supposed to let him? After five years of nothing? See? This is how I get when I try.

So the event itself. That is how I will tell you.

My father looked us over in the garage. Tommy, Bucky, and me. Home two months on that day. I remember Bucky smiling at him, all of us clueless.

Well, isn't this a motley crew, my father said.

This guy smashed up our racers, Tommy told him. *This is one A-one asshole.*

I did what? Bucky said.

No talking! Tommy yelled. He circled around Bucky's chair and fisted his palm like a boxer. He flicked Bucky's ears. He talked about cutting off his tongue and feeding it to a snake.

My father looked over at me. *What is this?* he asked and grabbed a plastic cup from above the freezer. *Is this your gang?*

I don't know, I said.

Bucky asked if he could be in our gang.

That's it, Tommy told him. *Tongue stew!* He grabbed a saw for its tongue removing capabilities.

Are you the master here? my father asked me. He pointed at Bucky. *Is this your little lion?*

This kid smashed up our racers, I said. *The one you gave me. The black and yellow one.*

At this, my father's face did not shift. His eyes didn't switch into focus. The comment instead simply flew right through him, his mind raked clean of my childhood. So he poured cold vodka into his cup. He watered his brain. Then he pointed at the wrench in my hand. *What do you plan to do with that?* he asked.

Nothing, I said.

We were going to pull off his nose, Tommy said. *Or turn it up-side down.*

I put the wrench on the trunk of our car.

Mr. Gilberto, Bucky said. *Were you really a lion tamer?*

Of course, he was, I said. *Don't be stupid.*

Are lions stronger than tigers? Bucky asked him.

Hey! Tommy yelled. *The prisoner does not talk.*

My father put down his drink and walked towards us. He said, *Easy soldier*, to Tommy and took the hammer out of his hand. He placed it on a bench. *Lions are the second strongest, second most powerful beast in the ring,* my father told us. *I am the first. The lion's tamer is the first.*

Elephants are the strongest, Tommy said.

My father circled in front of Bucky and leaned in close to his face. He put his hands on Bucky's thighs. *When they tell you to be quiet,* he whispered to him, *you don't have to listen. The lion is powerful. The lion should roar.* My father passed his hand through the air. *That is what the crowd wants,* he said. *This is what they pay for.* My father then smoothed his palm along Bucky's cheek and gave it a slap. Bucky growled and, at this, my father seemed pleased. He scratched the hair behind Bucky's ears. *A good cat,* he said.

My father then held up his index finger. He looked at each of us. *You see, good cats understand the first rule of the ring,* my father said and tapped at the tip of Bucky's nose. *The first rule*, my father told him, *is that I am your master.* My father then pushed his finger into Bucky Carter's nostril. He pushed it in hard, and I saw this. I know this to be true. Other things I can only imagine, but this I saw with my eyes. My father, knuckle deep, stretching the flesh of that boy. Bucky closed his eyes but did not resist this, even with the outline of my father's nail through his skin. *You see, it is only through my mercy,* my father whispered, looking into Bucky's eyes, *that you even have the power to serve me.*

My father removed his hand, and Bucky's eyes watered. A thin line of blood circled the bend above his lip. None of us said anything. I didn't *do* anything. I only remember thinking that Bucky would probably cry now, that he would act like a baby, and that I would hate him even more. But instead, Bucky took on that jewel-eyed look again, that idiot look I will never forget. He smiled, and this frustrated my father.

It is OK to get angry, my father said and pulled on Bucky's ear. *It is only through the strength of your anger that you deserve my attention.* My father then parted Bucky's lips and bared his teeth. He pressed his thumb against Bucky's canines. *The big cat roars,* my father said, *or else it does not exist.*

Tommy Newman laughed when he said this, and I did too, although now I don't know at what. My father heard us. He patted Bucky on the head and stood up straight to stretch his back. I watched him walk over to the sawhorse, the place I had slung the whip we tied Bucky with, the one I had taken from his footlocker that morning. He dangled it.

The red hide stock whip, he said. *A gentleman's whip.* He passed the snake of it over his forearm. *Five feet long. Australian. Kangaroo. A starter's whip.*

Tommy and I snuck grins at one another, and he made the crazy sign to me by circling his ear with his finger. We then watched my father drape the whip across his shoulders and walk back into the house.

Did you see that? Bucky said. *I am a lion.*

Shut up, Tommy told him. *Heinrich's dad is nuts. You are a butterball turkey.*

He's not nuts, I said. *We used to travel all over. My mom says he was the best in his profession. She says he's just waiting for a call. He's just waiting for another chance.*

Bucky then asked me if I had ever petted the lions. If, at some point in my past, my father ever brought them home.

That's enough out of you, Tommy told him.

We lived in a trailer, I said.

I am a lion, Bucky said.

After that Tommy and I threw the football around the garage, talking about what else we should do to Bucky. We threw it six inches from his face. We bounced it off his head. Tommy rifled a bullet at Bucky's chest, and the ball ricocheted under the car.

Good catch, Tommy said.

I could eat you if I wanted, Bucky told him and bared his teeth. This was the type of thing he was doing the whole time. It drove us crazy. We hated him back then. I mean, I can remember what it felt like to hate him. Now it is all different, of course it is. I can't imagine how lonely he must have been or what could have changed him from our bully, our worst nightmare, into that child sitting before us that day, having an acceptable time in my garage. To be in that chair, not even trying to get loose. I don't know that part of it. I can't explain about Bucky.

Let's go long, Tommy said, and so he and I walked out of the garage and into the street. We left Bucky there. We ran deep post patterns and made side-line catches like Montana to Rice. We played Sky-Dive Endzone where one of us jumped off the roof and the other threw a last-second prayer. We got bored. Tommy bet me he could throw a spiral through the open doors of a moving train, and so we walked toward the tracks. On our way out, I heard Bucky in my garage, roaring.

He is such a dildo, Tommy said.

I know, I said. *We should have dumped his bike in the river.*

There you go, Heinrich, Tommy told me. *Now you're thinking.*

We sat down on some lumber by the train tracks, the only hilly area in Fluker. And from there we could see over a tree line of pines and into the new carnival area, where construction was just under way. Tommy and I watched the supports of the Ferris Wheel get raised. We saw them haul trailers to the back of the lot. Tall Man walked around the place wearing striped pants. He argued with men driving bulldozers. He argued with men in construction hats. The whole place budded like a dream to us then.

You know what I was thinking? Tommy said. *I was thinking we should have been harder on Bucky. I mean, how did we get him back, really?*

We didn't, I said.

I loved that fucking Frog.

It was a good car, I said. The blue and green Frog. The puddle jumper. Off-road tires with rubber spikes. Roll bar. Every cool thing in the world wrapped in one.

You want to race me? Tommy said. *Down to the switch? I bet I could beat you.*

Where's a stupid train? I said.

Tommy took the blindfold from his palm where the rope had cut him. It wasn't bad. He flexed his hand a few times, and no more blood came. The sun was starting to fade then, and so he held his hand up to the light. *That dildo,* he said again and wrapped the blindfold back around it.

We sat there.

You know what else I've been thinking? Tommy said. *I think I'm going to start running everywhere I go. Like even if it is just to the kitchen or from the car to the house. I'm going to start hauling ass.*

I threw a few rocks at the train tracks.

Think how fast I would get if all I did was run, he said. *I bet I could get to your house in like forty-five seconds.* Tommy took off his watch and pressed a few buttons on the side. *If I started now, think about how fast I would be. Starting now, forty-five seconds. Starting now.*

Tommy clicked his watch and pumped his arms like he was running. I laughed and then felt tired. I let my thoughts roll down the hill and through the pines, and I imagined my dad starting work again, maybe walking through that construction site like Tall Man. I began to wonder if any lion would fear him or if he would now be eaten alive in the ring, his blood making mud out of dirt. I gave my next thoughts to what had happened in the garage that day, how hard he pushed his fingers into Bucky's face. I felt the strangeness of it all set in. What kind of person does that sort of thing, I wondered, and what sort of person lets them? I still think about this today. I wonder if even you, my wife, are aware of which type of these people I am. Then I began to think about my mother and what if she could cook like she used to. If she would make sausage and mashed potatoes every night so we could fatten my father back up, get that beard on his face as full as it had been. I then pictured him changing my mom's bed sheets, like I had been doing, and I wished he had never come home. So I pictured the phone at our house, yellow and push buttoned, the long cord that could stretch to the bedroom, and I begged inside myself for it to ring. If not from the new carnival, then from someplace else remote and un-returnable. I thought hard about that phone in our kitchen, and also of the prospects of its silence. Maybe it is ringing right now, I thought. Maybe right now.

OK, stop. Tommy said. *Now think about how long that could be if you were running.*

No trains came while we were out there, so we walked towards our houses for dinner. Before we parted at my neighborhood, Tommy told me not to worry, that we would get Bucky back better next time and maybe throw his bike in the river like I said. We shook hands like best friends do.

When I got back to my house, the entire street seemed dark but for the light on inside of the garage.

This is when I opened the garage door.

Best I can do here is to say my father was leaning over the car hood. Head on his forearms, the whip on his belt, a faded red suit on his body like ghost clothes. I remember the garage floor being cleared in a circle, the sawhorse right in the middle. Bucky was wearing my mother's fur coat, asleep on the concrete.

Bucky? I said, and my father crept to life. I could see in his eyes guilty furniture. A chair in one hand, a whip in the other. Bucky on ladders and stools.

Whose boy is this? my father asked me.

His mom is a secretary, I said. *I don't know her name.*

My father took off his coat and laid it on the hood. His suspenders were uneven and clipped to his pants. *I want you to call her,* he said. *Tell her to come pick him up.*

We're not really friends, I told him.

Don't argue with me, he said and turned back towards the house. He stopped at the door. *Do you still collect those baseball cards?* he asked.

Sometimes, I said.

Go get them. Bring them down.

My father walked inside, and I got on my knees. *Bucky?* I said. I shoved him until he woke up.

Is he gone? Bucky said.

Get up, I said.

I wasn't really sleeping, he said. *I think I made him mad.*

I asked Bucky what happened, and he told me. I won't repeat it all here. Your guesses are safe. And if you are hoping to get that bit out of me, then this writing idea is useless. You say you need to know why I won't have kids, why I don't return his calls, why I believe the very heart of me is a coward. That's what I'm saying. Don't ask me for more. I can't explain what Bucky was thinking. I can't explain my father.

I can only tell you how I acted. And I will be honest here instead of smart.

I wanted to hit him.

Why did you smash up our racers? I said.

I don't remember doing that, he said.

Bucky gave me his phone number, and I went inside to call his mom. She asked if everything was OK. I said yes. She told me she was starting to get worried. I hung up. I ran into my room and grabbed my baseball cards where I kept them in a three-ring binder with my name written on the cover. Each plastic sheet held nine cards, eighteen if you faced them front and back. I tore out the page with the Henderson rookie and shoved it under my mattress. I did this by instinct. I can still show you the card. I never made this right.

When I got back into the hall, I heard my mother's voice. Her bedroom door was cracked open and so I went to it. I saw my father standing over her. She was stroking his forearm. *Do you remember Munich?* she said. *Seven males in the cage with you. Three encores in one night.*

I've lost all my power, he said.

You are just tired, she told him. Her breathing was thin and short. *You are still full of power. You still have power over me.*

My father stared down at her. *We need you,* my mother told him. *Don't go.*

I have failed with the boy, he said. *I have failed with our son.*

No, David. You haven't.

Tell me I am full of power, he said.

Yes, David, you are.

He put his hand on her face.

Yes, she said.

And then my father began to press on her, gentle and calm, until her head sank into the pillow. *Tell me I never left here,* he whispered. *Tell me I am always your husband.*

I pushed opened the door but just stood there. I didn't do a thing. My mom said, *Honey,* to me under his palm. *Honey, please close the door.*

So I closed it.

Yes, David, I heard her say again from the hall. *You are.*

I ran back to the garage. Bucky was sitting on the sawhorse, still wearing my mother's fur coat. *Here,* I said and gave him the binder. *Take one.*

Am I in trouble? he asked.

Take all of them, I said.

Did you mean it when you said we weren't really friends?

That's all I have! I told him. *Jesus. Take them. I don't care.*

Up the road, I saw a car turn onto our street. I watched it drive by our house and then circle back around. I ran inside.

She's here! I yelled. *She's here!*

My father passed me in the hall. *Stay inside,* he said.

I went into their bedroom and locked the door behind me. My mom was struggling to breathe. She took my head in her hand and pulled me to her chest. I listened to her lungs, the sounds of loose paper in wind.

Make him leave, I said. *Tell him to go.*

Shh, she said, and her skin on my face was warm.

Why can't you tell him to go? I yelled. I was crying.

We need him here, she said. *Boys need fathers. One day you'll understand this.*

He doesn't even want to be here! I said, and then we just stayed like that for a while, only breathing. We heard voices in the garage. She petted me around my ears. She palmed my face with her hand, and I sniffed her in through my nose. And sitting there, I thought about those long moments that Tommy had talked about. How time could move so slowly if you ran. How much more you could accomplish with speed.

I suddenly wanted to churn my wheels like a freight train and drive right into my mother's palm, to sprint through the heat of her blood. I wanted to run back to that morning and fix things, to be done with Bucky before my dad walked in and to make it over to the tracks before the trains stopped. To see Tommy throw a few spirals through the car door, and to come back home in time to cook sausage and potatoes. To be so quick in the kitchen that my father couldn't even see me, and he would just eat the hot food because it lay there. I thought that maybe it could be like this every night, that it could work like this. Because then I could zip back into that bedroom like I was then, with my face in the cup of her hand, without her ever even knowing I had left.

But this didn't happen. Instead, my mother grew tired, and her hand stopped moving against me. I crawled onto the bed to lie next to her and, when I thought she was asleep, I pressed her head into the pillow. I felt for her breath. After a while, she kissed my palm, and I let go.

*   *   *

You are awake now, Susan. I can hear you turning on the water in the bathroom.

So, what else will you want to know, I wonder? What more can I answer before you ask? There was no law involved that I know of. I don't know what my father said to his mom. We never spoke of it again.

I only know that Bucky got held back a grade and that Tommy started running like he said he would. He ran up and down the halls at school. He ran everywhere he went. People began to make fun of him. We eventually stopped hanging out. Then Tommy joined the Army.

I also know that my mother lived for two more years after this and that she only did this for me.

You are the only woman I've told this to. You need to understand what I am saying. You see, I am stuck here, Susan, the son of my father. Still fourteen years old in the heart of me. Heinrich the Master of Nothing. Can't you see it how I do? That I am still standing outside of their bedroom, still quiet, in nearly every part of me that counts?

*   *   *

You just walked in here. I thought you had gone back to sleep. You always say you sleep so well, but you don't. You get up and eat peanut butter out of the jar with your fingers. You wander around the house. You wish you had a child to check on. I know this.

But I didn't realize you were behind me just now. My chest is still thumping. And you probably don't even remember, Susan, but you scared me when you did that. I was just sitting here. You put your hand on my shoulder, and I jumped. I got mad at you. I'm sorry. I was just thinking about my mother, and how I could describe her better. How maybe I could end this whole thing a few paragraphs ago, with the pad of her hand against my face.

But since I know you will be reading this, I might as well tell you. If I am ever alone in here like I was tonight, even if I am doing something else entirely, knock or something. Don't just barge in.

Don't just touch me.

CONTRIBUTORS

Graduates

Lindsay Allen graduated from the CWW in 2012. She is currently Director of the Academic Center & Writing Instructor at Friends Seminary in Manhattan. Her work has appeared in *Narrative Magazine, The Briar Cliff Review, The Adirondack Review*, and *Ellipsis.* "The Ending of the Duck Joke" was originally published in *[PANK]* in 2015.

Jamie Amos graduated from the CWW in 2012. She is currently Program Coordinator of the Intensive English Language Program at UNO. She has published stories in *The Greensboro Review, Cold Mountain Review, The Florida Review,* and others. "Spit" was originally published in *storySouth* in 2014.

Rebeca Antoine graduated from the CWW in 2004. She is currently a lecturer in the Merritt Writing Program at the University of California, Merced. She has published stories in *the strange fruit, Upstreet* and *Gulf Steam* and edited two books of Hurricane Katrina narratives, *Voices Rising: Stories from the Katrina Narrative Project Vols. I and II.* "Names on My Tongue" was originally published in *The Briar Cliff Review* in 2004 and was subsequently anthologized in *Aftermath: Stories of Secrets and Consequences* in 2012.

Tad Bartlett graduated from the CWW in 2015. He is an attorney at Jones, Swanson, Huddell, & Garrison, L.L.C. in New Orleans. His work has appeared in *The Chautauqua Literary Journal, The Stockholm Review of Literature, The Writing Disorder, The Carolina*

Quarterly, *The Oxford American*, and others. "Addressing You" was originally published in *Euphony* in 2015.

Robin Baudier graduated from the CWW in 2014. She is currently an editor at Tulane University School of Medicine and owner of Alligator Pear Publishing, LLC. Her work has appeared in *Ellipsis* and in *This I Believe II: More Personal Philosophies by Remarkable Men and Women* and aired on NPR's "This I Believe" and New Orleans radio station WWNO's "Storyville" series.

Andrea Boll graduated from the CWW in 2001. She currently works as an instructor at JCFA High School in Jefferson Parish, LA. She has published nonfiction in a number of publications. Her fiction has appeared in *Spout Magazine*, *City Works* and *Rio Grande Review*, and she is the author of the novel *The Parade Goes on Without You.* "When the Crazy People Get Their Checks" was originally published in *Eye Rhyme: Journal of New Literature* in 2006.

Carin Chapman graduated from the CWW in 2014. She is currently Instructor of English at Southeastern Louisiana University.

Hannah Choi graduated from the CWW in 2013. She is currently Education Chair for the Film Society of Northwestern Pennsylvania. She has published in *Erie Reader*, *New Orleans by New Orleans,* and *Glimmer Train.* Her novel excerpt from *Reap and Sow* was a *Glimmer Train* Honorable Mention in 2012.

Chrys Darkwater graduated from the CWW in 2006. He currently works as a bartender in New Orleans. He has published stories in *Gris-Gris* and *Black Heart Magazine.* "The Distance" was originally published in *Gris-Gris* in 2013.

Lea L. Downing graduated from the CWW in 2014. A dedicated educator, she is currently an adjunct professor of English at Southern University at New Orleans and a tutor at the Writing Center at Delgado Community College, among other jobs. "Mariposas" was first published in *Ellipsis* in 2014.

Zachary George graduated from the CWW in 2011. He works as a limousine driver in New Orleans and on his urban farm he calls, "9th Ward Dirt." He has published in *Inkwell Journal.*

Abram Shalom Himelstein graduated from the CWW in 2005. He has written for the *Daily Racing Form*, the *Houston Chronicle*, and *Next City*. He is the co-founder of the Neighborhood Story Project and is the editor-in-chief of University of New Orleans Press.

Skip Horack graduated from the CWW (low res) in 2011. He is currently Assistant Professor of Creative Writing at Florida State University. His work has appeared in *Oxford American, Epoch, The Southern Review,* and elsewhere. He is the author of the novels *The Other Joseph* and *The Eden Hunter* and the story collection *The Southern Cross*, which won the Bread Loaf Writers' Conference Bakeless Fiction Prize. "The Cryptozoologist" was originally published in *Narrative Magazine* in 2012.

Jennifer Ann Kuchta graduated from the CWW in 1998. She is currently Retained Instructor of English at the University of New Orleans. Her nonfiction has appeared in the anthologies *Where We Know: New Orleans as Home* and *Year Zero: A Year of Reporting From Post-Katrina New Orleans.* Her fiction has been anthologized in *Life in the Wake: Fiction from Post-Katrina New Orleans.* "Mosaic" first appeared in *Gris-Gris* in 2013.

A.C. Lambeth graduated from the CWW in 2005. She currently works as a yoga teacher in New Orleans. She has published work in *Passages North, Cimarron Review, Elephant Journal, Sojourn,* and *Short Story.* "Ich" was originally published in *North American Review* in 2005.

Casey Lefante graduated from the CWW in 2008. She currently works as a high school teacher of literature and writing in New Orleans. Her stories have appeared in *Third Coast, Slush Pile, Burlesque Press,* and *fwriction.* "Evolution of a Smart Girl" was originally published in *Zone 3* in 2008.

Bill Loehfelm graduated from UNO with an M.A. in English in 2005, taking many classes in the CWW. He makes his living writing. His nonfiction has appeared in the anthologies *Year Zero: A Year of Reporting from post-Katrina New Orleans, Soul is Bulletproof: Reports from Reconstruction New Orleans, Books To Die For: the World's Greatest Mystery Writers on the World's Greatest Mystery Novels,* and *Please Forward: How Blogging Reconnected New Orleans After Hurricane Katrina.* He has published short fiction in *Strand Magazine* and in the anthologies, *Staten Island Noir* and *Life in the Wake: Fiction from Post-Katrina New Orleans.* His novels include *The Devil She Knows, The Devil in Her Way, Doing the Devil's Work, Let the Devil Out, Bloodroot* and *Fresh Kills.* "Snake Hill" was originally published in *Staten Island Noir* in 2012.

Nicholas Mainieri graduated from the CWW in 2011. He is Assistant Professor of English at Nicholls State University in Thibodaux, Louisiana. His stories have appeared in *Southern Review, Southern Humanities Review, Salamander, Sou'wester, Midwestern Gothic, Hobart, Cheap Pop, fwriction:review,* and in the anthology in *Hobart Handbooks: Baseball.* He is also author of the novel *The Infinite.* "This Game Do That to You" was originally published in *The Southern Review* in 2010.

Craig T. McWhorter graduated from the CWW in 1997. He is currently a self-employed marketing consultant in Denver. He wrote the short film *Every Other Weekend* and has published stories and essays in *Evergreen Chronicles* and the anthologies *Men on Men 2000* and *Men for All Seasons.* "All There Is" was originally published in the anthology *M2M* in 2003.

Kyle Mox graduated from the CWW in 2002. He is Associate Dean of the Honors College at Arizona State University. Recent publications include "Decadence, Melancholia, and the Making of Modernism in the Salome Fairy Tales of Strindberg, Wilde, and Ibsen" in the anthology *Decadence, Degeneration and the End: Studies in the European Fin de Siècle.*

K.L. Owens graduated from the CWW in 2015. She works as a custom framer at Art Conscious, LLC, in New Orleans. Her work has appeared in *Fur-Lined Ghettos, The Riding Light Review,* and *freeze frame fiction.* "A July Story" was originally published in *Shimmer Magazine* in 2015.

David Parker, Jr. graduated from the CWW in 2008. He is currently a freelance writer and editor and Adjunct Professor of English at Nicholls State University. He has published in *Louisiana Literature, fwriction: review, Exquisite Corpse, The Nation, Maclean's* and *Fodors*, among others. "Feed the Head" was originally published in *Gris-Gris* in 2013.

Denise Patrick graduated from the CWW (low res) in 2015. She is Adjunct Instructor of Intermediate Writing at Nyack College in New York. She is the author of the short story collection *A Matter of Souls* and the novels *No Ordinary Sound* and *Finding Someplace.*

April Blevins Pejic graduated from the CWW in 2011. She teaches English at Nicholls State University. Her work has appeared in *Green Briar Review, Arcadia,* and *Furious Season.* Her essay "A History We Can Live With" was listed as a notable essay in the 2015 Best American Essays anthology.

Rachael Peralez graduated from the CWW in 2015. She is currently an instructor and academic advisor at Southeastern Louisiana University. She has published in *Lunch Ticket, Alchemy,* and the anthology *Sundress.*

Carolyn Ranu graduated from the CWW in 2014. She is currently an educator and a mother. She has published in *Yemassee* and *Oxford American.*

Maurice Ruffin graduated from the CWW in 2013. He is an attorney in New Orleans. He won the Iowa Review Fiction Award in 2014. His work has appeared in *Kenyon Review, Callaloo, Massachusetts Review, Cicada, the New Delta Review, Green Mountain Review, The Pinch Journal, Redivider, New Orleans Noir:*

the Classics, Scars: An Anthology, and *Unfathomable City: a New Orleans Atlas.* "The Ones Who Don't Say They Love You" was originally published in the Winter 2014/15 issue of *The Iowa Review.*

John Tait graduated from the CWW in 1997. He is currently Associate Professor of English at the University of North Texas. His work has appeared in *Prairie Schooner, The Sun, Fiction, Triquarterly, Michigan Quarterly Review* and elsewhere. "Reasons for Concern Regarding My Girlfriend of Five Days, Monica Garza" was originally published in *Crazyhorse* in 2006.

Jessica Viada graduated from the CWW in 2011. She is currently Development Officer for the MacDowell Colony in Peterborough, New Hampshire. She lives in Brooklyn, New York.

Jen Violi graduated from the CWW in 2007. She is a writer, editor and story mentor. She is the "For Here Please" columnist for *Sweatpants and Coffee.* She has published in *The Baltimore Review, Annapurna Living, Land Your Dream Job in Portland* and *Write Livelihood* and in the books *Behind Door #3: Choose With Your Eyes Wide Open* and *Frock Off: Living Undisguised, the Freedom Edition.* She is also the author of the novel *Putting Makeup on Dead People.* "Salvation" was originally published in *fwriction: review* in 2011.

Tawni Waters graduated from the CWW (low res) in 2009. She is a writer at Simon & Schuster, Sourcebooks and Burlesque Press and Creative Writing Instructor at The Elizabeth Ayres Center for Creative Writing. Her work has appeared in *Dr. T.J. Eckleberg Review, Blood Lotus, So To Speak, Siren Song, Burlesque Press, Poetry Collection* and elsewhere. Her novel *Beauty of the Broken* won The International Literacy Association Award for Young Adult Literature, among other awards. "Trade Secrets" was originally published in *Ellipsis* in 2009.

Missy Wilkinson graduated from the CWW in 2005. She is currently Special Sections Editor at *Gambit Weekly* in New Orleans. Her fiction, journalism and essays have appeared in *Punchnel's,*

The Bitter Southerner, xoJane.com, Neutrons/Protons, Jackson Free Press, Brides, Country Living, Thrillist and in the anthologies *Louisiana: In Words* and *New Orleans: What Can't Be Lost.* She is also author of the novel *Destroying Angel.* "Tear Sheets" was originally published in *The Rusty Nail* in 2012.

Larry Wormington graduated from the CWW (low res) in 2013. He is an entrepreneur and instructional designer in the Dallas-area town of Melissa, Texas. "Keyhole" was published by *Harpur Palate* in 2014.

Che Yeun graduated from the CWW in 2013. She is currently a graduate student in the Department of History and Philosophy of Science at the University of Cambridge. She has published in *The Pinch, Enizagam* and *Philadelphia Stories*, among others. "The Quiet Thing" was first published in *Kenyon Review Online* in 2015.

Faculty

Fredrick Barton directed the CWW from its founding in 1990 until 1992 and again from 2009-2014. He is currently Writer in Residence in the CWW. His books include the collection of essays *Rowing to Sweden* and the novels *The El Cholo Feeling Passes, Courting Pandemonium, Black and White on the Rocks* (originally published as *With Extreme Prejudice*), *A House Divided* (which won the William Faulkner Prize for fiction), and *In the Wake of the Flagship.* "Inky Holler" is a passage from *A House Divided.*

Amanda Boyden graduated from the CWW in 1995 and served on its faculty from 2003-2013. She is currently producing a television series for the Canadian Broadcasting Corporation. Her novels include *Pretty Little Dirty* and *Babylon Rolling.* Her passage here is an excerpt from her forthcoming novel *The Scientist's Daughters.*

Joseph Boyden graduated from the CWW in 1995 and served on its faculty from 2003-2013. He is currently producing a television series for the Canadian Broadcasting Corporation. His books include the story collection *Born with a Tooth* and the novels *Three Day Road, Through Black Spruce* and *The Orenda.* His many awards include the Rogers Writers' Trust Prize, the Canadian Authors Association Book of the Year, the Libris Book of the Year and the Scotiabank Giller Prize, among many others. "Born with a Tooth" is the title story of his story collection.

Barb Johnson graduated from the CWW in 2008 and began teaching in the program in 2010. Her fiction has appeared in *Glimmer Train, Washington Square, The Greensboro Review, 52 Stories, Guernica,* and *Oxford American.* Her nonfiction has been published in *Don't Quit Your Day Job: Acclaimed Authors and the Jobs They Quit* and *The Booklover's Guide to New Orleans.* She won *Glimmer Train's* Short Story Award for New Writers and *Washington Square*'s fiction competition. Her collection of short stories, *More of This World or Maybe Another*, was an IndieNext pick, a Discover Great New Writers selection, an Indiebound Notable Book, and the winner of the American Library Association's Barbara Gittings Literature Award. "Rider" was previously published in Yemassee 20.1

James Knudsen taught in the CWW from its founding until his death at age 54 in 2004. He served as program director from 2001-2003. His stories appeared in *Louisiana Literature, Something in Common, Contemporary Louisiana Stories, Denver Quarterly, Puerto del Sol, Sonora Review, Kansas Quarterly, Vermont Literary Review* and *North Dakota Quarterly,* among others. His books include the novels *Just Friends* and *Playing Favorites* and the story collection *Evening of Wonders.* "Magic Boxes" was first published in *Sonoma Review* in 1984.

Joanna Leake has taught in the CWW from its founding. She served as program director from 1992-2001 and again from 2003-2009. Her stories have appeared in *Apalachee Review, Louisville Review, The Panhandler,* and elsewhere. Her novel *A Few Days In Weasel Creek* was also made into a CBS Television movie starring Mare Winningham.

M.O. Walsh joined the CWW faculty in 2011 and became program director in 2014. His stories and essays have appeared in the *New York Times*, *The Guardian*, *Oxford American* and *The Southern Review*, among others, and have been anthologized in *Best New American Voices* and *Best of the Net.* His story collection, *The Prospect of Magic*, won the Tartt's First Fiction Prize. His novel *My Sunshine Away* was listed as a Best Book of 2015 by NPR, *Booklist, Kirkus* and Amazon and won the Pat Conroy Prize. "The Son of Gilberto Writes Letter to Wife" was originally published in *Epoch* and reprinted in his collection *The Prospect of Magic.*